THE SILENT SEA

THE SILENT SEA

A NOVEL OF THE *OREGON*® FILES

CLIVE CUSSLER
WITH JACK DU BRUL

LARGE PRINT PRESS
A part of Gale, Cengage Learning

GALE
CENGAGE Learning

Detroit • New York • San Francisco • New Haven, Conn • Waterville, Maine • London

GALE
CENGAGE Learning™

LIBRARY OF CONGRESS CATALOGING-IN-PUBLICATION DATA

Cussler, Clive.
    The silent sea : a novel of the Oregon files / by Clive Cussler with Jack Du Brul. — Large print ed.
        p. cm.
    ISBN-13: 978-1-4104-2194-4 (alk. paper)
    ISBN-10: 1-4104-2194-5 (alk. paper)
    1. Cabrillo, Juan (Fictitious character)—Fiction. 2. Intelligence service—Fiction. 3. Ship captains—Fiction. 4. Mercenary troops—Fiction. 5. Argentina—Fiction. 6. Antarctica—Fiction 7. Large type books. I. Du Brul, Jack B. II. Title.
PS3553.U75S52 2010b
813'.54—dc22   2010000197

ISBN 13: 978-1-59413-428-9 (pbk. : alk. paper)
ISBN 10: 1-59413-428-6 (pbk. : alk. paper)

Published in 2011 by arrangement with G. P. Putnam's Sons, a member of Penguin Group (USA) Inc.

Printed in the United States of America
1 2 3 4 5 6 7 15 14 13 12 11

The fair breeze blew,
the white foam flew,
The furrow followed free;
We were the first that ever burst
Into that SILENT SEA.

— *The Rime of the Ancient Mariner,*
SAMUEL TAYLOR COLERIDGE

Prologue

December 7, 1941
Pine Island,
Washington State

A golden blur leapt over the small boat's gunwale just as the bows met the rocky beach. It hit the water with a splash and plowed through the surf, its tail raised like a triumphant pennant. When the retriever reached land, it shook itself so that drops flew like diamond chips in the crisp air, and then it looked back at the skiff. The dog barked at a pair of gulls farther down the beach that took startled flight. Feeling its companions were coming much too slowly, the purebred tore off into a copse of nearby trees, her bark diminishing until it was swallowed by the forest that covered most of the mile-square island just an hour's row off the mainland.

"Amelia," cried Jimmy Ronish, the youngest of the five brothers in the boat.

"She'll be fine," Nick said, shipping his oars and taking the boat's painter line in his hand. He was the eldest of the Ronish boys.

He timed his leap perfectly, landing on the pebbled shore as a wave receded. Three long strides later he was above the tidal mark of flotsam and drying kelp, looping the rope around a sun- and salt-bleached limb of driftwood that was a crosshatch of carved initials. He hauled back on the line to firmly ground the fourteen-foot craft and tied it off.

"Shake a leg," Nick Ronish admonished his younger siblings. "Low tide's in five hours, and we've got a lot to do."

While the air was reasonably comfortable this late in the year, the north Pacific was icy cold, forcing them to unload their gear between the lapping waves. One of the heaviest pieces of equipment was a three-hundred-foot coil of hemp line that Ron and Don, the twins, had to shoulder together to get it up the beach. Jimmy was given charge of the rucksack containing their lunch, and as he was nine years old it was a burden to his slender frame.

The four older boys — Nick at nineteen, Ron and Don a year younger, and Kevin just eleven months their junior — could have passed for quintuplets, with their towheads of floppy blond hair and their pale blue eyes. They retained the buoyant energy of youth wrapped in bodies that were rapidly becoming those of men. On the other hand, Jimmy was small for his age, with darker hair and brown eyes. His brothers teased that he looked a lot like Mr. Greenfield, the town's grocer, and while Jimmy wasn't exactly sure what that implied, he knew he didn't like it. He idolized his older brothers and hated anything that distinguished him from them.

Their family owned the small island off the coast and had for as far back as their grandfather could remember, and it was a place every generation of boys — for the Ronishes hadn't produced a girl since 1862 — spent adventurous summers exploring. Not only was it easy to pretend they were all Huck Finns marooned on the Mississippi or Tom Sawyers exploring the island's intricate cave systems, but Pine Island had an inherent sense of intrigue because of the pit.

Mothers had been forbidding their boys from playing near the pit since Abe Ronish, great-uncle of the current Ronish brood, had fallen to his death in 1887. The directive was as inevitably ignored as it was given.

The real lure of the place was that local

legend told that a certain Pierre Devereaux, one of the most successful privateers to ever harass the Spanish Main, had buried part of his treasure on this far northern island to lighten his ship during the dogged pursuit by a squadron of frigates that had chased him around Cape Horn and up the length of the Americas. The legend was bolstered by the discovery of a small pyramid of cannon balls in one of the island's caves, and the fact that the top forty feet of the square pit was braced with rough-hewn log balks.

The cannonballs had long since been lost and were now considered a myth, but there was no denying the reality of the timber-works ringing the mysterious hole in the rocky earth.

"My shoes got wet," Jimmy complained.

Nick swiftly rounded on his youngest brother and said, "Damn it, Jimmy, I told you already if I heard one complaint outta you I'd make you stay with the boat."

"I wasn't complaining," the boy said, trying to keep from sniveling. "I was just saying is all." He shook a few drops from his wet foot to show it wasn't a problem. Nick shot him a stern look, his blue eyes glacial, and turned his attention back to the job at hand.

Pine Island was shaped like a Valentine's

Day heart that rose out of the cold Pacific. The only beach lay where the two upper lobes come together. The rest of the islet was ringed with cliffs as insurmountable as castle walls or was protected by submerged rocks strung like beads that could tear out the bottom of even the sturdiest craft. Only a handful of animals called the island home, squirrels and mice, mostly, who had been marooned there during storms, and seabirds that used the tall pines to rest and search for prey amid the waves.

A single road bisected the island, having been laboriously hacked twenty years before by another generation of Ronish men, who had made an assault on the island using gasoline-powered pumps to drain the pit, only to see their efforts fail. No matter how many pumps they ran or how much water they sucked from the depths, the pit would continuously refill. An exhaustive search for the subterranean passage connecting the pit to the sea turned up nothing. There was talk of building a coffer dam around the mouth of the bay closest to the pit, the thinking being that there was no other logical choice for the conduit, but the men decided the effort was too much and gave up.

Now it was Nick and his brothers' turn, and he had deduced something his uncles

11

and father had not. At the time Pierre Devereaux had excavated the pit to hide his treasure, the only pump available to him would have been his ship's hand-operated bilge pump. Because of its inefficiency, there was no way the pirates could have drained the pit with their equipment when three ten-horse pumps couldn't.

The answer to how the pit worked lay someplace else.

Nick knew from the stories his uncles told that they had made their assault during the height of summer, and when he consulted an old almanac, he saw the men had been working during a period of particularly high low tides. He knew that to be successful he and his brothers would have to try to reach the bottom at the same time of year Devereaux had dug the pit — when the tides were at their very lowest — and this year that fell at a little past two o'clock on December the seventh.

The older brothers had been planning their attempt at cracking the pit since early summer. By doing odd jobs for anyone who'd hire them, they'd scraped together money to buy equipment, notably a two-stroke gasoline-powered pump, the rope, and tin miner's helmets with battery-powered lights. They'd practiced with the rope and a laden bucket so their arms and shoulders could work tirelessly for hours. They'd even devised goggles that would let them see underwater if necessary.

Jimmy was only along because he had overheard them talking about it all and had threatened to tell their parents if he wasn't included.

There was a sudden commotion off to their right, an explosion of birds winging into the bright sky. Behind them, Amelia, their golden retriever, came bounding out of the tree line, barking wildly with her tail swinging like the devil's own metronome. She chased after one gull that flew close to the ground and then halted, dumbfounded, when the bird shot into the air. Her tongue lolled, and a string of saliva drizzled from her black gums.

"Amelia! Come!" Jimmy cried in his falsetto, and the dog dashed to his side, nearly bowling him over in her excitement.

"Shrimp, take these," Nick said, handing Jimmy the mining helmets and their satchels of heavy lead batteries.

The pump was the heaviest piece of gear, and Nick had devised a sling with two carrying polls like he'd seen on Saturday-matinee serials when natives carried the movie's hero back to their camp. The poles were lengths of timber taken from a construction site, and the four older boys hoisted them on their shoulders and lifted the engine from the rowboat. It swung and then steadied, and they started the first mile-long trek across the isle.

It took forty-five minutes to haul all of their equipment across the island. The pit was located on a bluff above a shallow bay that was the only feature to mar its otherwise perfect heart shape. Waves smashed into the coast, but with the weather so fair only an occasional drop of white spume had the energy to climb the cliffs and land near the pit.

"Kevin," Nick said, a little out of breath after their second trip to the boat and back to the bluff, "you and Jimmy go get wood for a fire. And not driftwood either, it burns too fast."

Before his order could be carried out, natural curiosity made all five of the Ronish brothers edge closer to the pit for a quick look.

The vertical shaft was approximately six feet to a side and perfectly square, and for as far down as they could see it was ringed with age-darkened timbers — oak, in fact, most likely cut on the mainland and brought to the island. Cold, clammy air climbed from the depths in an eerie caress that for a moment dampened their enthusiasm. It was almost as if the pit were breathing raspy, echoing exhalations, and it didn't take much imagination to think it came from the ghosts of the men who had died trying to wrest secrets out of the bowels of the earth.

A rusted metal grate had been laid over the mouth of the pit to prevent anyone from falling in. It was anchored with chains looped around metal pegs drilled into the rock. They had found the key to the padlock in their father's desk drawer under the holstered broom-handled Mauser he had captured during the Great War. For a moment Nick feared it would break in the lock, but eventually it turned and the hasp clicked open.

"Go on and get that firewood," he ordered, and his youngest siblings took off with a raucous Amelia in tow.

With the twins' help, Nick dragged the heavy grate away from the opening and set it aside. Next up was the erection of a wooden frame over the pit so the rope would dangle directly into the hole from a tackle system that would allow two of the boys to easily hoist a third. This was done with the wooden carrying poles and some metal pins fitted into predrilled holes. The butt ends of the lengths of lumber were nailed directly into the oaken balks ringing the shaft. Despite its age, the old timber was more than strong enough to bend a few nails.

Nick took charge of tying the knots that would literally make the difference between life and death while Don, the most mechanically inclined, tinkered with the pump until it was purring sweetly.

By the time everything was ready, Kevin and Jimmy had a nice-sized fire going ten yards from the pit and enough extra wood to keep it going for a couple of hours. They all sat around it, eating sandwiches they had packed earlier and drinking canteens filled with sweetened iced tea.

"The trick's gonna be timing the tide just right," Nick said around a mouthful of baloney sandwich. "Ten minutes before and after it's lowest is about all we've got before the pit floods faster than our pump can keep up. When they tried back in 'twenty-one, they never got it cleared below two hundred feet, but they knew from when they plumbed it that the pit bottoms out at two-forty. Because we're on a bluff, I figure the bottom will be maybe twenty feet below the low-tide mark. We should be able to plug wherever the water's coming in, and the pump'll do the rest."

"I bet there's a big ol' chest just bursting with gold," Jimmy said, wide-eyed at the prospect.

"Don't forget," Don replied, "the pit's been dragged a hundred times with grappling hooks, and no one ever brought up anything."

"Loose gold doubloons, then," Jimmy persisted, "in bags that rotted away."

Nick got to his feet, wiping crumbs from his lap. "We'll know in a half hour."

He put on thigh-high rubber boots and slung the battery pack for his miner's helmet over his shoulder before zipping into an oilskin jacket, feeding the power cord out his collar. He slung a second satchel of equipment over his other shoulder.

Ron lowered a cork bob down the pit on a string marked off at ten-foot increments. "One-ninety," he announced when the line went slack.

Nick donned a web harness and clipped it to the loop at the end of their thick rope. "Lower the hose for the pump but don't fire it up yet. I'm going down."

He tugged the rope sharply to test the tackle block's brake, and it held perfectly. "Okay, you guys, we've been practicing for this all summer. No more screwing around, right?"

"We're ready," Ron Ronish told him, and his twin nodded.

"Jimmy, I don't want you coming within ten feet of the pit, you hear? Once I'm down there, there won't be nothing to see."

"I won't. I promise."

Nick knew the value of his youngest brother's word, so when he shot Kevin a knowing look, Kevin gave him a thumbs-up. He would make sure Jimmy stayed out of the way.

"Two hundred feet," Ron said, checking his bob once again.

Nick grinned. "We're already at the deepest anyone's managed to get and we didn't have to lift a finger." He tapped the side of his head. "It's all in the brains."

Without another word he stepped off the rim of the pit and dangled over the mouth of the precipice, his body twisting kinks out of the rope until coming to stop. If he felt any fear, it didn't show on his face. It was a mask of concentration. He nodded to the twins, and they pulled a little on the line to release the brake and then fed rope through the tackle. Nick sank a few inches.

"Okay, test it again."

The boys pulled again, and the brake reengaged.

"Now, pull," Nick ordered, and his brothers effortlessly raised him up those same few inches.

"No problem, Nick," Don said. "I told you this thing's foolproof. Hell, I bet even Jimmy could haul you up from the bottom."

"Thanks but no thanks." Nick took a couple deep breaths, and said, "All right. This time for real."

In smooth, controlled motions, the twins let gravity slowly draw Nick into the depths. He called up to them to halt when he was just ten feet into the pit. At this shallow depth, they could still converse. Later, when Nick approached the bottom, they had devised a series of coded tugs on the plumb bob.

"What is it?" Don yelled down.

"There are initials carved on the oak timber here. ALR."

"Uncle Albert, I bet," Don said. "I think his middle name is Lewis."

"Next to it is Dad's JGR, and it looks like TMD."

"That'll be Mr. Davis. He worked with them when they tried to reach the bottom."

"Okay, lower away."

Nick turned on his miner's lamp at forty feet where the wooden supports gave way to native rock. The stone looked natural, as

19

if the shaft had been formed millions of years ago when the island was created, and was damp enough to support slimy green mold even though it was well above the tide line. He cast the beam past his dangling legs. It was swallowed by the abyss just a few yards beyond his feet. A steady breeze blew past Nick's face, and a single uncontrollable shiver shook his body.

Down he went, deeper into the earth, with nothing to support him but a rope and his faith in his brothers. When he looked up, the sky was just a tiny square dot high overhead. The walls weren't exactly closing in on him, but he could feel their proximity. He tried not to think about it. Suddenly, below him, he could see a reflection, and as he sank lower he realized he'd reached the high-tide mark. The stone was still damp to the touch. By his calculations he was a hundred and seventy feet belowground. There was still no sign of any way water could reach the pit from the sea, but he didn't expect to see it until the two-hundred-foot mark.

Ten feet lower, he thought he heard something — the faintest trickle of water. He gave the plumb line two tugs to tell his brothers to slow his descent. They immediately responded, and his speed was halved. The sound of water entering the pit grew louder. Nick strained to see into the darkness while droplets dripped off the walls, pattering his helmet like rain. An occasional drop was an icy flick against his neck.

There!

He waited a few more seconds to be lowered another eighteen inches, then gave the plumb a sharp pull.

He hung loose next to a fissure in the rock the size of a postcard. He couldn't estimate how much water was coming through it — surely not enough to defeat all the pumps his father and uncles had brought — so he decided there was at least one more channel to the Pacific. He carefully pulled a handful of oakum fibers from his bag and shoved them into the crack as deep as he could, holding them in place against the icy flow. As seawater saturated the fibers, they swelled until the surge dwindled to a drip and then stopped altogether.

The oakum plug wouldn't hold for long once the tide came back in, which was why his time on the bottom would be so short.

Nick tugged again and started down once more, passing clusters of mussels clinging to the rock. The smell was noxious. He plugged two more similar-sized clefts and when the third was dammed completely he could no longer hear water entering the pit. He pulled the plumb four times, and a moment later the flaccid hose attached to the surface pump puffed out as it started to suck the shaft dry.

A few moments later, the surface of the water appeared below him. He tugged to halt his descent and took his own plumb bob from his oilskin's pocket. He lowered it, and grunted with satisfaction when he saw that only sixteen feet of water remained in the shaft. Because the pit was a good two feet narrower at this depth, he figured the pump would clear it down to three feet in ten minutes.

He could see the surface receding by watching anomalies on the rock wall, and he realized his estimate was off. The pump was draining faster than he —

Something to his left caught his eye. A niche was slowly emerging as the water level sank. It appeared to be about two feet deep, and the same width, and he could tell immediately that it wasn't natural. He could see where hammers and chisels had bitten into the crumbly stone. His heart caught in his throat. Here was more definitive proof that someone had worked in the pit. This wasn't yet proof that this was the repository for Pierre Devereaux's treasure, but in the nineteen-year-old's mind it was close enough.

Enough water had been pumped from the pit for Nick to see some of the junk that had found its way to the bottom. It was mostly driftwood that had been sucked into the shaft through the channels, as well as branches small enough to fit through the grate. However, there were also some lengths of logs that been blown in before the grate was placed over the shaft. He could imagine his father and uncles throwing some of it into the pit in frustration after they failed to unlock its secret.

The pump on the surface continued its work, more than capable of defeating the small trickles escaping his oakum plugs. Off to his side the carved niche continued to grow in height. On a hunch, he had his brothers lower him farther, and he shifted his weight to start to pendulum at the end of the rope. When he swung low enough and close enough, he kicked a leg into the niche, reaching down with his foot. His boot found purchase in just a few inches of water. He let himself swing back once more and threw himself at the opening, landing solidly on both feet. He signaled for his brothers to stop the rope, and he unclipped it from the harness.

Nick Ronish was standing no more than a couple of feet from the bottom of the Treasure Pit. He could sense the loot just inches away.

The final obstacle was all the wood littering the floor of the pit in an impenetrable tangle. They would need to clear some of it in order to feel along the bottom for gold coins. He knew the work would go faster with two of them down here, so after tying a bundle of branches together and attaching it to the rope he pulled on the line to signal to his brothers to first haul it up and then send one of them down to him. Kevin and the remaining twin could operate the hoist, and, if needed, he was sure Jimmy could throw his bit of strength into the effort.

He chuckled as the dripping clutch of wood disappeared over his head. They could probably tie the rope to Amelia's collar and let the crazy dog haul them out.

He stayed with his back to the wall of the niche in case one of the branches slipped from the rope. From two hundred plus feet, even a glancing blow would be fatal.

Three minutes later an elated Don hallooed down from twenty feet over Nick's head. "Find anything?"

"Sticks and stuff," Nick called back. "We

need to clear some of it. But look where I'm standing. This was carved into the rock."

"By pirates?"

"Who else?"

"Hot damn. We're going to be rich."

Knowing the tide would turn shortly, the two teens worked like madmen, pulling apart the snarl of interlocked branches. Nick took off his climbing harness and used it as a sling to bind at least two hundred pounds of waterlogged limbs together. He and Don waited in the niche for the rope to return. Ron and Kev were working like men possessed. They unclipped the harness, pushed off the wood, and sent the rope back down in four minutes.

Nick and Don repeated the process twice more. It didn't matter whether they had cleared away enough of the trash. Time was running out. Leaving the rope draped over a spidery tree trunk sticking out of the water, they jumped down from the niche onto the pile. Wood shifted under their weight. Nick laid himself on a log as big around as he was and reached into the icy water. His hand brushed smooth stone. The very bottom of the pit.

Unlike his brothers, he had only half believed the stories about pirate treasure buried in the pit. That was until he saw the carved niche. Now he wasn't sure what he believed. When he'd set out, getting to the bottom and proving himself against generations of ancestors who had tried and failed would have been success enough. But now?

He swept his arm in a wider arc, straining to feel anything lying in the silty muck. Nearby, Don was doing the same, his arm buried to the shoulder between some branches, his mouth a tight line of concentration. Nick felt something round and flat. He plucked it from the ooze, thumbing away the grime before it had cleared the surface.

The expected glimmer of gold didn't materialize. It was nothing but an old rusted washer. He tried another area where he and his brother had cleared some debris. By feel, he identified twigs and soggy bunches of leaves, but when he encountered something he wasn't sure of he pulled it from the water. He gave a startled grunt as he stared into the empty eye sockets of an animal skull — a fox, he thought.

High above them pressure was building behind one of the oakum plugs, forcing water through the dense fibers. What started as a trickle quickly turned into a gush when the plug shot from the hole with enough impetus to smack the far side of the shaft. Seawater came tumbling down the pit, twisting like an electrical cable carrying live current.

"That's it," Nick shouted over the roar. "We are out of here."

"One more second," Don replied, nearly his entire upper body in the water as he continued to feel around.

Nick was struggling into his climbing harness, and looked over sharply when Don gasped oddly. "Don?"

Something had shifted. A second ago, Don had been lying on a tree trunk, and now suddenly he was pressed against the far wall of the pit with the length of wood pushed against his chest.

"Nick," he cried out, his voice strangled.

Nick rushed across the pit to his brother's side. His frantic motion must have shifted the whole pile further because Don suddenly screamed. The wood pushing into his chest slipped even more, and in the light of his miner's lamp Nick could see a dark stain forming on his brother's coat.

Water continued to hammer them from above, a torrent as bad as any summer rainstorm.

"Hold on, little brother," Nick said, grasping the tree branch. He felt an odd vibration coming from the wood, an almost mechanical sensation, as though the end hidden underwater was attached to some device.

No matter how he tried to pull it out, the branch was firmly lodged against something hidden below the water. It remorselessly continued to drive into Don's chest in a slow, steady thrust.

Don screamed at the pain. Nick screamed, too, out of fear and frustration. He didn't know what to do, and he looked around for some way to lever the bough out of his brother's body.

"Just hold on, Don," Nick said, tears mingling with the salt water sluicing off his face.

Don called his name again, weakly, for there was three inches of wood impaled into his flesh. Nick took his hand, which Don gripped, but quickly the strength afforded him by fear and pain began to ebb. His fingers slackened.

"Donny!" Nick cried.

Don opened his mouth. Nick would never know what his brother's final words were meant to be. A clot of blood erupted from Don Ronish's pale lips. The first eruption turned into a steady stream that turned pink in the spray as it ran down his neck and across his chest.

Nick threw his head back and roared, a primeval call that echoed off the pit walls, and he would have remained at his brother's side forever had the second of his oakum plugs not burst, doubling the flow of water pouring into the pit.

He fumbled with the rope in the deluge, clipping his harness into the loop. He hated what he was about to do, but he had no choice. He tugged on the plumb line. His other brothers had to know something was wrong because they started hauling him from the pit instantly. Nick kept his light trained on Don until the lifeless body was just a pale outline in the stygian realm. And then it was gone.

Don Ronish's memorial service was held the following Wednesday. The world had changed dramatically during the hours the five brothers were playing at being explorers. The Japanese had bombed Pearl Harbor, and the United States was now at war. Only the Navy had the kind of dive equipment necessary to recover Don's body, and their parents' request had fallen on deaf ears. His casket remained empty.

Their mother hadn't spoken since hearing the news and had to sit through the service leaning against their father to keep from fainting. When it was done, he told the three eldest to stay where they were, and he lead their mother and Jimmy to their car, a secondhand Hudson. He returned to the graveside, a decade older than he'd been Sunday morning. He said nothing, looking from one son to the next, his eyes red-rimmed. He then reached into the jacket pocket of the only suit he owned, the one he'd been married in and the one he'd worn to his own parents' funerals. He had three slips of paper. He handed one to each, pausing with the one he gave to Kevin. He kissed it before thrusting it into his son's hand.

They were birth certificates. The one he'd given Kevin had been Don's, who had been eighteen years old and thus eligible for military service.

"It's 'cause of your Ma. She never understood. Do our family proud and maybe you'll be forgiven."

He turned on his heel and walked away, his rangy shoulders hanging as though they supported a weight far heavier than his body could ever carry.

And so the three boys went to the nearest recruiters, all thoughts of boyhood adventure banished forever by the memory of their brother's unoccupied coffin, and then by the hellfires of war.

ONE

Near the Paraguay–Argentine Border
Present Day

Juan Cabrillo had never thought he would meet a challenge he would rather walk away from than face. He felt like running from this one.

Not that it showed.

He had an unreadable game face — his blue eyes remained calm and his expression neutral — but he was glad his best friend and second-in-command, Max Hanley, wasn't with him. Max would have picked up on Cabrillo's concern in a second.

Forty miles down the tea-black river from where he stood was one of the most tightly controlled borders in the world — second only to the DMZ separating the two Koreas. It was just rotten luck that the object that had brought him and his handpicked team to the remote jungle had landed on the other side. Had it come down in Paraguay, a phone call between diplomats and a little hush money in the form of economic aid would have ended the affair then and there.

But that was not the case. What they sought had landed in Argentina. And had the incident occurred eighteen months earlier it could have been handled effortlessly. Yet a year and a half ago, following the second collapse of the Argentine peso, a junta of Generals, led by Generalissimo Ernesto Corazón, had seized power in a violent coup that intelligence analysts believed had been in the works for some time. The monetary crisis was simply an excuse for them to wrest control from the legitimate government.

The heads of the civilian leadership were tried in kangaroo courts for crimes against the state involving economic mismanagement. The fortunate were executed; the rest, more than three thousand by some estimates, were sent to forced-labor camps in the Andes Mountains or deep into the Amazon. Any attempt to learn more of their fate was met with arrests. The press was nationalized, and journalists not toeing the party line were jailed. Unions were banned and street protests were met with gunfire.

Those who got out in the early chaotic days of the coup, mostly some wealthy families willing to leave everything behind, said what was happening in their country made the horrors of 1960s and '70s military dictatorships seem tame.

Argentina had gone from a thriving democracy to a virtual police state inside of six weeks. The United Nations had rattled its vocal swords, threatening sanctions but ultimately sending out a watered-down resolution condemning human rights abuses that the ruling junta duly ignored.

Since then, the military government had tightened their control even further. Lately, they had started massing troops on the borders of Bolivia, Paraguay, Uruguay, and Brazil, as well as along the mountain passes near Chile. A draft had been implemented, giving them an army as large as the combined forces of all other South American countries. Brazil, a traditional rival for regional power, had likewise fortified their border, and it wasn't uncommon for the two sides to lob artillery shells at each other.

It was into this authoritarian nightmare that Cabrillo was to lead his people in order to recover what was essentially a NASA blunder.

The Corporation was in the area monitoring the situation when the call came through. They had actually been unloading a shipment of stolen cars from Europe in Santos, Brazil, South America's busiest seaport, as part of the cover they maintained. Their ship, the *Oregon,* had a reputation as a tramp freighter with no set route and a crew that asked few questions. It would just be coincidental that over the next several months Brazil's police forces would receive tips concerning the cars' locations. During transit, Cabrillo had his technical team hide GPS trackers on the gray-market automobiles. It wasn't likely that the cars would be returned to their owners, but the smuggling ring would surely collapse.

Pretending to be larcenous was part of the Corporation's job, actually abetting in a criminal enterprise was not.

The center fore derrick swung over the hold for the last time. In the glow of the few dock lights left working at the little-used section of the port, a string of exotic automobiles glimmered like rare jewels. Ferraris, Maseratis, and Audi R8s all waited to be loaded into the backs of three idling semitrailers. A customs foreman stood nearby, his coat pocket bulging slightly from the envelope of five-hundred-euro bills.

The crane's motor took up the strain at a signal from crewmen in the hold, and a bright orange Lamborghini Gallardo emerged, looking as though it were already traveling at autobahn speeds. Cabrillo knew from his contact in Rotterdam, where the cars had been loaded, that this particular vehicle had been stolen from an Italian Count near Turin and that the Count had gotten it from a crooked dealer who later claimed it had been stolen from his showroom.

Max Hanley grunted softly as the Lambo gleamed in the weak light. "Good-looking car, but what's with that god-awful color?"

"No accounting for taste, my friend," Juan said, twirling a hand over his head to signal the crane operator to go ahead and lower the final car onto the dock. A harbor pilot was due to guide them out to sea shortly.

The sleek car was lowered to the crumbling concrete dock, and members of the smuggling gang unshackled the lifting sling, taking care that the steel cables didn't scratch what Juan had to agree was a damned ugly paint choice.

The third man standing on the old freighter's wing bridge had given his name as Angel. He was in his mid-twenties, and wore slacks of some shiny material that looked like mercury and an untucked white dress shirt. He was so thin that the outline of an automatic pistol tucked into the small of his back was obvious.

But maybe that was the point.

Then again, Juan wasn't really concerned about a double cross. Smuggling was a business built on reputation, and one stupid move on Angel's part would just about guarantee he'd never do another deal again.

"Okay, then, *Capitão,* that is it," Angel said, and whistled down to his men.

One of them retrieved a bag from a tractor trailer's cab and approached the gangplank while the rest started loading the hot cars into the rigs. A crew member met the smuggler at the rail and escorted him up the two flights of rusted stairs to the bridge. Juan entered with the others from outside. The only illumination came from the antique radar repeater that gave them all a sickly green pallor.

Cabrillo dialed up a little more light as the Brazilian set the bag onto the chart table. Angel's hair cream shimmered as much as his slacks.

"The agreed-upon price was two hundred thousand dollars," Angel said as he opened the battered duffel. That amount would almost cover the cost to buy one of the Ferraris new. "It would have been more if you had agreed to deliver three of them to Buenos Aires."

"Forget it," Juan said. "I'm not taking my ship anywhere near there. And good luck finding a captain who will. Hell, none would take a legit cargo into BA, let alone a bunch of stolen cars."

When Cabrillo moved, his shin hit the edge of the table. The resulting sound was an unnatural crack. Angel eyed him warily, his hand moving slightly closer to the pistol under his shirt.

Juan made a "relax" gesture, and stooped to roll up his pant leg. About three inches below his knee, his leg had been replaced with a high-tech prosthetic that looked like something out of the *Terminator* movies. "Occupational hazard."

The Brazilian shrugged.

The cash was in bundles of ten thousand. Juan divvied them up and handed half to Max, and for the next several minutes the only sound on the bridge was the soft whisper of bills being checked. They all appeared to be legitimate hundred-dollar bills.

Juan stuck out his hand, "Pleasure doing business with you, Angel."

"The pleasure is mine, *Capitão*. I wish you a safe —" A loud squawk from the overhead speaker cut off the rest of his sentence. A barely understandable voice called the

39

captain down to the mess hall.

"Please excuse me," Cabrillo said, then turned to Max. "If I'm not back when the harbor pilot gets here, you have the conn."

He took a flight of internal stairs down to the mess deck. The interior spaces of the old tramp freighter were just as scabrous as her hull. The walls hadn't seen fresh paint in decades, and there were lines through the dust on the floor where a crewman had made a halfhearted attempt at sweeping sometime in the distant past. The mess hall was only moderately brighter than the dim companionway, with cheap travel posters taped haphazardly to the bulkheads. On one wall was a message board bearded with unread slips of paper offering everything from guitar lessons from an engineer who'd left the ship a decade ago to a reminder that Hong Kong would revert to Chinese control on July 1, 1997.

In the adjoining kitchen, stalactites of hardened grease as thick as fingers hung from the ventilation hood over the stove.

Cabrillo walked through the unoccupied room, and as he neared the far wall a perfectly concealed door snicked open. Linda Ross stood in the well-appointed hallway beyond. She was the Corporation's vice president of operations, essentially its number three after Juan and Max. She was pixie cute, with a small, upturned nose, and a panache for varying hair colors. It was jet-black now, and swept passed her shoulders in thick waves.

Linda was a Navy vet who had done a tour on a guided-missile cruiser as well as spent time as a Pentagon staffer, giving her a unique set of skills that made her perfect for her job.

"What's up?" Juan asked as she fell in beside with him. She had to take two steps for every one of his.

"Overholt's on the phone. Sounds urgent."

"Lang always sounds urgent," Juan said, removing a set of fake teeth and some wadded cotton from his mouth that were part of his disguise. He wore a fat suit under his wrinkled uniform shirt and a wig of graying hair. "I think it's his prostate."

Langston Overholt IV was a veteran CIA man who'd been around long enough to know where all the skeletons, literal and figurative, were buried, which was why after years of trying to put him to pasture, a succession of politically appointed directors had let him stick around Langley in an advisory capacity. He had also been Cabrillo's boss when Juan was a field agent, and, when Juan left the Agency, Overholt had

41

been instrumental in encouraging him to found the Corporation.

Many of the toughest assignments the Corporation had taken on had come from Overholt, and the substantial fees they had collected were paid through black budget appropriations so deeply buried that the auditors for them called themselves the 49ers, after the California gold rush miners.

They reached Cabrillo's cabin. He paused before opening the door. "Tell them to stand by in the op center. The pilot should be here soon."

While the wheelhouse several decks above them looked functional, it was nothing more than window dressing for marine inspections and pilots. The wheel and throttle controls were computer linked to the high-tech operations center that was the real brains of the ship. It was from there that all thrust and maneuvering instructions were issued, and it was from there, too, that the array of deadly weapons secreted throughout the decrepit-looking scow was controlled.

The *Oregon* might have started out as a lumber carrier schlepping timber along America's West Coast and to Japan, but after Juan's team of naval architects and craftsmen were finished with her, she was one of the most sophisticated intelligence-gathering and covert-operations vessels ever conceived.

"Will do, Chairman." Linda said, and she headed down the passage.

Following a rather hairy duel with a Libyan warship several months earlier, they had found it necessary to dock the ship for extensive repairs. No fewer than thirty artillery shells had penetrated her armor. Juan couldn't fault his ship. Those shells had been fired at less than point-blank range. He'd used the opportunity to redo his cabin.

All the expensive woodwork had been stripped out, either by the Libyan guns or carpenters. The walls were now covered in something akin to stucco that wouldn't crack as the ship flexed. The doorways were modified so they were arched. Additional arched partisans were added, giving the seven-hundred-square-foot cabin a cozy feeling. With its decidedly Arabesque décor, the rooms looked like the set of Rick's Café Américain from *Casablanca,* Juan's favorite movie.

He tossed the wig onto his desk and snatched up the handset of a repro Bakelite phone.

"Lang, Juan here. How are you doing?"

"Apoplectic."

"Your normal frame of mind. What's up?"

"First of, tell me where you are."

"Santos, Brazil. That's São Paulo's port city, in case you didn't know."

"Thank God, you're close," Overholt said with a relieved sigh. "And just so you know, I helped the Israelis snatch a Nazi war criminal from Santos back in the sixties."

"Touché. Now, what's going on?" By the tone of Overholt's voice, Juan knew he had something big for them, and he could feel the first feathery traces of adrenaline in his veins.

"Six hours ago, a satellite was launched from Vandenberg atop a Delta III rocket for a low-earth polar orbit."

That one sentence alone was enough for Cabrillo to deduce that the rocket had failed someplace over South America, since polar shots fly south from the California Air Force base, that it was carrying sensitive spy gear which might not have burned up, and that it most likely had crashed in Argentina since Lang was calling the best covert operatives he knew.

"The techs don't know yet what went wrong," Overholt continued. "And that really isn't our problem anyway."

"Our problem," Juan said, "is that it crashed in Argentina."

"You said it. About a hundred miles south of Paraguay in some of the thickest jungle of the Amazon basin. And there's a good chance the Argentines know because we warned every country on the flight path that the rocket was overflying their territory."

"I thought we no longer have diplomatic relations with them since the coup."

"We still have ways of passing on something like this."

"I know what you're about to ask, but be reasonable. The debris is going to be spread over a couple thousand square miles in bush that our spy satellites can't penetrate. Do you honestly expect us to find your needle in that haystack?"

"I do, because here's the kicker. The particular part of the needle we're looking for is a mild gamma ray emitter."

Juan let that sink in for a second, and finally said, "Plutonium."

"Only reliable power source we had for this particular bird. The NASA eggheads tried every conceivable alternative, but it came back to using a tiny amount of plutonium and using the heat off its decay to run the satellite's systems. On the bright side, they so overengineered the containment vessel that it is virtually indestructible. It wouldn't even notice a rocket blowing up around it.

"As you can well imagine, the administration doesn't want it known that we sent aloft a satellite that could have potentially spread radiation across a good-sized swath of the most pristine environment on the planet. The other concern is that the plutonium not fall into the Argentines' hands. We suspect they have restarted their nuclear weapons program. The satellite didn't carry much of the stuff — a few grams worth, or so I'm told — but there's no sense in giving them a head start on their march for the Bomb."

"So the Argies don't know about the plutonium?" Juan asked, using the colloquialism for Argentines he'd picked up from a Falklands War vet.

"Thank goodness, no. But anyone with the right equipment will pick up trace radioactivity. And before you ask," he said, anticipating the next question, "levels aren't dangerous provided you follow some simple safety protocols."

That wasn't going to be Cabrillo's next question. He knew plutonium wasn't dangerous unless ingested or inhaled. Then it became one of the deadliest toxins known to man.

"I was going to ask if we have any kind of

backup."

"Nada. There's a team on its way to Paraguay with the latest generation of gamma ray detectors, but that's about all you can count on. It took the DCI and the chairman of the Joint Chiefs to convince the President to let us help you that much. I'm sure you realize he has a certain, ah, reluctance, when it comes to dealing with sensitive international situations. He still hasn't come to grips with the whole debacle in Libya a few months back."

"Debacle?" Juan said, sounding hurt. "We saved the Secretary of State's life and salvaged the peace accords."

"And damned near started a war when you went toe-to-toe with one of their guided-missile frigates. This has to go ultra-quiet. Sneak in, find the plutonium, and sneak right back out again. No fireworks."

Cabrillo and Overholt knew that was a promise Juan couldn't make, so instead Juan asked for details about the exact location at which the missile exploded and the trajectory of its fall back to earth. He pulled a cordless keyboard and mouse from a tray under his desk, which sent a signal for a flat-screen monitor to slowly rise from the desk's surface. Overholt e-mailed pictures and target projections. The pictures were worthless, showing nothing but dense cloud cover, but NASA had given them just a five-square-mile search area, which made the grid manageable, provided the terrain didn't go to hell on them. Overholt asked if Cabrillo had any idea how they were going to get into Argentina undetected.

"I want to see some topographical maps before I can answer that. My first instinct is a chopper, of course, but with the Argies ramping up activity along their northern borders that might not be possible. I should have something figured out in a day or two and be ready to execute by week's end."

"Ah, here's the other thing," Overholt said so mildly that Cabrillo tensed up. "You have seventy-two hours to recover the power pack."

Juan was incredulous. "Three days? That's impossible."

"After seventy-two hours, the President wants to come clean. Well, cleaner. He won't mention the plutonium, but he's willing to ask the Argentines for their help recovering, quote, sensitive scientific equipment."

"And if they say no and search for it themselves?"

"At best we end up looking foolish, and, at worst, criminally negligent in the eyes of the world. Plus we give Generalissimo

Corazón a tidy bundle of weapons-grade plutonium to play with."

"Lang, give me six hours. I'll get back to you on whether we're willing — hell — able to back your play."

"Thanks, Juan."

Cabrillo called Overholt after a three-hour strategy meeting with his department heads, and, twelve hours later, found himself and his team standing on the banks of a Paraguayan river, about to cross into God alone knew what.

Two

The Wilson/George Research Station
Antarctic Peninsula

The skeleton staff of the winter-over crew could feel spring coming in their bones. Not that the weather was much improved. Temperatures rarely rose above twenty below, and icy winds were a constant. It was the growing number of × marks on the big calendar in the rec hall marking the advancing days that buoyed their spirits after a long winter in which they hadn't seen the sun since late March.

Only a few research bases remain open year-round on the planet's most desolate continent, and those are usually much larger than the Wilson/George Station, run by a coalition of American universities and a grant from the National Science Foundation. Even at full staff during the summer months starting in September, the clutch of prefabricated domed buildings atop stilts driven into the ice and rock could house no more than forty souls.

Because of money pouring into global-warming research, it was decided to keep the station online all year round. This was the first attempt, and by all accounts it had gone well. The structures had withstood the worst Antarctica could throw at them, and the people had gotten along well for the most part. One of them, Bill Harris, was a NASA astronaut studying the effects of isolation on human relations, for an eventual manned mission to Mars.

WeeGee, as the team called their home for the past six months, was out of some futurist sketchbook. It was located near a deep bay on the shores of the Bellings-hausen Sea, midway along the peninsula that thrusts toward South America like a frozen finger. Had there been sunlight, a pair of binoculars on the hills behind the base was all one would need to see the southern ocean.

There were five nodes surrounding a central hub that served as the mess and recreation hall. The nodes were connected by elevated walkways that were designed to sway with the wind. On particularly bad days, people with the weakest stomachs usually crawled. The nodes were designed as laboratory space, storage, and dormitory-like rooms, with people sleeping four to a cell during the busy summer. All the buildings were painted safety red. With opaque panels in the domed ceilings and many walls, the facility looked like a group of checkerboard silos.

A short distance away, along a carefully roped path, sat a Quonset-type building that acted as a garage for their snowmobiles and the snowcats. With the weather so miserable during the winter, there had been little opportunity to use the arctic vehicles. The building used waste heat piped from the main base to keep it at a minimum of ten below so as not to damage the machines.

Most of their meteorological equipment could be remotely monitored, so there was very little for the crew to do during the sunless days. Bill Harris had his NASA study, a couple of them were using the time to finish their doctoral dissertations, and one was working on a novel.

Only Andy Gangle didn't appear to have anything to occupy his time. When he'd first arrived, the twenty-eight-year-old postdoc from Penn State had actively overseen the launching of weather balloons and had taken his study of the weather seriously. But not long after he'd lost interest in local temperatures. He still performed his duties, but he spent a great deal of time out in the garage or, when the weather permitted, trekking solo to the shore to collect "specimens," though no one knew of what.

And because of the strict privacy code needed to keep a group of people in isolation from getting on one another's nerves, everyone let him be. The few times his case had been discussed, no one felt he was succumbing to what the shrinks referred to as isolation syndrome but what the team called bug-eyes. In its severest forms, a person could suffer delusions as part of a psychotic break. A few seasons back, a Danish researcher lost his toes and more when he ran naked from his base on the leeward side of the peninsula. Rumor had it he was still in a Copenhagen mental hospital.

No, it was decided that Andy didn't have bug-eyes. He was just a sullen loner who the others were more than happy to avoid.

"Morning," Andy Gangle muttered when he entered the rec hall. The smell of frying bacon from the cafeteria-style galley filled the room.

The overhead fluorescent lights made his pallor particularly wan. Like most of the men, he'd long since stopped shaving, and his dark beard contrasted sharply against his white skin.

A pair of women at one of the Formica tables paused from their breakfasts to greet him and then returned to their food. Greg Lamont, the titular head of the station, greeted Andy by name. "The met guys tell me this will probably be your last day to head to the coast if you're planning on it."

"Why's that?" Gangle asked guardedly. He didn't like people telling him his business.

"Front coming in," the silver-haired ex-hippie-turned-scientist replied. "A bad one. It's going to blanket half of Antarctica."

Real concern etched the corners of Gangle's lipless mouth. "It won't affect our leaving, will it?"

"Too early to say, but it's possible."

Andy nodded, not in understanding but absently, as if he were reorganizing thoughts in his head. He passed through to the kitchen.

"How'd you sleep?" Gina Alexander asked. The forty-something divorcée from Maine had come to the Antarctic to, as she put it, "get as far away from that rat and his new Little Miss Perfect Bod as is humanly possible." She wasn't one of the researchers but rather worked for the support company hired to keep WeeGee running smoothly.

"Same as the night before," Andy said, filling a mug with coffee from the stainless urn at the end of the cafeteria line.

"Glad to hear it. How do you want your eggs?"

He looked at her, his expression almost feral. "Runny and cold, as usual."

She wasn't quite sure how to take that. Andy usually never said anything more than "scrambled," before taking his food and coffee to eat back in his room. She chuckled reproachfully. "Boy, aren't you a bundle of sunshine this morning."

He leaned across the dinner-tray track, speaking softly so the others in the rec room couldn't hear him. "Gina, we've got one more week before we can get out of here, so just serve me my damned food and keep your comments to yourself. All right?"

Not one to back down — ask her ex about that sometime — Gina leaned over so their faces were inches apart. "Then do yourself a favor, love, and watch me while I cook, otherwise I might be tempted to spit in your food."

"That would probably improve the waste." Andy straightened, his face scrunched as he thought for a moment. "Paste? No, damn it. Touch? Taste. That's it. It would probably improve the taste."

Gina wasn't sure what had gotten into him, but she laughed anyway. "Sonny boy, you need to be a little quicker for your insults to be effective."

Rather than wait around feeling foolish, Andy grabbed a handful of protein bars off the counter and skulked from the room, his bony shoulders hunched up like a vultures.' His ears rang with her parting call of "Bug-eyed twerp."

"Seven days, Andy," he said to himself as he made his way back to his room. "Keep it together for seven more days and you can kiss these suckers good-bye forever."

Forty minutes later, bundled under six layers of clothing, Andy inked his name on the whiteboard hanging next to the cold lock and stepped through the heavily insulated door. The difference in temperature between the interior of the station and the small anteroom that lead to the exit was a whopping ninety degrees. Gangle's breath turned into an opaque cloud as dense as any London fog, and each inhalation stabbed deep into his lungs. He waited for a few minutes to adjust his clothing and fit his goggles over his eyes. While the Antarctic Peninsula was relatively warm compared to the interior of the continent, any exposed skin would still get frostbitten in moments.

All the clothing in the world still wasn't enough to defeat the cold, not in the long term. Heat loss was inevitable, and, with the wind, inexorable. It started at the extremities — nose, fingertips, and toes — then spread inward as the body shut itself down to conserve its core temperature. It wasn't a matter of willpower, facing these extremes in temperature. One couldn't just bull through the pain. Antarctica was as deadly to human life as the hard vacuum of outer space.

With cumbersome overmittens covering his gloves, Andy needed both hands to turn the doorknob. The real cold hit him hard. It would take several seconds for the air trapped in his clothing to warm against such a thermal onslaught. He shivered for a moment, then rounded the corner that protected the exit from the wind. He clutched the handrail as he made his way down the stairs to the rocky ground. There wasn't much wind today — ten knots, maybe — and for that he was grateful.

He grabbed up a five-foot length of metal conduit pipe as thick around as a fifty-cent piece and headed out.

The sun was a pale promise that circled the horizon but wouldn't emerge above it for another week, but it gave enough light for Andy to see without using his headlamp. His moon boots were inflexible and made walking difficult, and the terrain didn't help much. This part of the Antarctic Peninsula was volcanic, and not enough time had passed since the last eruption for the elements to have eroded the rock to a glassy smoothness like he'd seen pictures of during orientation training.

Another thing he'd learned during his orientation was to never sweat outside. Ironically, that was the ticket to fast-onset hypothermia because the body shed heat so much faster when exertion opened the skin's pores. Therefore, it took Andy twenty minutes to reach his search area. If Greg Lamont was right and this was his last day to be outside until extraction, Gangle felt this might be the best spot. It was closer to the beach from where he'd made his discovery but in line with a low range of hills that afforded protection. For the next two hours, he walked back and forth, his goggled eyes sweeping the ground. Whenever anything promising appeared, he would use the steel pipe to probe the ice and snow or lever rocks out of the way. It was mindless work, for which he was particularly well suited, and the time seemed to slip away. His only distraction came when he felt the need to run in a circle for a few minutes. He managed to stop himself before he worked up a sweat, but his breath had frozen to the three scarves he had wrapped around his nose and mouth. He pulled them off to retie them so the icy snot was around the back of his head.

He figured this was a good enough time to call it a day. He studied the distant ocean for a moment, wondering what secrets it harbored below its iceberg-laden surface, then turned back to Wilson/George, the conduit slung over his shoulder like a hobo's pole.

Andy Gangle had made the discovery of a lifetime. He was content with that. If there were others out here, then someone else could find them while he spent the rest of his life basking in luxuries he'd never dreamt would be his.

THREE

Cabrillo gave the dark river another look before turning back to the abandoned hut they were using as a base. It was built on stilts partially over the water, and the ladder up to the single room was made of logs lashed together with fiber rope. It creaked ominously as he climbed, but it held his weight. The thatch roof was mostly gone, so the twilit sky was bisected by wooden trusses still covered in bark.

"Coffee's ready," Mike Trono whispered, and handed over a mug.

Trono was one of the Corporation's principal shore operators, a former para rescue jumper who'd gone behind enemy lines in Kosovo, Iraq, and Afghanistan to rescue downed pilots. Slight of build, with a mop of fine brown hair, he had quit the military to race offshore powerboats only to find the adrenaline rush wasn't enough.

Next to him slouched the large sleeping

form of his partner in crime, Jerry Pulaski. Jerry was a qualified combat veteran, and it would be his responsibility to lug the seventy-pound power pack once they found it. Rounding out the tight squad was Mark Murphy, also asleep.

Murph's main job in the Corporation was handling the *Oregon*'s sophisticated weapons, and he could fight a ship like no one Juan had ever encountered, though he'd never been in the military. He was an MIT graduate with a fistful of letters after his name, including Ph.D., who'd taken his genius into the development of military hardware. Cabrillo had recruited him some time back with his best friend, Eric Stone, who was the now *Oregon*'s chief helmsman. Juan thought of them as the dynamic duo. When they were together, he could swear they communicated telepathically, and when they spoke in the arcane vernacular of their oft-played video games, he figured they were speaking in tongues. Both young men considered themselves geek chic, though few on the crew were too sure of the chic part.

Mark had had his first real taste of close-quarter combat during the Corporation's rescue of the Secretary of State, and Linda Ross's assessment was that he handled himself like a pro. Juan wanted him along on this mission in case there were any technical issues with the plutonium-containment vessel. If there was a problem, Murph was the best the Corporation had at figuring it out.

In deference to the humidity, which made the air thick enough to practically drink, all four men were shirtless, their skin slathered in DEET against the hordes of insects circling just outside the mosquito net they had hung from the rafters. Sweat clung to the hair on Cabrillo's chest and snaked down his lean flanks. Where Jerry Pulaski had heavy slabs of muscle, Cabrillo had a swimmer's physique, with broad shoulders and a tapered waist. Not one to worry about what he ate, he kept himself trim by swimming countless laps in the *Oregon*'s marble-lined swimming pool.

"Another hour until sundown," Cabrillo said, taking a sip of the instant coffee cooked on a little folding stove. The taste made him look into the mug suspiciously. He'd grown accustomed to the gourmet Kona brewed aboard ship. "We have just enough light to get the RHIB ready. Leaving an hour later will put us at the border a little before midnight."

"Just before the third watch takes over and the second's thinking about their beds,"

Mike said, then kicked Pulaski's ankle. "Up, Sleeping Beauty, your breakfast awaits."

Jerry yawned broadly, stretching his thick arms over his head, his dark hair tussled from using his shirt as a pillow. "God, you sure are ugly to wake up next to."

"Watch it, my friend. I've seen some of the girls you've dragged home."

"Is that coffee?" Mark Murphy asked, rubbing sleep from his eyes. He usually kept his hair long, but for this mission Juan had had him cut it to a more practical length.

"Calling it that is being generous," Cabrillo said, and gave the weapons genius his cup.

After changing clothing they assembled under the ramshackle hut. Tied to one of the stilts, and lying dangerously low to the water, was their river conveyance, a matte-black ridged hulled inflatable boat, or RHIB. It was essentially a fiberglass-bottomed craft with inflatable fenders ringing its gunwale for added buoyancy. Two massive outboards hung over the boat's transom. The only crew amenity was a stand-up cockpit shielded by bulletproof glass in the center of the twenty-five-foot deck. It had been modified aboard the *Oregon* so it could fold flat.

They had airfreighted the RHIB in a steel

container into Paraguay and loaded the crate directly onto a rented truck. Juan had no idea if the Argentines had spies watching its neighbor's airports for suspicious activity, but if he were in charge of the military dictatorship, he would. The truck was driven to an isolated town about fifty miles upriver from the Argentine border, and it was there they unloaded it and all the other gear they had brought along. Their current location was another thirty miles south of the town.

Juan had opted for a riverine approach versus infiltrating Argentina by helicopter because radar coverage along the border was simply too tight, even flying nap-of-the-earth, and because a tributary of this river ran less than five miles from their search target. The clincher was the fact that the cloud cover he'd seen on the pictures turned out to be a massive slash-and-burn logging operation close to where the satellite fragment crashed. The chances of being spotted were too great.

He took a lesson from World War II, specifically Germany's Operation Greif at the outset of the Battle of the Bulge, in which English-speaking commandoes crossed through the Allied lines during the opening hours of the fight in order to change signposts, disrupt traffic, and generally create chaos among the Allied forces. Cabrillo recalled reading the story of one SS Corporal who was part of Operation Greif. He admitted that crossing the lines during the battle was the most frightening part of the plan because gunfire was directed at them from both directions. Once on the other side, the German had written, he carried out his duties without the slightest fear, knowing his disguise and command of English would protect him. He hadn't been captured and was eventually wounded defending Berlin against the Russians.

Cabrillo had no desire to get caught in a cross fire from nervous border guards, so rather than cross this particular line he was going to go under it.

The RHIB was loaded to the gunwales with iron plates — tons of them — enough to quadruple the shipping costs of sending the boat unladen. Mark Murphy and Eric Stone had figured out the exact amount needed to pull off Juan's stunt, and now they were about to find out if his two resident geniuses were right.

Wordlessly, they got to work. Jerry and Mike installed the engine covers and made sure they were watertight while Mark double-checked that all their dive bags full of equipment and weapons were securely tied down. After inspecting the open cabin for anything that might get damaged by emersion, Juan handed over the four Draeger rebreathers. Unlike Scuba tanks, there was no telltale trail of bubbles from the German-made device. They worked by scrubbing carbon dioxide from the closed-loop system and adding oxygen from a small tank when gas ratios tipped dangerously.

The men wore micro-thin black diving suits, not so much for thermal protection — the water was blood warm — but to cover their white skin. Their dive shoes had thick rubber soles and detachable flippers in case they needed to leave the water in a hurry.

"Would be nice if we could do this closer to the border," Jerry Pulaski commented. It was an observation hiding a mild complaint.

"Sure would be," Juan agreed, suppressing a grin. Satellite pictures showed the next town on the river was five miles downstream. Again, if he was part of the Argentine junta, he would pay some local wharf rat to drop a dime if he saw or heard anything suspicious. In this part of the world, patriotism was a poor substitute for a full belly, so the team was in for a long night. Cabrillo turned to Murphy. "You want the honors?"

"Hell no," Mark said. "If we got it wrong,

you're going to make Eric and me pay for the boat."

Juan shrugged. "Good point."

Standing chest-deep in the current, he reached over one of the inflatable fenders and opened a release valve. Air hissed from the valve under high pressure until the black rubber was limp. He nodded to Jerry to do the same on the other side, and soon they had half of them emptied. Water sloshed over the gunwale as the boat sank deeper into the river. Cabrillo and Pulaski pushed down on the hull. The boat sank farther and remained submerged, though the bow soon rose to the surface. More air was released until the RHIB was neutrally buoyant and perfectly balanced.

Not surprisingly, the calculations for the added ballast had been spot-on.

The team struggled into their rebreathers, fit full masks over their faces, and performed a communications check. There was little chance of running into crocodiles or caimans, but all had spearguns fitted into holsters strapped to their thighs.

Juan sliced the rope securing the RHIB to the hut and let the current take them. With each man holding a line attached to the boat, they swam their ungainly charge into the middle of the river. To Cabrillo, it felt like they were trying to herd a hippopotamus.

They stayed close to the surface for the first few miles, swimming lazily with the river's not-insignificant current. This far from the light pollution of any cities, the sky was a vaulted dome of glittering stars, so bright and so numerous it seemed as though night in this part of the world was silver and not black. It was more than bright enough to see both banks of the river and to keep the wallowing boat in the center of the channel.

Only when they neared the next village did the men dump air from their buoyancy compensators and take the RHIB down close to the bottom. Juan had taken a compass bearing before slipping below the surface, and he steered them by watching the dial's luminous face. It was an eerie feeling, swimming in water as dark as ink. With the temperature close to his own body's, it was as though he'd been denied all tactile sensation. They drifted for a mile, the men lazily finning to maintain steerage, before Cabrillo ordered them back to the surface.

The isolated village was well behind them, and they found they had the river to themselves. Even had there been traffic, their black gear, and the fact that only parts of their heads were exposed, would lead any native to believe the team was just a couple of branches being slowly swept down toward Argentina.

Hours rolled away. It was a faint glow emanating around the next bend that told them they were approaching the border. During their briefing, they had all seen satellite shots of the area. On the Paraguay side was a three-hundred-foot concrete quay fronting tumbledown warehouses and a customs shed. The sleepy little town was maybe four streets deep and equally wide. A white-steepled church was the tallest building. In response to the troop buildup, the local military commander had brought a detachment of soldiers to town. They were camped just north of the village in a field that ran right to the river's red-clay bank.

The Argentine side was almost identical, except there were at least five hundred soldiers garrisoned there, and they had strengthened their position by deploying search lights on spidery towers to sweep the black river, and strung thickets of concertina wire on the dirt road connecting the two towns. The satellite pictures showed two slim boats tied to the pier near where it looked like the military was headquartered. To Juan's eye they appeared to be Boston

Whalers, and, if he had to guess, they were probably armed with machine guns and possibly grenade launchers. They would be a problem if things got hairy.

Keeping close to the bottom, but not touching it so the hull didn't disturb the silt and leaves and kick up a telltale wake, the men swam through the formidable gauntlet. They knew they had reached the Argentine position when a shaft of light pierced the dark water. They were too deep and the river too muddy for anyone on shore to see them, but they steered away from the silvery glow anyway. On the surface, the two men in the tower watched whatever the beam revealed — empty water slowly flowing southward.

Cabrillo and the team remained submerged for another hour, only coming up when the border was miles behind them. It took another hour of drifting silently to reach a nameless tributary seen earlier from the satellite pictures. This time, the men had to work against the current, wrestling the unwieldy craft against the flow. Twenty minutes of struggle gained them only a hundred yards, but Juan called a halt, judging they were far enough upstream to keep them from potentially prying eyes.

He sighed as he stripped off the heavy

70

Draeger set and laid it into the half-sunk boat. "That feels good."

"My fingertips look like white prunes," Mark complained, holding them up to the moonlight.

"Quiet," Juan admonished in a whisper. "Okay, boys, you know what's next. The quicker we get it done, the more shut-eye we get."

The steel plates used to lower the RHIB's profile weighed fifty pounds each, a not-unreasonable load for men in peak physical condition, but there were hundreds of them that had to be lifted over the gunwale and dumped into the river. The men worked like machines, Jerry Pulaski especially. For every plate Murph or Mike Trono got over the side, he moved two. Slowly, so slowly, the boat began to emerge like some slimy amphibian from the primordial ooze. Once the sides cleared the surface, Murph engaged a battery-powered pump. The steady stream of water sounded like a babbling brook.

It took an hour, and when they were finished all four rolled onto the still-wet deck and lay like dead men.

Juan was the first to rouse himself. He told his men to sleep, and let Jerry know he would have second watch. The night sounds of the jungle were punctuated by the occasional snore.

Two hours later, shortly after dawn, the RHIB left the small tributary and returned to the river proper. The air cells they had emptied remained limp, but on such smooth water, and with such a light load, it wouldn't affect the boat's capabilities.

The four men now wore Argentine combat fatigues with the insignia of the Ninth Brigade and their trademark maroon berets. The Ninth was a well-trained and -outfitted paramilitary unit that answered only to General Corazón. In other words, a death squad.

Pretending to be a Ninth Brigade officer, Cabrillo knew he would be able to talk them into or out of any situation that could arise.

He stood at the RHIB's helm, wearing aviator-style glasses favored by members of the Ninth, his beret at a cocky angle on his head. Behind him, the twin outboards threw up a volcanic wall of white froth while the bow planed over the still surface like a rocket. Mike and Murph stood at his sides, Heckler and Koch machine pistols, a Ninth Brigade staple, slung across their backs. Jerry was still curled up on the fiberglass floorboards like a dog, somehow able to sleep despite the motor's roar.

The speedometer quivered just below forty miles per hour.

Twenty minutes downriver, they came to their first village. It was impossible to tell how long ago it had been destroyed — the amount of vegetation creeping into the burned-out shells of thatched huts led Juan to think months rather than weeks. Land behind the village that had been cleared for agriculture was also succumbing to the jungle's intractable advance.

"I know what those guys must have felt going upriver in *Apocalypse Now,*" Mike said.

There were no bodies lying on the ground — animals had seen to that shortly after the assault — but the savagery was still in clear abundance. The hamlet's score of cement-block buildings had been destroyed by high explosives. Chunks of concrete had been blown as far as the river's edge, and the few remaining sections of wall were riddled with machine-gun holes. There were countless impact craters from the mortar fire used to drive the frightened people into their fields, where the Argentines would have set up a perimeter picket of men. The villagers would have raced into a slaughter.

"Good God," Murph gasped as they

continued past. "Why? Why did they do this?"

"Ethnic cleansing," Juan replied, his mouth a tight, grim line. "This far north the villagers were probably Indians. Intel reports I've seen say the government in Buenos Aires wants to eradicate the last few pockets of natives remaining in the country. And to give you an idea of the characters we're impersonating" — he nodded in the direction of the little town — "that's most likely Ninth Brigade handiwork."

"Lovely," Mike spat. He'd tucked his beret into a shoulder epaulet, so his fine hair blew free around his head.

"Same thing's going on in the cities and towns. Anywhere they find natives, they drag them out and ship them off to either labor camps here in the Amazon or they just simply disappear. This place is a mix of Nazi Germany and Imperial Japan."

"How many Indians are left?"

"There were about six hundred thousand before the coup. God only knows how many have already been killed, but if this regime stays in power for a few more years, they're all going to end up dead."

They passed a ferryboat, lumbering its way slowly upstream. It was big enough for eight vehicles, and maybe forty passengers on its upper deck. The trucks aboard were all painted in camouflage colors, and the men lining the rail were soldiers. They waved over at the speeding RHIB, shouting greetings in Spanish. Keeping in character, the three men standing at the helm didn't deign to respond. When the Argentine soldiers were close enough to recognize the maroon berets, their happy calls fell to instant silence, and most of them suddenly had the need to see what was happening on the other side of the old craft.

There was little other traffic on the river, mostly hand-built pirogues with single paddlers working along the bank in search of fish. Juan felt bad when they were caught up in the RHIB's churning wake, but slowing down would have been the last thing a Ninth Brigader would do. Truth of it was, they probably would have aimed for the dugout canoes and rammed their occupants under the water.

Two and a half hours of hard running down the river brought them to a tributary about half the size of the main branch, the Rio Rojo, and because of the high iron content in the soils upstream the water was indeed a reddish brown, like a bloody stain that spread into the current. Pulaski was awake by now, and he and Mike had been scanning the river for any sign that they were being watched. There was nothing but the river and the jungle, which was a solid wall of intertwined vegetation.

"Clear," Mike called over the engines' growl.

"Clear," Jerry echoed at the bow, and lowered his binoculars.

Juan cut power just enough to make the sharp turn, and opened the throttles again as soon as the bow pointed upstream. The Rio Rojo was less than fifty yards wide, and the towering jungle seemed to meet overhead, filtering the sunlight with a greenish tinge. It was like they were making their way up a tunnel. Their wake caromed off the dirt banks, eroding clots of mud that fell into the water and dissolved.

They started upstream, keeping the speed down because, in less than five minutes, they came across an expected towboat hauling logs down from the highlands. The boat was a wooden-hulled, bow-heavy scow with black smoke belching from its exhaust and more smoke coiling from the engine housing at the stern. The tree trunks were left floating in the water with the perimeter logs chained together to keep the whole mass intact. Cabrillo estimated there were at least two hundred twenty-foot lengths of what looked to him to be mahogany. He figured a larger load would be too cumbersome in such a narrow river.

"No radio mast," Mark Murphy said.

"Probably has a sat phone," Juan replied. "But I'm not worried about them reporting us. He can tell we're Ninth Brigade, and he won't want any trouble from us."

They stayed far to the right side of the channel as they passed the lumber boat. Neither crew made any gesture of greeting. In fact, the tug's three-man crew kept their eyes pointed decidedly downstream the entire time.

Once clear, Juan opened the throttles further, but had to slow again just moments later. Another nearly identical boat appeared ahead. This one was making its way around a tight bend and was well into Cabrillo's side of the river. Tradition would be for Juan to idle his boat until the floating logjam made its turn and straightened out. But arrogant soldiers of an elite paramilitary group wouldn't care one bit about riverine customs.

In Spanish, Juan shouted, "Stop where you are and let us pass."

"I cannot," the boat's captain yelled back.

He hadn't bothered to look to see who was addressing him. He was watching the shifting mass of logs edging closer and closer to the inside bank. If they rammed into the shore, it was possible that his boat wouldn't have the power to pull them free. It wasn't an uncommon occurrence, and it could take hours for the crew to unchain some of the logs from the bundle in order to free themselves and hours more to set the load right again.

"I'm not asking, I'm telling," Juan said, letting anger drop his voice to a snarled hiss.

One of the deckhands tapped the boat's captain on the shoulder. The man finally looked over at the RHIB, with its crew of armed soldiers in maroon berets. He went a little pale under his two days' growth of beard.

"Okay, okay," he said with the resignation of the powerless in the face of oppression. He throttled back, and the current immediately slammed his load into the riverbank. A dozen logs as thick around as oil barrels were thrown onto shore. The impact snapped a section of chain, hurling bits of its rusted links through the air. The oily workboat slowly came across the current, pressing its load deeper into the bank while at the same time opening the channel for Cabrillo and the RHIB. Logs that had broken free were already drifting downstream.

Keeping in character, Juan threw the hapless men a mocking salute and firewalled the throttles.

Murph said, "It's going to take the better part of the day to clean that up."

"Had we waited for him to clear the corner, he would have been suspicious," Mike Trono countered. "Better them inconvenienced than us questioned. Juan speaks Spanish like a native, but I get lost with the menu at a Mexican restaurant."

They continued upstream, passing one more boat towing a mass of timber, before the handheld GPS said they were as close to the crash site as the river would take them. After cruising for another quarter mile, they found a small feeder stream, and Juan backed the boat into it. There was barely enough room for the RHIB's hull, and the jungle scraped against the vessel's rubber sides.

Jerry Pulaski tied a line around a moldering stump, and Juan cut the engines. After so many hours of their throaty roar, it took several seconds for Cabrillo to hear jungle sounds through the ringing in his ears. Without being told, the men set about camouflaging the boat, hacking fronds and leaves from different trees and bushes and creating an intricate screen over the RHIB's bow. When they were done, the craft was all but invisible from five feet away.

"Well, boys," Juan said as they gathered their communications equipment and other gear together, including a specially made harness for Jerry to carry the plutonium power cell, "our leisurely cruise downriver is over. Now the real slog begins. I'll take point. Mike, you've got the drag slot. Keep low and quiet. We have to assume the Argies have their own teams out here looking for the debris, or at least investigating. Stay sharp."

The men, their faces smeared with camouflage greasepaint, looking as fearsome as any native warrior, nodded silently as they stepped from the boat onto the spongy shore. They started inland, following a game trail that ran roughly parallel to the small stream. The temperature was a solid eighty degrees, with the humidity a few notches higher. In just a few minutes, their pores were running like faucets.

For the first mile, Cabrillo felt every muscle cramp and ache from their time in the river, but as they forged on the countless laps he'd swum over the course of his life began to show. He moved more lithely, his boots merely brushing the loamy soil. Even his stump was feeling good. He'd always been more accustomed to wide-open spaces — the sea or the desert — but his other senses were making up for what his eyes could not see. There was a faint trace of woodsmoke in the air — from the logging operation, he knew — and when a bird's startled cry carried down from the jungle canopy, he paused and waited to learn what had disturbed it. Was it startled by a predator or by something it saw walking the same path as Juan's team?

The mental acuity required for jungle stalking was as physically taxing as the effort to slide through the dense foliage.

Something off to his left caught Juan's eye. He immediately dropped to a knee, hand-signaling the men strung out behind him to do likewise. Cabrillo studied the spot that had attracted his attention through his machine pistol's iron sights. The quick squirt of adrenaline into his veins seemed to heighten his vision. He perceived no movement, not even a breeze rustling the leaves. This far below the canopy, air movement was a rarity. He cautiously swayed back, changing his angle of view in minute increments.

There.

A dull flash of metal. Not the slick black sheen of a modern weapon trained on him but the pewter shimmer of old aluminum left out in the elements. According to the GPS, they were still several miles from where the power cell was projected to have landed, and he wondered for a moment if this was other debris from the doomed satellite.

Still in a crouch, and with the MP-5 tucked hard against his shoulder, he moved off the trail, confident that what he was taking away from his own peripheral vision would be covered by his men. He approached with the patience of one of the jungle cats. Five feet away, he saw the outline of something large through the undergrowth. Whatever this was, it wasn't part of the doomed orbiter.

He used his weapon's barrel to move aside a clump of vines hanging from a tree and grunted in surprise. They had discovered what looked like the cockpit of a downed plane. The windshield was long gone, and creepers had infiltrated, snaking around seats and bulkheads like a cancerous growth. But what really held his attention was what lay in the copilot's seat. There was little left of the body, just a brown-green skeleton that would soon dissolve into its chair. Its clothing had long since rotted away, but lying in the pelvic girdle and shining brightly in the diffused sunlight was a brass strip that Juan knew had been the guy's zipper.

He whistled softly, and seconds later Mark Murphy and Jerry Pulaski approached. Mike would remain near the trail, watching their six.

"What do you think?" Juan asked quietly.

"Looks like this plane's been here awhile," Jerry said, swatting at a mouse-sized bug that had landed on his neck.

Mark's expression was thoughtful for a moment, and then his eyes widened. "This isn't a plane," he said with awe in his voice. "This is the *Flying Dutchman.*"

"Forgive my ignorance, but wasn't the *Dutchman* a ghost ship?" Pulaski replied.

"The *Flying Dutchman* was a blimp," Mark told him, and pointed. "Look between the seats. See that big wheel. That's for controlling a blimp's pitch. Rotate it forward, it engages the elevator on the fin assembly, and she goes nose down. Move it back, and the nose rises."

"What makes you think this is the *Flying Dutchman* and not some lost Navy patrol from World War Two?"

"Because we're a thousand miles inland from both the Atlantic and the Pacific, and the *Flying Dutchman* went missing while looking for a lost city in the jungle."

"Okay," Juan said. "Go back and tell it from the beginning."

Mark couldn't tear his eyes off the airship's shattered gondola. "When I was a kid, I kind of had a thing for blimps and zeppelins. It was just a fad, you know, a hobby. Before that, it was locomotives from the Steam Age." Seeing the expressions staring at him, he added, "Look, I admit it. I was a geek."

"Was?" Jerry deadpanned.

"Anyway, I read a lot of books about airships, their history. Like the story of the L-8, a Navy patrol blimp that took off from San Francisco in August of 1942. A couple of hours into a routine patrol, the two-man crew reported seeing an oil slick. A couple hours after that, the blimp floated back over the coast, minus the men. The only clue was that two life jackets were missing."

"What's that got to do with this?" Juan asked a little impatiently. Mark Murphy was the smartest guy Cabrillo had ever met, but with that came his tendency to go off on tangents that highlighted his near-photographic memory.

"Well, another lost-blimp story is the *Flying Dutchman*. I hope I am remembering this right. After the war, a former Navy blimp pilot and some of his buddies bought a surplus airship to use as an aerial platform to fly over the South American jungle in search of an Incan city, most likely El Dorado. They converted the blimp to fly on hydrogen, which is insanely explosive, but it was something they could make themselves using electrolysis.

"Treasure hunters?" Pulaski asked dubiously.

"I didn't say they were right," Mark replied on the defensive. "I'm only saying they were real."

"This is all well and good," Cabrillo said, backing away from the ruined cockpit and its grisly occupant. "I've marked the location on the GPS, but we've got a mission to perform."

"Give me five minutes," Mark pleaded.

Juan thought for a second. Nodded.

Murph grinned his thanks. He crawled through the opening where the gondola's door had been ripped off when the airship crashed into the jungle. To his left were the two pilots' seats and controls. To the right was the cabin proper. It had the neat economy and efficiency of a travel trailer. There were two bunk beds, a tiny galley with an electric burner, and a dozen storage lockers. He opened each in turn, rummaged around for any clues, and moved on when all he found were clots of mildew and mold or old surplus mess kits the men must have used to make their meals.

In one locker he found the metal remains of a climbing harness. The webbing and ropes had dissolved to goo, but the steel remained unchanged over the years. He knew instinctively that they had used the gear to lower one of their own out the gondola for ground reconnaissance. He finally hit pay dirt when he opened the rusted remains of a coffee can that had been left on the little dinette table.

He cursed himself for not realizing its significance immediately. The can would have tumbled to the cabin floor when the blimp crashed. There was no way it should be on the table unless someone had placed it there. A survivor. Inside, he discovered a white rubber sheath about six inches in length. It took him a moment to realize it was a condom. By the feel of it, there was something stuffed inside — papers, most likely — a final log entry? The open end had been knotted shut.

After sixty years lying out here, this wasn't the time or place to open it. He would need the preservation equipment on the *Oregon* if he had any chance of learning more. He carefully sealed the prophylactic in a waterproof pouch and tucked it into his fanny pack.

"Time's up," Juan said. The jungle was so thick that his voice was disembodied, yet he stood only a few yards away.

"I'm done." Mark emerged from the gondola. With a last look back, he vowed to find the names of the men who had crashed here and inform their surviving relatives.

FOUR

Wilson/George Research Station
Antarctic Peninsula

The winds had picked up, so the sky screamed over the domes, carrying with it curtains of blowing snow. Such was the oddity that was the planet's most isolated continent that much of it, though snow-covered, is considered a desert, with only trace amounts of precipitation. The peninsula saw far more snowfall than the interior, but it was possible the flakes raking the facility had fallen hundreds of years ago.

This wasn't yet the storm they were anticipating, just a subtle reminder that, no matter what, humanity is an interloper here.

Andy Gangle woke with a screaming headache. It wasn't the dull pain of too much time staring at a computer screen. Rather, it was the sharp stab of drinking something too cold too quickly, and no matter what he did — like pressing chemical hand warmers to his temples, as if to defrost his brain — nothing helped.

Not the darkened room, not the pain tablets he'd dry-swallowed moments after being struck with the crippling agony. Despite his vehement need for privacy, a low moan escaped his white lips, a plaintive, albeit unintended, call for help. He lay curled in a fetal position on the sweat-soaked tangle of sheets and woolen blankets. Opposite Gangle's bed, and staring down since his arrival, was the iconic image of Albert Einstein sticking his tongue out at the camera.

He'd won that picture in an eighth-grade science contest, and it had stayed on his wall through high school and had a place of honor in a succession of dorm rooms. It was a little tattered, but whenever he was troubled he would look at the photograph and find the absurdity in whatever was bothering him. If Einstein, with the burden of knowing his equations had helped decimate two Japanese cities, could laugh at the world, then there was nothing going to stop Andy Gangle.

He looked at it now and felt nothing but rage. A blinding rage fueled by the unmitigated agony searing his brain. What did Einstein know of burden? Andy thought. He'd made his mark in physics as a young man and spent the rest of his life doddering around. To hell with him. To hell with them all. Moving faster than he thought possible, Gangle uncoiled his gawky limbs, leapt from the bed, and clawed the poster from the wall. Clear tape adhered four little triangles of paper to the wall, but the rest came off in a sheet. Savagely, Andy tore at the poster, ripping at it with his fingers and teeth, damp confetti falling to the linoleum-tiled decking.

Gina Alexander was passing by Andy's door on the way to her place in the kitchen, thinking that in five days, if the weather held, a big beautiful C-130 Hercules airplane would land on the ice runway a quarter mile inland from the station and that she'd be out there waiting for it. Next stop Chile, then Miami, then . . . what?

She didn't know. Coming to Antarctica had been cathartic, and her time here had put the pain of her husband's betrayal and their divorce into a locked corner of her heart, but she didn't know what would come next. She hadn't thought that far ahead. She considered the possibility of moving closer to her parents, but the very idea of living in a place called Plant City, Florida, grayed her hair and made her fingers curl with imaginary arthritis.

A sound coming from Andy's room as she passed by had a reptilian quality, a dry, rasping hiss, like a monstrous snake or some giant lizard. She paused in midstride and listened. It did not come again. The thought of knocking on Andy's door and asking if he was okay came and went as fast as her mind could process it. If Andy Bug-eyes was having a problem, that was just too bad. He'd alienated the entire team with his odd behavior, and Gina was a firm believer in "you reap what you sow."

A minute later, she was greeting a few of the science types, as she warmed the griddle and dropped the first batches of bread into the restaurant-grade toasters.

It would have behooved Gina to check on Andy or tell Greg Lamont, the station commander, what she'd heard.

Andy had discovered a way to dull the pain in his head. It had happened in the frenzied seconds when he was shredding the poster. In his enraged fit to see it utterly destroyed, his coordination was off just enough so when his teeth clamped down on a section of paper, his incisors nipped the flesh to the side of his index fingernail. The blood was a warm combination of copper and salt, not unpleasant, but unexpected in

91

that as soon as it touched his lips the pain spiking behind his eyes dimmed, like an industrial lightbulb goes from glaring white to just an amber glow and then fades to nothing.

The morsel of flesh, as he chewed it, was rubbery, like a pencil eraser that had hardened over time. He contemplated what he was doing, as his finger dripped blood. He brought his hand up to his face, staring in fascination at the patterns the blood made as it dribbled across his skin. He waved his hand to make lines of blood across his palm. He giggled, dipping his finger into the blood and writing on the wall, red smears on clean white plastic. He wrote letters, formed them into words, into a concept he should have seen all along. It was so simple, so perfect. He admitted the line he'd written was crudely formed, blood not being as easy to work with as paint, but the meaning was perfectly clear.

Mime Goering for crow Nicole.

Some instinct, some sense of self-preservation buried deep in his brain, told him to clean himself before he went to find what he needed to carry out his plan. With his finger wrapped in masking tape from his desk and the worst of the blood wiped from his lips, Andy Gangle checked that the hallway was clear and stepped from his room.

FIVE

Juan held up a hand when he heard the distinct sound of approaching helicopters. The noise was muted by the jungle canopy, and he couldn't hope to spot them through the dense foliage that hung over the ground like a living shroud. But the best hunters in the world can spot the tiniest movement in the riot of vegetation, and he had no doubt that these were military choppers. They didn't have that refined sound of executive helos built to deliver the pampered. These sounded raw, stripped down to the bare essentials in order to pack in as many men and as much gear as possible. Yet the human eye perceives motion better than pattern, so the men waited, crouched along the game trail until the sound faded. Ominously, in the direction they were heading.

"What do you think, Chairman?" Jerry Pulaski asked.

"Our welcoming committee has arrived.

Let's make sure they don't have time to set up the party." Juan checked the handheld GPS. "The trail is taking us slightly east of where we need to go. Time to hoof it cross-country. Same formation."

By staying low, the men could duck under the thicker leaves and fronds, though Jerry, with his six-inch height advantage, found himself at a disadvantage in the jungle. After ten minutes, razor-sharp leaves had cut his face as though he'd been shaving with a month-old razor, and insects dove at him with the abandon of kamikaze pilots, in their hunger for such an easy meal.

To add insult to already injured bodies, the terrain started to rise. They were heading into foothills of mountains they'd seen on the recon photographs. And the smell of burning brush was growing stronger. The slash-and-burn logging operation was only a few miles away.

Juan did the best he could blazing a trail through the underbrush, and when he spotted what looked to be a large opening ahead he made the mistake of rushing through rather than checking it out first. He stepped onto a dirt road at the very instant a semi-trailer went roaring past, its engine beat muffled by the bend it had just rounded. Had Juan emerged a second later, the driver would have seen him though not in time to brake.

Cabrillo froze, windmilling his arms to prevent himself from taking a final step under the empty timber hauler's massive tires. The stakes used to contain the logs the big rig hauled down to the river flashed inches from his face, and the vortex they cut through the soggy air threatened to suck him into the hurtling steel.

And then it was past in a cloud of dust. Juan took what could have been his last step and exhaled a breath he hadn't realized he'd been holding. Training then bypassed the fear and shock, and he dove flat onto the deeply rutted road on the off chance the driver glanced at his rearview mirror. Cabrillo lay prone until the truck rumbled out of sight, then dodged back undercover.

"Close one," Murph remarked unnecessarily.

Juan knew his subordinate was teasing him but didn't rise to the bait.

When they were sure no more trucks would roar out of nowhere, the team dashed across the road in a tight pack, with Mike Trono trailing a hastily cut branch to obscure their boot prints.

Safely hidden on the other side, Juan withdrew the gamma detector from his pack. The piece of electronics was military grade, meaning it was as simple as the builders could get it. The machine itself was a matte-black box about the size of an old tape recorder. There was a simple on/off switch, one red light, and a clear panel that showed a single needle. When the red lamp came on, the machine was detecting gamma rays, and by sweeping it through three hundred and sixty degrees and watching the needle the user would learn in which direction the source lay.

Juan turned it on. The detector chirped once to tell him it was working, but the indicator light remained dark. They were still too far from the downed power cell to detect the trace amounts of gamma rays it emitted.

They started slogging higher into the hills, crossing and recrossing the same haul road as it switchbacked up the mountain. The smell of smoke was no longer an ethereal wisp carried on the breeze. The air was slowly filling with it, and white clouds clung to depressions in the land like noxious gas from a chemical attack.

Mark suggested flagging down the next truck they saw to ask for a lift and was only half joking. Juan knew the men were getting tapped out and decided that once they had the NASA cell in the shielded harness, they would find someplace to lay up for the night and make their way down to the boat and the hell out of Argentina the next morning.

It was noon when they reached the crest of the mountain. They approached it cautiously, on their bellies, so as not to show movement to anyone in the valley beyond. What greeted them was a scene out of hell.

What had once been a lush primeval forest was now a barren wasteland of mud and brush many miles across. Burn piles as tall as haystacks gave off towering pyres of smoke and fire while yellow excavators lumbered across the landscape, whole trees caught in their mechanical jaws. Amid the chaos, like ants, were men, moving from grove to grove, their saws keening, then straining, as they bit through timber that had taken generations to grow.

Off to the team's left, the clear-cutting was spreading like a cancer up the flanks of a mountain that had already been scarred with yet another recurring haul road. Something caught Juan's attention. He handed the gamma detector to Mark Murphy, grabbed binoculars from his pack, and checked that the angle of the sun wouldn't reflect off the lenses before putting them to his eyes.

In the distance he could see a flattened area halfway up the hill that was used to load logs onto the semis. There was an aluminum-sided construction trailer and several specialized timber-industry vehicles: grapple-claw crawlers and log skidders with cleated-steel tires. Just beyond sat the two choppers they had heard earlier, their rotors sagging in the afternoon sun, their camouflage-paint scheme nearly matching the jungle behind them.

Soldiers were assembled in a loose parade formation while two other uniformed men — officers, he assumed — were talking with a small group of loggers. At their feet lay a charred scrap of metal. Juan couldn't make out details, but it didn't take a great intuitive leap to guess it was a fragment of the downed rocket or its payload. As he watched, the civilians repeatedly pointed up the mountainside as if indicating that something important had happened near its summit or just beyond.

"What's going on?" Mike asked.

"The party's getting started," Juan said grimly.

"I got something," Mark said, sweeping the gamma ray detector.

"Where?" Juan demanded.

"Over there." Mark pointed. "Signal's

weak, but it's definitely where the Argies are having their little powwow."

Juan imagined the events leading up to this particular tableau. When the rocket exploded and rained debris across the jungle, something landed in the clearing and was recovered by the loggers. They dragged it to the staging area to show the foremen, who called in the military to investigate. At this moment, they were telling the soldiers that another piece of debris had crashed at or near the top of the mountain.

Major Jorge Espinoza of the Ninth Brigade liked orders. He liked receiving them, he liked giving them, and he liked to see when they were carried out. The nature of the orders never bothered him. Told to march through a swamp for seven days during the training for his coveted maroon beret or burn a hamlet of indigenous farmers to the ground, it made no difference. He carried out both with utter determination and dedication. In his years of military service, he'd never once questioned if his directives were moral. That played no part in his reasoning. Orders were given. Orders were executed. There was nothing else.

His men saw him as the perfect leader, one unfettered by emotion or doubt. But in his private moments, Major Jorge Espinoza admitted to himself that there were orders he preferred over others. He'd enjoyed slaughtering villagers a lot more than spending a week chest-deep in a leech-filled swamp.

His was a military family that had served Argentina for four generations. His father had been a Colonel in Intelligence during the glory days when the Generals ran the country. He had regaled his sons with stories about what they did to enemies of the state, of helicopter flights laden with bound dissidents over the icy South Atlantic. They made a game of heaving them though the open door from a thousand feet. The object was to throw the second man onto the frothing splash of the first, and so on with the rest of the prisoners.

It was the psychopath's version of ring toss, but Jorge never saw it that way.

He had been too young to see action when the British retook the Islas Malvinas, but had been trained by combat veterans and had been an exemplary soldier ever since. When the Ninth Brigade was formed after General Corazón led the charge against the weak former President, Jorge Espinoza had been one of the first to volunteer. His training was no easier than that of the younger enlisted men he now commanded, and for that he had forever gained their loyalty.

He was now the deputy commander of the entire brigade under General Philippe Espinoza, his father, who had come out of retirement for the position. Any rumors of nepotism were silenced by the sheer ruthlessness and efficiency with which the younger Espinoza carried out his duties.

And he was a commander who liked to lead from the front. Which was why he was here, deep in the Amazonian region of his country, talking to lumberjacks about something they had seen crash near their work site. The wreckage they had shown him certainly looked like part of the American rocket. It was made of lightweight aluminum, carefully riveted so not the slightest imperfection showed on its surface. The edges were torn as if by an explosion, and there were score marks on the white paint.

The junta saw the recovery of any piece of the rocket as potential to embarrass the United States. They didn't know what the payload had been. NASA claimed a weather satellite, but the Generals in charge couldn't ignore the chance that its purpose was espionage.

"We think another piece landed on the far side of the mountain," the lumber foreman said, pointing to the half-denuded hill behind them. He was nervous around so many maroon berets but had felt it his duty to call in the military. "It is past where you see those men logging on the hill. Some of them wanted to go find it, but I pay them to cut timber, not explore. It was bad enough they wasted an hour digging this one out of the mud."

Espinoza glanced at his aide, Lieutenant Raul Jimenez. Unlike the Major, who had light brown hair and blue eyes from his paternal grandmother, Jimenez maintained the Gypsy dark looks of his Basque ancestors. The two men had worked and trained together for nearly their entire careers. The difference in rank wasn't because of differing abilities but because Jimenez refused to leave his friend's side for a command of his own.

They needn't exchange a word to know what the other was thinking.

"Round up as many men as you can in fifteen minutes," Jimenez commanded. He had a drill instructor's voice that demanded action. "We will form a skirmish line and make our way up the mountain until we find what the *Yanquis* lost in the jungle."

The only sign that the logging company foreman was upset by the order was that he scratched under his filthy hard hat before nodding. "Anything for the Ninth Brigade."

The civilians moved off to roust their men, leaving Espinoza alone with his adjutant. Both men lit cigarillos, sharing a single wind-resistant match. "What do you think, *Jefe?*" Jimenez asked, exhaling a cloud of smoke that mingled with the pall already hanging over the camp.

"We'll find whatever these men saw," Major Espinoza said. "The only question is if it will be worth our while."

"Anytime we can show the world that the Americans aren't infallible is always good for the Ministry of Propaganda."

"World opinion is so against our government right now that I'm afraid a few bits of space junk won't change many hearts or minds. But orders are orders, yes? And this is a good training exercise for the men. They can grow soft clearing out villages from the comfort of our gunboats."

Cabrillo and his men were already on the move by the time the logging camp's foreman was ordered to gather his men. It would be a race to see who reached the prize first. Juan and the team had more ground to cover, but they would remain near the crest of the hills while the Argentine soldiers were forced to climb the mountainside. They would be further hampered by the need for a slow, deliberate approach to their search. The men from the Corporation had the gamma detector acting like a bloodhound to help pinpoint the power cell.

Knowing the competition was close goaded them on, allowing them to push past the aches creeping into their muscles and joints. If they could reach the power cell and retreat, then the Argentines would have no idea they were ever here.

The men moved swiftly but maintained noise discipline. There was no sound louder than the rasp of vegetation on cloth and the steady whisper of their breathing. The smoke billowing up from below, where the forest was being cleared, was just a thin veil at their altitude, but down where the soldiers were starting their skirmish line it was one more impediment to their search.

Juan didn't break stride when he heard the approaching whine of a helicopter's jet engine, but he couldn't help but feel his heart sink. He should have realized they would use aerial reconnaissance. A piece of space debris weighing seventy pounds and slamming into the earth at terminal velocity would leave an impact crater more than large enough to be spotted from the air. It was only a question of whether enough jungle canopy remained to hide it from above.

He had a feeling they wouldn't be that lucky.

"Signal from the detector's still looking good," Mark said. They had abandoned a normal separation for the fast trot around the mountain's top, so he was just a few paces behind the Chairman.

Forty hard minutes later, they were close to where the chopper traversed the jungle, searching for any sign of an impact. There was no way to know how the soldiers on the ground were doing with their assent. The men were forced to reduce their pace whenever the Argentine helo flew within visual range.

Juan wished their detector could give them a range to target. Without that information, he didn't know if they were near the power cell or had another mile to go. The noise from the chopper suddenly changed. It no longer Dopplered back and forth through the haze but held a steady rhythm. It was hovering about a half mile ahead. That could mean only one thing.

They were over the power cell's impact crater.

Cabrillo cursed. A team could fast rope

down from the helo, grab the cell, and be back aboard by the time he and his men had covered half that distance.

Without being spurred, the men put on a burst of speed, cutting through the jungle as if born to it. Juan ran with single-minded determination, starting to burn into the reserves of strength that had never let him down before. He knew that even after everything they'd been through to get to this point, he was capable of a six-minute mile. Mike Trono managed to keep pace, but Mark and Jerry were beginning to lag.

The chopper inexplicably veered out of its hover and beat south, toward the logging camp. Cabrillo took this as a good omen and slowed, the turbines and rotor beat no longer masking the sound of his running. His chest heaved, but he forced his breathing under control by taking huge lungfuls of air to resaturate his tissues with oxygen. He could almost feel the lactic acid dissolving from his muscles. He and Mike dropped flat and began to crawl on their stomachs, making their final approach with serpentine stealth.

The power cell had crashed into the earth at a shallow angle, tearing though the jungle and leaving in its wake a charred cone of foliage. The crater itself was a blacked ring of churned soil. Five Argentine soldiers had roped down to the site. Two of them were digging into the crater with shovels probably pilfered from the loggers while the others had set up a strong perimeter. All five wore distinctive maroon berets.

Juan knew from studying the Ninth Brigade in order to impersonate them that they operated in squads of six. There was another man out here with them, someone he couldn't see. He quickly triple-clicked his combat radio's mike. It was a command for everyone to hold in place and find cover.

He and Mike could take out the three sentries before they could radio a warning and then take out the shovelers, who had both stripped to the waists and piled their gear a few yards off. But the sixth man. The invisible man. He was a wild card that would have to be dealt with first.

Cabrillo unslung his MP-5 machine pistol from around his neck. It would be nothing but a hindrance while he was stalking. The pistol, too, would remain in its holster. Even had he brought a silencer, the sound of a muffled shot would startle the local wildlife into panicked flight and alert the Argentines.

He had known some men who preferred the intimacy of killing with a knife. He'd never liked or trusted any of them because of it, but he was familiar with the techniques and had employed them more than once. Killing with a knife was filthy work, and those that took to it, in his experience, did it more for the life they took than for furthering the goals of their mission.

It was difficult to survey the scene. His view was obstructed starting inches from his face, so it was difficult to place himself in the sixth man's mind and guess where he had positioned himself to secretly watch over his comrades digging to get the chunk of satellite.

At the ten o'clock position from where Juan lay, the undergrowth was thinner because several trees towered over it and blocked sunlight from nourishing the ground cover. This would give a gunman a better field of vision. Cabrillo decided that was where his man was waiting. He was just about to start out. He knew he would circle around, come at the Ninth Brigader from the back, then he and Mike would take out the rest. Juan drew his knife, made a fractional move to his left, and froze.

Voices.

A dozen or more, shouting and laughing, as they charged through the jungle like a pack of wild boars. It was a mix of soldiers and loggers, the men who had slogged up the mountain. The satellite's location had been radioed to them, and they had rushed to the scene.

Cabrillo stayed still. Any action now would be suicide. Wary of the still-missing sixth squad mate, he resisted the urge to use the radio to call up Murph and Pulaski. Better they all remain as motionless as possible and wait to see what opportunity would present itself.

For the hour it took the men to wrest the seventy-pound power cell from the earth, Juan watched silently while next to him Mike slept. Somewhere in the jungle behind them, he knew either Mark or Jerry was also catching some much-needed sleep.

They were close enough to the impact crater for Juan to overhear a Lieutenant's call down to the command post. "We have it, *Jefe* . . . I'm not sure. It's about half a meter long, rectangular, and weighs maybe thirty kilos . . . What? . . . I don't know, some sort of scientific apparatus if I had to guess. I have no idea what its function . . . No, sir. It will be easier if we carry it back to where they are loading logs. We saw that they have a couple of pickup trucks. We'll use those to get back down to the camp. The pilot should have found the electrical short in the chopper by the time we get there, and we can get back to base in time for cocktails at the O club."

Cabrillo had heard enough. He knew their plan, and that was the edge he needed. He tapped Mike on the shoulder. The former rescue jumper came awake instantly but silently. His combat awareness was acute even in sleep. Together, they backed away from near the impact crater, making sure not to disturb vegetation overhead and marking their position. They met up with Jerry and Murph a quarter mile back.

"They've got the satellite," Murph said. "I can tell it's on the move."

Juan nodded, sipping from his canteen. He hadn't dared take a drink since first coming across the Argentine Special Forces. "They're hiking it back to the trailhead, and then they'll drive it down to camp and fly out on the helos."

"And we're . . . ?" Mark arched one Goth-plucked eyebrow.

"Going to stop them."

Coming down the mountain in two parallel groups, the soldiers and the Corporation team were converging on a leveled-off section of hillside at least two acres across that the loggers had cleared to set up some equipment. There was an excavator with a grapple for loading logs onto the semis and a machine called a cable yarder. The tracked yarder had a tall mast supporting wires that ran two miles down the hillside to a mobile spar that was anchored by guylines at the base camp. From this long loop of cable dangled choker lines that the axmen could slip around the dressed trunks of felled trees. The logs were then hauled upslope to where they were placed on the tractor trailers, and the choker send down again for the next load.

The men who worked at this upper site had arrived from the base in the pickup trucks Raul Jimenez planned on procuring.

Juan was confident his four-man team could beat the larger Argentine group until they came across a cleft in the earth, the result of an earthquake that had split the land in two and caused part of the mountain to subside. Because of the jungle, it was impossible to know how far the fissure ran, so they had no choice but to treat it as an obstacle to be surmounted, not circumvented. In the geologic timescale, the tembler had struck just a short while ago — twelve thousand years, in fact. Enough time had elapsed that the sides of the fissure had eroded to a manageable slope, but they had to descend fifty feet and scramble up the other side using fingers and knees, brute strength, and muttered curses.

They were all winded by the time they reached the top, and, by Juan's watch, they had lost fifteen precious minutes. They ran on, hoping for the best but fearing the worst. Juan had known since accepting the assignment from Langston Overholt that he hadn't had the time to put together an appropriate plan and that was now coming to haunt him. They were facing two squads of Argentina's best-trained troops with nothing more than four machine pistols and the element of surprise. The odds of getting the power cell without engaging the soldiers were zero, and getting the cell and escaping back to Paraguay he put at no better than twenty/eighty.

Six

By the time Juan and the others reached the edge of the upper logging site, the soldiers of the Ninth Brigade had loaded their prize into the back of a pickup and were hopping into the truck with it. Half of them took a second truck. The vehicles' owner knew not to protest.

From where they crouched at the edge of the jungle, the range to the Argentines wasn't extreme, four hundred yards or so. But the team carried machine pistols, which were devastating weapons in close-quarter combat but would be useless at this distance. Juan suspected the Ninth Brigade chose to issue the wicked-looking MP-5 to its men because of its intimidation factor more than its utility in combat situations.

Juan had a choice to make and he quickly ran through his options. A head-on charge would be suicide, and the idea of slinking back into the jungle without the power cell was equally unappealing. They had come too far to fail now, and "quit" wasn't a word Cabrillo allowed himself to contemplate too often. It was why the Corporation was the best in the world at what they did. And the truth was, much of their success had stemmed from Juan's ability to think on his feet, to find a third option no one else would consider.

Ideas ran through his brain but were quickly rejected as unworkable, and no matter how fast he came up with new ones, events continued to unfold. The Ninth Brigade soldiers had finished leaping into the beds of the two pickups, and exhaust bloomed from both tailpipes. Next to them smoke exploded from the twin stacks of a semitrailer loaded with logs so newly cut that the bark glistened with sap.

"Chairman?" Mark Murphy said in a whisper. He had never seen Cabrillo take so much time.

Juan held up a fist to stem the questions and crawled forward in the long grass that was growing like a curb between the jungle proper and the compacted-earth staging area cleared by the loggers. He reached the far side and looked down the mountain to the one-lane road that curled around its flank as sinuously as a snake. Shimmering above it, and as seemingly thin as gossamer, was the loop of steel wire for the cable yarder.

The two mud-splattered pickup trucks started pulling away while the big rig's cab shuddered when the driver put it in gear and started after them.

There it was, he thought. Not perfect, but it was better than nothing.

He broke cover, waving for his men to follow. They emerged from the jungle and sprinted after Cabrillo. It was like the final lap of a race, when the exhaustion falls away and the body responds to chemical signals that it is "now or never." The dozen loggers left milling around the shed-sized cable yarder saw four more Ninth Brigade soldiers running out of the jungle, who had presumably gotten separated and were now chasing after their comrades in the just-departed pickups.

They didn't know anything was amiss until one of the new soldiers brought his rifle to his eye, shouting, "Down! Everyone get down, and stay down."

Juan didn't wait to see if his orders were being followed. He trusted his men would see to it that they were. He raced for the yarder's cab, a modified excavator that had had its boom removed and the cable tower

116

attached in its place. The driver was protected in the cab from flying debris by a mesh cage that had replaced the glass windows. The cab door was open, the driver sitting casually in his seat, a cigarette dangling between the first and second fingers of his left hand. He hadn't seen the Corporation team approach, and, with the diesel idling, hadn't heard the shouted commands, so when Juan reached into the cab and heaved the man out of his seat the surprise was total. He landed on the rutted ground, the impact forcing every molecule of air from his chest.

"Murph," Juan called. "Get over here and figure out the controls."

As a trained engineer, Mark had an intuitive sense of how things worked, stemming no doubt from his childhood hobby of taking things apart and putting them back together, a hobby his parents put a stop to when they came home one day to find his father's vintage Porsche in pieces.

Murph left Jerry and Mike to cover the loggers and jumped for the cab.

"Mike," Juan shouted as he made his way to the edge of the clearing overlooking what had once been prime forest and was now a smoldering moonscape. "Find the keys to that third pickup and get her started.

117

The choke line for the cable yarder was suspended from a block system that could raise or lower the thick loop of wire so when they were dragging a log clear it wouldn't snag on the stumps of already fallen trees.

Juan made sure his machine pistol was secure across his back and called Mark on the radio. He stepped onto the loop of the choke line and held on with one hand. "Do you know what I have in mind?"

"You want me to haul you down the mountain and drop you into the pickup with the power cell."

"Not quite," Cabrillo replied, and told Mark what he wanted done.

"Man, you're crazy. Inspired, but crazy."

It took Murph just one false start to learn the controls of what was essentially a simple machine to operate. The trick was to operate it well. He eased back on the choker, feeding braided steel wire into the block hanging from the main yarder line.

Cabrillo braced for the impact of the choker coming taut and had to give his weapons specialist credit as he was gently lifted into the air. Like a skier who didn't get off the lift at the top and now descending, Juan started sailing down the mountain, picking up speed as Mark surveyed the scene below, calculating tricky vectors in his head in order to get the Chairman to his target.

Juan soared fifty feet off the ground, zooming over a hillside made barren by the loggers. It was like a controlled zip line, and, had the scenery been better, he would have paid for the ride. Brush piles smoldered on either side of the yarder line, so he felt like he was flying over the very pit of hell itself. He crossed over the road in the wake of the three-vehicle convoy headed down to the base camp. The pickups had pulled far ahead of the fully laden eighteen-wheeler as he knew they would. The second time the line crossed over the road was two hundred yards ahead, directly over a hairpin corner the pickups were just about to clear.

If any of the soldiers clutching the bed's rail looked up, Juan was as exposed as he could be. He'd be nothing more than a human target. Mark must have changed his calculations because the choker block began to decelerate. Juan pendulumed forward, and the choker started to twist. He fought to keep facing forward. He could hear the semi's air brakes growl when the truck approached the sharp bend. Cabrillo accelerated again, swinging back and forth on the line as it twirled first one way, then the other. Moving through space on three axes

119

was disorientating enough, and he still had to time his landing.

The truck drove deep into the curve before the driver started to crank the wheel. Juan was fifty feet up the hill and coming fast. Too fast, he realized, and even as he thought it the choker block slowed and the line began to reel out, lowering him closer and closer to the timber hauler. It was a remarkable feat of depth perception and control on Murph's part, as he dropped the Chairman toward the loaded trailer, timing it so that the turn hid the descending block from the soldiers at the last critical second.

The wire loop Juan was standing on twisted hard enough to squeeze his foot with a crushing pressure that would have shattered bone and pulped flesh had he not been standing on his prosthetic leg. Even without having to deal with pain, he had to kick with all his strength to free the limb as he soared over the back of the truck. The logs just a few tantalizing feet below him were three feet in diameter, with bark as thick and rough as alligator hide.

The driver began to straighten out as he guided his load through the hairpin. In seconds he would pull away from the arrow-straight yarder cable, leaving Cabrillo hanging in space. Juan kicked again to free his foot but could do nothing until the choker wire twisted back. He was less than five feet from the rear of the trailer. Then three. He felt himself rotating clockwise again. He heaved on his foot and it popped free. Holding on with one arm, Juan found his spot on the topmost log and let go.

He landed a bit awkwardly, not fully adjusting to the rig's steady acceleration, and started rolling off the log. He reached out to find a finger hold in the irregular bark and came away with a fistful of crumbling wood. He slid farther, and spreading his knees to clutch the log with his legs did no good. He went over.

And immediately slammed into one of the steel supports used to contain the trunks. It hit in the small of his back. Had it not been for the minimal cushioning of his pack, he felt certain he would have broken bone. It took him a few stunned moments to recover from both the pain and the fact he hadn't fallen off the truck, then he scrambled back to the top log and, in a crouch, started making his way toward the cab.

"I'm on," he radioed Murph.

"I can see that. You blew the landing, but I'll still give you seven-point-five."

Cabrillo had always found humor in the absurd, and replied, "You gotta be kidding me. Didn't you see that half twist at the dismount? Degree of difficulty alone gives me an eight."

"All right. Eight."

"I want the three of you coming after me in the last pickup. What did you do with the loggers?"

"Jerry chained them to an old bucket-loader tire sitting up here."

"Good. Now, get your asses down here. I'm going to need you to bail me out."

Juan reached the front of the trailer. The road ahead continued straight for nearly a mile before it twisted back on itself through another hairpin. The pickups were just a dust cloud halfway there. To Juan's right was a two-hundred-foot drop, at the bottom of which ran the next loop of the switch-back road.

Looking down over the front of the trailer, he could see the tops of the semi's eight spinning drive wheels and, through the skeletal frame of the chassis, the graveled blur of the roadbed. A misstep would land him under twenty tons of exotic hardwoods.

Rather than leap, he climbed down the butt ends of the logs and stepped lightly onto the truck's chassis. He could see the driver's head through the cab's rear window, and if the man happened to glance at his rearview mirror he would see the Chairman. Juan stepped right onto a diamond-plate fuel tank as big around as a barrel. He clutched the handhold screwed into the cab directly behind the driver's door in his right hand and placed his other on the door handle. The driver's bearded face filled the big wing mirror in front of him.

The Argentine's eyes drifted left, and in the second it took his brain to register what he was seeing Juan threw open the door and grabbed the man by the collar. The door rebounded into Juan's arm but didn't have enough pressure to even slow the Chairman, as he yanked the hapless man from his seat and flung him far enough away from the semi that he wouldn't be caught under the wheels.

Juan pulled his machine pistol from around his back and leapt into the seat, noting that even with both windows wide open the cab smelled of stale sweat, spicy food, and a hint of cannabis. He had his foot on the gas before the rig had slowed more than a mile or two per hour. He checked his mirror to see the driver slowly getting to his feet. He was dazed, for sure, but didn't look permanently injured.

Now came the tough part, Cabrillo thought grimly. Glancing up at the road above, he could see a feathery plume that would be his men coming after him in hot pursuit. Down the slope, the road was still clear. The Ninth Brigade soldiers were probably just now entering the next hairpin on the long descent. Juan carefully steered the semi so its outside tires rode closer and closer to the edge of the road and the precipitous drop beyond. The ground was much less firm this far from the main ruts packed down over countless hundreds of passages. Gravel hissed from under the wheels and pattered down the stump-strewn slope.

There!

The height advantage of being on the upper section of the haul road let Juan see the oncoming pickups below. They weren't going nearly as fast as he expected them to, and he wondered if they had a little trouble negotiating the last corner. The thought gave him a newfound respect for the men who drove up and down the mountain a dozen times a day.

Juan took the truck even closer to the edge. The front tires were digging ruts out of the very lip of the shoulder while the outside drive tires and the outside tires on the right side of the trailer hung in space. At a closing speed of sixty miles per hour, but separated by two hundred vertical feet, the three vehicles raced toward one another.

Without taking his eyes off the road, Juan felt for the door handle and made sure it hadn't latched. It was all down to the timing. Too soon, they would stop. Too late, and he would miss.

Juan judged it as finely as he could. He cranked the wheel to the right and threw himself from the cab, landing hard on the road but tumbling across his shoulder like an acrobat, and came up on his feet.

The eighteen-wheeler teetered on the brink for another second before rolling off the road. It hit square on its side, its momentum plowing the grille though the churned-up ground until it smashed into the stump of a tree that must have stood for a hundred years before greed sealed its fate. Steam gushed from the ruptured radiator, and the windshield was punched out in two solid sheets that exploded into mounds of glittering glass chips.

At the violent impact, the trailer bucked and threw its load. There were thirty logs on it, most the width and length of telephone poles while others were monsters that weighed three tons apiece. They stayed in a tight bundle for the first few yards as they rolled down the hill, but once they started bouncing off stumps, all semblance of order vanished. Some bounced off stump after stump, changing directions as they fell. A few were upended by the impact and hurtled down the hillside like ballistic projectiles.

The driver of the lead pickup never saw the deliberate accident above his truck, and it wasn't until he heard cries of alarm from the men in back that he knew something was wrong. He studied the dirt track ahead and saw nothing amiss. The steepness of the hill above them prevented him from having the proper angle to look up and see the avalanche moments away from sweeping the truck off the road.

"Hector!" screamed his passenger, staring wide-eyed up the hill. "Stop! For the love of the Virgin, stop!"

The driver, Hector, stood on the brakes, holding the wheel steady against the truck's desire to fishtail. Then came a jarring impact as the second truck, driven by Raul Jimenez, slammed into their rear bumper. Hector had been wearing a seat belt, a habit drilled into him as a child, and no amount of macho grandstanding would get him to change.

The passenger — the team's Sergeant — had never worn a seat belt in his life. He was catapulted through the windshield, leaving a man-sized hole ringed in blood from where the glass sliced his face and arms. He landed a good fifteen feet from the front of the truck. Hector had no idea if the Sarge was alive or dead when a log as thick around as a man's chest rolled over him, crushing the man's body into the hard earth.

That's when Hector felt death touch his shoulder. Another log that had tipped end over end speared through the top of the cab and smashed into his leg. The huge piece of timber continued its journey, ripping off the pickup's roof as easily as a can opener.

The men not hurt in the crash leapt from the truck and started running downhill, all thoughts of staying with their comrades forgotten in their panicked flight. The truck took a pair of broadsides from the two largest logs and was tossed bodily off the road. The men too stunned or too injured to flee were thrown from the vehicle and crushed as it started barreling down the mountain.

Most of the soldiers on foot had made the mistake of running straight away from the truck and were soon caught up as it tumbled. The lucky ones were knocked aside with broken limbs. The others were killed outright. One soldier had the wherewithal to run down the slope at an angle and avoided being killed by the cartwheeling vehicle. He even managed to leap up in time to have one of the logs roll under him. A second one slammed into his knees, breaking both joints. It bounced and flattened him before his nerves could send the pain signals to his brain.

The second truck fared little better. It was knocked perpendicular to the road by a titanic collision and then shot forward when a trio of logs slammed into the tailgate. The engine had stalled when Raul Jimenez had hit the first pickup, and without power steering he was incapable of controlling the vehicle as it accelerated downward. He mashed his foot to the brake pedal and yanked the emergency handle, but gravity and momentum were too much for a tired machine that had better than two hundred thousand miles on the odometer. It slammed into a stump just off-center enough to kick the rear end around. The tires hooked and the truck flipped. Men were scattered like rag dolls. Raul managed to stay in his seat as his view through the windshield rotated again and again. His side window was smashed, but whatever had punctured the glass had missed him. Impact after impact rattled the truck and threatened to loosen his sanity, but one massive hit and everything turned still. What remained of the pickup was hard against a stump, and the avalanche of logs had ended.

"Nice shootin', Tex," Juan heard over his radio.

He looked back to see the truck carrying his team racing for him. If he felt anything for the men he had just killed and injured, he need only think back to the burned-out village and knew he'd done the world a favor.

Mike Trono was behind the wheel with Mark Murphy. Jerry stood in the bed and, as the truck came close, held out an elbow to hook Cabrillo's arm and lift him into the bed. Juan rapped on the roof of the cab, and Mike hit the gas.

It took two minutes to negotiate the hairpin and return to the site where the Ninth Brigade soldiers had been swept from the road. Moans of anguish rose from the wounded. The dead lay in such unnatural angles it was difficult to believe they had skeletons at all.

None of the real Argentine Special Forces questioned the presence of more unknown men dressed in their uniforms. They were simply relieved that help had arrived so quickly. Juan squatted next to one of them, laying a hand on the man's uninjured shoulder. The other had been wrenched from its socket.

"What truck had the piece of satellite?" he asked in Spanish.

"It was in back of ours," the soldier said through gritted teeth and lips so compressed they had gone white.

"The first one?"

"No. The second."

Juan called out to his men, *"Numero dos,"* and held up two fingers in case Trono's Spanish was as bad as he said.

It took ten minutes to find the plutonium power cell. It was a silver rectangular object, a foot and a half long and about as wide and thick as a dictionary. Its surface was made of some mysterious alloy that Murph might know about but was outside Juan's purview or interest. All he cared about was that they had it and, for the moment, the Argentines didn't. He marveled, though, that for all the abuse it had just endured there was only a minute dimple on one side. Murph ran the gamma detector over every square inch of it.

"It's clean, Juan," he pronounced. "No radiation above what it's been giving off all along."

"That's a relief," Pulaski said. "I might want to have more kids someday. Hate for the little buggers to have tentacles and flippers and such." He turned to Cabrillo. "So now what?"

Juan scratched at the stubble covering his jaw. Down at the base camp, he could see pandemonium had erupted. The "accident" had been plain for everyone to see, and the reserve Ninth Brigade soldiers were scrambling to get up the mountain in order to help the wounded. Loggers, too, were racing for vehicles to lend a hand.

A sly smile crossed Cabrillo's handsome face. The three greatest assets in combat — and it doesn't matter if it's two men squaring off or whole armies meeting on the field of battle — are numbers, surprise, and confusion. He didn't have the first, the second had already been sprung, and now the third reigned over his adversaries. Jerry had wrestled the power cell into the carrying harness and stood with it strapped to his back. The others wore his same questioning expression.

"Mike, how many hours do you have with Gomez?" Juan asked. George "Gomez" Adams was the pilot of the MD-520N helicopter hangared below the *Oregon*'s aft hold.

"Hold on a minute," Mike Trono protested. "We've only been working together a couple of months. I've only soloed twice.

131

And they didn't go so well. I bent a landing strut on one and nearly clipped the ship's rail my second time."

Juan looked at Jerry. "Do you really feel like lugging that thing all the way back to the RHIB?"

"Hell no."

"What do you say, Mr. Trono?"

If Mike couldn't fly them out of here in one of the Argentine's helicopters, Juan knew he would admit it. He selected each member of the Corporation not only for what they could do but also because they were aware of what they could not.

Trono nodded. "Let's hope my third solo's the charm."

SEVEN

Fooling the injured Argentine soldiers had been easy. Those men saw what they wanted to see. It was going to be something altogether different getting past the reserve troops below and making their way to one of the helicopters.

Juan thought for a second and found inspiration amid the moans of the wounded. "Okay," he said. "Back to the truck, but move like you're injured. Murph, lean against Jerry. Mike, pretend I'm helping you."

They crawled up the hill as though they were victims of the accident, moving stiffly but surprisingly quickly. Cabrillo had the three men crawl into the old pickup's bed while he got behind the wheel. Before engaging the manual transmission, he pulled a clasp knife from his pocket. The blade's edge was honed as sharp as a scalpel, so when he drew it across his forehead at his hairline he felt no pain, only the liquid rush of blood, which quickly began dripping into his eyes and cutting runnels through the dirt and grime that caked his face.

He glanced back through the rear window so his men could see what he'd done. They caught on immediately, and by the time he'd gotten the truck up to speed the three men in back looked like they'd just walked out of a slaughterhouse. They met a ragtag convoy of vehicles coming up the mountainside — pickups, mostly, but also ATVs, and a fire engine that had first been put into service in the 1950s. Juan slowed as he approached the lead truck. The driver was a civilian, but next to him was a man in uniform, a man who would be considered handsome in other circumstances but whose features were drawn by what he'd seen.

"What happened?" he shouted across the cab to Juan.

"A log truck overturned, sir," Juan replied. He wiped blood from his eyes, smearing it over his face to better disguise his features. "The men in back are the most seriously injured."

On cue, Jerry, Mike, and Mark moaned pitiably.

"The others have only minor injuries," Juan continued. "These should be flown out immediately."

"What about Lieutenant Jimenez and the recovered part of the satellite?" Major Espinoza asked.

"He has it up where the trucks overturned," Juan replied.

"And you, how bad are your injuries?"

"I'm okay to drive."

Espinoza made a quick decision. "All right, get these troops down to the chopper and tell my pilot to fly you back to our forward operations base. Make sure he radios ahead so medical staff are standing by."

"Yes, Major," Juan said, recognizing the insignia on the other man's collar. He took his foot off the brake and slowly passed the convoy on the narrow road. It took all his self-control to keep a grin off his face.

A few minutes later, they pulled into the base camp. Down here where the brush piles burned, the smoke haze was so thick they couldn't see more than thirty yards, and each breath was like inhaling razor blades. Juan knew they only had a tiny window to make their escape. As soon as the Argentine Major figured out he'd been tricked, his entire reserve force would come down the mountain like the hammers of hell. He drove toward where the choppers were parked.

They were Eurocopter EC-135s, a medium utility chopper with a ten-year history of some of the most rugged flying in the world. These were stripped-down troop transports with the doors modified so they could mount .30 caliber door guns. One of the choppers had a rear access panel open and the pilot half buried in the machine's innards. Juan assumed he was working on the fault he had overheard Lieutenant Jimenez mention.

He pulled closer to the second chopper. The pilot of this bird, sporting a bandanna around his nose and mouth to filter out the worst of the smoke, was asleep in his seat. Cabrillo got an idea; better to use a well-trained enemy than an amateur ally. He sounded the truck's horn, which turned out to be the only part of the old vehicle that still showed signs of life.

The man startled awake and lifted his sunglasses. His dark eyes widened when he saw the bloody apparitions stepping from the old pickup.

"We need an immediate evac," Juan called to the pilot, pausing to help Mike Trono and his Quasimodo-like gait.

"Not without the Major's permission," the pilot replied.

"Radio him," Juan said sharply. "He was the one who said to take off immediately. But fire the turbines first so we don't waste any time."

The pilot made no move to turn on the Eurocopter's engines. Instead, he reached for his helmet, with its integrated communication's system. Cabrillo glanced up the mountain. Through the smoke, it was difficult to make out details. It didn't appear the lead vehicles of the rescue convoy had made it to the crash scene, but he decided they'd wasted enough time.

He moved quickly, drawing an automatic from his hip holster and rushing forward to place the muzzle against the pilot's head before he could don the bulky helmet. The man froze.

"Start the engines now." The cold timber in Juan's voice was enough to command compliance.

"Take it easy, *amigo*. I'll get you and your buddies out of here." He carefully set the helmet back onto the copilot's seat and set about preparing the chopper for flight.

Juan turned back to his men. "Miguel," he said nodding to Mike Trono and then pointing to the cockpit. Trono knew immediately that the Chairman wanted him watching the pilot for any sign he was going to trick them. The pilot should be thinking that these were badly wounded and even more frightened comrades who needed medical care. It would come later that he'd realize he was being kidnapped.

The rest of the men climbed into the helo, strapping themselves into the web-canvas bench seats. Jerry carefully placed the power cell on the deck and found some bungee cords to secure it in place.

In the cockpit, the pilot hit the turbine starter. There was a loud pop followed immediately by the steadily increasing whine of the helo's main engine. In seconds, the chorus was joined by the second motor. It would take more than a minute for them to reach the proper temperatures to engage the transmission and start the blades turning overhead.

Juan kept glancing upslope. The convoy must have reached the injured men by now. He wondered how long it would take the Major to understand what had happened. An hour would be nice, Cabrillo thought ruefully, but the truth was that the Argentine officer appeared more than capable. He would consider them lucky to get off the ground before coming under fire.

There came a clunk as the rotors started turning. Slowly at first, they quickly began whipping the smoke-gorged air. A tinny voice came over the helmet's speakers. Even with the din filling the chopper, its strident tone was plain.

Time's up, Juan thought.

The pilot motioned for Mike to hand him the helmet. Trono threw back a thousand-yard stare, the look of a man so deep into his own pain that nothing in the outside world mattered. The Argentine reached over to grab it, only to feel the cold steel of Juan's pistol hard up against his neck.

"Leave it and just take off."

"What's going on?"

Mike suddenly shed his wounded persona and also had an automatic trained on the pilot.

"My friend here also knows how to fly this thing. Do what we say, and you'll walk away alive. Screw with me, and some poor slob is going to be hosing your brains out of the cabin for a week. *Comprende?*"

"Who are you people? Americans?"

"Do I sound American to you?" Juan shot back. Like any of the world's great languages, Spanish has diverse accents and dialects that are as regionally distinctive as fingerprints. Cabrillo also spoke Arabic, and no matter how he tried he couldn't shake a Saudi accent. But in Spanish he was a

139

perfect mimic. He could imitate royalty from Seville or a sot from a Mexico City slum.

What the pilot heard was the voice of a man from his own city of Buenos Aires. "I . . ."

"Don't think," Juan said. "Just fly. Take us south."

He spent a microsecond considering his options. The hard eyes on him said there was only one. "*Sí, sí.* I'll fly."

His hands moved to the controls. Cabrillo looked up the hill once again. Trucks were racing down the log-hauling road, kicking up dust that mixed with the smoke already fouling the air. It wasn't even going to be close. The chopper would be a mile away by the time the Ninth Brigade soldiers were in range.

Jerry Pulaski shouted Juan's name.

And saved his life.

The pilot of the second chopper had to have heard Major Espinoza's radio call. He stood just outside the Eurocopter with a raised pistol. He had seen the gun Juan had trained on the pilot and calculated that he was the greatest risk. When he heard Jerry yell, the Argentine shifted his aim and fired twice. From that instant, events happened in such rapid succession that it was impossible to know their order.

As a fine red mist enveloped the cargo area, Juan twisted and dropped the second pilot with a double tap to the chest that hit in such a tight group the penetrations overlapped. The man dropped where he stood, no dramatic flourish, no Hollywood contortions. One second he thought he was about to become a hero, and the next he was on the ground like discarded laundry.

Mike Trono fired across the cockpit when the pilot reached for his door, then took up the controls himself. He twisted the throttle, and the helo lifted from the ground. As it began to rotate around on its axes, he put in the opposite rudder, and the craft stabilized.

Juan turned, jamming his pistol against the pilot's head hard enough to break skin. Blood ran from his ear. "Fly this chopper or when we hit a thousand feet you'll fly out of it."

Mike's bullet had passed so close to the pilot's eyes that they stung from the heat and GSR, but he blinked through the pain and started flying the Eurocopter. With Trono covering him again, Juan turned his attention to Jerry Pulaski and Mark Murphy on the rear bench seat. Mark was bent over Jerry, who was slouched back with an arm clamped across his belly. Making sure the pilot wouldn't hear, Cabrillo asked, "How bad?"

The big man was going into shock. His face had lost all color, and he was shaking as though with fever.

"Gut-shot," Mark replied. "Both rounds. At such close range, I expect damage beyond the intestines. Kidney. Liver maybe."

Juan went numb. Such wounds were treatable at a level-one trauma center, but the nearest one of those was perhaps a thousand miles away. Out here, in the jungle, the chances of Pulaski surviving were zero. Cabrillo was looking at a dead man. And the pained eyes holding his knew it. "Stay with us, Ski," Juan said, the words as empty as the hollow in his chest.

"I ain't going anywhere," Jerry replied, taking rapid sips of air between each syllable, lying.

Down on the ground, Major Espinoza realized his quarry was getting away in the helicopter he gave them permission to take. He ordered the logger who was driving their pickup to stop. Espinoza threw open his door and jumped to the ground. He only carried a pistol, an ivory-handled Colt .45, but he had it out and trained on the fleeing helicopter as soon as his boots hit the dirt. He had no hope of hitting the chopper, but he cycled through the pistol's seven-round magazine as fast as he could pull the trigger, rage as much as gunpowder sending the bullets flying.

The men in the bed followed suit, filling the sky with autofire from their machine pistols. What they lacked in range they made up for in sheer weight of shot. In seconds, nearly two hundred bullets went chasing after the helicopter, and the men managed to reload and unleash another volley even as the first rounds began to swarm around the chopper like maddened wasps.

"Incoming," Mike shouted from the copilot's seat as he saw the constellation of muzzle flashes through the drifting smoke.

The pilot instinctively juked the nimble chopper, but with so many bullets in the air, and so many of them spreading far from their intended target, it was impossible to evade them all. Nine-millimeters peppered the Eurocopter, tearing sizzling holes through its thin aluminum skin. Most passed harmlessly through, but there was the ominous clang of rounds striking the engine housings and doing who knows what to the delicate turbines. The chopper suddenly veered hard over. Juan lost his footing and, had he not grabbed for the door stanchion, would have fallen out of the aircraft.

Jerry lost his stoic battle with pain when the helo's vibration shifted his center of gravity, doubling him over his bleeding belly and causing the bullet fragments to tear through yet more tissue. His scream lanced into Juan as if he'd been pierced by a dagger.

Cabrillo regained his footing, looking into the cockpit. Mike had firm control of the helicopter, his eyes scanning instruments and sky. The Argentine pilot was slumped in his seat. Juan swung around the back of the chair so he could better assess the man's wounds. There was a fresh bullet hole in the Plexiglas side window close to the one Trono had fired a moment earlier, but this one had the elongated look of a round flying upward. It had hit the pilot in the side of his head at such an angle that while gouging through skin and perhaps cracking bone, it hadn't penetrated the skull.

Like all head wounds, it bled copiously. Juan grabbed a balled-up rag from the floor between the seats, pressed it to the wound, and held it while his other hand reached back. Mark Murphy knew what the Chairman wanted and handed over a roll of surgical tape. Like wrapping a mummy, Juan wound four loops of tape around the pilot's head to staunch the flow of crimson blood.

"Mike, you okay?" Juan asked in English. The need for subterfuge was over. The pilot would be unconscious for hours.

"Yeah, but we've got problems."

Cabrillo glanced back to where Mark tended to Jerry Pulaski. "Don't I know it."

"We're losing fuel, and either this model doesn't have self-sealing tanks or they've failed. Add to that the rising engine temperature, and I think we might also have a broken oil line."

Juan turned aft and leaned out the window, holding his body rigid against the tremendous wind pounding his head and upper body. The sound was a roar in his ears as if he were at the bottom of a waterfall. Trailing the copter, like proverbial bread crumbs, was a greasy feather of smoke. He could see it stretching back from the rear rotor boom to the point in the sky where a round had severed the oil line.

The Argentines would be coming hard, and the smoke would last for twenty or thirty minutes because there was so little wind and the air was already so heavily laden with ash and soot.

"Yeah, she's smoking pretty badly," he reported when he swung back toward the cockpit. After closing the door, they only had to shout to one another to be heard rather than screaming as they had been.

"How's Jerry?" Mike asked. The two were not only combat partners but best friends.

Juan's silence was Trono's answer. Cabrillo finally asked, "Can we make Paraguay?"

"Not a chance. This bird had only half a tank when we started, and we've already lost nearly half that. If the engines hold together, the best we can hope for is maybe fifty miles. What do you want me to do?"

Thoughts poured like an avalanche through Juan's mind. This is what he did best. He considered options, calculated odds, and made a decision all in the time it takes a normal person to digest the question. The factors hanging over his call weighed heavily. There was the success of the mission, his duty to Mike and Mark, the odds Jerry would be alive when they landed, and what they would do if he was. Ultimately, it came down to saving Jerry's life.

"We go back. The Argies must have medical facilities at their base, and the other chopper will have the range to reach it."

"Like hell," Pulaski said, finding the strength in his anger to speak. "You're not going down because I wasn't fast enough on the draw, damn it."

Juan gave Pulaski his full attention. "Jerr, it's the only way."

"Mike, get this tub to the RHIB," Jerry shouted past Cabrillo. "Chairman, please. I know I'm dying. I can feel it getting closer and closer. Don't throw your lives away on a dead man. I'm not asking, Juan. I'm begging. I don't want to go knowing you guys went with me."

Pulaski held out a hand, which Juan took. The congealed blood on his palm cemented their skin together. Jerry continued. "It ain't noble, staying with me. It's suicide. Argies are gonna shoot you for spies after torturing you." He coughed wetly and spat a little blood onto the deck. "I got an ex who hates me and a kid who don't know me. You're my family. I don't want you to die for me. I want you to live for me instead. You understand?"

"I understand you copied that sentiment from *Braveheart*," Juan said. His lips smiled. His eyes couldn't.

"I'm serious, Juan."

For Cabrillo, time stopped for a few moments. The steady beat of the rotor and the whine of the turbine faded to silence. He'd known death and loss. His wife had been killed by a drunk driver — herself. He'd lost agents and contacts during his time at the CIA, and the Corporation had been visited by the Grim Reaper as well, but he'd never asked another man to die so that he could live.

He reached into his pack and handed the portable GPS to Mike. "The RHIB's at waypoint Delta."

"There's no place to land," Mike said. "You remember how thick that jungle was. And there's no way I can ditch this thing in the river without killing us all."

"Don't worry about an LZ," Mark Murphy shouted forward. "I got that covered."

Cabrillo knew to trust the eccentric Mr. Murphy.

"Swing us around and punch in waypoint Delta."

"Not Delta," Murph said. "Echo."

"Echo?" Juan questioned.

"Trust me."

The Eurocopter's navigational computer was self-explanatory, so Mike punched in the coordinates from the handheld GPS, then swung the chopper around to a south-easterly bearing. So far, his flying had been smooth and controlled, just as he'd been taught. Gomez Adams would be proud.

"Looks like we have enough fuel. Barely," he said.

"Chairman," Mark shouted. "Starboard side. Maybe three klicks back."

"What?"

"I saw the flash of sun off the other chopper's windshield."

Juan looked out the side window. He didn't see anything but he didn't doubt Mark's eyesight. The Argentines were coming a lot faster than he'd thought. Then he should have realized it. With their helo burning oil, they didn't have the speed to match the other bird. And the Argentine Major would tear the guts out of his aircraft in order to get his prey.

"Mike," he shouted. "Give us everything she's got. Company's coming."

The turbines kicked up a notch but didn't sound healthy. Metal was grinding someplace in the engine compartment, and it was only a matter of time before they shut down.

Juan looked around the cabin for additional weapons. The door-mounted .30 caliber was a better option than their H&K machine pistols, but only if the other helo came up on the port side where the gun was mounted. He found a medical kit under the bench seat and a red plastic box containing a large-bore flare pistol and four stubby projectiles. Juan knew the script for this mission didn't include a billion-to-one shot with a flare, so he left it on the bench.

"Mark, jury-rig a harness for me," he ordered as he set to work unbolting the old Browning machine gun from its webbing gimbal.

The gun was a thirty-pound, four-foot-long antique with a single pistol grip at the end of its boxy receiver. A belt of fifty brass cartridges dangled from the breach and made an almost musical chime when they clinked together. He was familiar enough with the weapon and knew it had a reputation for reliability as well as a recoil that could shatter teeth.

Juan stripped off his shirt. He wrapped the garment around the Browning's twenty-four-inch barrel and tied it off with the rest of the surgical tape.

Murph, meanwhile, shucked out of his combat harness and reconfigured the nylon webbing into a long loop that he clipped to a D ring just forward of the starboard door. He clipped the other end to the back of Cabrillo's combat harness. He used the strap of his backpack to make a second loop that would go around the Chairman's ankles. He would hold the other end to prevent

Juan from falling into the Eurocopter's slipstream.

"I see them in my mirror," Mike announced from the cockpit. "If you're going to do something, do it quick."

"How much farther?" Juan asked.

"Eight miles to Echo. And just so you know, I don't see anything below us but jungle."

"I said, trust me," Mark fired back hotly.

Juan looked at Pulaski. Had he not been shot, he knew his men would be bantering, not sniping at one another. Jerry's head lolled and, had Mark not strapped him in, he would have tumbled to the floor.

"They're opening their side door," Trono said. "Okay, I see a guy. He's got a Browning like ours. He's fired! He's fired!"

Accustomed to strafing unarmed civilians fleeing from their villages, the gunner had fired far too soon. Three numbers then came into play. Mike saw the muzzle flashes reaching him at the speed of light, about three hundred million meters per second. The stream of bullets was approaching from a kilometer away at eight hundred and fifty meters per second. The nerve impulse, from brain to wrist, traveled at only a hundred meters per second. But it only had a meter to go. One-hundredth of a second after the first round was fired, Trono cut the power to dump altitude. Gravity had more than a second to pull the helicopter earthward. The string of white phosphorus tracers arrowed well over the spinning disk of the chopper's main rotor.

Juan nodded to Mark. Murph hauled back on the starboard door until it locked against its roller stops, and then he grabbed the loop of webbing around Cabrillo's feet.

The Chairman let his upper body fall out of the helicopter, coming up short when he hit the end of his tether. The tremendous power of the wind nearly pushed him back inside, but he fought it with every muscle in his legs and back.

Because he was firing aft from the right-side door, he had to shoot offhand, his left gripping the trigger and his right clamped over his taped shirt. There was no help for the spent brass flying into the helo's cabin.

His sudden appearance had startled the Argentine pilot, but he was moments late taking evasive action. Juan used those seconds and opened fire. The .30 cal bucked in his arms like a jackhammer, and heat began seeping through the gun's barrel sleeve and the bundled shirt.

It was a miracle that the flapping ammo belt didn't jam as the machine gun chewed up cartridges at four hundred rounds per minute and spat out a metallic plume of empty shells that pattered to the deck like shiny hail.

The clear Plexiglas windshield of the fast-approaching helicopter turned opaque as round after round punched into it, spider-webbing the plastic until it was almost a solid sheet of white. The pilot veered sharply away, making the mistake of not passing behind the Corporation's pilfered chopper and giving Juan more opportunities to fire. He had no idea if the follow-up barrage struck his target, but it certainly caused the other helicopter to fly a miles-long arc away.

"LZ coordinates coming up," Mike said. If the prospect of landing the unfamiliar Eurocopter bothered him, it didn't come through in his voice. "What the . . . ? I'll be damned. Murph, how did you know?"

A quarter mile from waypoint Echo — the decaying wreckage of the blimp — was an area large enough to land the helicopter where the jungle vegetation was no more than a few feet high and composed mostly of immature shrubs and ground cover.

"When the *Flying Dutchman* crashed," Mark shouted back, "its rubber gasbag would have landed nearby. As it lay across the jungle canopy, it would have shaded the plants under it until they died. Nothing would grow there until the envelope decomposed, forty or fifty years later. Voilà, instant landing zone."

"Pretty slick," the Chairman told Mark with more than a little pride. "Even for you."

"Strap in," Mike warned.

Hemmed in by thick jungle that rose a hundred or more feet into the air, the clearing was coming up fast. Trono slowed the Eurocopter on his final approach, skewing the aircraft to the left, then too far right, before centering over the nearly open area. He eased off the power, and the chopper slowly lowered itself earthward. When a sudden gust threatened to push the main rotor toward the wall of trees, he chopped the throttle a little too much, and the four-million-dollar aircraft hit with a bone-jarring impact. He immediately killed the engines. The turbines wound down, but the rotor continued to whip the grass into a frenzy and caused the trees to sway as if caught in a gale.

"Everybody out," Juan commanded. "That other chopper will be back any second."

Mike unbuckled his harness, and Murph went to work on Jerry's.

"Forget it. I ain't going anywhere," the

big Pole muttered. His chin was covered with blood. He held up an object for the others to see. Somehow, he had managed to pull a wad of Semtex plastique explosives and a pencil detonator from the thigh pocket of his combat fatigues. "Give me one last shot."

"Ski?" Mike's eyes were pleading.

"Not this time, bud. I don't have it in me."

"Damn it, Jerry," Juan cursed. "I can carry you. The boat's only a couple miles away."

The sound of an approaching helicopter echoed across their little glen.

"I suck at good-byes," Pulaski said. "Just go."

"I'll make sure your family's taken care of." Juan tried to look his friend in the eye but couldn't. He shouldered his way into the seventy-pound harness for the power cell and jumped from the chopper. He took a moment to drag the unconscious pilot into the shrubs and found cover a short distance away, his machine pistol raised in the direction of the approaching Argentines.

"Give 'em hell, Jerr," Mark said.

"You, too, kid."

Tears welled unashamedly in Mike Trono's eyes.

"Good-bye," he said, and leapt from the Eurocopter.

Using Cabrillo's GPS, the three men started off toward the RHIB. The plutonium was half the burden to Juan as the guilt he felt leaving Jerry behind. They had fought side by side for half a dozen years and had had drinks in every seedy harborside bar from Shanghai to Istanbul. Never could he have imagined abandoning Jerry Pulaski in a godforsaken jungle so he could blow himself up and give the rest of the team a chance of escape.

With every pace he had to fight the urge to turn back.

The canopy overhead muffled the sound of the Argentine helicopter but couldn't dampen the staccato burst of machine-gun fire they heard ten minutes into their march. It seemed to go on forever as the Ninth Brigade soldiers vented their fury at the downed helo.

If Jerry hadn't already succumbed to his wounds, the withering fusillade would almost certainly be fatal. Juan's expression grew more grim, and he began to notice the weight of the padded nylon straps digging into his aching shoulders. The sling had been designed for Jerry's broader back, so the power cell hung low and uncomfortable.

A silent five minutes passed as the men

continued toward the river and their boat. The machine guns had silenced the jungle creatures, and the breeze didn't reach into the gloom of the forest floor. It was eerie, still, oppressive.

The blast that rang out wasn't the distant roll of thunder, but an immediate crash of noise that struck like a hammer. A moment later it was followed by a secondary explosion.

They knew what had happened. Jerry had held off until men were descending from the Argentine helicopter and then popped the C-4. The second blast was the detonation of what little fuel and vapors remained in their aircraft's tanks. There would likely be survivors among the Argentine commandos, but there would be no pursuit.

EIGHT

The radio link went dead. That wasn't true. There had been a concussive sound just before Lieutenant Jimenez stopped talking. Major Jorge Espinoza tried again, shouting out Jimenez's call sign, Jaguar.

He had stayed behind at the logging camp because between the two officers, Espinoza had more cross training as a medic. And his skills were sorely needed. They had six men killed outright and another three who would probably never walk again. Two more were in rough shape with multiple lacerations and broken bones. Only Jimenez had walked away from the crash unscathed. Espinoza had used up all the field dressings the men carried in their personal kits, and had taken the emergency gear from the second chopper, before sending Jimenez and five men from the reserve force after the thieves.

He knew it was the Americans. Who else could have tracked the satellite and dispatched a search team so quickly? But knowing it and proving it were two entirely different things. With Argentina's world standing so poor, accusing the *Yanquis* without evidence to back it up was simply a waste of breath.

He needed Jimenez to capture at least one of them. Preferably with the fragment of satellite.

Not for the first time, he wondered what was so important about the satellite that the U.S. felt the need to risk some of their Special Forces on a retrieval operation. According to his briefing, Espinoza was told that it was some science research mission, but their level of interest in it told him it was something else, something almost certainly military. If he had the fragment back, plus one of the soldiers, then the propaganda coup Raul had mentioned earlier wasn't so far-fetched.

"Jaguar, come in, damn it."

A burst of static squelched from his hand-held radio and forced him to pull the device away sharply. Jimenez had reported that they had pumped a couple hundred rounds into the downed chopper, waited for a few minutes to see if it was going to explode, and then sent three men down on fast-rappel ropes.

"Jimenez, is that you?"

"Jefe?"

"Jimenez, come in."

"It's me, sir. Not good."

"What happened?"

"They booby-trapped the helicopter. It blew just as my men were about to set foot on the jungle floor. The blast wasn't big, but it was enough to shove my chopper a hundred feet or so, and that saved my life because then the fuel tanks exploded. The fireball was enormous."

"What of your men?"

"The three on the ropes are gone, sir. Blown to ribbons. But we see another man on the ground who survived the blast."

Espinoza seized on this news and asked, "One of them?"

"No, sir. It's the other pilot, Josep. He appears injured, but it looks like they patched him up before taking off.

Defeat left Espinoza's mouth bitter. He thought for a moment. "You said you're about five miles from the Rio Rojo, yes?"

"That is correct."

"They have a boat," Espinoza said. "They must have snuck through the border last night when those worthless frontier guards were either asleep or too busy scratching themselves to notice."

"I don't think we have the fuel to chase them," Jimenez said. It was clear in his voice this was a disappointment. "And the pilot says the chopper might have been damaged by the first explosion."

"No matter, mark Josep's position on the GPS so we can send a team to get him, then head straight for the base. Radio ahead so our third EC-135 is ready to take off as soon as you land. They probably have a fast boat, but you should be able to catch them before they reach Paraguay. I'm also going to alert the border guards. They can send out some patrol boats and stop anyone who looks suspicious."

"We'll have them yet, *Jefe*." Jimenez's wolfish grin carried through the static-filled connection.

"We will," Major Espinoza agreed, and, if anything, his smile was more dangerous.

Juan and the two other survivors reached the RHIB a little over an hour later. It had remained undisturbed under its cover of foliage. Juan lashed the power cell to the deck while Murph and Trono stripped away the camouflage. The twin outboards came to life with a turn of the key. Juan knew their boat, with its performance-tweaked engines, could outrun anything on the river, but he

161

had no illusions that a reception wasn't already being planned for when they neared the Paraguayan border.

"Lines are clear," Mark said, coiling the dark nylon rope around a cleat. When the Chairman didn't react, he called out, "Juan?"

"Sorry. Thinking."

Juan bumped the throttles, and the boat emerged from its hidden lair. The river was clear of traffic, so a few moments later he had them skimming across the surface at better than forty knots, slowing marginally in the blind corners, then giving the RHIB her head once again.

Going with the current, it took them less time to reach the main river than when they'd come upstream earlier in the day. The men were drained by the events of the past twenty-four hours, yet they remained vigilant as they started northward. Mike stood facing aft, his eyes scanning the sky for pursuit, while Juan and Mark studied the river and its banks for anything out of the ordinary.

They saw nothing for an hour, but then Mark Murphy tapped Juan on the shoulder, handed him a small pair of binoculars, and pointed a few points off their bow.

Juan needed only a second to recognize

two Boston Whalers coming at them at full speed. He didn't need to see details of the occupants to know they were armed to the teeth.

"Mike," he yelled over his shoulder. "We've got company."

"No kidding," Trono called back. "There's a chopper crawling up our six."

Cabrillo didn't bother looking back. The Whalers were coming too fast for him to worry about the helicopter. With a combined closing speed of nearly ninety knots, the pair of boats would pass the RHIB in seconds.

Juddering lights winked at them from both craft. The Argentines had opened fire well before they were in effective range. Tiny splashes sprinkled the river well away from the charging RHIB.

Juan waited until the two boats were less than fifty yards off, ignoring the lead that was filling the air. He could see three men on each; the driver, and two riflemen lying in the bow. With the Whalers skipping across the water, none of the shooters could aim accurately. The little boats were just too unsteady.

Of course, Mark couldn't get off a meaningful shot with the RHIB bouncing along either.

"Hold on!" Juan shouted.

He cut both throttles and used his palm to crank the wheel over to its lock. Despite the deflated cells of the buoyancy ring, the assault boat did a perfect one-eighty, shouldering aside a wall of white water and coming to an almost complete stop.

Having practiced the maneuver countless times and knowing it was coming, Trono and Murph reacted instantly. Now that the RHIB was wallowing, they could anticipate her movements and compensate for them with their machine guns. They opened fire as the two Whalers flashed by less than a hundred feet away. The two drivers standing in the open cockpits took the worst of it. One was stitched from thigh to shoulder, the kinetic impact of the 9mm rounds hurling his body over the gunwale. The other took two to the head and slumped over the console.

With its engines still pouring out full power, the Whaler started to veer off course because of the weight of the dead driver on the wheel. The centripetal force pushed the body in the opposite direction, and he slipped from the cockpit, his hand still tangled in the wheel's spokes. The Whaler turned sharply, caught part of the wave that had been generated by the RHIB, and flipped over. It augered into the water and vanished under the surface only to float up again, its keel pointing skyward.

The second Whaler continued racing down the river, no one sure if there was anyone aboard still alive.

Juan spun the RHIB around again and slammed the outboards to their stops. The bow rose up in an instant, the deep V hull coming onto plane faster than about any boat afloat.

Raul Jimenez ignored the wind buffeting him as he stood in the helicopter's open door, incredulous that the first Boston Whaler had barrel-rolled and then sunk. The second border-patrol boat continued downstream behind them. At first he thought the cowards were running away, but then the Whaler slammed straight into the riverbank. It folded like an aluminum can. Its outboards tore from the transom and vaulted into the underbrush while the three men were tossed like mannequins. Jimenez neither noted nor cared if any of them was alive. All his attention was focused on the fleeing boat below.

He recognized the black craft as an RHIB, the type favored by the United States Special Forces, though it was also available on the commercial market and could easily be operated by a group of mercenaries. He needed just one of them alive. He wanted the others alive, too, but when he was finished with them they would be in no condition to be paraded in front of television cameras.

This chopper wasn't equipped with a door gun, but they had pulled the weapon from the one damaged in the explosion and concocted a makeshift mount using straps threaded through eyelets in the ceiling. Jimenez stood behind it now, watching the RHIB grow larger and clearer in his sights. Just a few seconds more and he'd tear away the back of the boat. While one of the thieves drove, the other watched the approaching helo with a machine pistol tucked up hard against his shoulder. The third man was flat on the deck, either dead or wounded. Either way, he didn't appear to be moving.

Ever since his boyhood, Raul Jimenez had loved to hunt. He'd made his first slingshot out of tubing and a forked piece of wood, and killed birds by the hundreds around his family's farm. With his first rifle, a gift on his tenth birthday, he went after larger and larger prey until taking a jaguar from a hunting blind with a nearly seven-hundred-yard shot his companions said couldn't be made.

But on the day he killed his first man, a deserter who then-Captain Espinoza had told him to track, Jimenez knew he would never find satisfaction hunting mere animals again. He had stalked the deserter for five days through some of the toughest jungle Argentina has to offer. The deserter had been wily, and made the hunt the best of Jimenez's life, but in the end nothing could keep him from his prey, and the man had died despite his cunning.

Jimenez felt that same sense of satisfaction as he lined up the sights on the black RHIB. Just as he squeezed the Browning's trigger, the nimble boat cut sharply, and the heavy .30 caliber rounds peppered the water, turning it into a constellation of tiny white fountains.

He cursed, lined up, and fired again. It was as if the driver fifty feet below was reading his mind because the bullets arrowed into the river off the RHIB's port flank. He was certain the boat would dodge left this time and let loose a hammering string of tracers. And like before, the driver outwitted him by veering farther right, going under the helicopter and emerging on its blind side.

"Spin around," Jimenez shouted into his headset. "Give me an angle."

The pilot pushed hard on the rudder, pivoting the Eurocopter on its axes as it continued to race up the river. It was flying almost sideways, crabbing across the sky, but more than able to keep up with the speeding RHIB.

In the three seconds Jimenez had lost sight of the boat, the man he thought was injured had gotten to one knee. Behind him was an open space in the deck that had been a covered storage locker. On the man's shoulder sat an ominous dark tube pointed straight at the chopper. The range was less than two hundred feet.

Jimenez and the man holding the rocket moved at the same time. Mike Trono lit off the Stinger missile the same instant the Argentine soldier unclipped his safety harness. The rocket's infrared system only had a fraction of a second to come to life, find the heat plume billowing from the helicopter's exhaust, and make a minute adjustment. Jimenez leapt from the chopper just before the missile slammed into the turbine housing directly below the spinning rotor. The six-pound warhead detonated. The bulk of the engine saved Jimenez's life, but he was still caught in a flaming overpressure wave that ignited his clothing and slammed him into the water as if he'd jumped from twice the height. Had he not landed feet-first in the roiling waves churned up by the RHIB's outboards, the impact would have been no different than landing on cement. The water extinguished his burning uniform and prevented the burns on his face and hands from going past second-degree. He came thrusting back to the surface, coughing up a lungful of river, his skin feeling like it had been dipped in acid.

Fifty feet ahead of him, the Eurocopter crashed into the river, smoke pouring out the doors and blown-apart windshield. Jimenez didn't have time to fill his lungs, as the craft tipped and the rotors hit the water. They came apart like shattering glass, shards of composite material filling the air. Several skimmed across the river surface inches above Jimenez's head and would have decapitated him had he not ducked under the waves.

Through the water he could see flames licking at the chopper's shattered carcass, a wavy, ethereal light that silhouetted the pilot still strapped in his seat. The dead man's arms swayed in the current like tendrils of kelp.

He struggled to the surface once again,

the roar of fire filling his ears. Of the RHIB, there was no sign, and with the chopper down and the border patrol's two Whalers destroyed the thieves had a straight run to Paraguay. As he started the painful swim to shore, his burned hands screaming with every stroke, Lieutenant Jimenez could only hope they would be stopped before they could sneak across.

"Nice shot," Juan shouted as the Argentine helicopter fell from the sky in their wake.

"That was for Jerry," Trono said, laying the Stinger on the deck to reload it with the second missile stored in one of boat's several secret weapons caches. Mark Murphy was at the bows, watching for anyone else coming at them. He asked, "Are we still going to stick to the original plan?"

Cabrillo thought about it for a moment. "Yeah," he replied. "Better safe than sorry. The cost of the RHIB will just become one more line item in the CIA's black budget."

While Juan continued to drive, and Mark acted as lookout, Mike prepared for the final part of the operation, so when they finally cut the engines five miles from the border with Paraguay all their equipment was ready. The men slipped into their wet suits again and strapped the bulky Draeger sets to their backs. Juan overfilled his buoyancy compensators because he would be carrying the power cell.

After slicing open the remaining air bladders ringing the boat, they opened the sea cocks. The RHIB began sinking by the stern, dragged under by her heavy engines. They waited aboard her even after she slipped under the surface, making sure she settled on the bottom. The current had pushed them south another quarter mile, but they needed to ensure the boat stayed under. The bottom of the river this close to the bank was a jumbled snarl of rotting trees. They tied off the bow painter line to one of the more sturdy limbs and then started northward, propelled through the water by near-silent dive scooters.

Fighting the current, it took them the better part of two hours to reach the border, and another two until they judged it safe to surface. The scooters' batteries were on their last bit of power and the rebreathers nearly depleted. But they'd made it.

The men took a break before starting out on the six-hour slog back to the elevated hut they had slept in thirty-six hours ago. There they had stashed a small aluminum boat with a motor that they had towed into place with the RHIB.

When they reached base, Mike set himself against a tree and promptly nodded off. Juan envied him. Though Trono had been closer to Jerry than Cabrillo, Mike wasn't shouldering any guilt for his death. Just sorrow. Mark Murphy, with his love of all things technical, studied the power cell.

Juan moved a little ways off and pulled a satellite phone from a waterproof pouch. It was time to check in.

"Juan, is that you?" Max Hanley asked after the first ring. He could picture Max sitting in the *Oregon*'s op center since the mission began, downing cup after cup of coffee and chewing on the stem of his pipe until it was nothing but a gnarled nub.

The phones were so heavily encrypted that there was no chance of them ever being listened in on, so there was no need for code phrases or aliases.

"We got it," he replied with such weariness it sounded as though he would never recover. "We're six hours out from waypoint Alpha."

"I'll call Lang right away," Hanley said. "He's been bugging me every twenty minutes since you started off."

"There's one more thing." Cabrillo's tone was like ice over the airwaves. "Jerry paid the butcher's bill on this one."

There was almost thirty full seconds of silence before Max finally said, "Oh, Jesus. No. How?"

"Does it really matter?" Juan asked back.

"No, I guess it doesn't," Max said.

Juan blew a loud breath. "I tell you, buddy, I'm having a real hard time getting my mind around this."

"Why don't you and I take off for a few days when you get back? We'll fly down to Rio, plant our butts on the beach, and ogle a bunch of hard bodies in string bikinis."

Time off sounded good, though Cabrillo didn't particularly relish the idea of leering at women half his age. And he knew that after three failed marriages, Max wasn't really on the prowl either. Then Juan remembered the crashed blimp and Mark's suggestion to give closure to the families of men who'd perished on her. That was what his soul needed. Not staring at pretty girls but offering a bunch of strangers a little peace of mind after fifty years of wondering.

"I like the concept," Juan said, "but we need to work on the execution. We'll talk about arrangements when we get back to the ship. Also, you might as well go into my office. In the file cabinet should be Jerry's last will. Let's get that ball rolling right away. He didn't have too much love for his ex-wife, but he did have a child."

"A daughter," Max replied. "I helped him set up a trust for her, and he made me the trustee."

"Thanks. I owe you. We should be home by dawn tomorrow."

"I'll have the coffee waiting."

Juan replaced the phone into its pouch and sat back against the tree, feeling like he was feeding every mosquito within a fifty-mile radius.

"Hey, Chairman," Mark called a few minutes later. "Check this out."

"What have you got," Juan crawled over to where Mark sat with his legs bent like pretzels.

"You see this here and here?" He pointed to two tiny indentations on the glossy metal surface.

"Yeah."

"These correspond with two matching holes in the nylon carrying harness. They're bullet strikes fired up at us from when we took off in the chopper."

"Those were nine-millimeter from point-blank range," Juan said. "Barely made a mark. That thing is as tough as NASA boasted."

"Okay, but look at this." Mark struggled

to turn the seventy-pound cell over so the top was facing up and then pointed at an even deeper pit gouged into the satellite fragment.

Juan gave his weapons expert a questioning look.

"Nothing matches it on the harness. That was put there before we got our hands on it."

"Something the Argentines did to it?"

Mark shook his head. "We watched them dig it up, and it was out of our sight for only a few minutes before they loaded it into the pickup. I don't recall hearing a shot. You?"

"No. Could it have happened when the logs slammed into the truck?"

"I don't think so. I have to do some calculations to be sure, but I don't think there was enough energy in the collision to cause something like this. And remember, the truck flipped into muddy ground. There wasn't anything hard enough and small enough to cause such a smooth divot."

A flash of understanding struck Cabrillo. "It happened when the rocket blew. More than enough energy there, right?"

"That's the answer," Mark replied as if he'd known that all along, but there was little triumph in his voice. "The problem is this is the top of the power cell. It would have been protected from the explosion by both the rocket's vertical speed and the bulk of the cell itself."

"What are you saying?"

"I'm not sure. I'd love to do some tests on this back aboard the *Oregon,* but we're turning it over to some CIA flack in Asunción. We'll never get answers."

"What's your gut telling you?"

"The satellite was intentionally shot down by a weapon that only two countries in the world possess. Us —"

"And China," Juan finished.

NINE

Houston, Texas

Tom Parker never knew what he was getting himself into when he joined NASA. In his defense, he'd grown up in rural Vermont, and his parents never had a television because the reception on the side of the mountain where they raised dairy cows was terrible.

He knew something was up on his first day at the Johnson Space Center when his secretary placed a beautiful blown-glass bottle on the credenza behind his desk and said it was for Jeannie. He'd asked her to explain, and when she realized he had no clue as to Jeannie's identity she'd chuckled and said cryptically that he'd soon find out.

Next came a pair of hand-painted bellows delivered anonymously to his office. Again, Parker didn't know what this meant and asked for an explanation. By now, several other women in the secretarial pool knew of his ignorance, as did his supervisor, an Air Force Colonel who was a deputy director in the astronaut-training program.

The last piece of the puzzle was an autographed picture of a man in his mid- to late fifties, with receding red hair and bright blue eyes. It took Parker a while to figure out that the signature was that of Hayden Rorke. Internet research was at its infancy then, so he had to rely on a local library. This lead him to eventually discover that Rorke was an actor who played a NASA psychiatrist named Alfred Bellows who was continually vexed by astronaut Anthony Nelson and the genie he'd found on a beach.

Dr. Tom Parker was a NASA psychiatrist, and the *I Dream of Jeannie* jokes never stopped. After almost ten years with the program, Parker had dozens of glass bottles similar to the one Jeannie called home, as well as autographed pictures of most of the cast and several of Sidney Sheldon's scripts.

He adjusted the webcam on top of his laptop to accommodate the request of Bill Harris, his current patient.

"That's better," Harris said from Wilson/George. "I was seeing a picture of Larry

Hagman but hearing your voice."

"He's better looking at least," Parker quipped.

"Leave the camera on Barbara Eden and you'll make my day."

"So we were talking about the other members of your team. You leave Antarctica in a couple of days. What's their mood?"

"Disappointed, actually," the astronaut said. "A front's closed in on us. The weather boys at McMurdo say it's only going to last a few days, but we've all seen the data. The storm's covering damned-near all of Antarctica. We're socked in for a week or more, and then it'll take a few more days to clear their runway and ours."

"How do you feel about it?" Parker asked. He and the former test pilot had spoken enough over the past months to have an honest dialogue. He knew Harris wouldn't sugarcoat his answer.

"Same as everyone else," Bill said. "It's tough when a goal gets pushed back on you, but this is what we're here for, right?"

"Exactly. I especially want to know how this has affected Andy Gangle."

"Since he can't wander outside anymore, he's pretty much stayed in his room. To be honest, I haven't seen him in twelve or more hours. The last time was in the rec room.

He was just passing through. I asked him how he was, he muttered 'Fine' and kept on going."

"Would you say his antisocial behavior has gotten worse?"

"No," Bill said. "It's about the same. He was antisocial when he got here and he's antisocial now."

"I know you've mentioned you've tried to engage him over the last few months. Has anyone else?"

"If someone has, they've been shot down. I said before, I think the screeners who allowed him to winter down here made a mistake. He's not cut out for this kind of isolation, at least not as a functioning part of a team."

"But, Bill," Parker said, leaning closer to his laptop camera for emphasis, "what happens if you're on the space station or halfway to the moon when you realize that the doctors who screened your crewmates made a similar mistake?"

"Are you saying you're going to screw up?" Harris asked with a chuckle.

"No," Parker grinned, "but the other members of the screening committee might. So what would you do?"

"Above all else, make sure the person is pulling their weight. If they don't want to talk much, fine, but they have to do their job."

"And if they refuse?"

Bill Harris suddenly looked over his shoulder as if he'd heard something.

"What is it?" the psychiatrist asked.

"Sounded like a gunshot," Harris replied. "I'll be right back."

Parker watched the astronaut get up from his chair. He was halfway to the open door of his room on the remote ice station when a sudden blur moved across the threshold. Harris staggered back, and then something hit the webcam, and Parker's view was completely blocked. He watched for several seconds. Soon the blackness on his laptop took on a faint purplish cast. As more time elapsed, the view turned lighter and lighter, going from the deepest plum to light egg-plant, and finally to red.

It took him a moment to realize what had hit the camera was a clot of blood that then oozed off the lens. Parker could make out few details because of the bloody film, but there was no sign of Bill Harris, and the audio feed was picking up the unmistakable wail of a woman screaming.

A full minute elapsed before her voice was cut off abruptly. Parker kept watching, but when something passed the doorway again it was an indistinct blur. It certainly looked like the outline of a man, but it was impossible to know who.

He double-checked that his computer was automatically recording, as he did all sessions with his distant patient. Everything was safely on the hard drive. As a precaution, he e-mailed the first part of the file to himself so he had backup imagery and cc'd his boss.

Leaving his computer recording the now-silent webcam at Wilson/George base, he picked up his phone and dialed his supervisor's direct line.

"Keith Deaver."

"Keith, it's Tom. We've got a situation at Wilson/George. Check the e-mail I just sent. Forward through the file until the last five minutes. Call me back when you're done."

Six minutes later, Tom snatched up the handset before it had finished its first ring. "What do you think?"

"I know for a fact there aren't any guns on that station, but I'm positive that was a gunshot."

"I think so, too," Parker replied. "To be sure, we need an expert to listen to it, do that stuff like you see on the cop shows. This is bad, Keith. I don't know if you overheard Bill and I talking, but McMurdo can't send in a plane for a week or more, not even to do a visual reconnaissance."

"Who has lead on that place?"

"Penn State is monitoring it full-time, if that's what you mean."

"Do you have a contact there?"

"Yes. Ah, I think his name's Benton. Yeah, that's it, Steve Benton. He's a climatologist or something."

"Call him. See if their telemetry's still coming through. Also, see if they have other webcams up and running right now. We should get in touch with McMurdo, let them know what's happening, and see if they really can't get an aircraft to Wilson/George sooner."

"I have a contact there, too," Palmer said, "at the U.S. Antarctic Program. They're run through the National Science Foundation."

"Okay. I want hourly updates, and make sure someone's watching your computer from now on. I'll send you warm bodies if you need them."

"I'll get my secretary in here while I make the calls, but I'll probably take you up on that offer later in the day."

As bureaucracies go, the amount of time it took to get things in motion was remarkably short. By the end of the day, a Houston police officer had listened to the audio from

183

the webcam but couldn't determine if the sound was a gun or not. He gave it a seventy-five percent assurance that it was but wouldn't say definitively. The tower dispatcher at McMurdo confirmed that all their planes were grounded due to weather, and no emergency was grave enough to risk a flight crew. Conditions were even worse at Palmer Station, the only other American base on the Antarctic Peninsula, so there was no chance of them checking in on Wilson/George. Feelers had gone out to other nations with research centers nearby, but the closest was an Argentine research facility, and, despite the common bonds among the scientific community, they had rebuffed the request in no uncertain terms.

By eight o'clock that evening, the news of the situation had been sent to the President's National Security Advisor. Because Wilson/George was so close to an Argentine base and there was inconclusive evidence of gunfire, there was the possibility they had been attacked for some reason. Ideas were discussed late into the night, and a request was sent to the National Reconnaissance Office for a satellite to be retasked in order to photograph the isolated research station.

By dawn, the pictures had been analyzed, and even their remarkable optics were defeated by the storm that was savaging half the continent.

And then, like all bureaucracies, the efficiency stopped there. No one knew what to do next. All the information that could be gathered and studied had been. A decision was needed, but no one could be found who was willing to make it. The early surge of activity came to an abrupt end, and the people involved began to take a wait-and-see attitude.

When he arrived at Langley a little past nine, Langston Overholt took a cup of coffee his secretary had ready for him and went into his private office. The view through the bulletproof window behind him caught a copse of trees in full leaf. The wind danced along the branches and made fractal shadows on the lawn below.

His office was spartan. Unlike many other senior officers at the CIA, Overholt didn't have an ego wall — a collection of photographs of himself and various dignitaries. He had never seen the need to advertise his importance to others. But with his legendary reputation, it really wasn't necessary. Anyone visiting him here on the seventh floor knew exactly who he was. And while many of his accomplishments remain deeply buried secrets, enough had leaked out over the years to secure his status within the Agency. There were only a few photographs on the wall, mostly portraits done during the holidays as his family grew, and one sepia-toned snapshot of him and a young Asian man. Only an expert would recognize that he was Tibet's Dalai Lama.

"Well, maybe a little ego," he said, glancing at the picture.

Overholt read the briefing report given to all senior staffers. It was an even more thorough version than that given to the President, who'd early in his administration made it clear that he didn't like to bother with details.

There was the usual news from around the world — a bombing in Iraq, oil workers killed in Nigeria, North Korean military posturing along the DMZ. The incident at the Wilson/George Station rated a paragraph on the second-to-last page, just below remarks about the near capture of a Serbian war criminal. Had this taken place at any other Antarctic base, he wouldn't have given it a second thought, but the report made it clear that the Argentines had a facility about thirty miles away, and their terse refusal to send out a team to investigate set Overholt's sixth sense into high gear. He requested the raw footage from Dr. Palmer's webcam.

He knew immediately what had to be done.

He checked in with the director of the South American section and was told that Cabrillo had reached Asunción the night before and turned over the power cell to a pair of Agency couriers and it was now on a charter flight nearing the California coast.

Overholt killed the internal call and dialed Houston to speak with Dr. Parker. After that, he placed a call to an overseas exchange.

TEN

After nearly an hour in the shower and a breakfast of eggs, toast, and herbal tea — Maurice, the ship's steward, refused Cabrillo anything with caffeine — Juan still felt restless. He should go to bed, but his goose-down duvet looked uninviting. He knew sleep would not come easily. Dr. Huxley had recommended something to help him after performing a brief physical, but he'd declined. He wasn't punishing himself for Jerry's death, but somehow chemical oblivion didn't seem fair to his friend's memory. If thinking about the big Pole was going to keep him awake, then that was the price Cabrillo was willing to pay.

He and the others had arrived aboard the *Oregon* three hours earlier after a flight back to Brazil from the Paraguayan capital. They'd spent the first hour talking with members of the crew about what had happened and how Jerry had sacrificed himself so they could get away. Already a memorial service was in the works for that evening. The kitchen staff was making traditional Polish food, including pierogi, *Kotlet Schabowy,* and *Sernik,* a popular cheesecake, for dessert.

Cabrillo usually led such a service, but because of their friendship Mike Trono asked if he could have the honor.

Juan left his cabin to do a slow inspection of his ship as she lay at anchor just outside the port of Santos. The tropical sun beat down on the steel decks, but the trade winds that blew through his white linen shirt kept him cool. Even to the most observant eye, the *Oregon* looked ready for the breaker's yard. Junk littered the deck, and any areas of paint that weren't chipped or peeling were applied so haphazardly and in such a myriad of off-putting colors that it almost looked like she wore camouflage. The central white stripe of the Iranian flag hanging over her fantail looked to be the only spot of brightness on the old freighter.

Juan approached an oil drum placed next to the ship's rail. He fished an ear microphone from his pocket and called the op center. The *Oregon* was wired with encrypted cellular service.

"Hello," answered the high-pitched voice

of Linda Ross, who had the conn.

"Hello yourself," Cabrillo said. "Do me a favor and activate the number five deck gun."

"Is there a problem?"

"No. Just giving the old girl a once-over." Juan was well aware his crew knew he inspected the ship whenever he was troubled.

"You got it, Juan. Coming up now."

The oil drum's lid lifted silently on an armature until it was completely folded over the side. An M-60 medium machine gun rose barrel first and rotated down so it was pointed out to sea. He examined the ammunition belt. The brass showed no trace of corrosion, while the weapon itself was well coated in gun oil.

"Looks good to me," Cabrillo said, and asked Linda to stow it once again.

Next, he ambled down to the engine room, the heart of his creation. It was as clean as an operating theater. The ship's revolutionary power plant used supercooled magnets to strip free electrons from seawater in a system called magnetohydrodynamics. Currently, the technology was still so experimental that no other ship in the world utilized it. The room was dominated by the cryopumps used to keep the magnets cooled to three hundred degrees below zero. The main drive tubes ran the *Oregon*'s length and were as big around as railroad tanker cars. Inside were variable-geometry impellers that, had they not been locked away in the guts of an old tramp freighter, would have served as the focal point of any modern-art museum. When water was being run through them, the whole space thrummed with unimaginable power.

The *Oregon* could reach speeds unheard of in a ship her size and stop as quickly as a sports car. With her powerful athwartship thrusters and directional drive outlets, she could also turn on a dime.

He continued on, ambling about the vessel with no direction in mind.

The hallways and work spaces were usually filled with lively conversation and banter. Not today. Downcast eyes had replaced ready laughter. The men and women of the Corporation performed their duties with the knowledge that one of their own was no longer with them. Juan could sense no blame from the crew, and that was what started easing the burden he carried. There was no blame because they all felt a measure of responsibility. They were a team, and, as such, they shared the victories and defeats in equal measure.

Cabrillo spent five minutes staring at a small Degas hanging in a corridor near where most of the crew's cabins were located. The discreetly lit painting showed a ballerina lacing a slipper up her ankle. In his opinion, the artist captured light, innocence, and beauty better than any painter before or since. That he could appreciate one of Degas's masterworks and the ugly functionality of a machine gun in the same tour was an irony lost on the Chairman. Aesthetics came in all forms.

In the forward hold he watched crewmen preparing to pull their spare RHIB from storage. When they were at sea and away from prying eyes, a deck crane would lift the RHIB from the hold, set it in the water off the starboard side, and it would be winched into the boat garage located at the waterline.

He checked in on the ship's swimming pool. It was usually his favorite form of exercise, and the reason he maintained his broad shoulders and lean waist, but after so much time in the water over the past two days he would probably use the nearby weight room for a while.

At the very bottom of the ship was one of her best-kept secrets. It was a cavernous room directly above the keel from which they could launch a pair of submersibles. Massive doors split open along the bottom of a moon pool, and the minis could be launched and recovered even when the ship was under way, though it was preferable that the *Oregon* remain stationary. The engineering needed to create such a space and maintain the hull's integrity had been Juan's single greatest challenge when he'd converted her from an old lumber carrier.

The hangar under the aftmost of the ship's five holds was deserted. The black MD-520N sat on her struts with her main blades folded back. Unlike a traditional chopper, this model didn't have a tail rotor. Instead, the jet engine exhaust was ducted through the tail to counter the torque of the overhead rotor. It made her quieter than most helicopters, and Gomez Adams said it made him look cooler.

The space had a cramped feel because of modifications they'd been forced to make when upgrading from the small Robinson R44 helicopter they'd once used.

In the infirmary he found Julia Huxley, their Navy-trained doctor, bandaging one of the engineer's hands. The man had sliced it while working in the machine shop and had needed a couple of stitches. Julia wore her trademark lab coat and ponytail fashioned with a rubber band.

"Lay off the rum rations until after your shift, Sam," Hux joked after finishing taping down gauze pads.

"I promise. No more drilling under the influence."

"You okay?" Juan asked him.

"Yeah. Stupid, though. My father taught me the first day in our garage never to take your eyes off your tools. So what do I do? I look away while I'm milling a piece of steel and the damned thing slips and, wham, it looks like I was slaughtering a pig down there."

Juan's headset chirped. "Yes, Linda."

"It's Max. Sorry to bother you, but Langston Overholt's on the line, and he says he'll only discuss something with you."

Cabrillo thought for a second and nodded to himself as if he'd made a decision. "I was done anyway. Thanks. Tell him to give me a second while I head back to my cabin."

"Hello?"

"Juan, sorry to call so soon after a mission but I'm afraid something rather peculiar has come up," Lang said in his usual understatement.

"Have you heard?" Cabrillo asked.

"I had to talk with Max before he relented

and put the call through. He told me about your man. I'm sorry. I know what you're feeling. For what it's worth," Overholt continued, "you did a magnificent job. The Argentines will complain to the UN and accuse us of everything under the sun, but, bottom line, we have the power cell back and they've got nothing."

"I have a hard time believing it was worth a man's life," Juan muttered.

"In the great scheme of things it probably wasn't, but your guy knew the price going in. You all do."

Juan wasn't in the mood for a philosophical discussion with his former case officer, so he asked, "What's this delicate situation you mentioned?"

Overholt told the Chairman everything he knew about the situation at the Wilson/George Station, including what he'd learned from Tom Parker.

When he finished, Juan said, "So it could be this guy Dangle —"

"Gangle," Lang corrected.

"Gangle could have gone off the deep end and killed the others?"

"It's entirely possible, although Dr. Parker's assessment from what he'd learned from the astronaut is this Gangle kid was just a loner with a chip on his shoulder."

"Lang, those are always the ones who take axes to their families or shoot sniper rifles from bell towers."

"Well, yes. But still we need to keep in mind that there's an Argentine base less than thirty miles away. As you know, they've been making noise about how all of the Antarctic Peninsula is their sovereign territory. What if this is the first play in a larger operation? There are other bases down there. The Norwegians, Chileans, the Brits. They could be next."

"Or it could be a deranged kid who's spent too much time on the ice," Juan said.

"The problem is, we won't have a definite answer for the better part of a week, maybe longer if the weather doesn't clear. If this is an Argentine play, then by the time we figure it out it will be too late."

"So you want us to head south and investigate what happened at Wilson/George."

"Exactly. It should be a milk run. A quick dash down, a little look-see, and then tell old Uncle Langston that he doesn't have anything to worry about."

"We'll do it, of course, but you have to know that Max and I aren't going."

"You have something planned?"

Cabrillo explained about discovering the *Flying Dutchman* and his desire to tell the families of the blimp's crew what had happened to their loved ones a half century ago.

"I think that's a tremendous idea," Lang boomed. "Just the thing you need to gain a little perspective. The crew won't need you two on this mission anyway. Max frets too much, and you should get out of your head for a while."

"Oh, before I forget, my weapons guy said there's a chance that satellite was shot down."

"Come again?"

"You heard me. There are a couple of dings on the power cell's outer casing. Two correspond to a pair of bullet strikes, but the third is a mystery. You need to have that thing gone over with a fine-tooth comb."

"We were planning on it, but thanks for the heads-up. And I doubt your guy's right. Argentina doesn't have the technology to shoot down a rocket that late into its flight, and why would they bother? It wasn't a military launch."

"I'm just telling you what he thinks. If he's wrong, fine. If not, well, that's something else altogether. Don't forget who has demonstrated they have the capability to shoot down a satellite and who, by the way, continually blocks more intense sanctions against Argentina at the UN."

That forced a long pause from Overholt. "I don't like what you're implying."

"Neither do I," Juan agreed. "But it's food for thought. Still want us in Antarctica?"

"More than ever, my boy, more than ever."

ELEVEN

The summons had been a single word, "come." Despite its terseness, Major Jorge Espinoza read a great deal into the message and none of it was good. It took nearly twelve hours to arrange transport from the northern border to his father's estate in the grassy pampas a hundred miles west of Buenos Aires. He had flown the last leg himself in his Turbine Legend, a prop plane that looked like the legendary Spitfire and had nearly the same performance. Lieutenant Jimenez, his burns heavily bandaged, had ridden in the rear seat.

When his father was given command of the Ninth Brigade, he had used family money to build them a new command center and barracks at the estate. The old runway a mile from the main house had been expanded and paved to accommodate a fully loaded C-130. The apron was also expanded for helicopter landing pads, and a huge metal hangar was erected.

The camp itself was so far from the big house that even mortar practice didn't disturb the General, his new, young wife, and their two children. It had housing for the thousand men who belonged to the elite unit, with support facilities for all their needs. Next to the parade ground was an obstacle course and a state-of-the-art fitness center.

With its wide-open grassy planes, dense forests, and two separate river systems, the huge cattle estate was perfect for keeping the men in top operational preparedness.

The nearby village of Salto was growing from a sleepy little farming community to a bustling town of people more than willing to take care of the soldiers' off-duty needs.

Espinoza typically buzzed the main house when he made his approach to the airfield. His half brothers loved his aircraft and begged him for rides incessantly. But not today. He wanted to attract as little attention to himself as possible as he soared over the estate, where the spring rains were turning the grassland green and lustrous.

The debacle in the rain forest would be a career ender for any other soldier, and it still might be for him. As both son and subordinate, he had let the General down.

Nine men had died under his command, and then Raul had finally stumbled into the border crossing he had reported that the four men with him in the chopper were gone and six more border guards were dead and their boats destroyed. They had also lost two expensive helicopters, with a third damaged.

But the worst of all for son and soldier was the fact that he had failed. That was the truly unpardonable sin. They had let the Americans steal back the satellite fragment from right under their noses. He recalled the bloody face of the American driving the pickup loaded with his "wounded" comrades. Despite the mask of gore, Espinoza knew every feature — the shape of the eyes, the strength of the jaw, the almost arrogant nose. He would recognize this man no matter where they met again or how many years would elapse.

He lined up the nimble plane on the runway and dropped the gear. A four-engine C-130 was parked next to the big hangar. Its rear cargo ramp was down, and he could just make out a small forklift trundling up through the rear door. Espinoza wasn't aware of any future Ninth Brigade deployments, and he was almost certain that after his meeting with the General he would no longer be part of the elite force's future.

The plane bumped once when it hit the asphalt and then settled lightly. It was such a delight to fly that every landing was a disappointment the trip was over. He taxied to the apron where his father kept his plane, a Learjet capable of getting him anywhere in South America in just a couple of hours.

While the General came from a military family, Espinoza's late mother had been born into a clan whose wealth stretched back to the very founding of the country. There were office towers in BA and vineyards out west, five different cattle farms, an iron mine, and a virtual stranglehold on the country's cell-phone system. All this was run by his uncles and cousins.

Jorge had enjoyed the benefits of such wealth, the best schools and expensive toys like the Turbine, but he'd never been attracted to its creation. He had wanted to serve in the military as soon as he understood that the uniform his father wore to work every day was a symbol of his nation's greatness.

He had worked with single-minded determination to make his childhood dream of being a soldier a reality, and now, at thirty-seven years, he was at what he considered the peak of his career. With the next promotion would come a desk job, something he looked upon with dread. He had operational control over Argentina's most lethal commandos. At least for another few minutes. The humiliation was like an ember burning in the pit of his stomach.

A Mercedes ML500 SUV painted in a matte jungle camouflage was waiting for him and Jimenez. Inside was plush leather and burnished wood. It was his stepmother's idea of roughing it.

"How is he?" Espinoza asked Jesús, his father's longtime majordomo, who had driven down to the runway to pick up the young master.

"Calm." Jesús said, and tapped the vehicle into gear.

Not a good sign.

The track up to the manor house was a dirt road but one so meticulously maintained that the ride was as smooth as the autobahn, and the heavy SUV kicked up just a trace of dust. Overhead a hawk spotted some prey on the ground, tucked its wings, and plummeted earthward.

Maxine Espinoza greeted Jorge at the top of the steps leading to the front door. His stepmother was from Paris, and had once been an employee of their embassy in the Cerrito section of Buenos Aires. His real mother had died three weeks after being violently tossed from a horse when Espinoza was eleven. His father had waited until he was out of military college before considering remarrying, though there had been a string of beautiful women over the years.

She was only a couple of years older than Jorge, and had the old man not met her first he would have dated her in a heartbeat. He didn't begrudge his father a young wife. He had honored Jorge's mother by waiting so long, and by the time Maxine came into their lives it was good to have a woman to blunt some of the General's rough edges, which had grown sharper over the years.

She wore riding clothes that showed bearing two more sons for the General had done no permanent damage to her figure.

"You are not hurt?" she asked, her Spanish laced with a French accent. He suspected the French women made their second language sexy no matter what it was. Maxine could make Urdu sound like poetry.

"No, Maxie, I'm fine."

Raul approached, and she noticed his bandages. She blanched. "*Mon Dieu,* what did those pigs do to you?"

"They blew up a helicopter I was in, *señora.*" Jimenez spoke to his shoes as if he wasn't comfortable around such wealth or the attention of his commander's wife.

"The General is very upset," Maxine said, linking her arms though those of the young officers. The inside of the house was airy and cool, with a painting of Philippe Espinoza wearing the colonel uniform he had sported two decades earlier dominating one wall. "He is like a stallion denied the mare. You will find him in the gun room."

Jorge saw three men conversing in one corner of the entry hall. One turned when they entered. He was Asian. In his fifties. He was a man Espinoza didn't recognize. Lieutenant Jimenez made to follow his Major, but Maxine would not relinquish his arm. "The General wishes to see him alone."

The gun room was at the back of the house, its floor-to-ceiling windows overlooking the yard, with its stream and waterfall. Hunting trophies hung from the walls. The head of a giant boar had the place of honor above the fieldstone fireplace. There were three separate glass-fronted gun cabinets and one locked safe where the General kept his automatic weapons. The floor was Mexican tile covered with Andean rugs.

This was the room where punishment had been meted out when Jorge was growing up, and over the smell of leather furniture and gun oil he detected the scent of his own fear that had lingered over the decades.

General Philippe Espinoza stood just under six feet, with a shaved head and shoulders as broad as a hangman's gallows. His nose had been broken when he was a cadet and never fixed, giving his face a masculine asymmetry that made it difficult to focus on his eyes. Being able to stare down others was just one of the tools he had used to thrive during the dictatorships of the 1970s and '80s.

"General Espinoza," Jorge said, coming to attention. "Major Jorge Espinoza reporting as ordered."

His father was standing behind his desk, leaning over, as he studied a map. It looked like the Antarctic Peninsula, but Jorge couldn't be sure.

"Do you have anything to add to the report I've read?" the General asked without looking up. His voice was clipped, abrupt.

"The Americans have yet to cross the border, at least not in their RHIB. Patrols have turned up no sign of it on either bank of the river. We suspect they sank it and extracted overland."

"Continue."

"The helicopter pilot they kidnapped says the team leader was named Juan, another called Miguel. The leader spoke Spanish with a BA accent."

"But you are certain they are American?"

"I saw the man myself. He might speak Spanish like us, but he" — Espinoza paused, trying to find the right words — "had that American look."

The senior Espinoza finally looked up. "I attended their special School of the Americas, same as Galtieri, only years later. The instructors at Fort Benning all had that look. Go on."

"There was one thing I left out of my report. We discovered the wreckage of an old blimp. The Americans found it first, and it looks as though they spent time examining it."

A faraway look crossed the General's face. "A blimp. You are sure?"

"Yes, sir. It was the pilot who recognized the type of aircraft."

"I recall when I was a young boy a group of Americans flying across the jungle in a blimp. They were treasure hunters, I believe. They went missing back in the late 1940s. Your grandfather met them at a reception in Lima."

"They're found now. When the thieves stole our helicopter, they landed near the crash site as if they knew of it. I think they discovered it on their way to the logging camp."

"And you say they examined the wreckage?"

"Judging by the footprints, yes, sir."

"Not something disciplined commandos would do?"

"No, sir. Not at all."

Jorge took it as a good sign that his father sat. The calm exterior which masked his anger was slowly giving way to something else. "Your performance in this matter is beyond reprehensible. I would almost say it borders on criminal negligence."

Uh-oh.

"However, there are things you aren't privy to at the moment that mitigate the situation somewhat. Plans that are known only at the highest levels of the government. Soon your unit will be sent south, and it wouldn't do to have its most popular officer in custody. And what I put the official report of the incident will depend on how well you perform in an upcoming mission."

"General, may I ask where we are to be deployed?"

"Not yet. A week or so and you will understand."

Jorge straightened. "Yes, sir."

"Now, go fetch your Captain Jimenez. I

208

think I have something for you to do in the meantime."

TWELVE

While the *Oregon* headed south under the command of Linda Ross, Cabrillo and Hanley flew north on a commercial flight to Houston, where the Corporation kept one of a dozen safe houses in port cities all over the globe. Each was loaded with just about anything a team could need. They considered this one a fairly central place for their search of the airship's crew.

By the time they reached the town-house condominium in a generic development twenty miles from the city center, Eric Stone and Mark Murphy had done the necessary legwork, or finger work, as the case may be, since the two were virtuosos when it came to Internet research.

As Murph liked to boast, "I've never met a firewall I couldn't douse."

Unlike some of the other Corporation properties — the penthouse in a Dubai high-rise was as opulent as any five-star hotel — the Houston safe house was spartan. The furniture looked like it came from catalogs, which it had, and the décor was mostly cheaply framed prints of nature scenes. The only thing that set it apart from the four hundred identical units in the neighborhood was that the walls, floor, and ceiling of one of the bedrooms were lined in inch-thick steel. The door, though it looked normal, was as impenetrable as a bank vault's.

Upon entering, Max made certain that the room hadn't been breached in the three months since it had last been checked. He added batteries to an anti-eavesdropping device kept in storage and swept the entire condo while Juan opened a bottle of tequila and added ice from the bag of sundries they'd picked up at a convenience store on the drive in from the airport. Only when they were assured the place was clean did he connect his laptop to the Internet and place it on the coffee table in the living room.

The early-evening South Texas sun beat through the windows and created a glare on the screen, so Max shut the drapes and helped himself to some of the duty-free liquor. He settled onto the sofa next to Juan with a sigh.

"You know," he said, running the chilled glass across his high forehead, "after years of using our own jet, first class is a disappointment."

"You're getting soft in your dotage."

"Bah!"

The computer came online. Juan double-checked the security protocols and called up the *Oregon*. Instantly, a picture of Eric and Mark popped onto the screen. He could tell by the giant video display behind them that they were in Eric's cabin. Stoney was an Annapolis graduate who had come to the Corporation after fulfilling his minimum time in uniform. It wasn't that he disliked the service, but a commander of his who had served in Vietnam with Max thought the bright young officer would better serve his nation by joining up with the Chairman's crew. It was Eric who suggested his friend Mark Murphy join, too. They had gotten to know each other while working on a secret missile program, where Murph was a designer for one of the big defense contractors.

Eric didn't have the look of a Navy veteran. He had soft brown eyes and an almost gentle demeanor. Where Murph cultivated a cyberpunk ethos with an in-your-face style of dress, Eric was more buttoned-down and serious. He wore a white oxford shirt opened at the collar. Mark had on a T-shirt adorned with a cyclopic smiley face. Both looked too excited to stay still.

"Howdy, boys," Juan greeted. "How's it going?"

"We're running hard, boss man," Eric replied. "Linda has us up to thirty-eight knots, and with so few countries trading with Argentina there's virtually no ship traffic for us to avoid."

"What's your ETA at Wilson/George?"

"A tick over three days, provided we don't hit ice."

"*Encounter* ice," Max corrected. "One encounters ice, one must never hit ice. Bad for the ship."

"Thanks for the tip, E.J.," Mark said, using the first two initials of the ill-fated *Titanic*'s captain.

"So what have you found?" Cabrillo asked.

"You're not going to believe who those guys were," Eric said excitedly. "They were the Ronish brothers. Their family owns Pine Island off Washington State."

Juan blinked in surprise. As a West Coast native, he knew all about Pine Island and its infamous Treasure Pit. It was a story that fascinated him as a boy, as it did all his friends. "You're sure?"

213

"No doubt," Mark replied. "And what do you bet they found a clue in the Teasure Pit that sent them off looking for something hidden in the Amazon rain forest?"

"Hold on. Let's not get ahead of ourselves. Tell it to me from the top."

"There were five brothers. One of them" — Eric glanced down at his notes — "Donald, was killed, get this, on December seventh, 1941, when they tried to reach the bottom of the pit. Right afterward, the three eldest joined the military. The fifth brother was too young. Nick Ronish became one of the most decorated Marines in Corps history. He took part in three island assaults, including being on the first wave at Iwo Jima. Another brother was a paratrooper in the Eighty-first. Ronald was his name. He went in on D-day, and fought all the way to Berlin. The last one, Kevin, joined the Navy, where he became a spotter on blimps flying patrols off the coast of California —"

Mark interrupted, adding, "A couple of years after the war, they bought a surplus blimp, which Kevin had gotten himself licensed to fly, and they headed off to South America."

"Is there any indication that they found anything on Pine Island?" Juan asked. "I seem to recall a big expedition there in the 1970s."

"There was. James Ronish, the surviving brother, was reportedly paid a hundred thousand dollars by Dewayne Sullivan to allow him to excavate on the island. Sullivan was like the Richard Branson of his day. He made a ton of money in oil and spent it on all kinds of crazy adventures, like yachting solo around the world or skydiving from a weather balloon from eighty thousand feet.

"In 1978, he set his sights on Pine Island, and spent four months excavating the Treasure Pit. They had a massive pumping capacity and built a coffer dam to prevent water from seeping into it from a nearby lagoon, but they could never drain it properly. Divers did find Donald Ronish's skeletal remains, which were later buried, and they hauled out a lot of debris. But then a worker was killed when they were refueling one of the pumps. He had left it running — it spilled gasoline and went up in flames. A day or so later, one of the divers got the bends and had to be airlifted back to shore. That was when Sullivan shut down operations."

"That's right," Juan exclaimed. "I remember now. He said something like, 'No mystery is worth a man's life.' "

Eric took a pull off a can of energy drink. "That's it exactly. But here's what Mark and I think. After the war, the brothers went back to Pine Island and cracked the pit. There wasn't any treasure there, or maybe enough to buy the blimp, though I can't imagine the Navy asked much for them back then. Anyway, they found something down there that led them to South America — a map or carvings."

"They crashed before they found it," Murph added.

"What about the youngest brother?" Max asked. "What ever happened to him?"

"James Ronish was wounded in Korea. Never married, he still lives in the house his parents left him when they moved from the Coast, and he still owns Pine Island. We have his phone number and address."

"As well as his financials." Mark glanced down at a piece of paper. "As of noon today, he has one thousand two hundred dollars in a savings account. Four hundred in checking, and a credit-card balance of nearly a grand. He's two payments behind on his taxes but current on a mortgage he took out on the house seven years ago."

"Doesn't sound like a guy whose family found pirate loot."

"Nope. Just an old man marking his calendar until it's time to take a dirt nap," Murph said. "We found something in the local newspaper's online database. A contractor in the area reported that he and Ronish were forming a partnership to make another attempt on the pit. This was five years ago. The contractor was going to put up the money and equipment, but then nothing ever came of it."

Juan thought for a second, sipping from his tequila. "I'm getting the feeling that whenever Mr. Ronish is short on funds, he opens up his island for exploration."

"Sounds about right," Eric replied. "I can track down the contractor to find out what happened to give him cold feet."

Murph leaned closer to the webcam. "I'll hack into his bank again and see what kind of money trouble Ronish had when the deal was announced."

"I'm nixing both ideas," the Chairman told them. "Neither really matters because we're not doing anything with the Treasure Pit."

Murph and Eric looked like a couple of kids who had their puppy taken away from them.

Juan continued, "We're here to tell him that we found his brothers' remains and

217

likely have a journal one of them wrote after the crash." No one had had time yet to read the condom-wrapped papers. They were still in Cabrillo's luggage.

"You can't be serious," Mark whined. "This could lead to a significant discovery. Pierre Devereaux was one of the most successful privateers in history. His treasure has got to be someplace."

Max grunted, "Most likely at the bottom of the ocean where his ship sank."

"Au contraire, mon frère," Mark countered. "There were survivors when his ship sank in the Caribbean. They had just come from rounding Cape Horn and said they were carrying no cargo. They said Devereaux spent time off our western coast with a handful of men, but when he returned to his ship he was alone."

"Or it's all crap to keep the legend alive."

"Come on, Max, where's your sense of whimsy?" Eric asked.

Hanley cocked a thick eyebrow at the odd choice of word. "Whimsy?"

"You know what I mean. Didn't you ever dream of finding pirate treasure when you were a kid?"

"Two tours in 'Nam pretty much crushed any whimsy I might have had."

"Sorry, fellas," Juan said with finality. "No

pirate treasure for us. We're just going to deliver the papers and tell Mr. Ronish where his brothers died."

"All right," they said in hangdog unison, making Cabrillo smile.

"Let me find a pen to write down his address, and Max and I will get ourselves up to Washington."

"Don't forget to bring garlic and a wooden stake," Eric said.

"What are you talking about?"

"Ronish lives outside of Forks. That's the town where the *Twilight* books take place."

"Huh?"

"It's a series of romantic novels about a teenage girl in love with a vampire."

"How would I possibly know that?" Cabrillo asked. "And, more telling, why do you?"

Eric looked sheepish while Max roared with laughter.

Because there was no real urgency to reach Forks, Washington, it didn't take much for Max to convince Cabrillo to enjoy an overnight layover in Vegas. Had he wanted, Juan could have made a nice living as a professional poker player, so he had no problem taking money from the amateurs at the table with him. Hanley didn't do as well at the craps table, but both agreed it had been a welcome diversion.

In the city of Port Angeles, on the Juan de Fuca Strait, they rented a Ford Explorer for the hour-long drive around the spectacular Olympic Mountains to Forks.

The place was typical small-town America — a cluster of businesses clinging to Route 101 backed by houses in various states of disrepair. Timber was the main industry in the region, and with the market so soft it was clear that Forks was suffering. A number of storefronts were vacant with leasing signs taped to the glass. The few people walking the streets moved with little purpose. Their shoulders were hunched from more than the cold wind blowing off the nearby North Pacific.

The darkening sky was filled with bruised clouds that threatened to open up at any moment.

In the center of town, Max nodded his head at a hotel as they neared. "Should we check in first or head straight to Ronish's?"

"I don't know how talkative this guy's going to be, and I don't know if the desk in a place like that stays open too late. So let's check in and then get to his house."

"Man, this sure ain't Caesars."

Twenty minutes later they approached a

dirt track off Bogachiel Way, six miles from town. Pine forests soared overhead, and the trunks were so tightly packed that they couldn't see lights from the house until they were almost upon it.

As Eric had said, James Ronish had never married, and it showed. The one-story house hadn't seen fresh paint in a decade or more. The roof had been repaired with off-color shingles, and the front lawn looked like a junkyard. There were several skeleton-ized cars, an askew satellite dish as big as a kiddy wading pool, and various bins of mechanical junk. The doors to the detached garage were open, and inside was just as bad. Workbenches were littered with uniden-tifiable flotsam, and the only way to reach them was by narrow paths through even more clutter.

"Right out of *Better Homes and Scrap-yards,*" Juan quipped.

"Five will get you ten his curtains are dish towels."

Cabrillo parked the SUV next to Ronish's battered pickup. The wind made the trees creak, and their needled tops whisper. The storm couldn't be more than a few minutes away. Juan grabbed the condom-wrapped papers from the center console. As much as he wanted to read them, he didn't feel it appropriate. He could only hope that Ronish would share their contents.

A blue flicker showed through a large picture window that was caked with dust. Ronish was watching television, and as they neared the front door they could hear it was a game show.

Juan pulled open a creaky screen door and knocked. After a few seconds of nothing happening, he rapped on the door a little harder. Another twenty seconds went by before a light snapped on over the door and it opened a crack.

"What do you want?" James Ronish asked sourly.

From what Juan could see, he was a big man, heavy in the gut, with thinning gray hair and suspicious eyes. He leaned against an aluminum cane. Below his nose was a clear plastic oxygen canula with tubing that lead to an O_2 concentrator the size of a microwave oven.

"Mr. Ronish, my name is Juan Cabrillo. This is Max Hanley."

"So?"

Friendly sort, Juan thought. He wasn't sure what he'd expected, but he supposed Mark was right. Ronish appeared to be an old man marking his calendar until he died.

"I'm not sure how to tell you this, so I'll

just come out and say it."

Juan didn't pause but Ronish interrupted anyway. "Don't care," he said, and made to close the door.

"Mr. Ronish, we found the *Flying Dutchman*. Well, the wreckage anyway."

Color drained from Ronish's face everywhere but from his gin-blossom nose. "My brothers?" he asked.

"We found a set of remains in the pilot's seat."

"That would have been Kevin," the old man said quietly. Then he seemed to rouse himself, and his guard was up in an instant. "What's it to you?"

Max and Juan shared a glance, as if to say this wasn't going as they'd planned.

"Well, sir —"

"If you're here about Pine Island you can just forget it."

"You don't understand. We were just in South America. We work for" — Juan had planned to use the United Nations as a cover, but he suspected that would make a guy like Ronish all the more suspicious — "a mining company doing survey work, and we discovered the crash site. It took a little research to realize what we'd found."

Just then, the rain started. Icy needles that pounded through the pine canopy and impacted the ground almost like hail. Ronish's porch didn't have a roof, so he reluctantly opened the door for the two men to enter his house.

It smelled of old newspapers and food on the verge of spoiling. The appliances in the kitchen next to the entry were at least forty years old, and the floor had the matte finish of ancient linoleum. The living-room furniture was a mousy brown that matched the threadbare carpet. Magazines were stacked atop tables and along the yellowed walls. There were fifteen or twenty portable oxygen bottles stacked near the front door. The exposed fluorescent bulb in the kitchen gave off an electric whine that to Cabrillo was as obnoxious as nails on a chalkboard.

The only other illumination was from a floor lamp next to the chair where Ronish watched television. Juan would have sworn it had a five-watt bulb.

"So you found 'em, eh?" Ronish didn't sound as though he much cared.

"Yes. They came down in northern Argentina."

"That's strange. When they left, they said they were gonna search along the coast."

"Do you know exactly what they were looking for?" Max spoke for the first time.

"I do. And it's none of your business."

An uncomfortable silence stretched for several seconds. This was not the feel-good moment Juan had been hoping for. There was nothing about James Ronish's reaction that was going to cosmically balance what had happened to Jerry Pulaski.

"Well, Mr. Ronish" — Juan held out the bundle they'd taken from the downed blimp — "we found this in the wreckage and thought it may be important. We just wanted to give it to you and maybe bring you a little closure over your brothers' fate."

"I'll tell you what," Ronish said, anger tightened the wrinkles around his eyes. "If it weren't for those three, Don would still be alive, and I wouldn't have had damned-fool ideas about romance and adventure when I volunteered for Korea. Do you know what it's like to have the Chinese blow your leg off?"

"Actually —"

"Get out!" he snapped.

"No. Seriously." Juan stooped to raise his jeans' cuff and lower his sock. This prosthetic leg was covered with flesh-colored plastic that still looked artificial under the uncertain light.

James Ronish lost some of his anger. "Well, I'll be. A fellow peg leg. What happened?"

"Blown off by a Chinese gunboat during the reckless days of my youth."

"You don't say. Well, there's irony for you. Can I get you boys a beer?"

Before they could reply, the screen door outside squeaked open and someone knocked.

Cabrillo looked over to Max, concern etched on his face. He hadn't heard anyone drive up, but with the rain thundering against the house it was possible he missed it. And what were the odds an old curmudgeon like Jim Ronish getting two visitors on the same evening?

Then he told himself to relax. This wasn't a mission. They were just giving some information to a harmless old man living out in the middle of nowhere. Max had been right. Juan did need a little time off.

"Damn. Now what?" Ronish grumbled. He reached for the doorknob.

Juan's instincts went into overdrive. Something was very wrong. Before he could stop him, Ronish had the door open. A man stood out in the rain, his wet face shining in the light over the front door.

Both the man and Cabrillo recognized each other instantly, and while one spent a critical microsecond considering the implications, the other reacted.

Juan was grateful he was carrying a Glock. They didn't have safeties to slow him down. He whipped the pistol from the holster under his windbreaker and fired around Jim Ronish's shoulder. The bullet hit the frame, gouging out a sizable chunk of wood.

The Argentine Major who Cabrillo had talked his way past at the logging camp jumped from view. The automatic's report had been concussive in the foyer, but Juan could hear voices outside. The Major wasn't alone.

Cabrillo ignored his mind's desire to understand what had just happened. He leapt forward and slammed the door closed. The lock was about the cheapest made and yet he threw it anyway. Every second could count.

Max tackled a stunned James Ronish so that they hit the floor together, Hanley's arm over the older man's back. Cabrillo ducked through into the kitchen, found the light switch, and flicked it off. He then padded into the living room and simply knocked the floor lamp onto its side. The dim bulb went out with a pop. Next, he snapped off the television, plunging the old house into complete darkness.

"What's going on?" Ronish wailed.

"More of my reckless youth coming back

to haunt me," Cabrillo muttered, and flipped over a moth-eaten couch for additional cover.

Seconds ticked by. Max helped Ronish over to Juan's makeshift redoubt.

"How many?"

"At least two," Juan said. "The one at the door is an officer of the Ninth Brigade."

"I figured since you shot at him that he wasn't selling Avon."

The front picture window exploded under a murderous onslaught of gunfire. Glass rained on the men as they cowered behind the sofa. The house's thin walls didn't slow the high-powered rounds, so smoking holes appeared in the wallboard. The bullets passed through the living room, and probably didn't stop until they hit trees in Ronish's backyard.

"Those are rifles," Max said. He had his pistol out now but looked at it dubiously. Judging by the rate of fire screaming overhead, they weren't just outgunned, they were outmanned as well.

"Do you have any weapons?" Juan asked.

To his credit, the old man answered quickly, "Yeah. I got a .357 in my bedside table and a 30.06 in the closet. The rifle's empty, but the ammo's on the top shelf under a bunch of baseball caps. Last door on the left."

Before Cabrillo could retrieve the guns, an Argentine round slammed into one of the oxygen tanks Ronish kept for when he ran errands. The bullet blew through the tough steel skin and fortunately the oxygen didn't explode, but the twenty-pound bottle took off like a rocket. It crashed into the dining-room table, snapping a leg and sending it crashing under the weight of old magazines.

Next, it hit the couch hard enough to shove it into the men hiding behind it and then punched a hole in the Sheetrock wall, before dropping to the floor. It spun like a top until the last of the gas escaped.

Juan knew how lucky they had been. Depending on the type of ammunition they were facing, the tank could easily have exploded and started a chain reaction with the dozen or more bottles next to them. They were sitting in what amounted to a death trap.

"Forget the guns," Juan shouted. "We need to get out of here."

"I can't make it," James wheezed. His lungs were working overtime but he wasn't getting enough air. "I need the oxygen. I won't last five minutes."

"We stay here, we won't last five seconds!"

Cabrillo said, even though he saw the truth. James Ronish couldn't be moved.

The firing subsided as the Argentines regrouped after the first frantic moments of the gun battle. The only thing that made sense was that they needed Ronish alive. Juan knew he and Max hadn't been trailed to Washington, so he assumed that the men outside had followed the same informational bread crumbs as he had. It meant they knew something about the *Flying Dutchman*'s fateful voyage that he did not. Some piece of information that only James Ronish had. And he felt certain it had nothing to do with Pierre Devereaux's pirate loot.

Cabrillo pulled the Glock's trigger three times, laying down suppressing fire to keep the Argentines pinned. Their next tactic would be to encircle the house and come in from multiple angles. Juan still didn't know how he was going to get the three of them out of this.

"Mr. Ronish," he said, "they're here because of something your brothers found in the Treasure Pit. Something linked to the blimp we discovered. What did they find?"

Another crackle of gunfire from outside drowned out Ronish's answer. Dust filled the air from the destroyed drywall, and sofa stuffing was falling like snow. Ronish suddenly stiffened and whimpered softly.

He'd been hit. In the darkness, Cabrillo put his hand on the older man's chest. Feeling nothing, he moved his hand lower. Ronish hadn't been hit in the stomach, so Juan moved to his legs. In just the few seconds since the round penetrated his body, the amount of blood pumping from his thigh told Juan that the bullet had severed Ronish's femoral artery. Without medical help, he'd bleed out in minutes. Juan transferred his pistol to his left hand and pressed into the wound as hard as he could, while Max fired out through the picture window. There were definitely fewer men on the front yard. One or two of the Argentines were flanking them.

"What did they find?" Juan asked desperately.

"A way to the junk" was the pained reply. "The mantel. I kept a rub."

Juan vaguely recalled a framed piece of art above the faux-brick fireplace. Had it been some sort of rubbing? He didn't remember. It had made barely a passing impression. He looked through the darkness in the direction of the mantel and fired. The muzzle flash revealed the outline of the picture on the wall but no details. It was much too big to be easily portable.

"Mr. Ronish, please. What do you mean 'a way to the junk'?"

"I wish they'd never gone to the island," he replied. He was in shock, his body's response to his plummeting blood pressure. "It all would have turned out different."

Max changed out an empty magazine. Both men had brought only two spares from the Houston safe house.

Juan could no longer feel Ronish's heart pumping blood against his hand over the wound. The old man was gone. He didn't feel responsible. At least not directly. The Argentines would have killed him with or without the Corporation's presence. But had Juan and his team not stumbled onto the wreckage of the *Flying Dutchman,* James Ronish would have lived out his final days in obscurity. And therein lay the indirect guilt.

A voice boomed from outside. He spoke English. "I compliment you on your mastery of my language. My pilot thought you were from Buenos Aires.

"And you sound like that Chihuahua from the taco ads." Juan couldn't resist. Adrenaline was seething in his veins like champagne bubbles."

The Argentine shouted a curse that brought into question the marital status of

Juan's parents. "I give you one chance. Leave the house through the back door and my men will not fire. Ronish stays."

A kitchen window shattered. A few seconds later, wavering light came from the archway connecting it to the dining room. They'd tossed a Molotov cocktail to hasten the decision.

Juan jumped from the floor, firing from the hip through the window, and swept the rubbing, or whatever it was, from the wall. He heaved it into the kitchen like a Frisbee. The frame caught on the jamb, breaking the glass, and it vanished from sight.

Max opened fire again, covering Cabrillo while he changed mags, and together the two men ran down the hallway leading to the bedrooms. The house was a standard ranch, like millions of others built after World War II, like the one Juan had lived in until his father's accounting practice took off, like the ones all his friends lived in, like the one Max had grown up in. The two men could navigate it with their eyes closed.

The master bedroom was the last door on the left, just past the single bath. Juan even knew where the bed would be placed, as it was the only logical location, and he jumped on it, bending his knees to absorb some of the spring, and leapt again. He covered his head with his hands when he smashed through the window.

He hit the wet, needle-covered ground, shoulder-rolled, and came up with his gun ready. The muzzle flash from a snap shot fired from the far corner of the house gave away the gunman's location. Cabrillo put two rounds downrange. He didn't hear the meaty slap of a strike, but a low, mounting wail rose from the patch of darkness where the shooter had been.

Max came through the window a second later, having paused to let Juan clear the area. His exit wasn't as dramatic as Cabrillo's, but he made it nevertheless. They moved through the downpour as fast as they could, the wind and rain masking the sound of their escape. There was barely enough light to see but enough so they didn't run headlong into any trees. After five minutes, and several random turns, Juan slowed and dropped to his belly behind a fallen log.

Max's deep chest pumped like a bellows next to him. "You mind telling me," he panted, "what the hell they're doing here?"

Cabrillo's breathing was far less labored, but he was twenty years younger than his friend and, unlike Max, knew what a workout routine was. "That, dear Maxwell, is the million-dollar question. Are you okay?"

"Just a small cut on my hand from going through the window. You?"

"Nothing's hurt but my pride. I should have had that guy with my first shot."

"Seriously, how did they get here?"

"Same as us. They followed the trail from the *Flying Dutchman*. What I really want to know is what they hoped to find."

"Unless they're as nerdy as Mark and Eric, they're not looking for Devereaux's treasure."

"And we'll never know. The rubbing burned up in the kitchen, and I'd already given the journal or log, or whatever it was, to Ronish."

Max fished around in his jacket pocket and tapped something on Juan's wrist. He felt the spongy mass of latex-sheathed papers. "I nabbed this when I tackled him."

"I could kiss you."

"Let me shave first so you really get to enjoy the experience." Humor had always been their way of decompressing from a high-stress situation. "So what's our play?"

Where Max had always been the dogged one, the person who would bull through any challenge, it had always been Cabrillo who came up with the plan. Hanley really didn't see what to do next while Juan had figured it out the moment he leapt up and tossed the picture frame into the growing kitchen fire. If he was honest with himself, he'd known the instant the Argentine Major had shown up on James Ronish's doorstep.

"It's simple really," he said, turning on his back so that the rain washed the taste of gunpowder from his mouth. "You and I are going to solve the mystery of the Pine Island Treasure Pit."

THIRTEEN

A group of five Latinos, one of whom was wounded, would have stood out in a town as small as Forks or Port Angeles, so Espinoza and his men were forced to return to Seattle. Their injured comrade, shot through the side, suffered in silence for the hours it took to drive to the city. It wasn't until they were in the seedy hotel on the outskirts of the city that they were able to treat the wound properly. It had been a clean in and out and hadn't perforated the intestine, so unless he developed an infection he should be fine. They loaded him up with over-the-counter medications and half a bottle of brandy.

Once his men were settled, Espinoza returned to the room he shared with Raul Jimenez. He asked his friend to excuse himself and powered up a satellite phone. He wasn't sure how his father would react to the call. He was nervous nonetheless.

"Report," his father said by way of greeting, no doubt recognizing the number.

Espinoza hesitated, well aware that the computers of the American NSA monitored nearly every wireless transmission in the world, trolling through the mountains of data for key words that would make the call of interest to the intelligence community.

"We ran into competition. The same man I saw a couple of days ago."

"I wasn't sure they would be interested, nor did I expect them to move so fast," the General said. "What happened?"

"The target was collateralized, and one of my men was grazed."

"I don't care about your men. Did you learn anything? Or have you failed me again?"

"I retrieved a document," Espinoza replied. "I think the American tried to destroy it by throwing it into a fire before making his escape. However, we entered the target's house before it was damaged. You said it was possible we'd find evidence that the target knew something about China, so when I saw it on the kitchen floor I grabbed it.

"It appears to be a rubbing of some kind, like when families make tracings of headstones. It shows the map of a bay, but no location is given. There are glyphs on it that almost look like some Asian language."

"Chinese?" The General's tone was eager.

"It looks like it."

"Excellent. If this leads where I think it might, we are going to change the world, Jorge. Were you able to speak to the target?"

The elder Espinoza hadn't explained what it was he was after, but the words of praise made his son swell with pride. "He was already gone when we got inside. We burned his house to the ground afterward. I doubt they will bother checking the body for any sign of foul play, so we're clear."

"Where are you now?"

"Seattle. Do you want us to return home?"

"No. Not yet. Tomorrow, I want you to overnight the rubbing to me." The General paused. Jorge knew his father was considering angles and odds. He finally asked, "What do you think the competition will do now?"

"It depends if they extracted any useful information from the target. I checked the hood of their truck when we reached the house. It was still warm, so they hadn't been there long."

"They were interested enough to reach out to the target," General Espinoza said, more for his own benefit than his son's.

"Will they continue on or have they had enough?"

"If I may hazard a guess . . . The men were obviously soldiers. I think it's most likely they came here to tell the target about his brothers as a military courtesy. A *Band of Brothers* type thing."

"You believe they will drop it?"

"I think they will tell their superiors what happened tonight, and it will be they who decide to drop it."

"Yes, that's most likely how the military would act. There is no obvious threat to national security, so the soldiers will be told to stand down. Even if they want to pursue it, they will have their orders to let it go. This is good, Jorge, very good."

"Thank you, sir. May I ask what this is all about?"

General Espinoza chuckled. "Even if we were alone together here at the house, I could not tell you. I am sorry. I can say that in a few days an alliance is going to be announced that will forever change the world's balance of power, and, if I am correct about your find, you will have contributed to its success. I sent you to hunt a wild goose and it may yet turn out to lay a golden egg."

His father wasn't one to use such a frivolous turn of phrase, so Jorge took it as a sign of his happiness. Like any good son, he was especially proud when he could bring his father joy.

"See to your injured man," the General continued, "and be ready to move at a moment's notice. I am not sure if you will come back home or if you will have another mission. It all depends what we learn from the rubbing." He paused to give weight to his following words. "I am proud of you, son."

"Thank you, Father. It's all I ever want you to be." Espinoza hung up. He had more on his mind than simply waiting for orders. He wasn't sure what the Americans had learned from the old man, but it wasn't unreasonable to guess they might show up at his private island.

Cabrillo had always held the belief that if you threw enough money at a problem, it would go away, and he figured getting to the bottom of the Treasure Pit should be no different.

He and Max spent two hours in the woods watching the cheery glow of the fire as James Ronish's little ranch house burned to the ground. They waited that long to make sure the better-armed Argentines had left the area. Nothing remained of the house

241

but a toppled chimney and smoldering ash piles that spat and hissed in the rain. As a parting gift, all four tires on their rented SUV had been shot out, forcing them to drive back to the motel on flats.

Before they could think about hot showers and beds, they had to cut up the tires to retrieve the bullets so when they brought the truck to a garage the mechanic wouldn't report the incident to the police. They also smashed a headlight and keyed dozens of random lines into the glossy paint. Coming on the heels of such a fatal fire, it wouldn't do to arouse any kind of suspicion in the sleepy little town. The truck looked like the victim of juvenile vandals.

It was this kind of attention to detail, no matter how minute, that made the Corporation such a success.

The next morning, while Max went to find a garage to get the truck repaired, muttering about 'those damned kids these days,' Juan set up a video conference with his brain trust. When he told Mark and Eric that he had no choice but to dive the Treasure Pit, they looked like they were ready to jump ship to join him.

"My question to you is: How do I do it? How do I duplicate what only the Ronish brothers managed to accomplish on the eve of World War Two?"

"Have you gone over the information you recovered from the *Flying Dutchman?*" Eric asked. Juan had caught them eating breakfast. Over Stone's shoulder, Mark Murphy was munching on a banana. "They could have left a clue there."

"I took a quick peek. Despite the protection, the paper is in pretty bad shape. I don't know if I'll be able to get anything off of it. Assume I can't, and tell me what you two think. The pit has thwarted a number of attempts. You mentioned one that used some pretty high-tech solutions and yet they failed. What do you think the brothers figured out?"

Mark swallowed a mouthful of food, and said, "We know their first attempt ended in disaster, so obviously one of them learned something during the war that gave him the answer."

"Which one?"

"I doubt the pilot. He was an observer on a blimp. I can't imagine that kind of job giving him much inspiration."

"So it's either the Marine or the Army Ranger," Juan said.

Mark leaned in toward the webcam. "Look, this is an engineering problem, hydrodynamics, stuff like that. The Marines faced some pretty tricky booby traps as they fought their way to Japan. My bet is, he saw something the Japanese had done and thought Pierre Devereaux had come up with it first."

Eric looked at him crossways, and said what Cabrillo was about to. "You still think this is about an old pirate? There's no way the Argentines would be this interested if the Treasure Pit turns out to be just that."

Murph looked a little defensive. "What is it about, then?"

"Obviously, I can't answer that question." Eric turned back to Juan. "Do you have any ideas, Chairman?"

"Nothing. Ronish died before he could talk. And Max and I weren't in any position to search his place. Come on, think. What did they figure out? How do we crack the Treasure Pit?"

Mark tapped his chin. "A device . . . a device . . . A booby trap . . . Something involving water . . . Hydrostatic pressure."

"You have an idea?"

Murph didn't answer because he didn't have one. "Sorry, man. I've been so wrapped up in the history, I never really thought about the technology."

Juan blew out a breath. "Okay. Don't sweat it. Max and I will think of something."

"May I ask what?" Eric said.

"God, no. I'm winging it here."

For the next hour, they created a list of equipment the pair might need and went about filling it. What couldn't be purchased in Port Angeles would be delivered from Seattle. By the time they were done, a delivery van was headed to Forks from Washington's queen city and a small ferry was under way from Port Angeles and would pick up Max and Cabrillo at the fishing pier in the town of La Push. That coastal village was just a few miles north of Pine Island. The only problem was that they would lose another day because the sophisticated underwater communications equipment was coming in as airfreight from San Diego.

When it was all said and done, there was an additional forty thousand dollars' worth of charges on the Chairman's Amex, but, as he'd always believed, problem solved.

Hopefully.

He asked about the crew's morale, especially Mike Trono's.

Eric said, "He spent an hour or so after the service talking with Doc Huxley." She was the *Oregon*'s de facto shrink. "He says he's fit for active duty. Linda cleared it with Hux, so he's back working with the rest of

245

the fire-breathers."

"Probably for the best. Staying busy is a hell of a lot better than sitting still." Cabrillo knew that he was taking his own advice. "We'll call you when we're set up on Pine Island. I assume you want video feed when we're there."

"Hell yes," they said in unison.

Juan killed the connection and refolded his computer. Their deliveries from Seattle and Port Angeles arrived late in the afternoon, so it wasn't until the following morning that Max and Cabrillo headed for La Push. The ferry was a couple hours late because of wind, but they made the transfer quickly, driving the re-tired SUV onto the boat from the dock. With a capacity of only four vehicles and a relatively flat bottom, the ferry was at the mercy of the sea. The ride down to Pine Island was a battle between the boat's diesel engine and the waves that crashed over the bow. Fortunately, the captain knew these waters and handled his charge very well.

He was also being paid to forget this trip ever took place.

The approach to Pine Island went smoothly because its only beach was alee of the wind. They could only get about forty feet from shore before they had to lower the front ramp. Juan estimated they were in at least four feet of water.

He looked across to see that Max was strapped in before backing the Explorer to the very back of the ferry. "Ready?"

Hanley tightened his grip on the armrest. "Hit it."

Juan mashed the gas pedal, and the Ford's tires chirped against the deck. The heavy truck shot across the ferry and raced down the ramp. It hit the ocean in a creaming wall of water that surged over the hood and then over the roof, but there was enough momentum to shoulder most of it aside. The weight of the engine dragged the nose down, allowing the front tires to find purchase on the shale seabed.

It wasn't elegant, and the motor was sputtering by the time the grille emerged from the water, but they made it. Juan bulled the SUV up onto the beach, shouting and cajoling the truck until all four tires were on solid ground.

"You enjoyed that, didn't you?" Max was a little paler. Juan shot him a grin. "And have you considered how we're going to load this thing back on the ferry when we're done?"

"As you may recall, I got the full insurance package when I filled out the rental forms. Today is not Budget Rent A Car's lucky day."

"Should have told me that, otherwise I would have bought retreads rather than new tires."

Juan blew out a breath like a long-suffering spouse. "We never talk anymore."

He parked just above the tide line. They had discussed the possibility that the Argentines would anticipate them coming to Pine Island and lay a trap. While Max got some equipment together, Juan scanned the beach for any sign that someone had come ashore recently. The shale tiles looked undisturbed. There were no depressions like the ones his feet made with every step. He knew from talking with Mark and Eric that this was the only place where someone could gain access to the island, so he felt pretty confident that no one had set foot here in a long time.

They had brought battery-powered remote motion detectors that could send a wireless alert to Cabrillo's laptop. He hid several of them on the beach, facing inland so the motion of waves hitting shore wouldn't trigger them. It was the best they could do with only two people.

The tract leading to the pit was heavily overgrown, and it taxed the SUV's off-road capabilities to the limit. Small trees and shrubs vanished under the front bumper and scraped against the undercarriage. They saw evidence that people did continue to visit Pine Island despite the property being posted off-limits. There were several fire pits where local teens camped. Detritus of parties littered the clearings, and long-faded initials were carved in some trees.

"This must be the local version of lovers' lane," Max remarked.

"Just so long as you don't get any ideas," Juan grinned.

"Your virtue is safe."

The area immediately around the pit was little changed from when the Ronish brothers came here that first time in December of 1941, with one notable exception. A steel plate had been bolted over the opening into the rock. It was badly rusted, having been exposed to the elements for the past thirty-plus years since it was installed at James Ronish's insistence, but still remained solid. Mark had warned them about this, and they had come prepared.

The real difference lay just offshore, where concrete pylons had been driven across the mouth of a narrow inlet. When Dewayne Sullivan tried to drain the pit, they had blocked off the bay because it was the most likely source of the water that defeated his pumps every day. The inlet had since refilled, but the water looked stagnant, meaning the cofferdam kept it from mixing with the ocean.

Juan started unloading equipment while Max lugged an oxyacetylene cutting torch to the large piece of steel. The plate itself was too thick to slice efficiently, so he attacked the bolt heads. With the torch burning at over six thousand degrees, the bolts didn't stand a chance. He cut off all eight, and silenced the hissing torch. The smell of scalded metal was quickly whipped away by the steady offshore breeze.

The tow hook on the winch attached to the SUV's bumper slipped over the metal plate, and when Hanley took up the slack the chunk of steel slid smoothly across the rocks and revealed the yawning opening into the earth that had intrigued people for generations.

"I can't believe I'm about to dive the Treasure Pit," Juan said. "When I was a kid, I followed Dewayne Sullivan's expedition in the papers, dreaming of being on his team."

"Must be a West Coast thing," Max replied. "I'd never heard of this place until Murph and Stoney's briefing."

"Besides, you have no whimsy," Cabrillo

teased, copying Eric Stone's earlier observation.

The dive gear they had ordered from Seattle was top-of-the-line. Juan would have a full-face dive helmet with a fiber-optic voice-and-data link to Max on the surface. A tiny camera mounted on the side of the helmet would allow Hanley to see everything the Chairman did. Diving alone, especially underground, was never a good idea, but if something happened to Juan when he was in the pit, Max would know about it and be able to haul him back up.

"You ready," Max asked when Juan finished cinching a utility belt over his dry suit.

Cabrillo gave him the OK sign. Divers never give the thumbs-up unless they are about to surface. "Keep watch on the computer for those motion sensors. If one goes off, get me up to the surface as fast as you can."

Max had his pistol secreted in the small of his back and Juan's on the seat next to him. "I doubt they're coming, but we're ready."

Juan clipped the winch hook to his belt and slowly eased himself off the steel plate and into the Treasure Pit. There was no sense of how high he was over the bottom because the shaft was inky black. He had yet to put on his helmet. The air was layered with the thick stench of rotting kelp and the iodine tang of the sea.

His halogen light pushed only a few feet into the darkness before being swallowed up.

"Ready?" Max asked.

"Lower away," Juan replied, and slipped his helmet over his head and locked it to the collar ring. The air from the tanks on his back was fresh and cool.

The winch paid out cable at a steady sixty feet a minute. Juan observed the rock walls below the thick wooden supports placed here some time in the past by person or persons unknown. Where the Ronish brothers had used oakum to block water seeps, the 1978 expedition had used fast-drying hydraulic grout to fill any crack or crevice, and from the look of them it was still doing the job. The walls were bone dry.

"How are you doing?" Max's question came down the fiber-optics.

Darkness sucked at Cabrillo's dangling feet. "Oh, just hanging on. How far down am I?"

"About a hundred feet. See anything yet?"

"Murk. Lots and lots of murk."

At one hundred and forty feet, Juan saw the reflection of his dive light off the surface of the water below him. The water was perfectly still. As he got lower, he finally saw evidence that the pit was still connected to the sea. The rock was damp from high tide, and mussels clumped like black grapes clung to the stone, awaiting the tide's return. He could also tell that the ocean's access to the pit had to be limited. The tidal mark was only a few feet tall.

"Hold on a sec," Juan ordered.

"Looks like you've reached the water," Max said, watching the scene on the laptop.

"Okay, lower slowly." Juan didn't know what lay under the surface and didn't want to be impaled. "Hold again."

When his foot made contact with the water, he kicked around, feeling for any submerged obstruction. It was clear.

"Okay, down another foot."

They repeated this until the Chairman was completely submerged and he could see for himself that the pit was clear. He dumped a little air from his buoyancy compensator so that he sank to the full stretch of the cable.

"Visibility is about twenty feet," he reported. Even through the dry suit, he could feel the cold Pacific's embrace. Without the dive light, he was in a stygian world. There wasn't enough sun from the surface to penetrate this deep into the pit. "Give me some slack."

Cabrillo finned deeper into the pit. When he approached bottom at eighty feet, he realized that Dewayne Sullivan had pulled a fast one. He had used the excuse of the two accidents to call a halt to his exploration when in fact it looked like they had hit bottom only to discover the pit was empty. They had removed all the debris and found nothing. He swept his hand over the thin layer of silt covering the rock floor. The coating was only knuckle-deep. Below it, the rock was smooth against his fingertips, as though it had been ground flat. The only interesting feature was a man-sized niche just above the pit's terminus.

"I think this is a bust," he told Max. "There's nothing down here."

"I can see that." Hanley adjusted the control on the laptop to sharpen the picture because of the cloud of silt Juan had kicked up. A squirrel paused as it scampered by, gave him an angry tail twitch, and ran off.

A noise suddenly caught Max's attention. It wasn't the motion alarm but something far worse. A low-flying helicopter was approaching. It had been coming on at wave-top height, so the island masked the beat of its rotors until it was almost atop him.

"Juan! Chopper!"

"Pull me up," Cabrillo shouted.

"I will, but this'll be over by the time you get up here."

This was a move by the Argentines that they had discussed but had no real defense against. Hanley had only seconds to react.

The helicopter sounded like it was headed for the beach where he and Juan had come ashore. It was the only logical landing site. Max mashed the control button to winch Cabrillo back to the surface, grabbed Juan's pistol from the seat next to him, and jumped from the SUV. He started running as fast as he could, drawing his own pistol from its holster.

He calculated the odds that the Argentines had brought their own pilot to the United States to be pretty slim, meaning the guy at the controls had been hired to fly them out to Pine Island. If Max could get there quickly enough, there was a chance he could stop them from landing.

His legs were burning after only a few hundred yards, and it felt like his heart was going to explode out of his chest. His lungs convulsed as they fought to draw air. The extra pounds he carried around his middle weighed him down like an anchor. But he pushed through the pain, running with his head down and his arms pumping.

The rotor beat changed. He knew the pilot was flaring the helo to land. Max actually growled as he charged down the overgrown track. His sixty-plus years seemed to melt away. His feet suddenly felt like they were dancing over the ground, barely making contact with the earth.

Hanley exploded from the forest. Ahead of him was the beach, and just above it was a civilian JetRanger helicopter. The water was being whipped mercilessly by the rotor downwash as it slowly sank earthward. Max saw the outline of a couple of men in the rear seats.

The range was extreme for the Glocks, and when he skidded to a halt his body trembled, but he raised the pistols anyway. He aimed away from the JetRanger's cockpit and started pulling the triggers, firing right and left so the report from each weapon turned into one continuous roar. In just a few seconds he put up a thirty-round curtain of lead.

He had no idea how many rounds hit the chopper, but he knew some had. The rear door was thrown open, and one of the Argentines prepared to jump for the ground, ten feet below the skids. The pilot reacted by increasing power and starting to veer away.

Max dropped the pistol in his left hand and thumbed the magazine out of the other. The man in the door slid forward, trying to compensate for the tilting aircraft. In the fastest change out he'd performed since Vietnam, Hanley had a fresh magazine in the Glock and the slide closed before the Argentine could jump.

He fired as quickly as before, his ears ringing with the concussive blasts. The guy in the open door suddenly jerked and fell free. He made no attempt to right himself as he plummeted into the surf.

Hanley could imagine what was happening on the JetRanger. The Argentine Major would be screaming at the pilot to turn back to the island, most likely threatening him with a weapon, while the pilot would want to put as much distance between him and the madman shooting at him as possible.

Max slid home another magazine, waiting and watching to see who would win the test of wills. After a few seconds, it was clear the chopper wasn't coming back. It flew due west, presenting as small a target as possible. In moments it was just a white dot against the gray sky.

The only question in Hanley's mind now was whether the Argentines would let the pilot live. He didn't like the man's chances.

They'd already proven themselves ruthless, and he doubted they would leave an eyewitness alive.

His chest was still pumping when he finally started walking toward the beach. The Argentine who'd fallen from the JetRanger lay facedown about fifteen feet from shore. Max kept his pistol trained on the man and waded into the frigid waters, sucking air through his teeth when it reached his waist. He grabbed the man's hair and lifted his head free. The eyes were open and fixed. Max turned the body. His shot had hit the guy square in the heart, and, had he actually been aiming there, it would have been a remarkable shot. As it turned out, though, it was just dumb luck.

There was no ID in the man's pockets, only a little cash plus a sodden pack of cigarettes and a disposable lighter. Max unburdened the man of his money and towed the body toward the beach. When it was shallow enough, Hanley started stuffing rocks into the man's clothes. It took him a few minutes, but eventually the body began to sink. Max dragged him back into deeper water again and let go. With the body weighted and the tide ebbing, the corpse would never be seen again. He grabbed up the pistol he'd dropped and started back.

While he wanted to run, his body simply wasn't up to it. He had to settle for a loping trot that still made his knees scream in protest. It had taken him less than seven minutes to reach the coastline, but it took more than fifteen for the return journey.

Max expected to see Juan, but there was no sigh of the Chairman. To his dismay, the winch hadn't reeled up the cable. He looked at the control box and realized he had hit the down button by mistake. A glance at the front bumper revealed that the cable drum had completely paid out the line.

He lowered himself onto the SUV's rear seat and settled the headphones over his mouth. He frowned when he saw the feed from Juan's camera showed nothing but electronic snow.

"Juan, do you copy, over?" Max should have been able to hear the Chairman breathing inside his dive helmet, but all he heard was silence, a silence with a sense of finality behind it. "Hanley to Cabrillo, do you copy, over?"

He tried three more times, his concern deepening with each unanswered hail.

He decided not to reel in the cable but instead jumped out of the Ford and hauled up the seperate fiber-optic line hand over hand. After just a few seconds, he knew it was no longer attached to anything. Thin filament tangled at his feet as he frantically yanked it from the earth.

When the end appeared at last, he held it up to examine the break. It didn't look like it had been sheared cleanly. The plastic coating around the delicate cable was shredded, like it had been abraded between two rough surfaces. He'd seen the video himself. There was nothing in the Treasure Pit that could have caused such damage. This was when he engaged the winch and stood fretfully as the cable slowly rose from the depths. Like the fiber-optics, the braided steel appeared severed.

Max bellowed down into the dank shaft until his throat went hoarse, but all that returned was the echo of a very worried man.

FOURTEEN

Against a backdrop of towering icebergs that had been carved into fantastic shapes by wind and wave, and a sky stained red from horizon to horizon, the *Oregon* still managed to look like a garbage scow. Even this pristine Antarctic environment couldn't add to the derelict tramp freighter's tired façade. Even a beautiful frame can't help an ugly painting.

Linda Ross had done a remarkable job driving them southward. Fortunately, the weather had cooperated, and they had encountered little ice until they were alee of the Antarctic Peninsula. Once there, Gomez Adams scouted a lane through the bergs in their MD-520. The severe storm front that had gripped most of the continent had finally died down, but he reported it was still some of the hairiest flying of his life — and this from a man who used to make his living inserting Special Forces teams behind enemy lines.

Linda looked at herself in the antique mirror in her cabin and decided she would make the perfect wife for the Michelin Man. She knew there was a hundred-and-sixteen-pound woman under all the layers of arctic clothing, but the mirror sure wasn't showing it. And she still had one more overcoat to go once she got down to the boat garage.

She glanced at her desktop computer, which was linked to the ship's sensor system. The outside air temperature was minus thirty-seven, with a windchill that would make it feel twenty degrees colder. The ocean was a tick above freezing. Atmospheric pressure was holding steady, but she knew that could change without a moment's notice.

It was everything she had left northern Minnesota for.

Linda had grown up in a military family, and it was never in doubt that she would also serve. She did Navy ROTC at Auburn and spent five years in the service. She had loved her job, especially sea duty, but she knew her career would have limitations. The Navy rewarded merit better than any other branch of the military; however, she knew that with her elfin looks and almost helium-high voice she would never be tapped for command. And a ship of her own is what she wanted most of all.

Following an eighteen-month stretch working for the Joint Chiefs, she'd been offered a promotion and another staff job. What strings she was able to pull would get her nowhere near a ship, let alone a command. Linda saw the writing on the wall and packed it in. Within a month, she was first officer on an oil-service boat in the Gulf of Mexico, with the understanding that it would be hers within a year.

But then her life took one of those quirky changes that set a person on a course they never anticipated. An Admiral she had never met before called her and told her about a job opening with a real hush-hush outfit. Asked why her, the Admiral had replied that the Navy had made a mistake not giving her what she deserved and this might be a way of making things right.

What Linda would never know was that Langston Overholt at the CIA had put out feelers among the top brass in all branches of the service for people they felt would serve the Corporation well. It was how Cabrillo had recruited most of his crew.

She clicked off her computer, the thought of such cold filling her with apprehension, and stepped out from the cabin. Her insulated boots made her walk like Franken-stein's monster.

The boat garage was located amidships on the starboard side. Linda took her time. One of the first rules of arctic survival was: Never perspire. Even with everything unzipped, she could feel her body temperature rising. A few of the crew she passed made comments on her size in the bulbous white clothing, but it was in good humor.

The door outside the garage was insulated, but when she pressed her fingers to it to push it open she recoiled at the numbing cold that soaked through. She zipped up her many layers before turning the handle.

The Teflon-coated launch ramp was down and the outer door open, so she was hit with the full force of the Antarctic climate. It made her gasp aloud and brought tears to her eyes. Outside the ship, the water was black and roiled by the wind. Small bergs, called growlers, drifted past. The rest of her three-person team was already waiting. Franklin Lincoln, easily the largest member of the crew, looked positively enormous. All she could see of him was his black face smiling from a mound of white fabric. Mark Murphy looked lost in his gear, like a little boy trying on his dad's suit for some family pageant.

A crewman handed her an outer overcoat and a full-face mask with integrated communications. He checked her over for any loose seams, using white duct tape to strap down her mittens, and then helped her on with her rucksack and handed her a weapon. They would carry L85A2s, the Heckler and Koch rework of the British bullpup assault rifle. These had been further modified by the ship's armorer. With the magazine behind the trigger, it was easy to remove the trigger guards to allow them to be fired without the shooter removing their mittens. Powerful halogen lights had been fitted under the stubby barrels.

"I am your father, Leia," Linc said in a perfect imitation of James Earl Jones's Darth Vader. With his mask on, he looked a lot like the archvillain.

"I'd just as soon kiss a Wookiee," she said, throwing a line from *Star Wars* back at him. "Comm check. You with us, Mark?"

"Um, yeah, but what's a Wookiee and who's Leia?"

"Nice try, nerd boy," Linc replied. "I wouldn't be surprised if you changed your middle name to Skywalker."

"Please, if anything it would be Solo."

"Eric," Linda called out. "Are you on the net?"

Eric Stone was at his customary seat at the navigator's station in the op center. He'd been on duty during the roughest passages of their journey down here for the simple reason that he was the best ship handler they had when the Chairman wasn't aboard. "I read you, Linda."

"Okay, as soon as we're away I want you to pull back until you're over the horizon. If we need fast evac, Gomez can come get us in the chopper. But until I know what we're dealing with I don't want the *Oregon* exposed to anyone onshore."

A private smile passed Linda's lips. Oh yeah, this was *her* command.

"Roger that," Eric said. "We'll be just another chunk of ice floating out to sea."

"Okay, guys, let's saddle up." Linda vaulted into the Corporation's spare RHIB.

A hydraulic ram could launch the boat out of the *Oregon* like a dragster if necessary, but they opted for a smooth descent into the frigid water. Linda fired the big outboards as soon as they were submerged. They had already been brought up to temperature in the garage, so she eased the throttles, and the RHIB's bow began to lift. They were five miles from shore, but in the bay where the Wilson/George Station was located was a sea of drifting bergs. She had to cut right and left to find a path through the ice. Most of them were not much larger than the RHIB, but several were mountain-sized behemoths that towered into the darkling sky.

Linda was dutifully impressed by the stark beauty of the earth's most isolated continent.

Off to the side of the boat, a disturbance in the water revealed itself to be the canine snout of a seal. It eyed them for a moment, then disappeared under the waves.

It took them twenty minutes to reach the coast. Rather than run up onto the beach, Linda steered them to a low cliff overhanging the water. It would hide the RHIB from casual observation and made it so they didn't have to wade ashore. Linc was the first one up. He tied off the boat's line around a stone outcrop and used his immense strength to hoist the other two out of the boat.

The beach was as forlorn as any Linda had ever seen. It was covered with a light snow, a remnant of the storm. A sudden gust knocked her into the immovable form of Franklin Lincoln.

"We need to put some meat on those bones, girl."

"Or keep me out of Antarctica," Linda

rejoined. "The station is about a mile inland."

They had discussed the possibilities ad nauseam and would make their approach assuming the base had been taken by hostile forces. It took an hour to make their cautious approach. They found a low ridge overlooking the station and studied it through binoculars.

The futuristic structure with its domes and interconnecting tubes looked abandoned. The sound of a generator should have carried to them, but all they heard was the whistle of wind and the occasional slap of a door moving on its hinges. It was the personnel entrance to the adjacent garage building that flapped in the breeze. The station's windows were all dark.

A chill ran down Linda's back that had nothing to do with the weather. Through the green optics of her night vision binoculars, Wilson/George Station had an eerie feel unlike anything she had ever seen. Blowing wisps of snow took on the shapes of earthbound spirits doomed to haunt this desolate place.

"What do you think?" Linda asked to break herself out of the dark visions.

Mark turned to her. "A couple of days ago, I thought I was on the set of *Apocalypse*

Now. Now I feel like I'm staring at the base from *The Thing.*"

"Interesting observation, but not what I'm talking about."

"I'd say no one's home," Linc said.

"Looks like it to me." Linda stuffed her binoculars back in her bag. "Let's go, and stay low."

Her arctic clothing was doing its job of keeping out the cold, but there was nothing she could do about the knot tightening in her stomach. The sense of foreboding built with each slow pace toward the station. Something bad had happened here, she felt, something very bad.

There were no tracks around the base, meaning nothing had moved here since the storm, though it was possible someone had come right before or during it. Linc climbed the stairs at the entrance, his assault rifle at the ready. Mark moved into position next to him, and Linda carefully reached for the handle. It pulled outward, revealing a dim vestibule beyond. The main entry door into the facility was ajar, meaning whatever latent heat that might have been trapped by the station's thick coating of insulation had long since dissipated. There was no hope of any of the scientists surviving such prolonged exposure.

Linda indicated that Linc take point. The former SEAL nodded and peered through the station's door. He recoiled slightly, then turned.

He mouthed, This ain't good.

Linda moved up to his side and looked for herself. The room was in shambles. Clothing was strewn across the floor. Lockers had been emptied and overturned. A bench where workers once donned their boots had been flipped onto an object that truly held her attention. It was the body of a woman, turned blue from the cold. She was wearing a hoarfrost death mask, tiny icicles that clung to her skin and made her eyes opaque. What was worse was the blood, a pool of it frozen solid on the floor under her. Her chest was covered in it, and streaks and splashes decorated the walls.

"Gunshot?" Linda whispered after taking off her face shield.

"Knife," Linc grunted.

"Who?"

"Dunno." He swept his weapon's light around the space, checking each square foot, before stepping into the room. Linda and Mark entered at his side.

It took ten tension-fraught minutes to confirm that everyone at the station was dead. There were thirteen bodies in total.

All of them showed similar signs of a gruesome death. Most had been stabbed and lay in hardened lakes of blood. A couple showed blunt force trauma, as if someone had taken a baseball bat to them. One of them showed defensive breaks to the arms — he had clearly put up a fight. The bones were splintered. Another looked like he'd been shot with a large-bore gun, though Linda had been assured that there were no firearms at the base. In fact there were none on the entire continent.

"Someone's missing," Linda told them. "Wilson/George had a winter staff of fourteen."

"It's gotta be our killer," Mark said.

"I'll go check the vehicle shed," Linc said. "How many snowcats should there be?"

"Two, and two snowmobiles."

A few minutes later, Linda was searching through a desk drawer when Mark called out to her from another module. His voice made her jump. To say the research station and its grisly inhabitants gave her the creeps was putting it mildly. The hair on her arms had yet to stand down. She found him in one of the small crew's rooms, his light trained on more bloody smears on the wall. It took her a second to realize the lines weren't random. It was writing.

"What does that mean?"

Mark read it aloud, " 'Mime Goering for crow Nicole.' "

"Was someone saying they were killed by Hermann Göring?"

"I don't think so," Mark said absently.

"It doesn't make any sense. No one stationed here was named Nicole. I checked their roster."

Murph didn't reply. His lips moved silently as he read the bizarre sentence again and again.

"What are you thinking?" Linda asked, as the seconds dragged out to a minute.

"Whose room was this?"

"I'm not sure." They looked around and found a book with "Property of Andrew Gangle" written on the flyleaf.

"Who was he?"

"I think a tech. A grad student, if I recall."

"He's also our killer, and confessed before he carried out the murders. He was also very sick."

"No kidding. Hello? Thirteen slashed-up bodies. He was sick, all right."

"I mean *ill*. He had aphasia."

"What's that?"

"It's a speech disorder where the victim can't process language properly. It's usually caused by a stroke or brain injury, or it can progress as a result of a tumor, Parkinson's, or Alzheimer's."

"And you're able to figure this out how?"

"There was a game I used to play with some neuroscience grad students back at MIT. We'd make up sentences as if we had aphasia and challenge the others to decipher them."

"You didn't go on many dates, did you?"

Mark ignored her jab. "We usually had to give a clue, like a theme to the sentence, otherwise it would be impossible to work it out. The clue here was the killings, the murder, okay."

"Sure, but what does 'Mime Goering for crow Nicole' have to do with murder?"

"What do you call a group of crows?"

"I don't know, a flock?"

"A murder," Mark said with a triumphant gleam. For someone who was always the smartest person in the room, he still enjoyed showing off his intellect. "A group of crows is called a murder. In Gangle's brain, the two words — 'murder' and 'crow' — were synonymous."

"So then we're looking for some Nazi other than Göring?"

"No. Aphasia doesn't work like that. The connections in the brain are messed up. It could be words that sound alike or words

273

that describe objects that go together or words that reminded Gangle of something out of his past."

"Oh, so Mime Goering sort of sounds like 'I'm going.' "

"Exactly. 'I'm going to murder.' Gangle wrote the word 'I'm going "for" murder' instead of 'to.' I'm thinking in his brain, two is half of four. Switch numbers with prepositions and you get 'I'm going to murder' instead of 'I'm going for murder'."

"Okay, smart guy, what's up with Nicole?"

Mark threw her a cocky grin. "That was the easiest part of all. Nicole Kidman stared in a horror movie called *The Others.*"

" 'I'm going to kill the others,' " Linda said, stringing together the complete translation. "Wait, does aphasia make you go nuts?"

"Not usually. I think the underlying illness that caused his aphasia also caused him to turn against his crewmates."

"Like what?"

"You'd have to ask Doc Huxley. I only know about the condition because of the word game I used to play."

There was a sudden sharp bang that made both of them jump.

"Linda, Murph, we got company," Linc's baritone echoed throughout the entire base.

Both grabbed up their assault rifles from where they'd laid them on the bed and rushed out of Andy Gangle's disturbing bedroom. They met Linc in the rec hall.

"What did you find?"

"Some weird stuff, but not now. There's a snowcat heading our way from the south. That's where the Argentines have their closest research base, right?"

"Yeah," Linda replied. "Maybe thirty miles down the coast."

"I saw it when I was on my way back. We've got less than a minute."

"Everyone, outside."

"No, Linda. There isn't enough cover." Concern etched Linc's face. "They'd see us, no problem."

"Okay, find a place to hide, and be quiet. Let's just hope they're doing a little recce and not planning on setting up housekeeping. If you're discovered, come out with guns blazing."

"What if these are just scientists checking on the station?" Mark asked. It was a reasonable question.

"Then they would have shown up here a week ago like our government had asked. Now, go!"

The trio split up. Linda returned to Andy Gangle's room. The ceiling was acoustical tile made of a cardboardlike material hanging from metal support tracks. As limber as a monkey, she hoisted herself onto a dresser and lifted one of the tiles with the barrel of her gun. There was a three-foot crawl space between the ceiling and the dome's insulated roof. She set her gun onto the ceiling and boosted herself up. Her heavy clothing made it an almost impossible job, but by twisting her hips and kicking her legs she managed to lever her upper body through the opening.

She heard the front door crash open and someone calling out in Spanish. To her ears, it sounded like shouted commands rather than inquiring hails.

She slithered her legs up into the crawl space and carefully set the thin tile back to its original position. There was an insulated Flexi-tube nearby connected to a ceiling grate that was used to feed warm air into the room. Linda pulled the silvery tube off the grate and peered downward. She had a pretty good bird's-eye view.

The adrenaline that shot through her system when she heard Linc's shouted warning was wearing off fast, and she became aware of the cold again. She didn't have to contend with any wind, but the crawl space was the ambient thirty-plus degrees below zero. Her face was numb, and her fingertips were starting to lose sensation despite the heavy mittens. Keeping still was the worst thing possible for her body right now, but it was exactly what she had to do.

More bursts of guttural Spanish sounded below. She closed her eyes, imagining soldiers scouting the base as she and her team had just done. What would they make of the massacre? Would they even care?

A man wearing a white arctic uniform and carrying a large pistol suddenly entered the bedroom. He wore a mask much like the one Linda had sported, so she could not see his features. Like Mark, he stared at the bloody writing on the wall.

It happened so fast, there was nothing Linda could do to stop it. A drop of clear fluid dripped from her nose and pattered against the man's shoulder. He brushed at it without turning his head and made to leave and continue his search.

As soon as he stepped out of the room, Linda was in motion. Like a spider keeping to its web, she moved hand and foot along the tile ceiling's support rails. They weren't meant to take the weight of a fully grown person, and she was afraid the wires that kept them in place would snap.

There came a sudden eruption of gunfire.

The tile where she'd been a moment earlier exploded in a fine powder and fell down into the bedroom. Two more shots boomed out and two more tiles disintegrated. Seeps of weak sunlight filtered through the holes the bullets had torn through the outer roof.

Linda used the sound of the blasts, and the momentary deafness sure to accompany them, to slide over a larger trunk line for the base's ventilation system. This tube was more than big enough to hide her. The safety on her rifle was off.

She knew not to hold her breath but to let it come slow and even. With her heart racing, she needed oxygen. The roof above her snapped into sharp focus under the beam of a flashlight.

The Argentine had realized something liquid had dripped on his shoulder, but with the base so cold any fluid would be frozen solid. He had become suspicious.

Breathe, Linda, breathe. He can't see you, and he's too big to crawl up here.

Ten of the tensest seconds of her life went by. Ten seconds that she knew he could fire a shot into the ventilation hose for the fun of it and put a round through her head.

There came the sounds of another man entering the room — heavy footfalls and a shouted question. A terse conversation followed, and suddenly the light went away, and she could tell the men had left the room below.

She willed her body to relax and ever so gently sniffled.

That would have beat all, Linda thought. Killed because of a runny nose. This was one story she knew she'd keep to herself. She buried her face in her parka's fur-lined hood and prepared to wait out the Argentine search party for as long as it took.

FIFTEEN

Cabrillo waited for the winch to start hauling him up, but nothing happened. Then he realized that wasn't true, more of the line was coming down the shaft and forming an ever-enlargening loop just below where he hovered in the water. Max had hit the wrong button. Juan tried to hail him over the comm link but received no reply. Hanley had gone off alone to deal with the Argentine threat. And in his haste had trapped Juan in the Treasure Pit.

The prudent thing to do would be to surface according to the dive tables he'd memorized decades ago and wait for Max to return. But Juan wasn't one to let opportunity go to waste, so he inverted himself and swam back for the bottom. There was no sense leaving until he was positive he'd missed nothing.

He examined the niche first, going so far as to press himself into it to see if it activated any kind of device. The chiseled stone around him remained innocuous. He sank lower still. The silt he'd kicked up earlier had settled back to the bottom. He cleared away an area where the wall met the floor. And something caught his attention. He pulled his dive knife from the sheath strapped to his calf and ran it along the seam. The tip vanished into a tiny gap between the floor and wall. He tried again at another spot and found the same thing.

Three more attempts convinced him that the floor of the Treasure Pit was fitted like a plug. There was something deeper in the earth, something buried below this false bottom.

He thought for a moment. There had to be a way to get there. The Ronishes had figured it out. Cabrillo swam a slow circuit of the floor, his dive light shining on the joint. It was in a corner. A stone was wedged tightly between the floor and a small irregularity projecting from the wall.

Juan didn't touch it. Instead, he pulled his knees up to his chest and thrust them down onto the floor. The impact sent pain shooting up from his heels but also made the entire floor of the pit bobble ever so slightly. He glanced back up at the niche.

Clever, he thought. Very, very clever.

He returned to the rock wedge and got himself ready. He had no idea how much time he had, but he assumed he'd have to be quick. Reaching out a hand, he pulled the stone free, then finned for the grotto as fast as he could. Where a second ago all he could hear was the sound of his breathing, the pit was suddenly filled with the scrape of stone against stone.

The bottom of the chamber was an enormous float, kept in place by the wedge. Juan threw himself into the niche just as the silt-covered floor reached it. He pressed himself as far back as possible. The pit's designers hadn't had bulky scuba tanks, so the fit was tight. He watched in awe as the floor rose higher and higher. It climbed past his knees, then waist, and continued upward. It wasn't so buoyant that it raced for the surface, but rather it ascended at a stately pace.

He realized that his fiber-optic cable was trapped between the float and the wall, and said a silent prayer that it wouldn't get cut. No sooner had he thought it than the frayed end drifted down over him, the plastic abraded away. A second later, the loose end of his lifeline drifted past, too.

He had no idea how the float would stop but he figured it must, otherwise the Ronish brothers would have perished down here seventy years ago.

One mystery was solved when he got his first look at the side of the giant float. The top layer was just a thin veneer of slate while the rest of it was metal. When he tapped it, it rang hollow. The metal had withstood centuries of immersion in salt water because the designer had covered it in a layer of fine gold flake. Gold never corrodes, and could protect the metal float for centuries.

There were marks in the gold, thin lines cut through it as if someone had scraped some away with a knife. He imagined it had been one of the Ronish boys thinking the whole drum was made of gold only to see it was just a patina not even a millimeter thick. Where the knife had left scars, Juan could see that the float was made of bronze. While this metal resisted corrosion better than steel, he figured in another couple of decades the sea would find a way to eat through the scar. The hollow float would fill with water, and the trap would never work again.

Cabrillo estimated the drum was ten feet tall, and when the bottom of it finally passed over his head it stopped in line with the top of the niche. It had to have hit another small projection from the shaft wall that he had overlooked on his way down. He marveled at the engineering it took to make this work.

He swam out of the niche and looked up. There was a handle on the underside of the float. He grabbed it and tugged. The buoyancy had been so perfectly calculated that he was able to pull the enormous contraption downward a bit. He knew he could get out by tying his lead weight belt to the handle and letting the float settle back to the bottom while he waited in the niche. He assumed that's what the Ronishes had done, only their weight had dropped away. He descended past where the bottom of the shaft had been and sank lower still.

In the exact center of the real floor of the Treasure Pit he found a pile of rocks from the beach. The Ronish brothers' counterweight. The bag that had once held them had long since been dissolved by the Pacific's salt water. The other discovery Juan made was far more intriguing. There was a low tunnel off the main vertical shaft.

Cabrillo entered it, his tanks tapping on the ceiling because the fit was so tight. The tunnel angled up sharply, forcing him to pause several times in order to let the excess nitrogen dissolve out of his system. He checked his air supply. If he didn't dawdle, he'd be okay.

His light suddenly flashed on a reflection above him. He was approaching the surface, though he was still many hundreds of feet belowground. He also estimated that a person could swim from the niche to this point on a single held breath if the tide was low enough.

Juan rose slowly, his arms extended over his head to probe for any unseen obstructions above him. His head emerged in a bedroom-sized grotto with a ceiling about seven feet high. He realized that all of this had to be a natural rock formation, otherwise it would have taken years to excavate.

His light zigged and zagged across the dank stone until settling on an object hanging from the wall.

"What the hell is that?" Cabrillo asked aloud, his voice muffled by awe and the surrounding rock.

Just above the waterline was a plaque made of some metal. Bronze, he supposed. On it were lines of characters that looked to him like Chinese and the outline of a coast showing a deep bay. He had surmised since the Argentines had shown up at James Ronish's house that the Treasure Pit had nothing to do with an eighteenth-century privateer, but he hadn't expected this. What was Chinese writing doing in this place?

More important, why did anyone else care?

Cabrillo had always known to trust his instincts. They had served him well with the CIA and even better when he formed the Corporation. For reasons unknown, someone had gone to great lengths to hide the plaque and yet made it possible to be found. Their logic eluded him, and he could only hope that the writing would explain their motivations. Juan knew he was onto something, and, while he didn't know what, he felt certain it went far beyond lost blimps and downed satellites.

With the fiber-optic severed, he couldn't use video to record an image of the bronze plaque, so he pulled a small digital camera from a bag tied around his waist and removed it from its waterproof case. He snapped dozens of pictures, the flash searing his eyes after so much time in the pit.

He ducked back under the surface and followed his light as he retraced his way back to the main shaft. He had to force himself not to think about the enigma and concentrate on the dive instead.

Once he reached the big floating plug, Juan unclasped his weight belt and buckled it around the handle the — Chinese? — had left just for that purpose. The mystery of the Treasure Pit went back more than a hundred years, he thought. When had the Chinese been to Washington State long enough to reshape the cave system to suit their needs?

Concentrate, Juan.

With the belt in place, the well-balanced hollow drum began to sink ever so slowly. He pushed himself into the niche and waited for the contraption to sink past him. He helped it along by pressing downward against its flank with his hands. In a few moments, he was clear to make his ascent to the surface. It was awkward without the weight belt, and he had to fight his positive buoyancy, especially at the decompression stops. By the time his head thrust clear of the water, he was sucking on empty tanks.

He stripped off his helmet and gulped the salty air greedily. The sun's angle had changed, and the tiny amount of light filtering down from the surface was a welcome sight. He swept the beam of his torch around, vainly trying to find the tow cable. The implications were too horrible to consider if something had happened to Max. A two-hundred-foot climb without the proper equipment would tax even his abilities. Worse, though, would be losing his best friend.

Juan yelled up the shaft. It didn't feel like he had the lung capacity to throw his voice that far upward. He struggled out of his gear and let the tanks sink into the pit. The dry suit flipped him so he was floating on his back. He shouted again and again. The thought occurred to him that if Hanley had failed, he was calling the Argentines right to him. Not that they wouldn't have figured it out anyway. The fact that he hadn't been sprayed with rifle fire from above boded well that Max had taken care of them.

"Hello," a distant voice shouted back.

"Max?"

"No. I am the Argentine Major."

It *was* Max. "Get me out of here!" Juan demanded.

"One second."

It took a few minutes to lower the cable and a further couple to haul the Chairman out of the Treasure Pit, but it was one of the best rides of his life. When he reached the surface, Max was there to give him a hand as he clambered out of the shaft. He quickly killed the winch so it wouldn't drag Cabrillo across the rocks.

"Well, this sure has been an interesting afternoon," Hanley said with nonchalance.

"What happened?"

"They tried to land near the beach, but

288

their pilot got cold feet when I fired off a few clips at him. I got one of them, too. Care to tell me where the hell you've been?"

"You wouldn't believe it if I did."

"Try me.

Cabrillo explained what he had found while they were packing up their gear and driving back to the beach. The last big item in the Ford's cargo area was an inflatable raft and an outboard. While Hanley got it ready for the crossing back to the mainland, Juan used his dive knife to spear the SUV's gas tank. The vehicle had been rented using an untraceable false ID, but there was forensic evidence on the truck so it would have to burn.

They waited on the beach to make sure nothing remained of the Explorer but a charred husk. It took less time to motor to shore and reach the native village of La Push than it did to find a ride back to a good-sized town. They ended up bumming a ride in the cab of a semi transporting a load of timber, which made Juan remember his recent adventure in the Argentine jungle with a nearly identical rig.

The roar of a big diesel engine outside signaled that the Argentines had fired up their snowcat and were leaving Wilson/

George Station. Fifteen minutes had passed since Linda had taken refuge in the ceiling crawl space. Now that she felt confident they had gone, she broke out a chemical heat pad and applied it to her face. She'd managed to keep her toes and fingers from going numb by curling them repetitively in her boots and gloves. However, the apples of her cheeks and her nose were moments away from frostbite. The pain when sensation started rushing back was excruciating but welcome because it meant there had been no permanent damage.

And since she'd heard no more gunfire, she knew the rest of her team had remained safely hidden.

Linda climbed stiffly from her perch and remained silent until she made her way to the station's main door to verify the snow-cat was gone. Linc and Mark appeared by the time she returned to the rec room.

"I heard shooting," Linc said, concern corrugating his broad forehead. "Are you okay?"

She nodded. "It was a close call, but yeah. Where'd you guys hide?"

"I just laid down next to one of the bodies," Mark said. "The guy checking the room didn't give me a second look."

"I was in the back of a closet under a pile

of clothes. I think they were pretty spooked by what they saw. Their search was cursory."

"I know how they feel," Linda agreed, trying not to think about the grisly tableau around her. "Linc, you said you found something in the vehicle shed?"

"Yeah, but you'll need to see it for yourself."

With their masks back in place, the three of them trooped along the staked trail to the arch-roofed building. The door still flapped in the wind, a metronomic rattle that was the base's only sign of life. The power was out, and the garage was so heavily shadowed that the back wall was lost in the gloom. Their flashlights cast brilliant beams that cut the murk like lasers. The two snowcats looked like a hybrid cross between tanks and passenger vans. The tops of the studded Caterpillar tracks came up to Linda's thigh. Bright orange paint covered the bodywork so they could be easily spotted out in the snowfields behind the station.

"Over here." Linc led them to a workbench along the side of the garage.

Amid the usual clutter — tools, oil cans, and frozen rags — was a trunk measuring three feet in length. Linc opened the lid.

It took Linda a moment to understand what she was seeing. There was another body in the trunk, but, unlike the others, it had clearly been dead and exposed to the elements for some time. It was more mummy than corpse, and much of the face had been eaten away by scavengers before the body became too frozen to eat. Its clothing was unfamiliar. It wasn't dressed in contemporary arctic gear but rather a padded jacket of brown wool and pants too thin for the environment. The hat perched atop frozen black hair looked odd. It had two peaks and a short brim.

"I'd say this guy's been down here for a hundred years or more," Mark said as he examined the body.

Linda said, "Maybe a whaler who got lost over the side of his ship?"

"Could be." Mark looked at Linc. "Did you go through his pockets?"

"Not me, man. I took one look and closed the lid. But our missing man sure did."

Linda had forgotten they hadn't accounted for all fourteen members of Wilson/George. "You found Andy Gangle?"

"Is that the dude's name? He's at the back of the garage. And he is messed up."

Andy had taken his own life in the end, driven to suicide by the same madness that made him kill his companions. He had sat down, with his back against a rack of spare tools, and pulled so hard on his lower jaw that he'd nearly broken it loose. He'd died, either from exposure or blood loss, with his fist stuffed into his mouth as if he were trying to get at whatever affected his brain.

Something glinted brightly in his other hand. Mark pried it from the stiff fingers. It was a piece of gold, misshapen now, but at one point it had to have been ornamental. There was a hammer on the floor next to Gangle's body. When Mark shone his light on it, he could see where bits of gold had transferred to the head.

"He smashed it with this hammer?"

"Why?"

"Why'd he do any of this? He was sick."

"What was it?"

"Hard to tell. A figurine of some sort."

"Is it pure gold?"

"I'd say at least two pounds. Say, thirty thousand dollars." Mark peered into a knapsack that also was within Gangle's reach. It made a sound like broken glass scraping together when he lifted it. He peered inside, then dumped the contents on the floor.

It was impossible to know what had been in the bag originally because all that fell out was opaque greenish sand and small bits of similar-colored rock. Like with the golden statuette, Andy Gangle had hammered at something until all that remained was dust and fragments no bigger than a thumbnail.

There was also an odd tube made of what looked like cast bronze in the bag. One end was closed off and the other was shaped like a dragon's open mouth. The body of the tube was scalloped to resemble a dragon's scaly skin. Mark examined it more closely.

"This is a pistol."

"What?"

"Look, here at the closed end there's a small hole for a wick or taper. It's a single-shot muzzle-loading pistol."

"Looks Chinese, with the dragon and all."

"And ancient," Linda added. "I assume all this stuff, whatever it was, goes with our mystery friend in the box?"

"That's my read," Linc replied.

"Weird," Mark opined.

Linc asked, "What now?"

"Report our findings back to the *Oregon* so we can let the CIA know what happened. My guess is, Overholt will want us to pay a visit to the Argentine base to see what's happening there. In the briefing material I read, it said no one has laid an eye on their facility in two years. I say we anticipate him and head out on our own."

"I'm not walking thirty miles across

Antarctica," Mark griped.

Linda tapped the front of the nearest snowcat. "Neither am I."

After making a radio call to their ship and fulfilling Dr. Huxley's request for tissue and blood samples from Andy Gangle and the mummy in the trunk, it took almost an hour to get one of the big vehicles fired up. Without electricity for the plug-in engine warmer, the oil had turned as viscous as tar. It had to be drained and warmed over a camp stove twice since the first time it cooled too quickly to crank the motor. Despite his nerd chic, Mark Murphy was a nimble mechanic.

Heat from the snowcat's ventilators was a welcome breath, and only a few miles from Wilson/George it was warm enough for them to unzip their outer parkas and remove the heavy mittens over their Gore-Tex gloves. Linc drove, and Linda relinquished the shotgun seat to Murph.

She decided they should circle out into the snowy expanse behind the base and approach the Argentine camp from the east. Compasses were useless this close to the South Pole, but the snowcat was equipped with satellite navigation. This, too, was a little spotty because the constellation of satellites used for triangulation was often hidden by the horizon. The system was not developed with polar navigation in mind. There were base relay stations to aid GPS, but most of them were on the other side of the continent where most of the research bases were located.

The landscape was an unbroken vista of white. Even the distant mountains were still covered in winter ice. Some would melt as the spring thaw deepened to reveal gray granite slopes, but for now they towered under a mantle of frozen snow.

Unlike other areas of Antarctica, where the ice was miles thick, there was little chance of driving into hidden crevasses here, so Linc drove fast, the crawler treads having little difficulty hauling them across the wind-scarred surface.

"It's believed," Mark said to cut the boredom, "that the mountains to our left are a continuation of the Andes in South America." He stayed quiet when no one engaged him.

Three hours of monotonous driving found them two miles behind the Argentine re-search station. Given the militaristic nature of the current regime in Buenos Aires, they expected there would be perimeter security of some kind, most likely patrols on snow machines. Linda judged two miles was close enough. From here, they would proceed on foot.

Linda and Linc tightened up their arctic clothing. Mark was to remain with the snowcat so he could start the engine occasionally to keep it warm and also to be able to move it if trouble approached. They grabbed up their weapons and leapt to the ice. It was dark but the clouds had moved on, allowing the moon's glow to glitter off the snow.

The night had an eerie stillness. It seemed the only sound in the world was their breathing and the crunch of their boots. It was as though they were walking on another, inhospitable planet. And in a sense they were, because without their protective suits they wouldn't last five minutes.

Linda had pocketed a bunch of nuts and washers from a storage bin in the snowcat. She dropped one every fifty or so feet. The metal looked black against the ice and was easily seen. She carried a handheld GPS, but the little trail of metal bread crumbs was her low-tech backup.

They'd gone a mile when Linc suddenly dropped flat. Linda threw herself to the ground and started scanning the horizon.

"I don't see anything," she whispered.

Linc wiggled forward on his elbows. She

matched him move for move and then she spotted what he'd seen. There were tracks in the ice from a snowmobile. They'd been right to be cautious. The Argentines did patrol around their base.

"Makes you wonder what they're protecting," Linc said.

"Let's find out."

They got to their feet again and continued onward. As a former SEAL, Franklin Lincoln was always on guard, but he moved with even more vigilance than usual. His head turned side to side as he studied the barren terrain around them, and every couple of minutes he would pull down his parka's hood to listen for the telltale buzz of an approaching snowmobile.

The back of the Argentine base was protected by low jagged hills. Here the snow and ice had been blown away in spots to reveal rocky crags as black as midnight. It wasn't a particularly difficult climb, but they moved with slow deliberation. Their thick boots weren't suited to the task, and they were on constant lookout for patrols.

They reached the top and got their low-light binoculars ready before peering over the crest.

Linda didn't know what to expect. She assumed the Argentines would have something similar to Wilson/George, but what lay below them between the hills and the sea was astonishing. It wasn't an isolated little research station as had been claimed, but rather a sprawling town so cleverly camouflaged it was impossible to tell its size. There were dozens of buildings built on what at first looked like an ice shelf but was in fact an artificial construct made to look like ice. Because nature abhors a straight line, all the buildings were constructed with curved shapes to hide their outlines from satellite observation.

Huge white tents hid even more of the base. She imagined these were made of Kevlar to withstand the elements. They had also constructed a large dock with several piers, again made to look like ice.

The natural bay the facility abutted was ice-free, except for a dozen tall iceburgs. She zoomed in on one. Something wasn't right about it. It looked real enough, but it was too tall for its base. It should have toppled over during the latest storm. They all should have. That's when she realized they were artificial, too.

Oil platforms. That's what they were — small offshore oil-drilling rigs.

Now that she understood the nature of what the Argentines had built here, she recognized that three odd hills near the pier were actually giant storage tanks that had been buried under earthworks redoubts. These weren't just exploratory wells out there. They were about to go into full-scale production. The dock may not be large enough for the latest-generation supertankers, but it could certainly handle a hundred-thousand-tonner.

She knew what she was seeing flew in the face of one of the most important treaties in existence. Since the early 1960s, the Antarctic Treaty had maintained that the continent was a scientific preserve and that no nation could claim sovereignty over any part of it. The accord also stated that it was illegal for signatories to mine for raw materials or drill for oil, on land or offshore.

Linc tapped her on the shoulder and pointed farther south. She saw what he was pointing at, a separate building away from the others, but she wasn't sure what piqued his interest. She shot him an inquiring glance.

"I think that's a missile battery."

If he was right, that was another violation, she believed. She clicked off more than a dozen pictures with her camera, shooting through the night vision binoculars. They weren't the best pictures, but they were at least proof.

Linc slithered back over the crest of the hill. "What do you think?" he asked when they were clear.

"I'd say the Argies have been busy. Did you notice the icebergs in the bay?"

"Yeah. Oil derricks."

Linda nodded. "We've got to report this."

A wind was starting to pick up. It wasn't enough to cause a whiteout, but visibility was down dramatically, and after so much time exposed Linda felt the cold starting to seep through her clothes. Remarkably, she could still see her trail of nuts and washers.

Linc continued to scan all around them, so he was the one to spot the snowmobile. He pushed Linda to the ground hard enough to cause the air to explode from her lungs. They didn't know if they'd been spotted, and a tense few seconds passed as the machine's single headlamp bounced through the darkness.

Time stretched, and it looked like the driver hadn't seen them moving, or, if he had, he though it was a trick of the wind. The sled's motor was a piercing whine, but he continued to angle away from them. At the last second, the sentry jerked the handlebars hard over and drove straight for the prone pair.

Linc cursed, and brought his assault rifle to his shoulder.

He couldn't see what the driver was doing because of the glare of its headlamp, but the crack of a shot carried over the engine's beat. The shot went wild because the snowmobile was racing over rough terrain. The snowmobile was almost on them. Linc fumbled in his oversized mittens to flick off the safety, and when he realized he wouldn't have time he lurched to his feet and swung the rifle like a baseball bat.

The gun hit the driver in the neck, and the kinetic energy of his forward motion coming against Linc's tremendous strength ripped him off the back of the machine and sent him sprawling across the ice.

Without its driver, the snowmobile's engine automatically cut out when the safety key, which was tethered to the man's wrist, was ripped from the dash. It rolled onward for a few feet and came to a stop, its headlight reflecting flakes of snow drifting on the wind.

Linda ran to the downed Argentine. He lay completely still. She peeled off his helmet. The way his head flopped when she did it told her his neck had been broken by the brutal impact. She stood.

"Dead?"

"Yes."

"Him, her, us," Linc said with a career soldier's fatalism.

He lifted the body and brought it closer to the snowmobile. He set the corpse gently on the ice and took hold of the handlebars. Bracing his legs, he flexed his muscles and threw the five-hundred-pound machine on its side as if it were no more than a toy. He adjusted the body to fit what would look like a tragic accident.

"Wish we could take it and ride it back to the snowcat," Linda said, although she knew they couldn't.

"Walk will do you good," Franklin Lincoln grinned.

"First, I need meat on my bones, and now you say I need exercise. Which one is it?"

Linc knew that answering that was a trap, even if she was teasing, so he wisely said nothing and continued the long slog to Murph and their warm ride back to Wilson/George.

SIXTEEN

In Bremerton, Washington, the only requirement Juan and Max had for their hotel was that it have an Internet connection because Cabrillo wanted to transmit the pictures he'd taken in the pit to Eddie Seng aboard the *Oregon* and get a translation as quickly as possible.

By the time they'd finished stuffing themselves on Wallapa Bay oysters and Dungeness crab at a nearby restaurant, Eddie had a preliminary report for them.

Seng was another former CIA agent and had been with the Corporation almost since its inception. Ironically, though they had served at the same time, he and Cabrillo had never met in the halls of Langley. Born in New York's Chinatown, Eddie was fluent in both Cantonese and Mandarin.

He regarded the world through heavy-lidded dark eyes, and in them Juan could see Eddie had discovered something interesting. Behind the Corporation's chief of shore operations, Juan could see the back of the op center, so he figured his image was on the main display above the helm and weapons stations.

"You were right, it is Mandarin, but an older form. It reminded me of having to read Shakespeare back in high school."

"So what is it?"

"Are you familiar with Admiral Zheng He?"

"Some kind of Chinese explorer in the 1400s. He sailed as far west as Africa and as far south as Australia."

"New Zealand, actually. He went on seven voyages between 1405 and 1433 in what would be the largest ships built until the eighteenth century. He had over two hundred of them in what they called the Treasure Fleet, and twenty-eight thousand men."

"Are you saying that the Chinese discovered America seventy years before Columbus?"

"No. Zheng didn't place that writing in the pit. But the Admiral who *did* had been inspired by Zheng and embarked on a remarkable voyage of his own. There were three ships, and they left China in 1495 headed east. In command was Tsai Song. Admiral Tsai had been commissioned by the Emperor to trade as far and wide as he could. And because Zheng had found a continent to the west, Africa, he was convinced the earth had symmetry and there would be another to the east."

"So they reached North America, but it was already a couple of years after Columbus did," Max said, relieved that they wouldn't have to rewrite the history books.

"Actually, from what I can tell, they landed in South America first. But there was a problem. As Tsai writes, one of the ships was cursed while they were in a 'hellishly cold cove.' I assume Tierra del Fuego."

"What happened?"

"The crew was overcome by evil. That's what Tsai writes. An evil so powerful that he felt it necessary to order the vessel destroyed and the stricken crew left to die. They sank it with an explosive charge placed against the hull."

Hanley asked, "How big were these ships?"

"Over three hundred feet, with a crew of four hundred."

Max gave a low whistle, impressed with medieval Chinese naval architecture.

"Does he say the nature of this evil?"

"No. The whole purpose of the pit, though, was to give a clue as to the ship's location. He wrote that the evil surrounding it should never be approached, but he was also a pragmatist. There were untold riches aboard her, treasure they had planned to barter with any natives they came across.

"Tsai left two markers, one honoring the gods of the underworld — the one in the pit — and another to honor the gods in heaven."

"Something underground and something above," Juan mused aloud. "What is the second marker?"

"Tsai only writes that it can be seen from the heavens. And that they left it two hundred days from the Treasure Pit."

"Two hundred days?" Max groused. "What the hell is that?"

"I assume," Eddie said evenly, ignoring Max's sarcasm, "that it means two hundred days' sailing south of Pine Island. Obviously, the Ronish brothers thought it was around the twenty-fifth parallel."

"Hold on a second," Juan said. "If they were looking for a marker left by a Chinese Admiral, what were they doing so far inland? Whatever the marker was, surely it would be near the coast."

"I don't know."

"We need to work on those papers you found at the crash site," Max suggested.

"The answer could be in their log."

"We need to learn more about this Admiral Tsai." This came from Eric Stone, who had been sitting at the helm station but had walked around the op center so that he stood behind Eddie. "And what was aboard his ship. This could be a significant archaeological find."

"Actually," Max said, "we need to ask ourselves if this is worth pursuing further. What's this to us, anyway?"

"I think the answer is pretty clear," Stone replied. "This is something of interest to the Argentine government, a regime currently at odds with the United States. Whatever their agenda, it can't be good."

"I agree," the Chairman said. "The *Generalissimos* have an interest in this thing, and until we know their angle we should keep at it. What about the drawing of that cove or inlet?"

"That is the outline of the area where their ship was sunk, and, before you ask, I've already got Eric here running a computer match of South America's coastline, including all couple hundred islands that make up Tierra del Fuego. It's going to take some time."

"Okay. What's the latest on Linda and her team?"

"They're still in the snowcat. You're not going to believe what they found. What was supposed to be a small Argentine research station turns out to be a full-blown oil field."

"A what?"

"You heard me. They're drilling for oil off the Antarctic Peninsula."

The news rocked Cabrillo, and he blurted stupidly, "But that's illegal."

"Well, yeah. Apparently they don't care."

"Have you reported this to Overholt?"

"Not yet. Linda said she snapped some pictures. She wants to include them with her report."

"This is getting weirder and weirder," Max said. "They're taking a hell of a risk pulling a stunt like that."

"Not really," Eric Stone countered. "They're already an international pariah, so what's a little more bad will?"

"Bad will, my butt. The U.S. is going to send an armada down there. It'll be like the Falklands War all over again."

"Are you sure?" Stone asked, one eyebrow arched.

Hanley opened his mouth to reply but thought better of it because he wasn't sure. With the U.S. military spread thin around the world and the current occupant of the White House more focused on domestic issues, it was possible that the government's response would be weak protests and another round of UN sanctions.

"Now we have to ask ourselves if a six-hundred-year-old Chinese ship has anything to do with current global events," Eric said.

"If things hold true to form," Juan replied, "we can count on it."

Eddie asked, "What do you want us to do once Linda returns? Should we stay down here or start heading north?"

Cabrillo considered the options and came to a quick decision. "Get the ship out of there. We have no idea what the Argentines are planning in Antarctica, but if the balloon goes up and war breaks out I want the *Oregon* clear. Also, we need to get into position for the Kuwaiti Emir's visit to South Africa. He's hired us as additional security, and that's one lucrative contract."

"You got it," Eddie said. "They should be back in a couple of hours and then we'll head northward again."

"Call me when they're back. I want to hear Linda's full report."

Juan killed the connection and brought up his electronic Rolodex. There were more than a thousand names listed, from the direct lines of heads of state to some of the most shadowy characters in the world. He thought it ironic that when listed alphabetically, Langston Overholt's entry was next to a French pimp who also trafficked in information.

It was three hours earlier on the East Coast, so he wasn't worried about the time difference. A deep baritone answered on the second ring. "Hello?"

"Mr. Perlmutter, this is Juan Cabrillo."

"The infamous Chairman. How are you?"

Though the two had never met and had spoken on the phone only once, each was well aware of the other's reputation. St. Julian Perlmutter was a living encyclopedia of all things maritime and owned the largest private collection of books, manuscripts, and folios about the history of ships and shipping. His Georgetown home was quite literally packed to the rafters with his well-thumbed trove.

It had been one of Perlmutter's research projects a few months back that eventually sent the crew of the *Oregon* to Libya and led to the rescue of the Secretary of State, Fiona Katamora.

"Fine, sir. Yourself?"

"A bit peckish, as the Brits might say. Dinner's still in the oven, and the aroma is mouthwatering." Perlmutter's second-greatest love was food, and to meet him one could see he dined with gusto. "Tell me you're here in the States, and I can finally get a tour of your ship."

"Max Hanley and I are here, as a matter of fact, but the *Oregon*'s at sea." There was no reason not to tell Perlmutter where the ship was other than that Juan didn't know if the other man's phones were clean. "I was wondering if I could pick your brain."

"Good God, man, you're starting to sound like Dirk. All he ever calls for is information. At least his kids have the decency to bring me a little something when they come to pump their old uncle St. Julian for his knowledge."

"Max and I are in Washington State, we'll send you some of their famous apples."

"Make it Dungeness crab instead, and you have a deal. What do you need to know?"

"The Chinese Treasure Fleet."

"Ah, Admiral Zheng. What about it?"

"Actually, I'm talking about Admiral Tsai Song."

"I'm afraid that's a myth," Perlmutter started, and then stopped speaking for a moment. "Did you find evidence that he really existed? He's real?"

"Are you familiar with the Pine Island Treasure Pit?"

"Yes, of course," Perlmutter's voice suddenly shot up a couple of octaves. "My God. That was Tsai?"

"There's a secret chamber off the main shaft. He left a plaque there, giving a hint to where they abandoned one of their other ships."

"So it wasn't pirate loot at all. I never believed it was, but this is fantastic. Tsai Song's voyage was thought to be nothing more than a story, most likely invented in the eighteenth century as a way of claiming national pride when China was in the throes of unrest due to British meddling."

"Kind of 'Look at us, we once had an empire bigger than yours.' "

"Exactly. Listen, Captain Cabrillo —"

"Juan, please."

"Juan, I'm not really the person you need to be speaking with. All I know is that there was a claim that Tsai sailed to America and back sometime around the end of the 1400s. I am going to put you in touch with Tamara Wright. She's a Chinese history scholar who wrote an excellent book about Admiral Zheng's voyage to India and Africa and has pieced together a history of the Admiral Tsai legend. Can I call you in ten minutes?"

"Sure." Juan gave him his cell number and

glanced at Max. "You just witnessed history, my friend. Dirk Pitt told me that in all the years he's known Perlmutter, he's never been able to stump the man."

Not knowing St. Julian, Hanley was underwhelmed. "I'll mention it next time I'm at NUMA."

Juan's phone trilled a few minutes later. "Bad news, I'm afraid. Tamara's on vacation and won't be back to her office at Dartmouth until next Monday."

"For reasons I can't discuss," Juan said, "time might be of the essence. We only need a couple of minutes of her time."

"That's just it. She's unavailable. The grad student who answered at her office said Tamara left her cell phone behind."

"Do you know where she's vacationing? Maybe there's a way we can track her down."

"Is it really that important?" Perlmutter asked, and then spoke again before Juan could reply, "Of course it is or you wouldn't have asked. She's on a Mississippi River jazz cruise aboard the *Natchez Belle.* I have no idea where they are right now, but you can probably get that information from the cruise line."

"I'm already logging on to their website," Cabrillo said. "Thank you, Mr. Perlmutter."

"You can forget my crab and send me a translation of that plaque, and we'll call it even."

"Done and done."

"So?" Max asked.

Juan spun the laptop so Hanley could see. The image on the screen was a beautiful white paddle wheeler with smoke coming from her two skinny stacks and people waving from her three wedding-cake-like decks. In the background was the famous St. Louis Arch, one of her usual ports of call.

"Up for a little riverboat gambling?"

"I left my derringer at the safe house." Max shot his cuffs. "But I should be able to find a few spare aces. Where is she now?"

"We can catch her in Vicksburg and get back off again in Natchez, Mississippi," Juan said, taking back the computer to book them on the overnight trip and make the flight arrangements to get them there. "After that, we'll hook up with the *Oregon* again in Rio and either head to the assignment in South Africa or see where the Fates blow us."

"You're having fun, aren't you?" Max was pleased.

"Apart from getting shot at and left at the bottom of a two-hundred-foot pit for a while, yeah, I am."

Hanley chuckled. "You liked those parts, too."

Juan just grinned.

SEVENTEEN

The closest large airport to Vicksburg was in Jackson, Mississippi, fifty miles to the east. The wall of humidity Cabrillo walked into when he stepped out of the terminal made him think he was back in the Amazon. The air shimmered with heat, and he couldn't seem to fill his lungs. Beads of sweat popped up on the dome of Max's balding head, and he had to mop his brow with a bandanna.

"My God," he said. "What is this place, like, ten miles from the sun?"

"Eighteen," Juan replied. "I read that in the airline magazine."

What made it worse is that both men had donned jackets after retrieving their pistols from the checked baggage.

Rather than bother with the formalities of renting another car, they opted to take a cab instead. Once they found a driver and agreed on a price, the bags went into the trunk and the men settled in the arctic comfort of the taxi's air-conditioning.

With traffic, it took a little over an hour to reach their destination, but they arrived in plenty of time. The *Natchez Belle* wouldn't leave for its namesake city for another forty minutes.

She was moored behind a structure made up to look like a side-wheel steamer that housed one of the casinos in the shadow of the Vicksburg Bridges, a pair of skeletal steel spans that stretched across the muddy Mississippi. Her boarding gantry was lowered right onto the parking lot. A white tent had been set up nearby, and the brassy beat of jazz music carried to where the men stood, as the cabbie headed back home again. Dozens of people milled around with plates of hors d'oeuvres and drinks in their hands. A few of the boat's staff were in attendance, dressed in period costumes.

"What do you know, more gambling." Max no longer noticed the heat.

"Forget it, you lost enough in Vegas. You know, it doesn't seem right to me. Vicksburg's the site of one of the most famous battles of the Civil War. I have a hard time putting casinos here. It's like if they put Euro Disney on the Normandy beaches."

"A lot of locals agree, I'm sure, but a lot

more are grateful for the revenue and jobs."

Juan conceded the point with a nod. "It just occurred to me. I have no idea what Tamara Wright looks like." He was reaching for his phone to call Perlmutter when it started to ring.

"Chairman, St. Julian here."

"Your ears must have been buzzing because I was just reaching for my phone to call you. We don't know what Professor Wright looks like."

"She's tall, I'd say six feet, and a light-skinned African American. Her hair was straight the last time I saw her, but that was several years ago. The best way to spot her is she always wears a gold Tijitu pendant.

"A what?"

"It's the Taoist symbol for yin and yang. One half black, the other white. Listen, that's not important. Her grad student just called me again. She says she had another call last night from a man asking about Tamara. She just thought to call me now."

Juan's gut tightened. "What did she tell this man?"

"Everything. She didn't think she was breaking any confidences."

"Did the man identify himself?"

"Yes, he said he was a fellow scholar visiting from Argentina and wanted to set up a meeting with Tamara."

The tightness spread to Cabrillo's chest. He started looking around the small parking lot, expecting to see the Argentine Major at any second.

Perlmutter continued, "This isn't good, is it?"

"No. No, it isn't. It means Professor Wright's life is in danger."

At hearing this Max Hanley also started scanning faces.

"Thanks for the warning, St. Julian," Cabrillo said, and folded his phone.

"Persistent buggers, aren't they?" Max said.

"They've been an hour behind us the whole way."

"How do you think they found out about Professor Wright?"

"The same way we would have if I didn't know Perlmutter. I Googled her last night after you went to bed. She's world renowned for her knowledge of ancient Chinese shipping and commerce. If I wanted to learn more about Admiral Tsai, she's the person I'd want to talk to."

"I guess this means that rubbing you threw into the kitchen at Ronish's house survived the fire," Max remarked.

"What can I say? It was a lousy toss. Come

on, let's go check in, then find Dr. Wright. I feel like I've got a target pinned to my back, standing out here."

Despite her antebellum look, the *Natchez Belle* was a modern ship built with every conceivable amenity for the seventy passengers she could handle at a time as she made her way back and forth between St. Louis and New Orleans. Her two tall, spindly stacks were for show, as was the massive red stern wheel that churned the waters rhythmically. Propellers under her fantail would actually move the vessel.

The interior was as decorative and ornate as the outside. Woodwork gleamed under countless rounds of hand polishing, and all the brass looked as bright as gold. The carpet under their feet, as they stepped to the reception desk, was as plush as any aboard the *Oregon.*

The duo checked in. Juan was down to his last fake identification thanks to the need to burn their rental in Washington. He asked about Dr. Tamara Wright, but the receptionist, in her hoopskirt and tight bodice, said they didn't give out information on other passengers. They would have to find her themselves.

Their wood-paneled cabin was tiny, but at least they had a balcony overlooking the

Louisiana side of the river. Max made a comment about the bathroom being smaller than a phone booth, to which Cabrillo replied that they weren't here to enjoy the cruise. They didn't unpack their bags and left the cabin quickly.

Before boarding, they had checked the people at the cocktail reception on the quay. Dr. Wright wasn't among the guests, so the next logical place would either be her cabin or up on the sundeck. They hoped they could find her, convince her that she was in danger, and get her away from the stern-wheeler before the Argentines showed up. If not, they would guard her until the next port of call and make their escape then.

There was a bar at the aft section of the upper deck, overlooking the paddle wheel as it turned idly in the current. It was covered by a large white tarp to ward off the last rays of the setting sun. A few passengers were seated around it, and several others sat in nearby sofas, but none matched Tamara Wright's description. Farther forward, in the shadow of the *Natchez Belle*'s ersatz smokestacks, was a sunken hot tub big enough to seat ten. Like the bar, it proved popular with passengers, but there was no sign of Dr. Wright.

"What do you think?" Max asked.

"I think we're going to Natchez," Juan replied.

"We might as well get dressed for dinner."

The men hadn't bothered packing suits, so they made due with fresh shirts and the sports jackets they'd been wearing. By the time they emerged from their cabin, the gangway was being levered into its position along the ship's flank. An old-fashioned steam whistle — or at least an electronic version of one — signaled that the stern-wheeler was about to get under way.

While many passengers lined the upper rails or stood on their balconies to wave good-bye to Vicksburg, Cabrillo and Hanley scoured the *Natchez Belle* for Tamara or the Argentine hit squad. They found neither.

Both men felt a sense of relief. When the Argentines came, as they no doubt would, it wouldn't be until they reached their next destination. By then, Tamara Wright would understand the danger she was in, and they'd be able to sneak her off the ship. Cabrillo had already worked out a plan for that.

They sauntered up to the main-deck bar again, where most passengers were enjoying another predinner drink and listening to the house jazz band. A concert by legendary jazz pianist Lionel Couture was scheduled for after the meal.

Max suddenly slapped Juan's chest with the back of his hand and pointed. "I think I'm in love."

Most of the people they'd seen were older couples out blowing their children's inheritances, so Cabrillo didn't understand what his friend could be talking about. He didn't think it was the mustached bartender wearing the white suit. At least, he hoped it wasn't. The bartender shifted position, and Juan had a clear view of the woman sitting on the opposite side.

He got it now.

"That's her, isn't it?" he asked.

"Notice the necklace. Just like Perlmutter said."

Tamara Wright had to have been a ravishing beauty in her day, and, in her mid-fifties, she was still a striking woman. She had unlined café au lait skin and shoulder-length hair that was as shiny black as a raven's wing. She was smiling at something the bartender said, showing a mouthful of the whitest teeth Juan had ever seen. She wore a patterned spaghetti-strap dress that showed off her toned arms.

He had pictured a cloistered academic when St. Julian first mentioned her and he was delighted to admit how wrong he was.

Juan had to stretch his pace to keep up with Max's bull-in-a-china-shop charge to get to her.

"Dr. Wright," Max said with as much gallantry as he could muster. "My name is Max Hanley."

A puzzled but pleased look set her smile at just the right angle. "I'm sorry. Do we know each other?"

Before Max could start in on what could prove to be a lengthy assault on her virtue, Juan stepped in. "No, ma'am. You don't know us, but we're here because St. Julian Perlmutter said you'd be here."

"You know St. Julian?"

"Yes, we do, and he said you'd have some insight into a Chinese Admiral that he, as much as it pains him to admit, doesn't."

Now she was really intrigued. "Who are you?"

"Cabrillo. My name is Juan Cabrillo, and a couple of days ago my associate here and I discovered writing at the bottom of something called the Pine Island Treasure Pit that had been put there by Admiral Tsai Song in 1498."

Her mouth hung agape for a moment before she realized she was staring. She took a steadying sip of her white wine. Hanley and Cabrillo didn't look like the types to play a practical joke. They looked deadly serious.

"It really is true?" Her voice was a wonder-filled whisper.

"Yes." Max said, grinning that he was able to provide her with information she obviously relished.

"Wait," she said suddenly. "Isn't Pine Island where some privateer supposedly buried his treasure?"

"The reality is even more amazing than that legend," Juan told her. He had already decided to get as much out of her as he could before telling her about the Argentine threat. He didn't want to risk her becoming uncooperative. "Please, what can you tell us about Admiral Tsai?"

"The reason so little is known about him is that when he returned to China, a new Emperor was on the throne, one who didn't believe his subjects should leave the Middle Kingdom, and he put Tsai and his crew to death so they couldn't pollute the people with tales of the outside world. One of the men managed to escape, and it's from him we know about the voyage." She spoke with a real passion on the subject. And while Juan had asked the question, she was directing most of her attention to Max.

"Tell us about the ship they were forced

to leave behind. Tsai wrote that his men were set upon by an evil but didn't say what really happened."

"Yes, that was the *Silent Sea*. Tsai was forced to sink her and kill all her crew because they had gone mad."

"Where did this happen?" Max asked.

"The survivor was a lowly seaman, not a navigator. He only said that where it took place was a land of ice."

"Curious," Juan said. "How does —"

"A black woman become an expert on Chinese maritime history?"

"No, I was going to ask how the story was preserved for so long, but since you brought it up . . ."

"My father was an electronics engineer who spent most of his career in Taiwan. I was raised in Taipei. That's where I got my undergraduate degree. It was only after I finished that we returned to the States. As for how the story persisted, the survivor, Zedong Cho, wrote it down when he was an old man. He lived in Taiwan when it was just anther province. The manuscript was handed down through the family, but by the time a few generations had passed it was seen as a piece of fiction, the fantasy of an old ancestor with a good imagination. I learned about it because my roommate all four years at university was Susan Zedong, Cho's nine-times-removed granddaughter.

"Of course, there was no way to prove Admiral Tsai ever existed because the Emperor erased all evidence of him and all his men, so the story has remained just that, a story."

"Until now," Max reminded.

"Until now," she smiled at him.

Cabrillo could definitely sense some sparks here, and as much as he'd like to give them time alone, time was a luxury they didn't have.

"Does he say what caused the madness?" He was thinking about Linda Ross's report. Coincidence was a four-letter word in their line of work.

"The *Silent Sea* got separated from the other two ships for a month on its way to South America. They stopped at a remote island — please don't ask which — and they traded for fresh food from the natives. That's the only deviation from what the other ships encountered, so I've always believed the food was tainted somehow."

"Would you excuse me for a moment," Juan said, and stepped away. Max couldn't have been happier.

Juan dialed the *Oregon* and asked to be put through to Dr. Huxley.

"Jules, its Juan."

"Hey, where are you guys?"

"Believe it or not, on a Mississippi river-boat."

"It's warm and sunny, isn't it?" There was envy in the ship's medical officer's voice.

"The sun just set, but it's still about eighty."

"And you're calling to gloat. That's cold, Chairman, even for you."

"Listen, have you had a chance to check those samples you asked Murph to bring back from Wilson/George?"

"Not yet."

"Test them for prions."

"Prions . . . seriously? You think Andrew Gangle had mad cow disease?"

"A form of it, yes, and I think he got it from the other body. Prions don't die, right?"

"They're just proteins, so they aren't really alive. But, yes, in a sense they don't die."

"So someone could become infected if prions are introduced into the bloodstream by, say, accidentally jabbing yourself with the bone of a corpse riddled with them?"

Julia didn't hesitate. "Theoretically. Where'd this brainstorm come from?"

"A Chinese ship that isn't where it was supposed to be. Do me a favor and tell

Mark and Stoney to quit studying the map. I found the bay." He left it at that and rejoined Max and Tamara, who was laughing at some joke Hanley had just cracked.

"What was that all about?" Max asked.

"Playing a hunch about what tainted the food aboard the *Silent Sea*." Cannibalism was a common occurrence on several Pacific islands, and, if he was right, he knew what kind of meat the Chinese had bartered for. "What cargo did the ship carry?"

"She was loaded with everything from gold and spices to silks and jade, all the items that the Chinese held in esteem. They wanted the best in their dealings with natives they met on their voyage, so they brought only their best. What else did Admiral Tsai write?"

"I have a translation down in my cabin. It would be my pleasure to get you a copy."

It was only because the band had stopped that Juan heard the low throb of powerful engines. He knew what it was even before he sprang to his feet. His sudden action alerted Max.

Juan raced to the side of the stern-wheeler and peered down into the dark waters. There was enough glow left in the sky for him to see that a forty-foot cigarette-style boat had pulled alongside the *Natchez Belle*.

In it were four men dressed in dark clothes with ski masks pulled over their faces. So many things gelled in his mind at that moment, so many implications of what their dogged pursuit meant. But he didn't have time to dwell on them.

Already one of the men had leapt the narrow gap from the cigarette boat to the lowest deck of the lumbering pleasure boat.

They had four men. One would have to stay with their vessel, meaning three would board the *Belle.* Juan and Max had faced worse odds, but he had to consider the other passengers' safety. From what he'd seen of the Argentines, they weren't above targeting civilians.

"Max, stay with her. Jump over the side if you have to."

Hanley hadn't drawn his pistol but his hand was at the ready in his jacket.

"What's happening?" Tamara asked, her body sensing the tension in her new companions.

"You're in danger," Max said. "You have to trust us."

"But I don't —"

Max cut her off. "There isn't time. Please, trust me."

Juan had made his way to the main stairwell down to the lower decks when he heard

331

screams coming from below. The Argentines were all aboard now, he guessed, and brandishing weapons. He could see a panicked mob, surging for the stairs. There was no way he'd be able to fight his way down through the mess of clamoring people.

He turned instantly and rushed forward. Next to the hot tub was a peaked skylight made up of dozens of pieces of emerald-cut glass set in a wrought-iron frame. He kicked at a few of the panes, shards of glass cascading onto the dinner table below. More shrieks came from startled early diners who hadn't heard the commotion.

Cabrillo jumped through the opening he'd created and hit the table a little off center. It collapsed, tossing him to the floor in an avalanche of food, cutlery, and plates. His momentum knocked a matronly woman back in her chair so her thick legs were pointed at the ceiling. They bicycled comically as she tried to right herself.

Juan got to his feet, stinking of wine and collard greens. His ankle gave a slight twinge. It wasn't sprained, but he'd twisted it in the fall. While some passengers stared, the husband of the woman he'd knocked over started yelling at him. He made to push Cabrillo in the shoulder, but Juan sidestepped his attempt, rotating in place and pushing the man on the back in a maneuver that looked like a matador turning a charging bull.

It happened so fast that the irate husband took two steps before he realized he was past his target. He spun to up the fight's ante but stopped dead when he saw Juan had drawn his pistol. Cabrillo didn't aim it at him, though he made sure the guy got a good look at it and rethought how best to defend his wife's honor. She still hadn't managed to get her legs down or her backside out of the overturned chair.

The glass doors leading into the dining room were suddenly smashed open. Two of the gunmen burst through. Screams erupted when the passengers saw the assault rifles. Cabrillo recognized them as Ruger Mini-14s, among the best civilian rifles made. He didn't have a clear shot because of the people scrambling to get away from the armed intruders. Some dove under tables while others seemed rooted where they stood, ashen and unsure.

The men swept the room, looking for Tamara Wright. They would easily have gotten a picture off the Internet, something Cabrillo had forgotten to do. Juan turned slightly and crouched so they wouldn't get a look at his face.

"Everybody line up against the back wall."

Cabrillo recognized the voice of the Argentine Major.

There was a waiter standing next to the kitchen doors. He slowly tried to sneak his way through and escape. The second gunman saw the movement and fired without hesitation. The bullet caught him square in the chest, its speed sending it straight through him and on into the kitchen, where it ricocheted off some piece of equipment.

The passengers' screaming built into a crescendo of noise that filled the dining room. In this fresh surge of panic, Cabrillo made his move. He knew that once the gunman got control of the room he was a dead man, so he launched himself toward the big picture window overlooking the inky river. He took four paces before the Argentines reacted. A string of rounds from the semi-automatic rifles buzzed around him. Glassware and dishes exploded off the tables when they were hit. One round caught a tuxedoed man in the arm. He was so close to Cabrillo that his blood splashed Juan's sleeve.

Several other bullets hit the window, starring the glass and weakening it enough so that when Cabrillo threw himself against it it failed spectacularly. He crashed into the

Mississippi in a hail of shards, forcing himself as deep as he could.

The water was pitch-black just inches below the surface. By feel, he swam along the hull as the *Natchez Belle* continued southward. He could sense the vibration of her props through the river and hear the relentless churning of her decorative stern wheel.

Juan surfaced just under where the hull and deck met, in an area protected from above. The boat was moving at about four knots, and its passage pulled him through the water at nearly the same speed. He jammed his pistol into its holster to free up his hands.

Like on a traditional stern-wheeler, there was a rocker arm protruding over the side of the ship, like the pistons that drive a locomotive's big wheels. On the *Belle,* it wasn't functional, only an additional element to make her look authentic.

Juan reached out of the water and grabbed one of the support brackets. There was nothing for him to climb higher once his torso was free of the river, however. This part of the ship was a sheer wall. He was partially aboard the ship but trapped along her waterline. The rocker arm lowered him back into the river like a tea bag before drawing him out again. The repetitive motion was nauseating. More shots pierced the night from inside the superstructure. Time was running out, and he knew what he had to do.

Hand over hand, he inched his way slowly aft, until the thirty-foot-diameter wheel loomed over his shoulder and tore at the water next to his waist. Unlike the original vessels where the paddles were made out of wood on a steel framework, the *Belle*'s wheel was all metal.

Juan watched it in the glow of lights shining over the fantail, judging its rotation and the rhythm of the rocker arm, until he was certain.

He lunged for one of the paddles with both hands, managing to get his fingers in position the instant before it sucked him under. The drag against his body threatened to pull his arms out of their sockets, but nothing in the world would make him let go. Just as quickly as he'd been pulled below the surface, he emerged again, streaming water. He was facing away from the ship, so, in the seconds he had, he twisted around so that when he reached the apex of the wheel he was looking at the windows of the Presidential Suite, just below the topside lounge.

Momentum threw him against the glass with more than enough force to shatter it. He landed on a king-sized bed and bounced to his feet. A woman wrapped in a towel was just coming from the bathroom. She screamed at Juan standing there, shaking off glass chips and water.

In moments like these, Juan was usually good for a one-line quip, but he was too stunned by the impact and the wild ride around the stern wheel. He gave the woman a charming smile, and strode from the cabin.

Only ten minutes had passed since he'd dived in the river. Ten minutes in which Max was alone, outgunned three to one. Juan pulled his pistol, racked back the slide to drain it, and blew into the receiver. It was the best he could do, but the Glock was a hardy weapon that had never failed him before.

The hallway outside the woman's cabin was deserted. Orange flicker bulbs meant to look like candles cast bizarre shadows from the wall sconces. It gave the dim hall the feel of a haunted house. Juan's shoes squelched with each footfall, and he was leaving a trail of stinking river water in his wake. A door suddenly opened a crack, and an eye peered out.

"Close the door and stay inside," Juan said. The person didn't need to be told twice. Even if he hadn't been armed, Juan's voice demanded compliance.

The screaming had stopped, which in a hostage situation means the gunmen now had complete control and the crowd had become docile. That wasn't a good sign.

Juan found a stairwell, ducked his head around quickly, and then committed himself when it was clear. He eased his way up until he could see the floor of the topmost deck. From this vantage, it looked deserted, so he climbed a little higher. Despite the sultry air, he felt chilled in his sopping clothes.

There were a cluster of people standing and kneeling around a prone form. Cabrillo's heart felt like it had stopped in his chest. There were no Argentine gunmen here, just passengers, and with a sickening dread he knew who was down.

He raced from his cover position. A woman yelled when she saw him running toward them, a pistol dangling from his hand. Others turned, but Juan ignored them. He burst into the circle of people.

Max Hanley lay flat on his back, blood coating half his face and forming a black puddle on the polished wooden deck. Juan scooped up his head and pressed his fingers against his friend's neck in the vain search for a pulse. Surprisingly, it was there, and strong.

"Max," he called. "Max, can you hear me?" He looked up at the crowd staring down on them. "What happened?"

"He was shot, and the gunmen grabbed some woman and took off downstairs."

Cabrillo used his coattail to wipe away the blood and saw a long oozing trench along Hanley's temple. The bullet had grazed him. Max probably had a concussion and would certainly need stitches, but chances were he would be fine.

Juan got to his feet. "Please look after him."

He raced back down the stairs again, anger and adrenaline making him reckless. The Argentines had approached the *Belle* from the port side, so he raced across the ship and descended another flight of steps to the main deck.

In front of him was the entry door where just hours ago he and Max had boarded the stern-wheeler. It was open, and through it he could see the dark silhouette of a man. He shouted, and when the man turned and confirmed he was wearing a ski mask, Cabrillo fired a double tap to the torso. The man fell back, his head hitting something with an empty thud, and then he splashed into the water.

Marine engines roared an instant later. Juan ran to the open door to see the back of the cigarette boat pulling away, a rooster tail of white water forming in its wake as it gained speed. He raised his pistol in a two-handed combat grip but held his fire. It was too dark to see anything but shapes, and he couldn't risk hitting Tamara.

He doubled over, breathing hard, and fought to control his emotions.

He'd failed. There was no other way to look at it. He had failed, and now Tamara Wright was going to pay for it. He turned away in disgust with himself, and, out of stupid testosterone-fueled anger, punched a decorative mirror hanging on a nearby wall. His reflection went crazy in the shattered glass, and his knuckles came away bloody.

Juan took another couple of deep breaths to compose himself and start his brain thinking rationally again. The list of favors he would need to call on to get him and Max out of this mess was going to be monstrous.

For now, though, the important thing was Max. He felt his phone vibrate as he rushed back up the stairs, but he ignored it. That it had amazingly survived its dunking was a fact of so little importance that it never entered Cabrillo's mind. The feel of the ship had changed, and the seaman in him told him the *Belle*'s captain had slowed so they could turn back for Vicksburg, where every cop on duty would be waiting.

It was going to take some fast talking to keep himself out of prison. The shootings would eventually be proven justified, but there was still the fake ID, the unregistered guns, and the fact that he and Max had lied to customs to get into the country in the first place. This was why Juan preferred to work in the Third World. There, a judicious bribe in the right hands bought your freedom. Here, it tacked another couple of years to your sentence.

Up on deck, people were still clustered around Max, but Juan could see that his friend was sitting upright. The blood had been cleared from his face, and a man was holding a bar towel to the side of his head.

"I'm sorry," he said when Juan squatted down at his side. "I went to pull Tamara behind me, and the guy just opened fire. One went wide, but the second . . ." He pointed to his head. "I went down like a sack of potatoes. They get her?"

"I got one of them, but, yeah, they got her."

"Damn."

"That's putting it mildly." Juan's phone vibrated again. This time he pulled it out to check who was calling. "This can't be good."

"Langston, you've got lousy timing," he said to the veteran CIA agent.

"You're not going to believe what happened about two hours ago."

Juan had put it together when the gunmen stormed the ship, and said, "Argentina just announced that they're annexing the Antarctic Peninsula, and China has already recognized their sovereignty."

"How could you . . . ?" Overholt's voice trailed off in incredulity.

"And I can guarantee that when this comes up at the UN tomorrow, the Chinese will use their veto power as permanent members of the Security Council to kill any resolutions condemning the annexation."

"They've already announced they would. How did you know?"

"That's going to take a little explaining, but first I think I'm going to need a favor. Do you happen to know anybody in the Vicksburg Ph.D.?" Cabrillo asked this as the ship's purser showed up with two goons from the engine room carrying wrenches the size of baseball bats.

A second later, he was facedown on the

342

deck, with one goon sitting on his back while the second gorilla pinned his legs. The purser was holding the Glock like a tarantula in one hand and had Cabrillo's cell in the other. Juan hadn't bothered putting up a fight. He could have taken out all three, but he had Max to consider.

He just wished Overholt had answered him, otherwise this was going to be a long night.

EIGHTEEN

In total, they lost eighteen precious hours. Max spent most of these under guard at the River Region Medical Center, where his head was scanned and stitched up. Juan was the guest of the Warren County Sheriff's Department. They kept him up all night in a windowless interrogation room, where detectives and uniformed cops grilled him relentlessly.

It took them two hours to determine that his identification was bogus. Had Cabrillo expected any kind of background check, he could have brought papers that would prove legit no matter how hard the authorities studied them. But he hadn't expected this kind of trouble, so his identity was breachable. Once they learned he wasn't William Duffy of Englewood, California — the name on his second set of papers — the questions came harder and faster.

And while his story about a woman being

abducted off the *Natchez Belle* had been confirmed by other passengers and the crew, the police seemed more interested in the hows and whys of his and Max's presence to try to thwart the attack.

There was nothing Juan could say to convince them that he wasn't part of the plot. And when the rushed ballistic report came back proving that the dead John Doe wearing a ski mask who'd been fished from the river had been killed by the gun the crew took from him, murder-one charges were threatened. They delighted in pointing out that Mississippi was a death-penalty state.

The FBI arrived at around nine the following morning, and for an hour, while jurisdiction was established, Cabrillo was left alone. Just for the fun of it, he pretended to pass out. Four cops, who'd been watching through the two-way mirror, rushed in. The last thing they wanted was for their prisoner to escape justice by dying on them.

It was around two-thirty, by his estimate — his watch had been taken upon his arrest — when two gray men in matching gray suits showed up. The cops and FBI agents, who were arrayed against Cabrillo like a pack of dogs slobbering over a fresh bone, looked nervous. They were told by the gray men that this was a matter for the Department of Homeland Security.

The salivating looks evaporated. Their bone was being taken by an even bigger dog.

Juan's cuffs were removed and replaced by a pair the Homeland agents had brought. Then he was given his belongings, including his suitcase from the *Belle,* and escorted outside. The bright sunlight felt wonderful after so many hours under the nauseating glow of fluorescent lights. They led him wordlessly to a black Crown Victoria that screamed *government vehicle.* One of them opened the rear door. Max was sitting in the back bench seat, half his head swaddled in bandages and tape.

"How's the noggin?"

"Hurts like hell, but the concussion's mild."

"Good thing they shot you in the head, otherwise they could have hit something important."

"You're all heart."

As soon as Cabrillo was settled next to Max, the car pulled away from the sheriff's office. The agent in the passenger's seat turned and held up a key. Juan wasn't sure what he wanted until he recognized it as the key to his cuffs. He held up his hands and they were freed.

"Thanks. We won't give you any trouble.

Where are you taking us?"

"Airport."

"And then?"

"That's up to you, sir. Though my orders were to recommend you leave the country."

Max and Juan exchanged knowing smirks. Langston Overholt had done it. God only knew how, but he'd gotten them out of that quagmire. Juan wanted to call him right away, but his cell phone had finally died from its soak in the river, and Max's hadn't been returned to him.

The agents dumped them at the curb in front of the Jackson-Evers terminal. Juan hailed a taxi as soon as they'd pulled out of sight.

"I take it we're not going to follow their advice?" Max asked.

"We are, but I don't want to hear you grumble about flying commercial. There's a charter service here."

"Now we're talking."

Twenty minutes later, they were in the general-aviation terminal waiting for their plane to be fueled. Juan was using his laptop to act as a telephone. His first call was to Overholt.

"I take it you're out?" the old CIA agent asked.

"Charter jet's fueling as we speak. Max

and I both owe you one. How'd you do it?"

"Suffice it to say, it's done, and leave it at that. How could you possibly know about Argentina and China?"

Juan wanted to tell him about Tamara Wright's abduction, but for now even someone as powerful as Overholt couldn't do anything more than was already being done by local law enforcement and the FBI.

He explained what Linda Ross and her team had discovered when they checked into the Argentine research station. He also told him about the gruesome find at Wilson/George.

"Okay, so I understand your thinking that Argentina's going to make a play for the peninsula; they've been rattling sabers over it for years, even before the current junta. But China? That caught the CIA, State Department, and the White House completely by surprise."

"Here's the thing. When I spoke to you last night, Max and I were with a woman named Tamara Wright —"

"The one they kidnapped?"

"You've read the police report?"

"Just bits and pieces. They're taking it seriously, but there are no leads. The speedboat was discovered in Natchez, where a van was stolen from a plumber's house. The

APB is out, but so far no hits."

"I figured it would be something like that. They're smart. I bet that van will be found wherever they stole the cigarette boat. They'll have their own set of wheels back and could be just about anywhere."

"Agreed. China?" Overholt prompted.

"Dr. Wright told us about a Chinese expedition in the late 1400s that sent a fleet of three ships to South America." Juan paused, expecting Overholt to question the validity of such a claim, but the wily case officer knew when to keep quiet. "One of the ships was afflicted by a disease that drove the crewmen insane. Sound familiar?"

"The guy at Wilson/George," Langston breathed.

"They ate tainted food provided by island natives. I think it was human flesh, most likely brain, and they got a dose of prions. The ship was scuttled with the crew aboard, and the remaining two ships ventured northward and eventually back to China.

"Five hundred years later, along comes Andrew Gangle, who finds a mummy some-place near their base. It's carrying gold and jade. Somehow, he gets infected, most likely he accidentally stabbed himself on a shard of bone. Now he's got a prion disease rotting away his mind until he snaps and goes berserk."

"That scuttled ship is off the coast of Antarctica? Dear God," Overholt exclaimed as he made the intuitive leap that Cabrillo had had the night before. "If they can prove that Chinese explorers discovered Antarctica a couple hundred years before the first European, they . . ."

"Exactly," Juan said. "They'll lay claim over it, or at least the peninsula. But with Argentina already so well entrenched, the smart move for them is to partner up and share the spoils. I believe this has been in the works for some time, long before we got involved. I think the Argentines were courting the Chinese because they would need the protection of a superpower and the patronage of someone in the UN. It was the chance discovery of that blimp and the subsequent events, like getting their hands on tangible proof that the Chinese had visited South America, that cemented the deal."

"Do the Argentines or Chinese know the location of the third ship?"

"Not yet, but they'll be able to figure it out with enough research. Admiral Tsai's drawing was pretty specific. A good computer program and Google Earth should do it. But here's the thing: even if they don't find it, they can still claim the ship visited Antarctica. Who's to stop them?"

"We are."

"What's the official White House position?"

"Events are unfolding too fast. They haven't said much, beyond the usual condemnation."

"What does your gut tell you?"

"I honestly don't know. China currently holds the lion's share of our national debt, so they have us over a barrel in that respect. Also, logically, are we willing to go to war over a part of the world only a handful of people care about?"

"This is about principles," Juan pointed out. "Do we stick to our ideals and risk lives for a bunch of penguins and a forty-year-old treaty or do we let them get away with it?"

"That's it in a nutshell, and I don't know what the President will do. Hell, I don't know how *I* feel. Part of me says to kick the bastards back to Beijing and Buenos Aires, but what's the point? Let them have the oil and the penguins. It's not worth putting our military personnel in harm's way."

"Dicey call," Juan agreed, though in his mind the decision was a no-brainer. Argentina broke a binding international treaty by invading neighboring territory that didn't belong to them. They deserved the full wrath of the United States, and any other signatory to the Antarctic Treaty. He suddenly remembered something. "Has NASA had a chance to analyze the power cell we recovered from their downed satellite?"

"Yes, and it is possible it was shot down, like your guy suggested, though they hedged and said the cause was indeterminate."

"Why would they risk it?" Cabrillo mused. "Why, with everything at stake, would they take the chance and intentionally shoot down one of our birds?"

"If you want a real head-scratcher, it wasn't a spy satellite and was never rumored to be one. It was designed to monitor carbon dioxide emissions and was going to be used to make sure countries stay within their targets when and if a new treaty is implemented to replace the Kyoto Protocol."

Juan remained quiet for a moment, thinking. "Of course," he said. "They can hide the thermal signature of their Antarctic activities using sea water, but oil-and-gas exploration would produce a dense plume of carbon dioxide in a place that shouldn't have any. Once that satellite went active, we'd have known exactly what they were up to."

"If they were going to annex the peninsula only a week after shooting down the satellite, why bother?" Overholt asked.

"You haven't been paying attention, Lang. The deal with China was only cemented in the last couple of days. Without that alliance, Argentina would need to keep their activities secret for months, maybe a year. China might have helped them shoot it down as a good-faith gesture or to guarantee they get the bulk of the crude that's pumped from those new wells. Either way, it shows they've been in bed together for a while."

"I should have thought of that."

"I've spent the last eighteen hours under police interrogation and *I* saw it, so, yeah, you should have." Juan was teasing, which at a time like this was an indication of the depths of his exhaustion.

"What are your plans now?"

"I've got to make contact with the *Oregon* before I know where we're heading, but I'll keep you updated. Please do the same."

"Talk to you soon."

Max had listened to Juan's end of the conversation. "You don't know where we're going?"

Juan pulled the microphone from his ear. "Do you honestly think I'm going to trust the locals to find Tamara Wright? We got her into this mess and we're damned sure going to get her back out. I've rented the plane with the greatest endurance they have here, so we're going to get her no matter where she is."

"That's why I love you. You'll spare no expense trying to get me a date."

Cabrillo grinned at Max's shamelessness and replaced the Bluetooth headset to call the *Oregon.* He asked Hali Kasim, their communications specialist, to patch him through to Eric Stone.

"Why did you pull us off our search for the mystery bay?" Eric asked.

"Because you've already found it."

"I have?"

"It's within snowcat distance of Wilson/ George, maybe closer."

"How could you know that?"

"Because I'm the Chairman." Juan really was exhausted. "Do me a favor, I want you to check the logs of Jackson-Evers field for any private jets that flew out of here between, say, midnight and noon today."

In the pre-9/11 days, he probably could have charmed that information out of the pretty receptionist at the general-aviation counter, but not anymore.

"Give me a second." Over the connection, he could hear Stone's fingers flying over his keyboard.

Juan was playing a hunch, one he felt reasonably certain about.

"One last firewall," Eric said absently, then a triumphant, "Got it. Okay, there were two. One was an Atlantic Aviation charter to New York City that left at nine o'clock this morning. The other was a private jet that filed a flight plan for Mexico City that took off at one-thirty this morning."

"What can you tell me about that plane?"

"Hold on. That's another database." It took him less than a minute. "The plane's owned by a company registered in the Cayman Islands."

"A dummy front?"

"No doubt. It's going to take some time to . . . hold on a second. I'm checking its past flights. It arrived in the United States at Seattle-Tacoma International three days ago from Mexico City."

"Then flew here yesterday," Juan finished for him. That was their plane, and if they were heading to Mexico City it was only to refuel. "Thanks, Eric."

Juan turned to Max. "They're taking her to Argentina."

NINETEEN

The horse was a big Arabian stallion with such taut muscles that veins showed in relief under its glossy skin. It was streaked in sweat and blew heavily, and yet was game to keep charging across the Argentine landscape, its hoofs pounding the ground in a thundering drumbeat. Its rider barely moved in her saddle, her slouch hat hanging off her throat by a strap.

Maxine Espinoza was a superb horsewoman, and raced for the stream five miles from the mansion as though she was gunning for the Triple Crown. She wore tan riding breeches and a man's white oxford unbuttoned enough so that wind caressed her skin. Her boots had a worn look that bespoke of countless hours riding and an almost equal amount of time being lovingly polished.

It was that perfect moment of late afternoon, when the sun dappled the ground under the occasional tree and slanted so the grass looked like burnished gold.

Movement to her left caught her eye, and she turned quick enough to see a hawk lift off from the ground with its dinner clutched in its razor-sharp talons.

"Ha, Concorde," she cried, and firmed her grip on the reins.

The horse seemed to love these wild rides as much as his mistress, and he lengthened his stride. They were of one mind, and existed almost as a Centaur rather than two separate beings.

Only when they neared the band of forest that lined both sides of a stream did they slow. Maxine entered the glen at an easy walk, the big stallion beneath her heaving great lungfuls of air through his flared nostrils.

She could hear the stream gurgling over rocks and songbirds in the limbs of trees. She ducked under a branch and weaved Concorde deeper into the woods. This was her sanctuary, her special place, on the sprawling estate. The clear waters of the stream would sate her horse's thirst, and along the bank was a bed of grass where she'd slept during countless siestas.

She legged over Concorde's back and lowered herself to the ground. She needn't worry about him wandering off or drinking too much. He was better mannered than that. From her saddlebag she pulled a blanket of the finest Egyptian cotton. She was just moving to spread it on the grass when a figure emerged from behind a tree.

"Excuse me, *señora.*"

Maxine whirled, her eyes narrowing in anger at the intrusion. She recognized the man. It was Raul Jimenez, her stepson's second-in-command. "How dare you come here? You should be on the base with the rest of the soldiers."

"I prefer the company of women."

She took two steps forward and slapped him. "I should tell the General of your impudence."

"And what would you tell him about this?" He grabbed her smoothly and drew her body to his. He kissed her, and for a few seconds she resisted, but it was too much, and soon she had her hand on the back of his head as her hunger grew.

Jimenez finally pulled back. "God, I've missed you."

Maxine's reply was to kiss him again, even more passionately. Now that they were alone, all pretense of his shyness around her was gone. They gave in to their desires.

It was much later that they were lying side

by side on the hastily spread blanket. She gingerly touched the burn scars on his face. They were still red and looked painful.

"You are no longer so beautiful. I think I should find myself another lover."

"I don't think there is another in the regiment who would dare do what we just did."

"Are you saying I am not worth a court-martial?"

"To me, you are worth death itself, but you forget I am the bravest man in the Army," he joked. And then a shadow passed behind his eyes.

"What is it, darling?"

" 'Bravest,' I said." His voice filled with bitterness. "It takes little bravery to gun down villagers or kidnap American women."

"Kidnap Americans? I don't understand."

"That is where your husband sent us, to America, where we grabbed a woman who's an expert on Chinese ships or something. I have no idea why. I tell you, though, it's not what I joined the Army to do."

"I know my husband," Maxine said. "Everything he does is planned, from eating breakfast to commanding your regiment. He has his reasons. This must be why he took off for Buenos Aires just as you and Jorge returned."

"We met him at your apartment in the

city. He had some men with him — Chinese, I think."

"They're from the embassy. Philippe has been meeting with them quite a bit recently."

"I'm sorry, but I still don't like it. Don't get me wrong. I love the Army and I love Jorge, but these past few months . . ." His voice trailed off.

"You may not believe this," Maxine said, her voice crisp and firm, "but I love my husband very much, and I love this country. Philippe may be many things, but he is not reckless. Whatever he is doing is for the greater good of Argentina and its people."

"You wouldn't say that if you'd seen some of the things he's ordered us to do."

"I don't want to hear about it," she said stubbornly, the romantic cocoon they had built for themselves dissolving.

He placed a hand on her bare shoulder. "I'm sorry. I didn't mean to upset you."

"I'm not upset," she replied, but had to wipe at her eyes. "Philippe tells me very little, but I have always trusted him. You should, too."

"Okay," Jimenez said, and reached for her.

Maxine slithered out of his grip. "I must be getting back now. Even with Philippe in BA, the servants talk. You understand?"

"Of course. My servants are always gossiping." They both laughed because he had come from a poor family.

Maxine moved off to dress. She climbed aboard Concorde, who had stayed near them the entire time.

"Will I see you tomorrow?" he asked, stuffing the blanket back into the saddlebag.

"So long as you promise not to discuss my husband or his work."

"I will be the good soldier and do as you order."

The chopper pilot was relieved that his passengers had paid cash because when he saw their destination he knew any check they wrote would have bounced. As it stood, he considered radioing his business partner and having him make sure the money wasn't counterfeit.

He was taking the two men from Rio's Galeão International Airport to a cargo ship a hundred miles offshore. From a distance, it looked like any of the dozens of vessels that approached Brazil every week, but as they neared and details came into focus he could see she was a floating heap of rust barely held together by duct tape and baling wire. The smoke from her stack was so black, he suspected she burned bunker fuel and lubricating oil in equal ratios. Her cranes looked like they could barely hold themselves up, let alone lift any cargo. He glanced over his shoulder at the younger passenger as if to say: Are you sure?

The man had the sallow look of someone who hadn't slept for days, and whatever burden he carried was just ounces away from crushing him. And yet, when he realized the pilot was looking at him, the passenger winked one of his bright blue eyes, and the mask of consternation melted away.

"She's not much to look at," the passenger said over his mike, "but she gets the job done."

"I don't think I can land on the deck," the pilot said, his English tinted with a hint of Portuguese. He didn't add that he thought the weight of his Bell JetRanger would probably collapse a hatch cover.

"No problem. Just hover over the fantail, and we'll jump."

The second passenger, a man in his late fifties or early sixties with a bandage on his head, groaned at the prospect of leaping from the helicopter.

"You got it." The pilot turned his attention back to flying while the passengers gathered up their luggage, which consisted of a laptop case and a battered canvas shoulder bag. Everything else had been dumped in Mississippi.

Juan Cabrillo never tired of looking at the *Oregon*. To him, she was as fine a piece of art as any of the paintings hanging on the walls of her secret passageways. He had to admit that homecomings were sweeter when a mission was complete, not like now, with Tamara Wright in the hands of an Argentine death squad and her exact whereabouts unknown. The cocky wink he had thrown at the pilot was just that — cockiness. Her fate lay like a stone in his stomach.

To the Brazilian pilot's credit, he held the skids of the helicopter a foot off the deck when first Max and then Juan jumped to the ship. The two men ducked low in the pounding rotor wash until the JetRanger peeled away and clawed skyward. When it was a glittering speck on the western horizon, the helmsman — Juan assumed it was Eric Stone — killed the smudge generator that gave the illusion the ship was powered by traditional, albeit poorly maintained, marine diesels.

He gave the Iranian flag hanging from the jack staff his traditional one-finger salute and followed Max toward the superstructure.

They were met at a watertight door by Dr.

Huxley and Linda Ross. Hux immediately started escorting Max down to Medical, muttering about the butcher job they had done on him in the hospital.

"Welcome back," Linda greeted. "That sure wasn't the relaxing couple of days you'd expected."

"What's that line: 'No good deed goes unpunished'? That was a great job you did in Antarctica."

"Thanks." There was an edge of bitterness in her voice. "We got the intel to Overholt less than twenty-four hours before the Argentines took over, so it didn't do much good."

"What's the latest?"

"There's been no contact with any of the other stations on the peninsula. We believe that the Argentines grabbed up the remaining interntional scientists and are going to use them as human shields at the oil terminal."

Juan frowned. "Borrowing Saddam's playbook."

"The *Generalissimo* plays dirty, that's for sure."

"I asked Overholt if they have any assets in Argentina who could find out where they took Tamara Wright. Has he gotten back to you?"

"Not yet. Sorry."

Cabrillo's scowl deepened. "This never would have happened if . . ." There was nothing to be gained by venting his feelings so he didn't continue. He motioned for Linda to enter the ship. The *Oregon* was picking up speed, and the wind was starting to howl across her deck.

"We'll be off the coast of Buenos Aires in thirty hours. With luck, Overholt will have something for us."

"God, I hope so." Juan raked his fingers through his hair. "I need to burn off some of this restless energy. If anyone needs me, I'll be in the pool."

One of the two enormous ballast tanks the Corporation used to raise or lower the ship depending on her disguise was tiled in buttery Carrara marble and lit with a combination of fixtures that approximated sunlight. It had taken a pounding when the *Oregon* went toe to toe with a Libyan frigate, but the artisans who'd made the repairs had done a masterful job.

Cabrillo shrugged off his robe and strapped four-pound weights to his wrists. The water wasn't kept that deep because the ship was racing for Argentina, so he shallow-dove, barely submerging his entire body, and came up in a breaststroke that he knew from experience he could maintain for hours.

The water had always been his refuge, and it was from here he could free his mind and let himself relax. The repetition of his thrusting limbs and the slow burn building in his muscles was like meditation.

The following morning, after a sumptuous breakfast in the dining hall, Juan stood his watch in the op center. He arrived early and relieved Eddie Seng, who'd had the dog shift. Eddie gratefully relinquished the command chair once he'd briefed Juan on shipping around the *Oregon* and the weather, which was about to turn nasty. The main view screen, all eight feet of it, showed the seas as if they were on the actual bridge several decks above them. The sky was a sunless gray, full of ugly, roiling clouds, while the sea was as black as slag from a foundry except where the wind tore at the tops of the waves and threw up custard-thick spume.

Water regularly burst over the bows in sheets that raced for the scuppers. A crewman was up on the forecastle, securing a hatchway. He looked as small as a child and nearly powerless in the face of the elements. Juan breathed a little easier when the man returned inside the ship.

Hali Kasim, the ship's communications expert, was at his station along the wall to Cabrillo's right near the now-dim waterfall display for the *Oregon*'s sonar system. In these seas, and at the ship's speed, it was impossible to hear acoustical signals, so the sonar was off-line.

"Call for you, Chairman," Hali said. His hair stuck up at odd angles because of the old-fashioned headset he preferred. "It's Overholt at the CIA."

"About damned time," Juan muttered, and hooked a Bluetooth over his ear. "Langston, what have you got for me?"

"Morning," Overholt grunted. In that one word, Cabrillo knew the news was going to be bad. "The President's National Security Council meeting just broke up. The DCI called me no more than five minutes ago."

"What's happening?"

"The Joint Chiefs reported that a Chinese fast-attack submarine was detected off the coast of Chile. Course and speed will put her in the waters around the Antarctic Peninsula in a day or two."

"They're playing for keeps," Juan remarked. The move didn't come as a surprise.

"Sure are. The Argies confirmed they have our scientists from Palmer Station as well as more than a dozen others from Russia, Norway, Chile, and Australia. The numbers are thankfully low because these are the small winter-over crews."

"What's our official response to this? What's the President going to do?"

"China's announced that any attempt to censure Argentina at the UN will be vetoed immediately. There will be no resolutions or sanctions."

"Gee," Juan said sarcastically, "that's a major setback. How will we ever stop them without the UN throwing harsh words their way?"

Overholt chuckled through his exhaustion. He shared Cabrillo's low opinion of the international body. "Here's the really bad news. The President will not authorize the use of force. England and Russia are rattling their sabers, but the political will in Parliament and the Duma just isn't there. The leadership in the House and Senate have also indicated they aren't willing to defend the Antarctic Treaty with American lives."

"So that's it?" Juan said with disgust. "We call ourselves a moral nation, but when it comes to fighting for an ideal the politicians ram their heads in the sand."

"I would say they've rammed their heads

in a far less hospitable place, but, yes, that's it."

"We are backing down from our moral and legal obligation. I'm sorry, Lang, but this decision is wrong."

"You're preaching to the choir, my boy," Overholt said affably. "However, I serve at the discretion of the President, so there's not much I can do. For the record, my boss thinks we should kick the Argentines out of Antarctica, as does the Chairman of the Joint Chiefs. They also see the dangerous precedent this sets."

"What happens now?"

"Why, nothing. We'll craft some UN resolution that the Chinese will shoot down — and that's about it, I'm afraid."

Now that he had Antarctica, Paraguay and Uruguay would be next on Generalissimo Ernesto Corazón's list. Cabrillo thought that the only thing sparing Chile was the difficulty of moving an army across the Andes. In Venezuela, Chávez had built up his military with oil-for-weapons deals with Russia, and he had been looking for an excuse to unleash it on Colombia. Iraq's teetering democracy would fall like a house of cards if an emboldened Iran started throwing its weight around.

Juan wanted to say all of this to Overholt,

but he knew it was wasted breath. The President's advisers, he was sure, had already laid out the same scenarios and had been unable to sway the man's opinion.

"Tell me some good news," Juan said wearily.

"Ah, that I have as well." Overholt's voice perked up. "We have an asset in Argentina who says that your missing professor is being held in Buenos Aires."

"That narrows it down to a city of twelve million."

"Ye of little faith," Overholt chided. "She's in a fifth-floor penthouse apartment in the Recoleta District just off Avenue Las Heras."

"If I remember correctly, the Recoleta District is the swanky part of town."

"The apartment belongs to General Philippe Espinoza, the commander of the Ninth Brigade."

"Ninth Brigade, huh?" That wasn't welcome news.

"I'm afraid so. The General is interrogating her personally. I would guess with the help of whatever spooks the Chinese have in Buenos Aires."

The image of Tamara Wright strapped to a chair flashed through Cabrillo's mind, and he winced. "Download whatever intel you have on the building. We should be off the coast by sunset."

"How are you going to get her out?"

"As soon as I come up with a plan, you'll be the second to know." Juan cut the connection and leaned back, absently rubbing his chin. He hadn't been joking. He had no idea how to save the professor.

TWENTY

Foul weather dogged the *Oregon* as she pounded her way southward. Ship and crew took the abuse stoically, as if it were penance for Tamara's capture. At least that's how Cabrillo felt about it. Some of the waves reached almost the height of the bridge, and, when her stern rose high, water exploded from the pump jets in twin lances that shot nearly a hundred feet.

Juan had assembled the senior staff in the Corporation's boardroom. The space had been destroyed by a direct hit from the Libyan frigate, and in the reconstruction Juan had gone for a modern glass-and-stainless-steel look. The table was embedded with a microscopic mesh of electrical wires that, when activated, created a static charge that kept papers in place no matter the sea's state. With winds blowing force seven outside, the table was cranked up to keep the dozens of notes and photographs from being dumped on the floor. On the head and foot walls hung large flat-screen displays running a slide show of photographs of the target house and its environs.

The beautiful apartment building looked like it had been taken apart stone by stone in France and erected on a broad avenue in South America. In fact, much of BA's older architecture was in the French Empire style — with mansard roofs, ornate stonework, and innumerable columns. Because of the wealth in the Recoleta District, there were countless parks dominated by statues of past leaders. Many of the main streets had been built to accommodate the turning radius of eight-horse teams when wagons were the dominant mode of transportation.

Because he admittedly lacked any tactical ability, Max Hanley wasn't part of the meeting and stood watch in the op center. With Cabrillo were Mark Murphy, Eric Stone, Linda Ross, Eddie Seng, and Franklin Lincoln, their lead gundog. While civilian attire was the preferred mode of dress aboard ship, Eddie, Linda, and Linc wore black tactical uniforms. Mark had thrown a grunge-era flannel shirt over his St. Pauli Girl Beer T-shirt.

Juan took a sip of coffee and set the cup back into a recessed swivel holder. "To recap, we're not going to bring the ship within Argentine waters, so that leaves us with a submersible infiltration, yes?" Heads nodded. "I recommend we use the bigger ten-person Nomad 1000. We probably don't need the room, but better too much than too little."

"Who's tail-ended Charlie and gets stuck babysitting it?" Linc asked.

"Don't know until we firm up our plans. We have to assume a building like this will have a doorman. He might be our key. Not sure yet."

Eddie raised his hand despite Juan's repeated admonishments that he could interrupt whenever he liked. "If she's held on the top floor, wouldn't going through the roof make more sense?"

"It's slate, for one thing," Eric said. "And you can best believe that the substructure is going to be substantial. The cribbing and decking to support such a shallow pitch is going to be thick and sturdy."

"It's gotta be some god-awful exotic timber that's harder than steel," Murph added. "The building predates the use of metal girders as a support structure, so there are fundamental flaws in its design and construction. Explosives in the right place would topple an exterior wall."

"I'm looking for the velvet touch here," Juan said, "not a sledgehammer. We have to remember that Argentina is a police state, and, as such, there will be cops on every corner with the authority to arrest anyone at any time. And every third pedestrian's a snitch. I don't want to have any reason for anybody to give us the hairy eyeball. We need to be subtle."

"There's always the sewers," Linda suggested. "And if that's how we do this, let me go on record and volunteer to stay with the minisub."

"That's taking one for the team," Eddie teased.

"It'll be a sacrifice," Linda said with as straight a face as she could muster. "But you know me. I'll do anything to help."

Ideas were floated, analyzed, and dissected for the next two hours. The five of them had planned countless missions together, and in the end they could come up with nothing better than a slight variation on Mark Murphy's sledgehammerish suggestion. There were too many variables — like the number of men guarding Tamara — to try anything with more finesse.

The space where they could launch either of the two minisubs they carried buzzed with activity when Juan entered through a watertight hatch. The massive keel doors, as large as those on a barn, were still closed, and the moon pool was empty, but the air was heavy with the smell of the ocean.

Technicians swarmed over the sleek Nomad 1000. The mini looked like a scaled-down version of a nuclear submarine, only its nose was a convex piece of transparent acrylic capable of withstanding depths of more than a thousand feet, and robotic arms hung under its chin like the claws of some enormous sea monster. The conning tower was only two feet tall, and lashed behind it was a large black rubber boat. They wouldn't be going very deep on their run to shore, so the Zodiac had been filled with air already. All their gear was stored internally and would be transferred to the inflatable when they were closer to shore.

The extraction team consisted of Cabrillo, Linc, Linda, and Mark Murphy. Juan wouldn't have minded another gunner along, but he wanted to keep the group as small as he could. Mike Trono would drive the sub and stay with her when the others motored to the coast.

Kevin Nixon waved him over. The former Hollywood special-effects guru ran what the crew called the Magic Shop. He was responsible for creating any disguises the shore operators would need, as well as providing documentation. Though he himself wasn't a master forger, he had two in his division.

"These should pass, no problem," the tall, bearded Nixon said. He handed Cabrillo a folder.

Juan thumbed through the papers. There were Argentine IDs for the four of them, plus travel and work permits. All the documents looked authentic and properly aged. The thick sheaf of cash was real.

"First-rate, as usual," Cabrillo said. "Let's just hope we never need to use any of this stuff."

"Batteries are fully charged, nav and sonar check out, and life support is set," Trono reported when Juan approached. "Wish I was coming all the way with you."

"We don't know what condition Dr. Wright's going to be in, so I need Linc in case we have to carry her back to the Zodiac."

"I know, but, well . . . You know what I mean."

Juan laid a hand on Mike's shoulder. "I understand."

Max Hanley arrived. "Seas aren't going to get any calmer, so you might as well launch."

Cabrillo raised an eyebrow. "Here to see us off?"

"No, just to make sure you bring her back. I wasn't kidding about wanting to take Tamara out on a date. She's dynamite."

"The future of your love life is in capable hands. Were you serious about the weather?"

" 'Fraid so. Rain's coming down in buckets and won't let up until tomorrow night. Do you want to delay?"

Launching and recovering one of the submersibles was tricky enough in calm weather, but Juan wasn't tempted. Every second counted. "No. Not this time."

"Good luck," Max said, and turned to head back to the op center.

Cabrillo was neither superstitious nor a fatalist, yet somehow Hanley's wish made him uneasy. Wishing luck to someone going into danger was just bad luck. He roused himself. "Okay, people, let's saddle up."

He was the last one through the Nomad's hatch and he spun it closed, tightening the seal until an indicator light in the cramped conning tower flicked to green. Mike would see the same indicator in the high-tech cockpit. A second later the technician on launch control used the heavy machinery to lift the submersible off its rack while at the same time opening the controls that flooded the moon pool.

The lighting in the space switched from fluorescent tubes to red bulbs to help the crew adjust to the coming darkness. When the artificial basin was full, hydraulic rams opened the keel doors. Water in the moon pool sloshed dangerously, washing across the deck and dousing one technician with spray. The submersible held steady in its cradle.

It was slowly lowered into the water, waves splashing against the acrylic dome. It was too rough to risk divers in the moon pool, so a worker leapt across to the top of the sub and detached the cables while she was still floating inside the ship. Mike immediately dumped air, and the minisub dropped clear of the ship.

The water was pitch-black, and at this shallow depth they could feel the powerful South Atlantic surging above them. Until they were about fifty feet down, the Nomad dipped and swayed in a nauseating random ballet.

"Everyone okay back there?" Trono called over his shoulder after setting a westerly heading.

"There should have been a sign back there that said I was too short for this ride," Linda said. She massaged her elbow where it had been slammed into the steel hull.

Juan climbed through the austere cabin and plopped himself in the copilot's seat to Mike's right. "What's our ETA?"

"One second." Mike finished punching numbers into the navigation computer. It spit back the answer instantly. "We've got five hours in this can, provided we don't stumble on any Coast Guard or Navy ships."

"They'll never hear us in this slop." Juan leaned back so he could see the others. "Five hours. Might as well catch a few z's."

"Mark, you can share my bench," Linc said. "We can spoon."

"Forget it, Colossus. You never let me be the little spoon."

The ride in was uneventful. There was no shipping into or out of Buenos Aires and no military patrols. They surfaced a mile from shore. The proximity to land had calmed the waters somewhat, though rain fell steadily. Through the murk they could see the lights of the downtown high-rises as a spectral aura announcing the city. What was known as the Latin Paris looked ominous in the storm. A mile from them was a place of malice and fear, where the state controlled every aspect of its citizen's lives. To be captured would mean their death.

Juan organized the loading of their gear into waterproof bags. He lashed each one to the Zodiac as it was passed up to him from below. He suspected they were taking too much equipment, but there were variables within variables, and they needed to be ready for anything.

He fitted a headset over his ears. "Comm check, comm check, how do you read?"

"Five by five," Mike answered from the submersible's cockpit.

"Mind the shop while we're gone."

"You got it, Chairman."

Juan waited until the other three had clamored out the hatch and settled into the inflatable before releasing the lines that had kept it secured. As they floated free, he eyed another bundle of equipment they had left lashed to the deck and hoped against hope they would not need to use it.

The Zodiac's electric motor made a whine that was lost to the storm, and with its low profile they were all but invisible. Juan had to steer a few degrees off point because of the current of the mighty Rio de la Plata, the river that first attracted Spanish settlers to build BA.

They made their way toward the heavily industrialized port area where big freighters lay idle since so few countries maintained trade ties with the rogue nation. Cabrillo noticed that the ships here were registered to nations such as Cuba, Libya, China, and Venezuela. He wasn't surprised.

Because of the weather, there was virtually no activity on the docks that they could see from their low vantage in the inflatable raft. The big gantry cranes were immobile and the tower lights were off. He motored them under an unused pier whose concrete pilings were covered with mussels and sea growth that stank of iodine. The water was remarkably free of trash, thanks to the river.

Linc tied off the Zodiac while Juan cut the motor.

"Hi, honey, I'm home," Mark quipped. They all wore foul-weather gear, but Murph had a particular drowned-rat look to him.

Cabrillo ignored the joke. He had his game face on. "Okay, we all know the plan. Stick to it. We'll call when we've cased the building."

"We'll be ready," Linc replied.

Juan and Linda stripped out of their nylon rain pants and jackets. Under his, Cabrillo wore a thousand-dollar suit, which he quickly wrapped in a Burberry trench coat. His shoes looked like wingtips but were in fact combat shoes with nonskid rubber soles. Linda had on a red cocktail dress that was slit up high and cut down low. Her trench coat was black, and she wore boots that nearly reached her thighs. Like Juan's shoes, these were designed for ease of movement and traction. Only another woman would notice they weren't quite the apex of fashion. They had no heels.

Juan climbed the ladder built into the dock pylon first, and Linda shot her two crewmates a look that said, Peek up my dress and you'll regret it, before following him. She pulled a little feminine umbrella from her coat pocket and popped it over her head. Because he stood a solid ten inches taller, Juan couldn't fit under it with her, and as they started down the quay he had to duck several times to avoid having one of its thin metal ribs gouge out an eye.

It took them fifteen minutes to cross the sprawling port facility and reach the main gate. Flickering light from inside the guardhouse meant the security men were watching television. Juan and Linda strolled leisurely past, and a few minutes later found a taxi cruising the deserted streets. Cabrillo gave an address a few doors down from General Espinoza's building. One of the junta's laws mandated that the cabbie write down their names and addresses from their travel papers. It was one more way for the government to keep track of its people. The lack of freedom made Cabrillo's skin crawl.

He grabbed the newspaper someone had left on the backseat and used it to cover his head when he and Linda got out of the cab.

They walked the last few feet to their destination once the taxi had disappeared around a corner. The first floor of most of the buildings were leased commercial spaces — boutiques catering to the wealthy women of the neighborhood mostly, but a few restaurants that were closing up at this late hour. There were no other pedestrians on the broad sidewalk. The cars parked along the curb represented every German luxury-automobile company.

Falling rain slashed silver and gold in the lights cast from apartment windows above.

Espinoza's corner building had a glass-and-brass revolving door that Juan and Linda sped through like happy lovers, laughing at how wet they were and how glad they were to be home.

Cabrillo pulled up short almost immediately and laughed. "Oops. Wrong building," he said, grinning drunkenly. He escorted Linda back outside. The doorman barely had time to step from behind the counter before the well-dressed couple was gone. In all, they had spent seven-point-one seconds inside the building.

More than enough.

"Talk to me," Juan said as soon they were outside.

"The doorman's wearing a gun in a shoulder rig," Linda said. "There was one camera covering the front door."

Juan stopped dead in the street, disregarding the rain. "That's all you saw?" His tone was both mocking and disappointed.

"What? What did you see?"

"Okay first, the gun under his shoulder was obvious. His suit was tailored to highlight it. Anyone passing by was meant to see it. It's a deterrent. What you weren't supposed to see — and what you didn't — was the pistol strapped to his ankle. His pants flared like bell-bottoms to hide it, but not well enough. Guy that carries two pistols will probably have a submachine gun behind the counter. He's definitely Ninth Brigade and not the regular doorman. Tell me about the cameras."

"Cameras?" Linda asked. "We were in there for two seconds. Like I said, I only saw one camera, and it was covering the front door."

Juan took a breath. He had no desire to teach a lesson in this kind of weather, but he felt that to bring Linda along to the next level he had no choice. "Okay. We were in the lobby for a tick over seven seconds. From now on, you need to be precise. You observed one guard and one camera. Yes?"

Linda didn't want to reply, but she mumbled, "Yes."

"There was a second camera inside, just above the revolving door, that covers the elevator and also the counter where the doorman sits. It looks like it was just installed. The feed wires are exposed and just sort of strung up. Dollars to doughnuts, it was put there when they brought Professor Wright to this building, and it's monitored from the penthouse suite."

"How did you see it?"

"Reflection off the mirror next to the elevator doors."

Linda shook her head. "When I saw the mirror, the only thing I saw was us. Well, me, actually."

"Human nature," Juan replied. "First thing people always look in a mirror or in a photograph for is themselves. It's simple vanity."

"So what do we do now? Check the back service door?"

"No, it'll have cameras, too. We can get away with the tipsy, lost couple once, not twice. If they saw us again, they'd call the police, or just take us into custody themselves."

"We're going with Mark's idea?"

"Sledgehammer it is." They found a vestibule a few doors down that sheltered them from the rain. The street was so quiet that they'd spot an approaching police car long before they could be seen. Juan raised Linc on the tactical radio. "We're a go. How are you guys doing?"

"Mark's out on the street and already has a car hot-wired," Lincoln reported. "I've found what we need and am just waiting for the word from you."

"Mount up. About how long to get here?"

"So long as the harbor cops don't give me any trouble and we don't get pulled over, we should be there in an hour."

"See you when you get here." Juan switched frequencies. "Mike, you out there?"

"Just chilling with the fishes."

"Move to waypoint Beta." All locations had been worked out long in advance.

"On my way." There was a slight catch in Mike Trono's voice. He knew the Chairman was getting a bad feeling.

"Why reposition the sub?" Linda asked.

"It occurred to me that with this weather, there are going to be a lot of police with little to do. Once the alarm's sounded, we're going to have every cop in BA after us."

Linda suddenly had Juan's bad feeling, too.

They circled around the block, moving only when they were certain no one was watching. Once, they had to hide behind trash Dumpsters near a construction zone when a patrol car eased by. The officer wasn't scanning the curbs. He was just focused on driving through the downpour. A miserable man walking a little dog was the only person they saw, and neither group acknowledged the other. The weather was just too nasty for pleasantries.

Juan touched the Bluetooth in his ear. "Go ahead, Linc."

"Wanna let you know that things are going smooth. Bluffed my way past the guards, no problem, even if my Spanish is rusty and I look about as native as a rhinoceros. Tell people you need to borrow something for the Ninth Brigade and the questions come to a halt."

"That's the beauty of a police state. No one will stick his neck out. They've learned it can get chopped off."

"Mark's right ahead of me, and we're getting close."

"We'll see you coming."

Fifteen minutes later, a strange convoy rounded a far corner and started approaching. Murph was in the lead, driving a nondescript compact sedan. Emergency flashers on the roof were strobing a rhythmic orange beat as if to announce the vehicle behind him. Which was the point. Linc was behind the wheel of a mobile crane emblazoned with the logo of the Buenos Aires Port Authority. The vehicle really didn't have a body but rather a turret like an Army tank's, mounted on a heavy-duty chassis. Its wheels were twice the size of a car's tires. The collapsible boom was at its shortest but still protruded from the crane like a battering ram.

They would have to act fast because a big crane in the middle of a posh residential neighborhood would attract attention. Juan stripped off his overcoat and suit jacket and tore away the white oxford shirt. The clip-on tie went flying. It was a disguise, after all. Under it, he wore a black long-sleeved T-shirt and two empty shoulder holsters. He slipped on a pair of tight black gloves.

Linda was at the sedan's driver's-side door before Mark had come to a complete stop. She killed the two battery-operated flashers and plucked them off the roof. The suction cups used to hold them in place made an

389

obscene smacking sound. Murph ran for the crane at the same time as the Chairman. While Mark was heading for the cab, Juan leapt for the industrial hook dangling from the boom and climbed his way atop it.

He was met there by Linc, who handed over an MP-5 as well as a pair of Fabrique Nationale Five-seveN automatic pistols, Cabrillo's weapon of choice because the small 5.7-millimeter bullets could defeat most body armor at close range. The extralong suppressor on the end of the submachine gun made it unwieldy.

The team was moving as though they had been choreographed. Juan jammed the pistols into his shoulder holsters at the same time Mark settled into the crane's cabin and Linda legged into the sedan. Sitting astride the boom, Franklin Lincoln tightened his grip with his thighs a second before Murph hit the hydraulics to extend it upward.

It was happening this fast.

That was the plan.

The boom telescoped up toward the fifth floor. Mark kept the engine noise to a minimum, sacrificing speed for stealth, but to Juan the crane sounded like a snarling animal. He and Linc rose atop the boom as it aimed for one of the dark apartment windows. A light snapped on a floor below their target as a homeowner was woken by the noise outside his bedroom. Thankfully, Espinoza's windows remained black.

Mark rammed the tip of the boom through the glass, and Linc and Cabrillo launched themselves into the room beyond. They landed as agile as cats, and both had their weapons ready when a man wearing camouflage opened the door to see what was happening. Both guns spat, and the man went down.

Linc whipped a pair of plastic ties around the guard's wrists. The bullets they were using were hardened rubber — nonlethal, yet hitting with enough force to incapacitate a fully grown man. It was essentially the same as a blow from a baseball bat. They had considered using tranquilizer darts instead, but even the best drugs needed precious seconds to knock someone out.

This would be the duty guard watching the video feed from the lobby, Juan thought as he flipped the man's pistol under the four-poster whose huge size made him think this was the master suite. And the General is out tonight, which means the Chinese interrogators were probably out with him. He guessed there would be no more than three other guards watching over Tamara Wright. They'd caught a break.

Beyond the bedroom door was a hallway with mahogany floors and an Oriental runner. Light spilled from an open door a few paces away, and by its gray hue Juan knew it was where the guards had their monitor station. The ceiling in the hall was at least eleven feet, and the crown molding was the most intricate Cabrillo had ever seen.

Another door opened. The man wore nothing but boxer shorts and was wiping sleep from his eyes. Juan gave him a double tap to the forehead that would put him down for hours. With Linc covering his six, Juan peered into this new room. There were two beds, but only one had been slept in. The random thought that the lady of the house couldn't be too thrilled about soldiers sleeping on her fine linen popped into his head.

He opened the next door a crack and saw a tiled bathroom with a tub big enough to swim laps. He swung the door open just a bit more to let in light from the hallway and spotted three razors on the vanity and three toothbrushes sitting upright in a cut-crystal glass.

One more to go. The next door was a closet filled with towels and sheets, and the one after that was the General's study. The desk was enormous, and behind it, on a credenza, was a stuffed and mounted jaguar. From the size, it looked to be an adolescent female. Cabrillo was liking Espinoza less and less.

A gun went off behind him, a loud report that echoed off the tall ceiling. Linc twisted around the doorjamb as another round blew some molding into expensive slivers. Juan slung the MP-5 behind his back and pulled one of the FN pistols. Unlike the machine gun's, these bullets were hot-loaded with lead. His wet shoes squelched, but he suspected the gunman's hearing was compromised.

He ducked his head around the corner, low to the ground, and drew a snap shot that went high but gave away the Argentine's position. He was hiding behind the door at the end of the hall. A light was on in the room, and Juan could see the outline of his foot in the space between the door and the floor. He laid his automatic on the carpet runner and fired two quick shots. The spent brass arced inches from his face.

The scream echoed almost as loud as the gunshots. The bullet hit the gunman's foot and shattered the delicate bones. As he hopped onto his other foot, Cabrillo fired again. This bullet grazed the bottom edge of the door but still carried the energy to plow through flesh. The Argentine fell to the ground, moaning at the agony radiating up from his ruined feet. Linc moved fast, covering the unseen gunman with his own pistol held ready.

He swept into the room, checking corners automatically and kicking aside the fallen gunman's pistol. "We'll have you out of here in a second, ma'am," he said to Tamara Wright, who was handcuffed to a bed and gagged. She wore the same dress she had on aboard the *Natchez Belle.*

Juan came in right after him, and when she recognized the Chairman the panic and fear that swelled in her eyes subsided. He untied her gag and tossed it to Linc, who quickly wound it around the wounded guard's mouth to stifle the sounds of his agony.

"How did . . . ? How are . . . ?" So overwhelmed, Tamara couldn't get a question out.

"Later" was all Juan said.

Linc carried a heavy pair of bolt cutters in a scabbard on his back. He pulled them free like a samurai drawing his katana. It didn't take one tenth of his strength to cut the chain binding Tamara to the bed. They would remove the cuffs back on the *Oregon.*

"Have they hurt you?" Juan asked.

"Um, no. Not really. They've just been asking me questions about —"

"Later," he repeated. Getting to her was the easy part of the operation. Getting them all back out was going to be tricky. "Do you know how to swim?"

She could only stare at such an apropos-to-nothing question.

"Can you?"

"Yes, why? Never mind. I know, *later.*"

Juan admired her spirit and didn't blame Max one bit for wanting to date her. Tamara Wright had an inner core of strength that even the past few days of terror couldn't diminish.

He tapped his comm link. "Sitrep."

Linda's elfin voice filled his ear. "The doorman made a call as soon as he heard the shots. I figure we've got a minute, tops, before the cops arrive."

Cabrillo guessed less. "We're on our way."

"Mark's ready."

The three Americans retreated back the way Juan and Linc had assaulted the apartment. The hook hovered just outside the broken window. Linc lifted Tamara over the broken glass and set her directly atop a metal platform encircling the crane's cable just above the hook. While it made a perfect perch for them, its purpose was to prevent rats from climbing the cable in what was a millennia-long battle between rodents and mariners.

Lincoln climbed on directly behind her, shielding her body and holding her steady. "Don't you worry. Uncle Franklin's got you."

"Don't you mean Nephew Franklin?" she said.

As soon as Juan wrapped his gloved fist around the cable, Mark dropped them toward the sidewalk as smoothly as an Otis elevator. Linda had the car pulled over to the curb with the doors already opened. The windshield wipers beat furiously at the rain.

Mark jumped from the crane's cab, and he and Linc sandwiched Tamara Wright in the backseat. The feet wells were packed with equipment, forcing Linc's knees up by his head. Linda had slid over to the passenger's side, leaving Juan at the wheel. Sirens sounded in the distance. He put the sedan in gear and eased away from the curb as if they didn't have a care in the world.

Maybe the hard part is over, Juan thought, but he knew not to say it aloud.

The fates heard him anyway.

A big black town car raced into the intersection and slid to a stop a few feet from their bumper, forcing Cabrillo to jam on the brakes. Doors were thrown open, and a large bald man wearing a dress uniform erupted from the back of the Cadillac. He had a pistol in his hand and opened fire immediately.

The people in the sedan ducked as bullets cored through the windshield. Juan cranked the transmission into reverse and reached up to adjust the rearview mirror. A bullet whizzed close enough to his wrist that he could feel its hot passage, but now he could see behind them without exposing his head.

They backed up for fifty feet, beyond all but an expert's ability with a handgun, before Juan mashed the emergency-brake pedal and spun the wheel. The wet asphalt helped him pirouette the woefully underpowered car in a slide worthy of a Hollywood chase.

He released the brake, dropped the car into first, and accelerated away. One more bullet hit the car, a wild shot that mangled one of the wing mirrors.

"Is everyone okay?" he called without taking his eyes off the road. It was like driving through a continuous waterfall.

"Yeah, we're fine," Mark replied. "Who was that?"

"General Philippe Espinoza, whose house we just raided. He must have been on his way back from dinner when the doorman called."

"That was the man asking me questions," Tamara told them, "him and the creepy Chinese guy named Sun. I could tell he was from Beijing, and I'm pretty sure he was State Security."

"Here in Argentina on a diplomatic passport, no doubt." The sirens were getting closer. Juan slowed. The only way out of this was to not attract attention and hope they could lose Espinoza, because the General was surely coming after them. "Mark, are you ready with our bag of tricks?"

"Say the word, Chairman."

Juan was thinking about chain of command. Espinoza doubtlessly knew someone in the police — a chief or commissioner, most likely. Fifteen minutes would pass by the time the General called his friend, who would in turn call someone lower in the police hierarchy, and so on, until a description of their car made it to the patrols out on the streets. If they could elude Espinoza and not draw attention to themselves, they would be halfway across the city before the APB went out.

He glanced in the mirror just as the town car careened around the corner one block back. Juan was driving an overloaded Mitsubishi and had no illusions that he could outrun the big American V-8 even if the car was carrying armor, which it probably was.

Juan made two quick turns, and slowed as a police car with lights flashing went streaking past followed closely by another unmarked car.

His confidence evaporated when he saw both cars brake heavily in his mirror. It took them a few moments to turn around on this narrow street, forcing Espinoza to stop completely. Obviously, the General knew someone a lot lower down on the food chain than Cabrillo had estimated. He should have figured a man like Espinoza would know the neighborhood precinct's commander.

In seconds, all three cars would be in pursuit, and the little Mitsubishi's description would be on police radios all across Buenos Aires. He'd been right about one thing. Getting Tamara out of the apartment was the easy part of the night's work.

They turned into a narrow alley, and Juan shouted, "Now," to Mark Murphy.

Murph already had his windows down, and he began pulling pins on smoke grenades as fast as he could. These were of the Corporation's own design and produced faster and denser smoke than even those used by the U.S. military. After the third one hit the street, Juan could see nothing behind him but a thick haze that even masked the streetlights and the illumination from second- and third-floor windows.

"Enough," Juan said, and he made another series of random turns. His throat felt as dry as dust, but his hands remained loose on the wheel and his focus never wavered.

"Just curious," Linc said from the backseat. "Does anyone know where we are?"

"Linda?" Cabrillo said.

She had a handheld GPS and studied the screen intently. "Yeah, I've got a pretty good idea. We're heading in the general direction of the docks, but up ahead is a maze of streets. We need to cut to our left where there's a pretty big avenue.

The town car emerged from a cross street without warning. It slid neatly behind the sedan, pressing so hard on its suspension and tires that a hubcap came loose and spun across the sidewalk like a Frisbee. The driver knew this neighborhood better than even the police who patrolled it, and had outguessed Cabrillo.

Gunfire spat from the passenger's window, where a bodyguard leaned out with a big pistol in his hand. Linc twisted his considerable bulk and unleashed a full magazine from his machine gun. The rubber bullets were useless against the Caddie, but the psychological impact of a full-auto attack forced the chauffeur to brake hard and crank the wheel over. They scraped against a series of parked cars and set off a chain reaction of shrieking alarms and flashing lights.

Linc dropped the H&K and unholstered his Beretta. If the town car was armored, the pistol would do no more damage than rubber bullets, but it was better than nothing.

"What about more smoke?" Mark suggested.

This street was too wide to block with the grenades, so Juan said nothing and watched his mirrors. By the time the Cadillac took up the chase again, it was being tailed by the police cruiser. There would be dozens more converging on the elegant streets of the Recoleta District. They needed to ditch the car and find another.

There was a construction site to their left. The street had been torn up by large yellow excavators, and scaffolding spiderwebbed across the façade of a columned building. Juan looked closer and realized it was a large ornamental gateway. He assumed there was a park through the closed gates and turned for it, pushing the little four-cylinder for everything it had.

The car maintained traction across the muddy ground, and Juan lined up the nose.

"Brace yourselves!"

They flashed through the scaffold latticework, bounced up one low step, and slammed into the gate. Cabrillo had expected a cataclysmic impact, but the gates were being repaired and had been leaned into place at the end of the work shift. The chain holding them together stayed in place, but the ornate wrought-iron panels crashed to the ground, and the Mitsubishi roared over them. The collision didn't even deploy the air bags.

Juan realized his mistake instantly. This wasn't a park, and it took a few seconds to understand what it was. Laid out in neat grids like a Lilliputian city were thousands of beautiful buildings made at about one-fifth scale. They were as ornate as any they had seen all night, with marble columns, bronze statues, steepled roofs, and all manner of religious iconography.

This wasn't a park. It was a cemetery, and those weren't miniature buildings but, rather, grand mausoleums.

After Arlington National in Washington

and Père Lachaise in Paris, the Cementerio de la Recoleta was perhaps the most famous cemetery in the world. All of the city's most wealthy and prominent figures, including Eva Perón, were laid to rest in some of the most decorative and stunning aboveground crypts ever built. It had become a tourist destination almost as soon as it had opened.

It was also a maze too tight for a car and was walled in on all four sides.

Juan had led them into a dead end.

TWENTY-ONE

They had no choice but to make the best of his mistake.

"Mark, pop smoke! Everything you've got."

As Murph started heaving more smoke grenades in their wake, Juan committed them to one of the wider lanes through the ranks of mausoleums. The cobbled path was tough on the car's overtaxed suspension, and the path was so narrow that a slight miscalculation cost the Mitsubishi its remaining wing mirror.

They had gone no more than fifty feet when the footpath narrowed even further because of an oversized marble crypt. They couldn't turn around. Juan glanced over his shoulder. Another path met this one at a diagonal. He put the car in reverse and backed into it, scraping paint off the doors against the statue of some politician or other. The only saving grace was that the rain was finally letting up a bit. Visibility was still poor, especially with the smoke drifting eerily around the tombs, but it had improved. The other consolation was neither the police car nor the Cadillac would be able to follow them.

He wondered if they would chase after them on foot and decided they probably would. The rage he had seen on Espinoza's face could only be slaked with blood.

The car clipped a marble bust and tore it off its memorial. The stone head rolled across the cobblestones like some misshapen bowling ball. It took all of Juan's defensive driving lessons to keep the car from caroming into the crypt on the opposite side.

He saw the path divide again and backed into the wider-looking route. It narrowed almost instantly, with a mausoleum that looked like a replica of a local church. He pulled forward and then backed down the other way. With so little light, it was next to impossible to keep straight, and again they scraped against one of the decorative monuments. He said a silent apology to the person's ghost and kept going.

To his left flashed a larger alleyway. The turn was so tight that it took him several tries, and a lot of smashed marble and crumpled sheet metal to make it. If they somehow got out of this, Cabrillo promised himself that the Corporation would make an anonymous donation to the cemetery's keepers.

A cat, for which this place was famous, dashed out of its hiding place right in front of the car, its fur soaked to its skin, in the glow of the only functioning headlight. Juan slammed on the brakes instinctively. The feline gave him a contemptuous look and slunk off.

The world suddenly went white. It took a second for Juan's eyes to adjust. Overhead, an unseen helicopter had thrown on its searchlight and created an oasis of daylight in the otherwise stygian cemetery. An amplified voice echoed down from above.

Cabrillo didn't need to translate for the others. Any order from a police chopper was pretty universal.

"Linc, do something about him, will you."

Franklin cranked down his window and thrust his machine pistol skyward. There wasn't enough room to lever his big torso out of the car, so he opened fire without sighting in on his target.

Seeing the tongue of flame flickering from the car was enough to convince the chopper pilot to back off, much like Espinoza's chauffeur had done. The searchlight vanished for only a moment before the helo came back again, flying aft of them and at a greater altitude.

The trail through the tombs turned sharply, but Juan managed to scrape the car through without having to stop.

If there was any coordination between the air and ground units, the pilot would be vectoring the cops from the patrol car to their position. Juan kept a sharp eye out, craning his neck left and right, as they sped past narrow passages. He saw nothing, and was moving fast enough that even had an officer been approaching from the side he would only have time for one snap shot that would surely miss.

Then they caught a break. The path branched, and they found themselves driving on the perimeter walkway that bordered the cemetery's exterior wall. After negotiating such close quarters, it seemed as wide as a highway.

Their second break came almost immediately. As part of the cemetery's refurbishment on the main gate, a section of wall had also been removed. A temporary barrier of plywood and wooden studs stood in the opening. The angle was all wrong to get any sort of speed, but Juan went for it anyway.

"Brace yourselves," he warned for the second time in five minutes.

The car hit the barricade with its front fender and splintered the wood but couldn't punch through. The wheels spun furiously on the slick cobbles, bowing the partition more and more until some critical point was met. The plucky little Mitsubishi tore through the wall and raced across a deserted sidewalk before Cabrillo could throw it into a four-wheel drift.

They had escaped the cemetery but not the chopper, which was doubtlessly radio-ing their position.

"Linda, get us back to the docks."

She was hunched over the GPS with her fingers dancing across the screen. "Okay, turn left at the second cross street, then get into the right lane for another sharp turn."

Juan did as she ordered, but, no matter what they did, they drove in a corona of hard-white light from the chopper. In his mirror, he saw two patrol cars suddenly ap-pear. They were racing hard, their sirens ris-ing and falling like banshee wails. There was no way on earth to outrun them.

Linc smashed out the rear window with the butt of his H&K and sprayed a fusillade of rubber bullets. The cops kept coming.

Either they knew about the nonlethal ammo from previous attacks or they just didn't care.

The lead car came up on their rear corner and tried to bump them into a skid. Juan countered the maneuver, his hands a blur on the wheel. Linc switched to his pistol and put two rounds through the patrol car's passenger's window. There was only the driver, and his courage failed him. He dropped back to a more respectful distance.

Cabrillo was beginning to recognize his surroundings. They were getting closer to the docks. "Mark, show Tamara how to use the pony."

"Already on it," Murph replied.

Juan tapped his radio. "Mike, are you in position?"

"I await your arrival," Trono said breezily.

"We're coming hot."

The sub operator became more serious at hearing the Chairman's tone. "I'm ready."

Shots rang out from behind them — big, concussive booms from a handgun. The passenger in the second cruiser was leaning out and firing his sidearm. A lucky shot punctured the trunk and erupted through the backseat in a flurry of foam rubber. Tamara shrieked. Linc and Mark Murphy just exchanged a look, and the big former SEAL turned to fire back.

"Next right," Linda called over the roar of wind whistling through the car. "That's the dock."

Juan took the turn so fast that the car slid into the guard shack hard enough to shatter the plate-glass window on the side of the building. The men inside dived for the floor, thinking they were under attack. The two cruisers were seconds behind them.

"Lower all the windows," Juan ordered as he guided the car around rows of shipping containers.

That last impact had damaged something vital. The car rose and fell on its suspension like the swaying of a camel. The rear axle had been damaged by the collision and Cabrillo's frantic driving, and it snapped. The two ends dug into the pavement and threw up fountains of sparks whenever they crossed sections of concrete roadway or the steel railroad tracks for the dock's big overhead cranes. The front-wheel drive motored on gamely despite the damage.

Juan patted he dash affectionately. "I'll never denigrate another Japanese compact again."

The pier was almost a thousand feet long, half its width shielded by a corrugated-metal roof on an open I-beam framework.

Juan wrestled the car down its length. He didn't look over when Linda tapped him on the shoulder and handed him an object about the size of a water canteen but with a hose and mouthpiece attached to one end. He clamped the mouthpiece between his teeth.

Keeping his foot to the floor, he raced them to the edge of the pier. There was no need to shout a warning. Everyone could see what was coming up.

The car hit the end of the dock and shot off into the darkness, arcing nose-first because of the weight of its engine. It hit the water in an explosion of white froth, the impact no worse than any of the others they had been put through tonight. Because all the windows were open and the rear window gone, the car filled quickly with frigid water.

"Wait," Juan cautioned.

Not until the roof had gone under did he lever himself out his window. He hovered at the passenger's door, holding on with one hand and helping Tamara out after she had crawled over Linc. It was too dark to see anything, but he gave her hand a squeeze, and she squeezed back. He could feel bubbles from her regulator rise past his face. Her breathing was a bit elevated, but, given the circumstances, so was Juan's. Remark-

411

able woman, he thought.

The pony bottle contained enough air for just a few minutes, so when the others struggled out of the sinking car Juan led them back under the pier, where a tiny speck of light beckoned.

It was a penlight attached to a pair of scuba tanks with multiple regulators. The tanks themselves were strapped to the top of the Nomad 1000 submersible. Had things gone smoothly, they would have met the minisub a couple miles from shore in the Zodiak, but there was always the contingency that the raid wouldn't go as planned so Juan had come up with an alternative. He had ordered Mike Trono to waypoint Beta — under the pier where they had tied the inflatable.

As soon as the group of swimmers reached the sub, Juan placed one of the regulators in Tamara's hand and motioned for her to switch off from the pony bottle. Given her ease in the water, he rightly assumed she'd been diving before. There was just enough light for him to indicate that Linda should cycle through the air lock and into the Nomad with Tamara.

As he waited for his turn, Juan could see flashlights playing across the surface of the water where air continued to escape their dauntless Mitsubishi. He wondered how long before the cops sent in divers, then decided it didn't mater. They would be long gone.

Ten minutes later, with the sub creeping away with the current, Cabrillo released the inner hatch on the minisub's cramped air lock and stepped over the coaming. Everyone was lined up on the benches huddled in foil blankets. Tamara and Linda had toweled off their hair and somehow managed to tame it.

"Sorry about that," Juan said to the professor. "We had hoped it would go a lot smoother. Just bad luck the General showed up when he did."

"Mr. Cabrillo —"

"Juan, please."

"All right, Juan. Just so long as you got me away from those" — she paused because the invective she was about to use wasn't for polite company — "horrible people I wouldn't have cared if we had to crawl our way over hot coals."

"They didn't hurt you?" he asked.

"I was telling Linda that I didn't give them a reason. I answered everything they asked me. What was the point of holding back information about a five-hundred-year-old ship?"

Juan's face turned grim. "You probably hadn't heard, but Argentina annexed the Antarctic Peninsula, and China is backing them. If they can find that shipwreck it will further solidify their territorial rights. This is also a bid for oil, and I'm guessing the reserves are substantial for such a big risk. Once that starts flowing, they can use the revenue to buy up votes in the United Nations. It'll take some time, but I bet within a couple of years their seizure of the peninsula will be legitimized."

"I didn't tell them where the ship sank," Tamara said. "Because I don't know. They believed me."

"There are other ways. I guarantee they're looking for it as we speak."

"What are we going to do?"

The question was almost pro forma, asked without really thinking. Just something a person says when faced with an obstacle. But to Juan, it was loaded with meaning. What *were* they going to do? He'd been wrestling with that since Overholt told him the White House refused to get involved.

This wasn't their fight. As Max would say, "This dog don't hunt."

However, there was his sense of right and wrong. He certainly didn't feel a responsibility to help out, that was never his motivator.

Instead, he was bound by a code of ethics that he would never compromise, and it was telling him the right thing was to get involved — to take the *Oregon* down into those icy waters and take back what had been stolen.

The rest of his crew was looking at him as expectantly as Tamara Wright. Mark cocked an eyebrow, as if to say "So?"

"I guess we're going to make sure they don't find that ship."

TWENTY-TWO

"Welcome to the Crystal Palace, Major. I'm Luis Laretta, the director."

Jorge Espinoza stepped off the rear ramp of a big C-130 Hercules cargo plane and grasped the man's outstretched glove. Laretta was so heavily swaddled, it was impossible to see his features or discern his stature.

Espinoza had made the mistake of not lowering his goggles before moving into the frigid air and he could feel the cold trying to solidify his eyeballs. The pain was like the worst migraine imaginable, and he quickly pushed the goggles into place. Behind him his men stood at attention, all of them kitted out for cold-weather combat.

The flight down from Argentina had been monotonous, as most military flights were, and, except for landing on skis on a runway made of ice, there was little to distinguish it from the hundreds he had taken before.

They were here to spearhead security in the wake of the annexation announcement. If the United States or any other power was going to attempt to force the Argentines out of Antarctica, it would happen soon, and most likely be attempted using commandos air-dropped by parachute. With a Chinese Kilo-class submarine recently purchased from Russia patrolling the choke point between the extreme tip of South America and the peninsula, an air assault was the only viable option.

Espinoza and a hundred members of the Ninth Brigade were sent southward on two transports to stop them.

The rationale was simple. When Argentina invaded the Maldives in 1982 — the islands the British called the Falklands — the English had telegraphed their intentions to retake them with a months-long deployment of ships from their home ports. This time, the Argentine high command believed, there would be no warning. The reprisal would be a lightning-quick attack by Special Forces troops. If they could be met with an equally prepared group of soldiers, the first attempt to retake Antarctica, if repulsed, would most likely be the last.

"You have to love the Army," Lieutenant Jimenez said as he strode up to Espinoza's side. "A couple days ago, we were sweating our butts off in the jungle, and today they're turning colder than frozen hams."

"I was all that I could be," Espinoza replied, a private joke between them referencing an old American Army slogan.

Jimenez called out to a Sergeant to see to the men while he and Major Espinoza followed Laretta on a tour of the installation.

They had timed their landing in the brief period when weak sunlight poured over the horizon. It wasn't much more than twilight, but it was better than absolute darkness. The shadows they cast on the ice and snow were indistinct, more like murky outlines than hard silhouettes.

"How many men are down here?" Espinoza asked. Laretta had a warmed-up snowcat waiting at the edge of the airfield. The men would have to hike the mile to the facility, though their gear would be transported on towed sledges.

"Right now, only four hundred. When we ramp up oil production, there will be better than a thousand here and out on the rigs."

"Amazing. And no one knew a thing about it."

"Two years of construction, under the worst conditions imaginable, and not a hint of rumor about what we were doing." There was well-deserved pride in Laretta's voice. He had been in charge since the beginning. "And we lost only two men the entire time, both from the sorts of accidents you see on any large construction project. Nothing to do with the cold at all."

Laretta peeled down his goggles and pushed back his parka as soon as they were settled in the big-tracked vehicle. He had a wild mane of silvery hair, and a thick beard that spilled onto his chest. His face was pale from so many months without sun, but the deep wrinkles around his dark eyes gave him a rugged quality.

"Of course the trick about building down here is fuel, and since we were tapping an offshore natural gas well almost from the beginning we had a steady supply. We were asked early on by the Antarctic Authority about the ship we used. We told them it was for drilling core samples, and they never bothered us again." He chuckled. "They neglected to ask why it didn't move for more than two years."

It took just a few minutes to reach the base, and almost as long for Espinoza and Jimenez to grasp the scale of what their countrymen had accomplished. So cleverly camouflaged and so artfully laid out that even the keenest observer wouldn't see it unless they were right on top of it. The only thing out of place was the matte-gray Argentine warship sitting at anchor in the middle of the bay. There was a faint glow from her bridge, but otherwise the cruiser was dark.

Laretta pointed. "Under those three big hills right on the edge of the bay are oil storage tanks big enough to fuel every car in Argentina for a week."

"How is it the bay is free of ice so early in the summer?" Espinoza asked.

"Ah, my dear Major, that is my pride and joy. Parts of it actually never freeze. There is a series of pipes strung out along the bottom. It is very shallow, by the way. We pump superheated air through the pipes and let it escape out of millions of tiny holes. The bubbles not only heat the water but when they break the surface they crack any thin ice that's forming. You can't see it because it is too dark, but the bay's entrance is narrow enough for us to run a continuous curtain of hot air to keep the water mixing with the rest of the Bellinghausen Sea."

"Incredible," Espinoza breathed.

"Like I said, with limitless fuel anything's possible down here. You see where the buildings are set. It looks like ice, yes? It's not. The entire facility sits on a polymer-composite sheet with the same refraction spectrum as ice, so from the satellites it appears that the beach is frozen. It's a petrochemical we actually make here. After getting the natural gas plant up and running, it was our first priority. All the buildings are made of the same material, except for the large geometric tent that shelters our vehicles. That's woven Kevlar. We needed it to withstand the winds."

"I feel like I'm looking at some kind of moon base," Jimenez said.

Laretta nodded. "For all intents and purposes, it is. We have created a working environment in the most inhospitable place on the planet."

"Tell me about the defenses," Espinoza invited.

"I've got an eight-man security force. Well, seven men. One was killed in a Ski-Doo accident. They're all ex-police. They patrol the camp perimeter, break up fights among the workers — that sort of thing. Then there's the *Admiral Guillermo Brown* out in the bay. She's loaded with antiship and antiaircraft missiles as well as two twenty-millimeter cannons. We also have four fixed antiaircraft missile batteries here on shore. And now we have all of you. The captain of the *Brown* is in overall charge of at least his ship and our missiles. I'm not sure about . . ."

"We take orders directly from Buenos Aires. The captain knows this."

"Sorry," Laretta said, "I don't know much about military command. When I was a kid and other boys were playing soldier, I sat in my room and read histories of Roman engineering feats."

Espinoza wasn't listening. He was thinking about what a big fat target the cruiser was, just sitting out in the bay. If he were the opposing commander, the first thing he'd do after his Special Forces made contact was to hit the warship with a cruise missile from a submarine and then take out the shore-based batteries with radar-homing missiles launched from an aircraft. Not a carrier plane. Sending an aircraft carrier would telegraph their intentions. No, he'd stage the plane out of McMurdo, using aerial refueling. If need be, then, the attacking commandos could be augmented with troops flown in on C-130s like the one he himself had arrived aboard.

He needed to discuss this with his father and have it relayed to the *Brown*'s captain. Once the shooting starts, the ship should be moved and the shore batteries' radars turned on only intermittently.

This was all contingent on the Western powers responding to the annexation militarily, which wasn't a foregone conclusion. And that, he believed, was the genius of what they had pulled off. With China backing them, there was a strong chance that no one would send a force south to dislodge them and that his country had gained one of the biggest oil reserves in the world as easily as taking candy from a baby. The double threat of the Kilo-class submarine, and the ecological devastation if the base was attacked strictly by bombs and missiles and its oil spilled, was a strong deterrent to ensure they went unmolested.

Espinoza was torn. On the one hand, he wanted them to come. He wanted to test himself and his men against the very best in the world. On the other, he wanted to see his country's bold strategy so intimidate the West that they didn't dare retaliate. As director Laretta prattled on about the facility, he realized he had no right to be torn. He was a warrior, and as such he wanted the Americans to send their finest troops. He did not want merely to repulse them. He wanted to humiliate them. He wanted to turn the ice red with their blood.

"Tell me, Luis," he interrupted, just to stop the director from speaking on and on about the facility, "have our guests arrived?"

"Do you mean the foreign scientists from the other bases? Yes, they are being guarded by my small security force in a maintenance shed."

"No. I mean our friends from China."

"Oh, them. Yes. They came in yesterday, with their equipment. I assigned them a workboat. They've been getting it ready. Is there really an old Chinese ship sunk someplace in these waters?"

"If there is," Espinoza replied, "then we can forget any chance of a reprisal. Our claims to the peninsula would be legitimized by history. I would like to meet them."

"Certainly."

He steered the snowcat off the escarpment overlooking the base and down a track worn into the ice. When they were in the facility itself, Espinoza was amazed at the level of activity. Men in arctic gear were working on oddly shaped buildings and countless personal snowmobiles zipped about, many towing sleds laden with what he assumed was oil-drilling gear. Where the natural snow had blown away in spots, he could see the composite mats made to look like ice, fitted together like the artificial runways he'd seen erected in the jungle. It could easily take the weight of their big vehicle.

There were several workboats tied up on a quay easily large enough to accommodate the *Admiral Brown*. They were all about forty feet long, steel-hulled, with large open spaces on their sterns and blocky pilothouses hunched over their bows. They were painted white, though much of their cargo areas had been so scraped up by material they transported out to the disguised rigs that bare wood shone through. Service boats like these were ubiquitous at offshore drilling sites all over the world.

Laretta parked alongside one of the crafts. Men bundled against the cold were working on a torpedo-shaped device sitting in a cradle under an A-frame crane mounted to the stern. None looked up from his task as the three men approached. One of them finally glanced at them when their weight made the boat bounce as they stepped aboard. He detached himself from the group and came over.

"Señor Laretta, to what do we owe the pleasure?" The man was covered head to foot, and his voice was muffled by scarves wrapped around his face. He spoke accented English.

"Fong, this is Major Espinoza. He's the commander of our augmented security force. Major, this is Lee Fong. He heads the

425

technicians sent out to find the *Silent Sea.*"

The two men shook hands so heavily gloved it was like grabbing a balled-up towel. "Is that a sonar unit?" Espinoza asked.

"Side-scan," Fong replied. "We'll tow it behind this boat, and it profiles a hundred-meter swath of the ocean floor."

"You have a rough idea where the wreck is located, yes?"

"From what I understand, we have you to thank for it."

Espinoza wasn't sure if he liked the fact that the Chinese knew of his exploits, but then he realized his father had been bragging about him to their newest allies and he felt pride replace his trepidation. "We got lucky," he said.

"Let's hope we stay lucky. Wrecks are a funny thing. I've had GPS coordinates, loran numbers, and eyewitnesses, and I've still failed to find one. Other times, I've found them on the first pass with no information other than the ship had sunk in the general area."

"Will the cold affect your gear?"

"That's the other factor. I've never searched in waters like this. We won't know how well the sonar will work until we get it in the water and test it here in the bay. We're hoping for today, but the light's going, so it will probably have to be tomorrow."

"From what I gather of the situation, we have more than a little time," Espinoza said. "The Americans are still reeling from our announcement, and they're too afraid of your country's reprisal if they launch a counterstrike."

"Fortune favors the bold," Fong said.

"That's attributed to Virgil," Luis Laretta told them. "It's a Latin expression, *Audentes fortuna juvat*. There's another, by Julius Caesar, that's also apt — *Jacta alea est*. He said it on his march to Rome when he crossed the Rubicon River."

Raul Jimenez surprisingly supplied the translation: "The die is cast."

TWENTY-THREE

With no landmass to break its cycle, winds circled the earth at the lower latitudes in endless loops that built and built. Below the fortieth parallel, they were called the Roaring Forties. Then came the Furious Fifties and the Screaming Sixties. A constant wind of eighty miles per hour wasn't unusual, and gusts of a hundred were an everyday event. The effect this had on the sea was ferocious. Waves built to forty and fifty feet, huge rolling masses of water that tossed aside everything in their path. Even the great icebergs that calved off the mainland glaciers were no match for the ocean when the winds came up. Only the superbergs, as large as cities and sometimes small states, were immune.

It was into this hell that Juan Cabrillo drove his ship and crew. Everything that could be tied down had been, and all activity except essential services was suspended.

Although the ship had crossed southward only a week earlier, the weather then had been downright tranquil compared to what was hitting them now.

Any other ship would have turned back or faced being torn apart by the waves. But Juan had so overengineered his beloved *Oregon* that she was in no real danger. Her hull could take the stresses, and there wasn't a seam topside that the wind could exploit to start peeling back sheet metal. The davits holding her two lifeboats would not fail even in a category five hurricane. Though, right now, she only carried one of them. The other had been set adrift with a ping locator activated so they could recover it later.

But there was a real danger. Not from the ocean but from the prowling Chinese fast-attack submarine. She was somewhere between the tip of South America and the Antarctic Peninsula. This was a choke point much like the GIUK Gap that NATO used to box in Soviet submarines at the height of the Cold War. They had set up pickets of subs, like fishermen, between Greenland, Iceland, and the United Kingdom, and waited for their catch to come to them.

Juan had laid a course toward Antarctica by staying close to the South American coastline, as if the *Oregon* were making for the Drake Passage around Cape Horn, and then heading dead south into the Bellinghausen Sea, the area the Argentines and Chinese had said was now forbidden to shipping.

Now he had to put his mind into that of the Chinese sub captain. With a couple hundred miles to patrol, Juan had to guess where he would be. The obvious answer was the middle of the narrows between South America and Antarctica. That would give him maximum coverage. But any ship making a dash southward would make that assumption and avoid the middle like the plague. So do they stay close to the peninsula or run a westward end around. The sub couldn't be in both places. A wrong guess would put them square in the Kilo-class's sights.

Cabrillo remembered an old school-yard saying. Never play chicken with a stranger. Meaning, if you don't know your opponent, you can't control the outcome.

He sat in the command seat in the middle of the op center, his body swaying with the roll of his ship. All on-duty personnel were strapped into their chairs with lap and shoulder harnesses. He hadn't shaved this morning — water wouldn't stay in the sink — so when he ran a hand across his chin, his beard rasped. East or west, he thought. East or west?

"Radar contact," Linda Ross called out.

"What have you got?"

"Aircraft flying south at twenty-five thousand feet. Speed three-eight-five. Range twenty miles."

Juan looked at her sharply.

"He must have dropped out of the clouds."

It had to be a big Hercules aircraft heading down with more supplies for the Argentines, Cabrillo thought. "Helm, show me the rear-deck camera."

Eric Stone typed a command into his computer, and the image on the main view screen switched to a camera mounted just below the jack staff at the very stern of the ship. Even in such heavy seas, the *Oregon*'s wake was a white slash through dark gray water leading right up to the ship. They couldn't announce themselves more if they had put on every light and broadcast across every frequency.

Juan's decision about east or west was moot. He knew the plane would radio their presence to the Argentines, who would pass that information on to the Chinese submarine. The Kilo-class would be coming after them like the hounds of hell.

"Can we jam his radios?" he asked.

"As long as he's in range," replied Hali Kasim, their communications specialist. "As soon as he moves on, he'll be free to report our position."

"We can shoot him down," suggested Mark Murphy from the weapons station next to helm control. "I can have SAM lock in in fifteen seconds and splash him ten seconds later."

"Negative." As tempting as it was, Juan wouldn't consider it. He had always been a firm believer in letting the other guy throw the first punch. He toggled his microphone to make a shipwide announcement. "This is the Chairman. There's a real good chance we were just spotted, and that means the sub knows where we are. We're already at combat stations, but I want all hands to be extrasharp."

"What does this mean, Juan?" Tamara Wright asked. He had forgotten all about her, as she sat strapped in to one of the damage-control stations over his shoulder.

He spun around in his chair to look her in the eye. "It means I should have gone with my gut and forced you off the ship when I had the chance."

Her chin lifted slightly and her eyes narrowed. "You would have had to knock me unconscious and truss me up."

"I know, and I should have done it."

"And left me alone in that little lifeboat of yours in these conditions? No way and no how," she countered. "Besides, there's a lot you don't know about me, and one thing is I never walk away from a fight."

"This might not be a fight but a turkey shoot. That submarine has all the advantages going for it."

"Then if my fate is to die with all of you, I am ready to accept that."

"Sounds like Eastern fatalism to me."

"I grew up in Taiwan, remember." She slipped her yin-and-yang pendant from under a blouse lent to her by the Magic Shop. "I'm a Taoist. It's not fatalism I believe in, just fate."

"You're as stubborn as Max. I can see why he has a thing for you." Over Juan's other shoulder, he heard Max Hanley groan aloud and the sound of his palm slapping his forehead. He swiveled to look at his second-in-command. "Sorry, Max, was that a secret?"

Max's blush started at the base of his throat and didn't stop until the crown of his head was as red as a cherry. Snickers filled the op center. Juan felt bad for teasing Hanley like this, but he needed something to relieve the tension.

"Mr. Hanley, I had no idea." Tamara's smile was genuine. "Come to think of it, my Mississippi cruise was cut short because of you. I think it only fair that, when this is all over with, you find some way to make it up to me."

Married and divorced three times, Max had always been comfortable around women, especially the ones he found attractive, but for the first time Cabrillo could remember his friend was tongue-tied.

"Helm," Juan said to get their heads back in the game. "What's our current speed?"

"Twenty-one knots. That's the best we can manage in these seas."

"I'll get you an extra ration of grog if you can get us a few more knots. Also, alter course to one-zero-five for the next ten minutes, then back to eighty-five. The old zigzag worked for allied convoys, so lets hope it works for us."

The *Oregon*'s two torpedo tubes were flooded, though their outer doors were still closed. Linda Ross was covering their sensor suite, and they were doing everything they could to confound the Chinese sub. There was nothing left to do but wait and hope they snuck through.

Juan didn't know how he did it, but the

ship's phlegmatic chief steward suddenly appeared at his shoulder with a big thermos of coffee and Styrofoam cups with plastic lids.

"What, Maurice, no Royal Doulton?" he teased, knowing he'd never get a rise out of the English septuagenarian.

"Considering the circumstances, I thought a less delicate alternative was more appropriate. If you wish, I can return to the pantry for a proper china service."

"This is fine. Thank you. I know I could go for a cup."

Maurice managed to pour cups all around and not get a single drop on his snowy-white apron. And how he maintained traction in spit-polished wingtips was a mystery for another day.

"I gather from your announcement, Captain, that the first watch will be on for the duration?" Maurice had retired from the Royal Navy and wouldn't abide by calling Cabrillo anything but Captain. He was as much a stakeholder in the Corporation as any of them, but this was a ship, and its commander was called Captain and there would be no argument about it.

"Looks that way."

"I will make sure to bring you dinner at six. Again, taking the weather into consideration, I think it best I serve something you don't need utensils to eat. Perhaps burritos?" He said the last word with ill-disguised disgust.

Juan smiled. "Whatever you think is best."

"Very good, sir." With that, he slipped away as silently as a cat.

The hours dragged on. There was minimal conversation, just an occasional whispered word, a quick order, and then silence once again. The only real sounds were the swoosh of air through the ventilators and the noises made by the ship and sea as they fought against each other. The hull would creak. Waves would slam. And all the while water sluiced through the ship's drive tubes under enough force to speed her up to twenty-five knots.

Juan had put off going to the head for as long as he could possibly take it. The nearest facilities were just beyond the op center's back door, but he didn't want to leave for even the minute it would take.

He had just unsnapped his shoulder harness and was reaching for his lap belt when Linda cried. "Contact! Sonar. Bearing two seventy-one degrees. Range, five thousand yards."

Cabrillo could hardly believe she could hear a submarine at that distance in these conditions, but Linda Ross knew her job.

Juan forgot all about his bladder. "Do you have a depth and heading?"

She had one hand pressed to her earphones and the other danced over her keyboard. Above her was the electronic green wash of the waterfall display. "Still working on it, but I definitely have prop noises. Okay. Hold on. Got you. She's at one hundred and twenty feet. Still bearing two seventy-one."

No change in her bearing meant they were heading straight for the *Oregon.*

"Helm, full emergency stop, then turn us with the thrusters until we're at ninety-one degrees," Cabrillo ordered. That would take them directly away from the sub and minimize the time her flank was exposed. The Chinese wouldn't know what to make of a contact that could pull off such a maneuver. He wondered if the Argentine aircraft had gotten a good enough look at them to know their target was a merchantman and not a naval vessel.

The magnetohydrodynamics wailed as Stone brought up full power and reversed the variable-pitch impellers in the drive tubes. As the speed bled off, the ocean swells attacked the *Oregon* as if angered that their power was being challenged. The ship heeled over nearly forty degrees when they were broadside to the waves, and water swept her decks from stem to stern.

Using the bow and stern thrusters, they turned as tightly as a bottle cap, and as soon as they were on the correct heading, Eric changed the impellers again and kept the engines firewalled.

"Range?" Cabrillo called out.

"Four thousand yards."

The sub had gained almost a mile on them as they were turning. Juan did a quick calculation, and said, "Mr. Stone, just so you're aware, the Kilo's coming at us at twenty-three knots."

In response, Eric dialed in emergency power.

The ride was brutal, like being on a bucking bronco. The ship shuddered so badly that Juan feared his fillings would loosen, while each climb up a wave was a vertiginous journey surpassed only by the gut-wrenching descent. Cabrillo had never called on his ship to give him more.

"Range?"

"Four thousand one hundred."

A cheer went up. Despite it all, they were pulling away from the submarine. Juan patted his armrest affectionately.

"Contact," Linda cried. "Sonar. New

transient in the water. Speed is seventy knots. They've fired! Contact. Sonar. Second torpedo in the water."

"Let go countermeasures," Cabrillo ordered.

Mark Murphy worked his magic on the keyboard, and a noise generator was released from a pod under the keel, though it remained attached to the ship on a lengthening cable. The device emitted sounds like those the *Oregon* was making and was designed to lure the torpedo away from the ship.

"The first torpedo's coming strong. The second has slowed. It's going into standby." The Chinese captain was keeping one of his fish in reserve in case the first missed. It was good naval practice. "Range is two thousand yards."

In combat, time has an elasticity that defies physics. Minutes and seconds seem interchangeable. The tiniest increments can go on forever while the longest duration is gone in an instant. It took the torpedo a little over two minutes to halve the distance, but for the men and women in the op center it seemed hours had elapsed.

"If they go for the decoy, it should happen in about sixty seconds," Linda announced.

Juan caught himself clenching his muscles and forcibly willed his body to relax. "Okay, Mr. Stone, cut power and go quiet."

The engines spooled down evenly, and the ship began to slow. It would take at least a mile to come to a stop, but that wasn't the goal. They wanted the torpedo to concentrate solely on the decoy they were towing.

"Thirty seconds."

"Take the bait, baby, take the bait," Murph urged.

Juan leaned forward. On the big monitor, the sea behind the *Oregon* looked as dark and ominous as ever. And then a geyser, a towering column of water, erupted from the surface and rose nearly fifty feet, before gravity overcame the effects of the explosion and the geyser began collapsing back in on itself.

"Scratch one decoy," Mark crowed.

"Eric," Juan said calmly, "turn us about with ten percent power on the thrusters. The acoustics are going to be scrambled for a while, but keep it quiet. Wepps, open the outer doors."

Mark Murphy opened the ship's two torpedo doors, as they came about and pointed their bow at the approaching submarine.

"Linda, what's he doing?"

"He's slowed down so they can listen, but he's maintaining his depth. And that second torpedo's still out there someplace."

"He'll want to hear us sinking," Juan said, "rather than surfacing. Mark, oblige him."

"Roger that." He typed in commands on his computer, and an electronic track began to play. The speakers were attached to the hull and they pumped out the sounds of a ship in its death throes.

"It just occurred to me," Cabrillo said. "We should have the speakers on a wire we can lower from the hull. It'd be more realistic." He looked over at Hanley. "Max, you should have thought of that."

"Why didn't you?"

"I just did."

"A little late to help us now."

"You know what they say —"

"Better late than never."

"No. They say, Wepps, fire both tubes."

Mark hadn't been fooled by the repartee, and he launched the torpedoes the instant the order came.

Jets of compressed air blew the two-ton weapons from the tubes as their electric motors came online. In just a few seconds, they were homing in on their target at sixty-plus knots. Cabrillo used the keypad on his chair to switch the view screen to the forward camera. The torpedoes left twin wakes of white bubbling water that streaked away from the ship.

"That second fish will be after us in about three seconds," he said. "Open the forward redoubt for the Gatling gun, and crank it up."

A cleverly hidden door at the bow crashed open, and the multi-barrel snout of the Gatling emerged. The cluster of barrels was spun up until they were just a blur. Capable of firing four thousand 20mm tungsten rounds a minute, the weapon had the capability of tearing through enough water to reach the torpedo as it homed in on the ship. They had stopped a similar attack in the Persian Gulf when an Iranian submarine had taken a shot at them.

"Contact. Sonar. Their fish has gone active. Oh, no!"

"What?"

"She's at three hundred feet."

Juan understood the implications immediately. Unlike their last fight with a Kilo-class, where the water had been shallow, here the Chinese captain had the sea room to order his torpedo deep and come up on them where a ship is most vulnerable — along the keel. A modern vessel can survive a massive explosion along her flank — witness the USS *Cole* — but a blast under the hull will snap its spine and usually result in it breaking into two pieces and sinking within minutes.

"Who's going to win the race?" Cabrillo asked.

"Their fish is inside ours by a hundred and fifty yards and coming at us four knots faster. It'll hit us a full minute before ours hits him."

Juan considered and rejected option after option. There simply wasn't enough time to maneuver away, and the seas were too rough for the *Oregon*'s unparalleled speed to be a factor.

"Wepps, sound the collision alarm. Eric, I'm transferring helm to my station."

Over the electronic warble of the alarm came another mechanical sound.

Max, who knew the ship better than anyone, was the first to realize that Juan had opened the big moon-pool doors. He quickly grasped what the Chairman intended. "Are you out of your mind?"

"Got a better idea? So long as that torpedo uses a contact fuse rather than a proximity signal, there's a chance we can pull it off."

"And if he does detonate just under the keel?"

"Having the doors open or closed won't

change a thing." Cabrillo turned to Linda. "You're my eyes. Guide me into position."

"What do you want me to do?" She still didn't understand.

"Thread the needle with that torpedo. I want it to come up directly below the moon pool. With a little, no, with a lot of luck, that thing will fly clear when it broaches. That should snap its guy wires. After that, it's nothing but a big paperweight."

"You are nuts," she said, and looked at Max. "He is."

"Yes, but it actually might work."

She returned to her display. "Depth is still three hundred. Range, one thousand yards."

The torpedo maintained its track, staying deep as it raced for the *Oregon*. Because of the guy wires running back to their sub, the Chinese couldn't take evasive maneuvers against the two torpedoes tracking them. Juan had to hand it to the Chinese captain. If the roles were reversed, he would have gotten out of there as soon as he heard he was under attack.

"Range, four hundred yards. Depth, unchanged. Time to impact, about forty seconds."

The Chinese commander wouldn't alter the torpedo's depth until it was directly under the ship, and then he would send it straight up on its killing charge.

"Range, one hundred yards. Depth, unchanged. Juan, it's about twenty feet to starboard of our center line."

Cabrillo kicked on the thrusters to push the *Oregon* laterally through the water. With the sea heaving so much, it was going to take more than the lot of luck he'd mentioned. It was like threading a needle, only the hand holding the needle was wracked with tremors.

"That's good. Okay, she's coming up. Depth, two-fifty. Range, twenty yards."

The sonar dome on the underside of the hull was thirty feet back from the bow. Cabrillo had to keep that in mind. The torpedo was twenty yards from the sonar but ten from his ship. The moon pool was directly amidships of the five-hundred-and-sixty-foot freighter.

"Depth, one-eighty feet. Horizontal range from the bow is five yards." A second later, she amended, and said, "Depth, one-fifty. Range, three yards."

Juan ran the vectors in his head, calculating the torpedo's glide slope as it arrowed in on them, his ship's speed and position, and how the waves were affecting her. He had one shot or they were all going to die. There was no margin for error. And there

445

was no hesitation. He slammed on full power for less than two seconds and then threw the impellers into reverse. The ship lurched forward, shouldered aside a big breaking wave, and slowed once again.

"Depth, fifty feet. Range is zero."

Eric keyed on a fish-eye camera attached high up on a bulkhead, overlooking the moon pool. Water surged from the hole in the ship in black glossy mounds that spilled over onto the grated floor and sank to the bilge.

"Depth zero," Linda said in an emotionless monotone.

Like Leviathan rising from the deep, the bulbous nose of the Chinese torpedo exploded out of the moon pool. Meeting no resistance, its motor thrust the weapon fully out of the water. Its quick last-second acceleration was enough to snap the two guy wires trailing miles back to the sub. It crashed back into the water, ringing like a bell when it hit the edge of the pool. And then it sank from sight. With no control inputs coming from the mother ship, the onboard computer shut the weapon down.

A victorious roar filled the op center and echoed throughout the ship, where other crew members had been watching video monitors. Max slapped Cabrillo on the back hard enough to leave a red handprint. Tamara hugged Juan briefly, and then Max much longer.

Cabrillo made to leave the room. "Chairman," Linda called to stop him. "What about the sub? Our torpedoes hit in forty-five seconds."

"I'll be in the head if they need me."

He was in the restroom, sighing contentedly, when another cheer went up. The fish had done their job, and the route to Antarctica, and the end of this affair, was open.

TWENTY-FOUR

A light touch on the shoulder woke Jorge Espinoza. Like any good soldier, he was awake instantly. His aide, Corporal deRosas, stood over him, holding a mug of what he hoped was coffee.

"Sorry to wake you, sir, but a large ship has appeared at the mouth of the bay."

"A warship?"

"No, sir, a freighter. It's beached."

Espinoza threw off the thick sheaf of blankets and regretted it immediately. Though the overseer, Luis Laretta, had boasted that fuel wasn't a problem for the facility, the air in the building they used as a billet had a perpetual chill that seeped into everything. Espinoza pulled on two pairs of long johns before donning fatigue pants. On his feet went three pairs of socks.

"Has anyone aboard tried to make contact?"

The aide opened the metal blinds to let in

what passed for sunlight in this godforsaken deep freeze. The room was barely big enough for the bed and a dresser. Its walls were painted plywood. The single window overlooked the back of another building just three feet away. "No, sir. The ship appears abandoned. One of its life rafts is missing from the davits, and, judging by how beat-up it is, it looks like it was deserted some time ago. Sergeant Lugones scoped it with a thermal sight. Nothing. The ship's stone-cold."

Espinoza took a swig of the strong coffee. It didn't go well with the film in his mouth, and he made a face. "What time is it?"

"Nine A.M."

Three hours of sleep. He'd survived on less. He and Jimenez and a couple of Sergeants had been out most of the night, scouting the hills behind the base for ambush sites. The fractured terrain was a natural fortification, with hundreds of places to position fire teams. The only problem was keeping them warm. Today was going to be dedicated to seeing how long the men could stay in position and still maintain combat efficiencies. The Sergeants guessed four hours. His estimation was closer to three.

He finished dressing and downed the rest of the coffee. His stomach rumbled, but he decided to investigate the mystery ship before breakfast. "Wake Lieutenant Jimenez."

It took just fifteen minutes in one of the workboats to cross the bay. The effect of the warm air bubbler was amazing. Not only was the bay ice-free, the air directly over it was a warm fifty degrees, while at the base it had been a bone-chilling ten below. Beyond the bay, a crust of ice rose and fell with the waves as the first inkling of summer tried to melt it away. There was a clear path out to the open ocean, where an icebreaker continuously plied back and forth to maintain a vital link back home.

The workboat passed close enough to one of the oil platforms to see that its camouflage was thin sheets of riveted metal designed to make it look like an iceberg. From fifty yards away, the only way to know it wasn't the real thing was the massive steel support columns that peeked out from under its white skirt.

At the narrow entrance of the bay, they passed over an area of agitated water. This was the curtain of warm air rising up from the pipes that prevented ice from flowing into the harbor. For the few seconds it took to cross, Espinoza was warm for the first time since arriving in Antarctica.

He turned his attention to the ship. It was old, that was for sure, and possessed a haunted quality even if he hadn't known it was abandoned. The hull was a mishmash of marine paint, blotchy and streaked, as if applied by children. Her upper works were mostly white, and her single funnel a faded red. She had five cranes, three fore and two aft, making her what seamen call a "stick ship." Since containerization had taken over maritime commerce, such ships were considered outdated, and most had long since been turned to scrap.

"What a rust bucket," Lieutenant Jimenez commented. "I bet even the rats abandoned her."

As they got closer still, they could see that she wasn't a small ship. Espinoza estimated her length at well over five hundred feet. Her name was difficult to make out because the paint had faded and was streaked with rust, but he could see she was called the *Norego*. Twenty feet of her prow was hard up on the pebbled beach. There was another workboat pulled up next to the massive bows, and a group of men standing around. One was erecting an aluminum extension ladder that looked tall enough to reach the rail, barely.

Espinoza's boat pulled up alongside the

first, and a crewman threw a line to one of the soldiers. He heaved the boat in as close as he could while another crewman lowered a gangplank that was nothing more than a twelve-foot piece of lumber.

Sergeant Lugones snapped a salute as soon as the Major's padded boots touched the rocky beach. The sky was clear, for once, and the temperature was a relatively balmy ten below zero.

"Quite a sight, eh, Sergeant?"

"Yes, sir. Damnedest thing I've ever seen. We spotted it at first light and came out to investigate. Begging the Major's pardon, but I thought it best you stay in bed and get some beauty rest."

From anyone else, that would have been gross insubordination, but the gristly Sergeant had more than earned the right to tease his commanding officer from time to time.

"You'd need a thirty-year coma to help that mug of yours," he called back, and the men who heard snickered.

"All set, Sarge," the soldier working the ladder called over.

Espinoza was the first to climb up, with two men bracing the base in case of a wind gust. He had modified his outer gloves so he could peel back the index finger, and when he unholstered his pistol he could get his finger through the trigger guard. He peered over the gunwale. The deck was a mess of loose clutter, oil drums, and scrapped pieces of nautical gear. He saw no movement, so he climbed over and signaled for the next man to join him.

Wind moaned though the crane's rigging, a warbling keen that sent shivers down his spine. It sounded like a dirge. He looked up at the bridge windows but saw nothing but the reflection of the sky.

Raul was at his side a moment later, followed by Lugones. The Sergeant carried a machine pistol with a powerful flashlight secured under the stubby barrel. They crossed the deck, moving carefully, and with one of them always covering the advance of the others. There were no hatches on the forward bulkhead under the bridge, so they moved to the starboard rail and proceeded aft. Here, they found a door just a few feet away. Above them were the two skeletal arms of the empty davit. A steel cable hung from each.

Jimenez undogged the latches, and when he glanced at Espinoza, who nodded, he pulled open the door. Sergeant Lugones had his weapon at the ready.

The interior hallway was dim, so he

snapped on his light. The paint job inside was about as bad as the exterior. The linoleum floor was badly chipped in places and looked like it had never seen a mop.

Their breaths formed halos around their heads.

"Looks like nobody's home."

"A wry observation, Lieutenant. Let's get to the bridge. If there are any answers to this mystery, that's where we'll find them."

The men climbed up several decks, checking rooms as they went. Judging by the way the furniture had been tossed around, it was clear the derelict had seen some heavy weather. Beds had been overturned, and a great number of the wooden pieces had been smashed. They found no evidence of the crew, living or dead.

The bridge was broad and dim because of the rime of salt on the windows. Again, they found nobody, but on the chart table behind the helm was a piece of paper that had been placed in a plastic sleeve and heavily taped in place.

Lugones used a combat knife to cut the paper free and handed it to his superior.

Espinoza read aloud: " 'To anyone who finds this, we were forced to abandon the *Norego* when the pumps failed and the sea poured through a breach in the hull caused by a rogue wave. Chief Engineer Scott did everything in his considerable power, but they would not restart. The decision was not an easy one to make. These are treacherous waters far from any shore. But a floating lifeboat is better than a sinking ship. I pray for my men. If we don't make it, please tell my wife that I love her and our boys very much. It is safe to assume that goes for all the men and their families.'

"It's signed 'Captain John Darling of the Proxy Freight Line,' and, get this, it's dated January of last year. This old girl's been adrift for twenty months."

"Think the crew was rescued?" Lugones asked.

Espinoza shook his head. "No idea. I'm wondering why the ship didn't sink. For a captain to abandon his vessel, he should be damned sure of his reason. I want to check the engineering spaces."

It took several minutes and more than a few wrong turns to find a stairwell that led down into the guts of the ship. As soon as Jimenez pulled the door open, a six-inch surge of icy water washed over their boots. Lugones trained his light into the stairwell. It was completely flooded. The water was thick with oil and flashed rainbow spectrums at them.

"That answers that," the Sergeant said. "She's flooded, all right."

"I wonder what she was carrying." Jimenez mused. "If I remember my salvage law, whoever finds her gets to keep not only the ship but her cargo."

"And when did you study salvage law?" Espinoza asked sarcastically.

"Okay. I saw something on TV about it."

"Tuck your larcenous hands back in your pockets. We're soldiers, not scrap dealers. More than likely, this heap will drift off again at the next high tide or when another storm brews up."

"Think we should pop some more holes in her to make sure she sinks for real this time?"

Espinoza considered Lugones's question. "You know what? No. Let her keep wandering. If she's survived this long, more power to her."

A deck below where the three men stood, Juan Cabrillo relaxed back into his chair. He hadn't thought the Argentine Major, whose face he was beginning to see in his dreams, had a romantic side. That had been his one main concern — that they would use the *Oregon* for target practice. These soldiers were once boys who probably liked to blow stuff up. The only difference is, now they had plastique explosives rather than firecrackers. The crew had defeated the thermal imaging by cutting the heat to the "public" parts of the ship, lowering the temperature in the rest, and letting the flooded ballast tanks shield them from the scan. The trick with the flooded staircase had been accomplished by simply closing the bottom hatch and pumping in some bilgewater.

Cabrillo looked over at Max Hanley, who was shaking his head. "What?" he said. "I told you I could hide the ship right on their doorstep."

"This doesn't count," Max groused.

"The more outrageous the lie, the more easily it's accepted. By rights, they should be suspicious as hell, and look at them. They called off the search after ten minutes, and our good Major is practically in tears."

"I'll give you this, Juan. You are one crafty SOB. So now what? You got us here. What's your plan?"

"To be honest, I hadn't thought much past this point. You did notice the piece of cargo under the tarp on the second boat?" The outside cameras had been watching the soldiers since the first group arrived at sunup.

"Seems about the right size and shape for a side-scan sonar probe."

"Means they're going to be looking for the Chinese wreck."

"I assume we're going to beat them to it?"

"See, the plan reveals itself," Cabrillo said with the self-satisfied grin of a kid pulling one over on his parent. He really hadn't thought much beyond getting the *Oregon* into position.

Max nodded toward the image of the soldiers milling around near the bow. "We'll need to wait until that lot sods off before we can empty enough ballast to open the moon-pool doors."

Juan nodded. "I suspect they'll start searching today, so as soon as they pass by in the workboat, we'll do our thing. When Tamara wakes up, ask if she'd like to join us. The least we can do is show her the fabled Treasure Ship before we destroy it."

That was the first Hanley had heard about that, and he stared at the Chairman for a moment before seeing the logic. "It'll be a shame, but you're right. It can't be helped."

"I know. We can't afford to give the Chinese even the slimmest chance of staking a claim down here."

An hour later, Juan released the clamps holding the thirty-two-foot Discovery 1000.

The three-person submersible didn't have an escape trunk like her big sister, but no one had any real desire to swim in water that was just a fraction of a degree above freezing.

Cabrillo sat in the reclined pilot's seat with Tamara on his right. Linda Ross had drawn the lucky number to accompany them, although with the temperature chilly enough for them to see their breaths in the cockpit she wasn't sure how lucky she felt.

"Can't we crank the heat a tad?" she asked, blowing on frozen fingertips.

"Sorry, but the bay we identified off the satellite pictures is at our maximum range. We need the endurance more than the comfort."

"Won't the Chinese already be there?" Tamara asked. She was bundled in an arctic parka, with another draped over her long legs.

"Nope. They went the wrong way. There are two similarly shaped bays around here. One to the north and one south. Because of the body Linda and her team found at Wilson/George, we know the wreck has to be in that direction. Those guys are going to spend the next week or so surveying fifty miles from where they should."

For the next three hours, they cruised at

twenty feet. Because of the weak polar sun, it was nearly black even this shallow. Juan relied on the sub's sonar and lidar systems to navigate. At least the seas were calm. Had the weather been foul, running so close to the surface would have been like taking a ride inside a clothes dryer.

Linda and Juan kept Tamara entertained with some of the crazier stunts the Corporation had pulled off, making certain each story painted Max in the best light. If she suspected they were putting on the hard sell for their friend, she didn't let on. They drank sweetened tea and ate gourmet sandwiches prepared in the *Oregon*'s world-class galley.

"The nav computer says we're coming up on the bay," Cabrillo informed his passengers. "The depth here is five thousand feet, but the bottom will come up sharply."

Juan had been thinking about where in the fjordlike cove the Chinese ship would have been sunk. He assumed they would have been as close to shore as possible, and in the satellite pictures he had spotted what he believed to be the best area. There was a beach of sorts, or at least an area where the towering mountains and glaciers were much lower.

He steered the submersible into the mouth

of the bay and plotted a course to the spot. He kept one eye on their side-scan sonar. As he had predicted, the bottom was rising at better than a sixty percent gradient. It remained featureless rock without so much as an outcropping. Had the incline below them been above water, it would have been nearly impossible to scale.

"I can't believe we're doing this," Tamara said for the third or fourth time. "Just a few days ago, I was half certain Admiral Tsai Song and the *Silent Sea* were just legends, and now I'm about to see her for myself."

"If we're lucky," Juan cautioned. "A lot could have happened in the past five hundred years. She could have been ground into toothpicks by the ice."

"Oh. I hadn't thought of that. Do you think that happened?"

"Not really. Eric and Mark, you met them on the bridge —"

"The two who don't look old enough to shave?"

"That's them. They're crackerjack researchers. They looked into archives from the 1957–58 International Geophysical Year, the last time anyone took measurements of this area. The mountains around the bay were never named, but a survey team checked the glaciers and found them to be about the slowest moving on the continent. If the ship is in deep enough water, she wouldn't have been affected even when the surface froze over."

Cabrillo rubbed his hands together to restore some circulation. He checked their battery level and determined they had more than enough but left the heat control untouched. He would rather spend more time surveying the bottom on this trip than have to go through it all over again tomorrow.

They saw their first sign of life when a leopard seal swooped in close to the acrylic view port. It pirouetted in front of them, its body trailing a wreath of bubbles, and then it vanished as suddenly as it appeared.

"Cute little fellow," Linda remarked.

"Not if you're a penguin."

Juan eyed the bottom profiler. The slope they had been traveling over was leveling out as it neared the shore, which was still about three miles away.

"Whoa," Linda called.

"What do you have?"

"I just got a strong hit off the magnetometer to starboard."

Cabrillo eased over the aircraft-style yoke, and the submersible swung right, not as elegantly as the seal, but she responded much better than their big Nomad. "Check out the sonar," he said.

Directly in front of them was what to the electronics looked like a solid wall measuring three hundred and eight feet long and forty high. It was three hundred yards away — still too distant, in the poor lighting. The motors purred sedately as they neared. When it was fifty feet off, Juan toggled the floodlights mounted over the pressure hull.

Tamara put her hands to her mouth to stifle a gasp. In seconds, tears coursed down her smooth cheeks.

Though he hadn't invested a lifetime studying the subject, Juan couldn't help but feel emotional as he gazed across time and distance at the massive Chinese junk lying on the bottom of the Bellinghausen Sea.

The masts had long since vanished, most likely broken off by a passing iceberg, and there was a huge hole in her hull just below where her bottom had been clad in copper. Other than that, she looked perfectly seaworthy. The low salinity and frigid temperatures meant there was little life in these waters to attack the wood. She couldn't have been better preserved if she'd been left in a windless desert.

Just above her waterline were dozens of ports. Juan asked about them because he doubted they were windows.

"For oars," Tamara replied. "A ship this size would probably have twenty to a side, and each one would have at least two rowers, sometimes three. She would have had probably six or seven masts that were square-rigged like all junks."

Nearer still, they could see that the long superstructure that ran almost the entire length of the ship had been painted a buttery yellow with red trim and possessed pagoda-like architectural details.

"The Emperor would have insisted that his ships be as ornate as possible," Tamara continued, "in order to show off the wealth and sophistication of his kingdom. Only the finest artists and craftsmen would have been allowed to work on them."

"And you said she was loaded with treasure?" Linda asked.

"You showed me that lump of gold you recovered. And those shards of jade."

"The crewman who survived the sinking and died near Wilson/George must have pocketed them from the stores," Juan said, and flew them up and over the huge ship. "It's possible the prions hadn't progressed that far yet, and he still had his wits about him." Dr. Huxley had confirmed that the Chinese mummy and Andy Gangle were riddled with them.

Over the bow were two large cannons shaped like dragons. They were scaled-up versions of the pistol they had found next to Gangle's corpse. There was so little slime on them that Juan could see teeth etched around the bore and wings carved along their flanks.

The aft deck was actually three stories taller than the main, and there was a square house dead in the middle with an elegantly sloped roof. Tamara pointed toward it. "That would be for the captain's use."

"His cabin?"

"More like an administrative office."

Juan brought them down again and nosed the submersible up to where Admiral Tsai had placed the explosive charge that scuttled the ship and killed its ill-fated crew. The xenon lights threw what little of the interior they could see into sharp relief. The decks were wooden, as were the walls. The room they were looking into was too broad for them to see the far side and contained a veritable forest of support columns. Too many, in fact, and it was Tamara who recognized what they were seeing.

"This is one of the crew's berths. They hung hammocks from the columns."

Juan added, "They were still doing it that way into the twentieth century, at least on warships."

"This is just amazing," Tamara breathed. Her eyes were wide with wonder.

"Now for the bad news," Juan said. She looked at him sharply. "We have to destroy it. I brought you along so you could see it with your own eyes, but we can't let the Chinese find her."

"But —"

"No buts. I'm sorry. Once we convince the Argentines that it's in their best interest to abandon their plans here, we can't leave a window open for Beijing to fill the vacuum. They're riding on the Argentines' coattails because they have no claim. This gives them one. A damned big one, at that. They discovered Antarctica three hundred and eighty years before the first European laid eyes on the continent."

"I . . ." Tamara's brow furrowed. "I hate politics. This is one of the most significant archaeological finds in history and it has to be sacrificed so some power-hungry men can't get their hands on a bunch of oil."

"That's it in a nutshell, I'm afraid," Juan said as kindly as he could. "The stakes are too high for anything else. Our government has decided it doesn't want to play the role of world cop, but we need to show people that there are still consequences for breaking international law. One of the ways we have to do it is to destroy that wreck."

She didn't look at him, or even speak, but after a second she nodded slightly.

Juan laid a hand on her shoulder for a moment, then went back to the controls. He vented some water out of the ballast tanks, and as the submersible rose toward the surface the light slowly became brighter.

When they broached, Juan climbed out of his seat and over Linda to reach the topside hatch. "Back in a second."

He stood to the side when he spun open the locking wheel to avoid the deluge of freezing water that cascaded to the deck. He climbed up the integrated ladder, his hands going numb on the wet steel. He popped his head out of the hatch. The chill took his breath away. Needles of agony pierced his sinuses, and it felt like his eyes were being seared. Juan ignored all this and concentrated on his surroundings. A tongue of ice stood poised in the gap between two black mountains that soared at least two thousand feet into the sky. The ice formed a vertical wall between them that ran right to the water. The bottom edge had been partly eroded by waves and tides, but the rest looked like a solid massif.

"You'll do," he said aloud, his words torn

from his mouth by the wind, and then he ducked back into the relative warmth of the submersible.

His first act when he retook his seat was to crank the heater to maximum, power-reserve requirements be damned.

TWENTY-FIVE

A team lead by Mike Trono was heading to the bay where the *Silent Sea* lay on the bottom even before Juan and the others returned to the *Oregon*. Juan had radioed his instructions for them to take the larger Nomad back up north and get to work on making the wreck disappear. Mike had five others with him and almost a ton of gear crammed into the submersible.

They were in for a cold, miserable night.

After what was the longest, hottest shower of Juan's life, and learning that the Argentine's survey boat hadn't spent more than an hour in the wrong location before coming back to base, he met with his department heads to go over the next phase of their operation. The meeting went quickly. In the idle hours motoring back from the wreck site, Cabrillo had developed a plan that needed little refinement. He was back in the moon pool less than two hours after returning home.

Rather than take the time to recharge the Discovery's batteries, technicians swapped them out for fresh ones, and they changed the carbon dioxide scrubbers and refilled all her air tanks as well. For this mission, Juan chose Franklin Lincoln to accompany him. He wasn't expecting any gunplay, but the big former SEAL moved like a wraith despite his size and had been on more covert insertions than almost the rest of the crew combined.

By the time they were ready to leave, Kevin Nixon arrived with arctic clothing his staff had modified to closer resemble the gear the Argentines wore. Once they were bundled into the jackets, pants, hoods, scarves, and goggles, they would be completely anonymous.

It took them ten minutes to enter the narrows. Even submerged, they could see the aura of lights on the far shore. With machinery on the oil platforms banging and whining, the waters sounded like a wrecking yard. The industrial clatter masked the sound of their motors, so there was no need for stealth as they started across.

"What's that noise?" Linc asked as they were gliding along at thirty feet.

"The oil platforms?"

"No. Like a low-frequency gurgling sound. It was really strong when we first entered the bay, and, while it's gotten quieter, I can still hear it."

Juan concentrated, and he, too, picked up the strange tones. He chanced turning on one of the weaker floodlights. From the surface, it would look like the moon's reflection off a wave. In its glow, he saw curtains of tiny bubbles rising up from the seafloor. And as his eyes adjusted further, he and Linc spotted the lattice of pipes laid across the ooze and how they were the source of the bubbles.

He killed the lights, and the two men shared a look.

"Any ideas?" Linc finally asked.

"That's how they keep the bay free from ice." He checked one of the computer displays. "Yup. That's it. The water temperature is near sixty degrees. They must use the vent gas from the oil platform to heat air and force it through the pipes. Pretty ingenious, when you think about it."

Moments later, they passed within a hundred yards of the big cruiser resting at anchor.

"Any thoughts about what we're going to do about her?"

Juan could almost sense its dark presence

in the inky water, like some great predatory shark. A fight between the *Oregon* and the cruiser would be short and brutal and would most likely end with both ships on the bottom. "Hopefully, inspiration will strike tonight."

Twenty yards short of the piers, Cabrillo extended the Discovery's low-light television periscope. It was no bigger than a pack of cigarettes, and the pictures it took went to an HD display in the sub as well as aboard the *Oregon*. A dozen sets of eyes studied the docks as Juan panned the camera back and forth for the next few minutes. Other than the workboats tied to the pier, there was nothing to see but concrete pylons. It was simply too cold for men to stand watch for any significant period of time.

Cabrillo also suspected that, for now, the Argentines were feeling good about their accomplishment and didn't believe they were in any danger yet. Later, perhaps, there would be an armed response, but for the next few days the world would continue to reel from their audacious play.

He guided the sub under the dock and slowly brought her to the surface. Less than eight inches of her hull broached, and the coaming around her hatch was a mere five inches taller. With her hull painted a deep blue, the submersible was all but invisible. Add to that, an observer aboard the workboat would have to be on his knees and looking under the pier, so their chance of detection was virtually zero.

The two men felt like a couple of contortionists when they donned their parkas, but a few moments later Linc popped the hatch and climbed up onto the deck. There was little clearance, and he had to work stooped over as he tied off the submersible so it wouldn't move when the tide changed. Cabrillo stepped off the minisub and onto the port side of one of the workboats. Linc climbed up next to him, and, as if they didn't have a care in the word, they moved onto the dock and approached the Argentine base.

This was the first good look Juan had of the facility, and he was amazed by its size and scope. He knew from Linda's pictures that there was room around the bay to more than triple its size. Given free rein, there would be a real town here before too long.

The first order of business was to locate where the Argies were keeping the international scientists they had kidnapped and were using as human shields. It was eight o'clock at night, and, as they suspected, there were hardly any people about. They saw an occasional shape moving amid the buildings, but most people were wisely inside. When they peered through the occasional lit window, they could see men lounging around on sofas watching DVDs or playing cards in rec rooms or in their own private bedrooms reading books or writing letters home. The first area they checked seemed to be dorms for the oil workers, an unlikely candidate.

They searched several warehouses, thinking the scientists could be tucked into a back room, but found nothing but oil equipment and hundreds of drums of a drill lubricant called mud.

When they were coming out of one of the buildings, a dark figure was waiting by the door. "What were you doing in there?" he demanded, his voice muffled by a scarf but the accusatory tone unmistakable.

"Trying to figure the place out," Juan answered in Spanish. The stranger was dressed as a civilian, so he went on the offense. "If we're to defend you guys, I need to know every square inch of this place. So if you don't mind, we will get back to it."

"Yeah?" He was still suspicious. "Then why skulk around at night?"

Juan made a gesture to Linc that said, Can you believe this guy, and replied, "Because I very much doubt the Americans will be sporting enough to attack during the day, and what looks like cover when it's bright may not be so good in the dark."

With that, Juan shoulder-bumped the guy as he passed, and he and Linc moved on without a backward glance. When they were out of sight behind the rounded corner of a dormitory, Juan did look back and saw their interrogator had vanished.

Linc chuckled. "My Spanish may be rusty, but that sure sounded like a line of the purest bull I have ever heard."

"I was just telling Max that the more outrageous the lie, the more likely it'll be believed."

Because the facility was designed to be camouflaged from satellite observation, it was not laid out in a neat, efficient grid. It wasn't until they were at the very southern edge of the base, near where Linc had earlier spotted a hidden SAM battery, that they saw a lone building on stilts shaped like an igloo lozenge. Light spilled from the window in front, but the rest were darkened.

They climbed the steps. Juan opened the outer door, and he and Linc stepped into a vestibule lined with pegs on the wall for parkas and racks for overboots. Neither man made to remove their clothing, and they just casually opened the door into the structure. Two soldiers were on their feet, both with pistols drawn. They had heard the outer door open and close and were on alert. When they saw it was two soldiers wearing Argentine gear, they relaxed. The room had all the charm and ambiance of a broken-down trailer.

"What are you guys doing here? We've got duty until twenty-two hundred hours."

"Sorry. We're not here to relieve you," Juan said. "We were sent to look for the Major. Has he been around?"

"Espinoza was here checking on our prisoners about two hours ago." The guard gestured to a locked door behind him. "Haven't seen him since."

Now Juan had a name to go along with the face. "Okay, thanks." They turned to go.

"Hold on. Who is that under there, Ramón?"

Bold as brass he said, "No, Juan Cabrillo."

"Who?"

"Juan Rodriguez Cabrillo. I just transferred into Ninth Brigade from MI." Meaning military intelligence, meaning, I'm probably an officer so you'd better cut your questions short.

"Yes, sir," the trooper said, swallowing hard. "If I see Major Espinoza, I'll be sure to tell him you're looking for him."

It was difficult to put menace in his voice because he was so bundled up, but Juan managed when he said, "Best if this discussion didn't take place, Private. Understood?"

"Sir. Yes, sir."

Linc and Cabrillo returned to the blistering-cold night, where the stars shone so brightly that the surrounding ice glowed.

"Bingo," Linc said.

"Bingo indeed. Now we just have to rescue the hostages, close this place down, and neutralize an eight-thousand-ton cruiser without the Argentines realizing we were ever here."

The two men continued to reconnoiter for another three hours, moving freely about the base. It seemed nothing was off-limits, with the exception of the makeshift jail. Juan was acutely interested in the oil-and-gas-processing plants. They were located in huge hangar-sized buildings that were covered in insulating layers and then snow and ice. Inside each was an industrial-sized tangle of pipes and conduits that joined and diverged in a system only an engineer could understand. One of the plants was set well back from the beach. The other was partially built over the water on stilts driven into the seafloor. Not only was natural gas processed in this structure, but they discovered the massive furnace used to keep superheated air flowing though the pipes under the bay. Everything appeared fully automated, but such importance was placed on this key system that a workman sat watch in an enclosed office a short distance away. He nodded to what he thought were two soldiers when he spotted Linc and Cabrillo. They waved back, and the worker returned to his anatomy magazine.

By the time they returned to the dock, it was past eleven. Both men were exhausted and chilled to the core. They jumped for the workboat, and Juan was just ducking under the pier to get onto the submersible when a guard shouted, "Stop right there! What are you doing out after curfew?"

Juan straightened. "I forgot my iPod this afternoon when I went out with the Chinese surveyors."

"I don't care what you forgot. No one is allowed outside after curfew. Get up out of there. You're coming with me." He brought up his machine pistol.

"Easy, pal," Juan said calmly, thinking it was just rotten luck they were found by the most dedicated soldier in the Argentine Army. "We don't want any trouble."

"Then you should have stayed in your bunk. Move it!"

Linc was the first to step onto the dock. The guard unconsciously backed off a pace when he saw the size of one of his prisoners. Linc was almost a full head taller, and looked like a polar bear under his thick arctic clothing.

Juan came up next to him, but before the guard could issue any more orders the Chairman lunged forward and pushed on the Heckler and Koch to ease off any pressure the Argentine had on the trigger and at the same time he swung his right fist into the man's face. His hand hit the sentry's goggles, which crushed into his nose, drawing equal measures of blood and tears.

Linc moved in, stripping away the weapon and crashing a boot into the man's knee. The man went down, with Cabrillo staying on top of him to smother his cries. Juan didn't hesitate. The stakes were too high. He got his hand over the guard's nose and mouth and held them closed as the man struggled to free himself. It lasted less than a minute.

"Damn. I didn't want to have to do that," he panted, and stood. His hands were bloody.

"What do we do with him? If we take him

with us, it might look suspicious. This isn't the kind of place you desert from."

Juan pulled back the guard's parka hood and stripped off a woolen balaclava. He then smeared the man's blood on a nearby bollard and positioned the body so it looked as though he had tripped, knocking himself unconscious and loosening his head protection. Ten minutes in such an exposed position was all it would take for the cold temperature to kill.

"Problem solved. Let's go home."

The following morning Cabrillo was awakened by the sound of a telephone. The mound of blankets over his bed weighed a ton, and he'd slept in sweats. Still, he felt cold. It reminded him of those frosty Kazak mornings when he had infiltrated the Baikonur Cosmodrome back in his CIA days. He snaked a hand out from under the covers and grabbed the headset from his bedside table.

"Hello." It was a quarter past eight. He'd overslept.

"Where are you?" It was Overholt at Langley.

"In bed, actually."

"Are you anywhere near Antarctica?" The tone was sharp, accusatory. Whatever pressure Langston was under, he was making sure Juan felt it, too.

"We're halfway to Cape Town for the Emir of Kuwait's visit," Cabrillo said so smoothly he half believed it himself.

"You sure?"

"Lang, I've got a couple million dollars' worth of navigational gear crammed into the *Oregon*. I think I know where we are. Mind telling me what has your tighty-whities in a twist?"

"You know that sub the Chinese sent down to protect the Argentines?"

"I recall you mentioning they were headed that way."

"The People's Liberation Army Navy has lost contact with her after she was ordered to investigate a ship wandering into their exclusionary zone. That was thirty-six hours ago."

"I promise you, we were east of the Falklands by then, halfway to St. Helena Island."

"Thank God."

Juan had never heard his friend so despondent. "What's going on?"

"Since losing that sub, the Chinese have been on a tear. They claim we sank it, but they have no proof. They say that any overt act against the Argentines, no matter who does it, will be seen as an attack by the

United States. If something does happen down there, they will recall all outstanding American debt. That's three-quarters of a trillion dollars. We'll be ruined completely because everyone else holding treasuries and bonds will call them, too. It'll be like the bank runs at the start of the Depression.

"Through diplomatic channels, we got word to them that if they did call the debt we would slap them with tariffs so no one here would buy their goods. In essence, they dared us. They don't care if their people are out of work and starving. When it comes to economic attrition, they can bury us. We've outsourced and borrowed ourselves into a corner and now we're going to pay the price."

"They said 'overt act'?"

"Overt. Covert. It doesn't matter. They have us over a barrel. End of story. The President has ordered any U.S. warships in the Atlantic to stay above the equator, and he's recalling all our fast-attack submarines to show the Chinese that we won't interfere with what they and the Argentines have done. As of today, the United States has ceded its superpower status to the Chinese."

Coming from a man who had played a significant role in ending the Soviet Union's bid for world domination, those last words were especially painful to hear. Juan didn't know what to say, and as of this moment wasn't sure what he was going to do.

The right thing was to keep with his plan and let the chips fall where they may. However, he had to consider what would happen to the people back home. What Overholt described would make the Great Depression sound like a boom time — sixty or seventy percent unemployment, hunger and the violence it inevitably spawned, the breakdown of the rule of law. In essence, it would be the end of the United States.

He finally found his voice. "Well, you don't have to worry about us. Like I told you, we're on our way to South Africa."

"I guess I'm glad to hear it," Langston said wearily. "You know, Juan, we still might not get out of this so easily."

"What do you mean?"

"We can placate the Chinese, but North Korea's demanding we draw down the number of soldiers we have in the south or risk a military confrontation. And last night a small bomb went off near the Presidential Palace in Caracas. The Venezuelans are claiming it was an assassination plot perpetrated by Colombian Special Forces. They've vowed revenge, and a check of satellite imagery shows them moving troops to the border. Interestingly, they started a couple of days ago."

"Which means they probably set it off themselves for a pretext."

"That's my read on it, too, but it doesn't matter. China's heavily invested in Venezuela, so you can imagine our reaction if they do invade Colombia."

"Thumb twiddling?"

"That might be seen as too provocative," Overholt said with gallows humor. "We'll probably sit on our hands instead. Listen, I've got a full slate of meetings this morning. I'll talk to you later about any new developments. Give my best to the Kuwaiti Emir if we don't speak before you get there."

"I'm sure we will," Juan replied.

He replaced the handset and threw off his blankets. The floor was as cold as a hockey rink, and just as slippery under Juan's woolen hunting sock. He wasn't sure who was better at playing the game. Him for lying to Overholt or Langston for trying to manipulate him. The veteran CIA minder did think that the *Oregon* was heading for Cape Town, but he'd told Juan about North Korea and Venezuela to get him to turn back.

"Do the right thing," Juan's father had

often told him. "The consequences are easier to deal with, no matter what you think."

He dressed quickly and was in the op center with a cup of coffee from a silver urn on a back table. With the ship firmly grounded, Maurice had pulled out their finest Royal Doulton. It was the steward's subtle way of getting back at him for his earlier crack. If Juan recalled properly, the cup in his hand had cost seventy-five dollars.

"How did Mike and his team make out?" he asked. Murph and Stoney were in their customary seats toward the front of the room.

"They got back at about four this morning," Eric Stone replied. "He left word that it went well, but they need at least one more night. But there's a problem."

"Isn't there always?"

"The workboat with the sonar gear went south this morning."

Juan cursed. If he could find the wreck in a submersible so quickly, it was a safe assumption that the Chinese would, too. "I bet the other bay is iced over, so they're checking on the right one."

"What do you want to do about it?" Mark asked.

"Not sure," Juan replied. "We can't catch them in either of the submersibles, and if we go after them in an RHIB they might radio back to base about an unknown craft approaching them."

Hali Kasim was sitting at his customary station. He offered, "So what if they find it today? All they'll be able to do is take some grainy underwater pictures. It proves nothing, and by this time tomorrow the wreck will be destroyed."

"Playing devil's advocate," Eric said, "if they find the wreck, who's to say they don't stay overnight? That'll mess up our schedule."

Juan felt the beginnings of a headache and rubbed his temples absently. Of course there was the other problem that he had no idea how to tackle. He'd already run his idea by Kevin Nixon, but the special-effects master said any fakes he made would be spotted in a second. It was the real deal or nothing. For their plan to work so the Argentines never suspected a thing, Cabrillo needed to find eighteen human skeletons.

The headache was morphing into a migraine.

Twenty-Six

"Who do you love more than me?" Linda Ross asked when she strode into the op center fifteen quiet minutes later. She carried a slim manila folder and a wide grin.

"Megan Fox," Mark said at once.

"Beyoncé," the duty tech at damage control called out.

"Katie Holmes," Hali said.

"I've always had a thing for Julia Roberts," Eric added.

"Chairman," Linda asked, "care to be a sexist pig, too?"

"The only woman I love more than you is my mom."

The other men jeered him softly.

Linda smiled. "Touché."

"Remind me again why I love you so."

"Because I've found that less than a hundred miles south of here is a Norwegian whaling station abandoned back in the 1930s."

"We don't need whale bones."

"It has been preserved as a World Heritage Site — wait for it — because it has a chapel with a graveyard that is the final resting place for twenty-seven whalers who'd died in these waters. You told me to find you some bones, I give you bones."

Juan was on his feet in an instant and at her side in two strides. He had to bend way over to lay a kiss on her velvety cheek. The migraine suddenly vanished, and the pall that had formed over him lifted. What had him so down was the fact that if they hadn't found a bunch of skeletons, he would have had no choice but to leave the hostages to their fate. He doubted they were going to be an Argentine priority once things heated up, so to leave them behind meant to let them die.

"Chairman, I'm picking up a transmission from the Chinese workboat," Hali said, turning back to his bank of computers.

"Jam it!"

He worked his keyboard for a second. "I've isolated the frequency. They're dead. The computer will automatically keep following them as they search for a signal up and down the dial."

"Okay. Good. If they have any news to report, they'll have to go back to base.

That's two problems down in under a minute. Well done, everybody."

Max and Tamara strolled into the op center, their hands so close together that Juan suspected they'd been holding them just seconds earlier. The bullfrog and the princess, he thought, but was happy for them both.

"Perfect timing, my friend."

Hanley looked at him like a buyer eyes a used-car salesman. "I've got a bad feeling about this."

Cabrillo smiled broadly. "And so you should. I need you to play Igor and go rob a churchyard."

Tamara looked aghast. "You want him to do what?"

"You know," Max said, shaking his head from side to side. "I have to admit there was a part of me that hoped this piece of the operation wouldn't pan out."

"Come on," Juan teased, "fresh air, open skies, decomposing Norwegians. It'll be great!"

"What are you two talking about? Decomposing *who?*"

Max turned to her. "In order for us to rescue the hostages so the Argentines don't know they're missing, we have to leave something behind to fool them."

"But?"

"Once we get them out of the building," Juan said, "we'll torch it. All they'll find are eighteen sets of charred bones. Only a pathologist would know they weren't the original men and women. We're just grateful the sizes of the winter-over crews are so small, otherwise we'd need to come up with an alternative."

"Like what?" Her mind reeled.

"A small nuke, maybe."

From what she'd seen of the Corporation so far, she wasn't sure if Cabrillo was joking or not. She wouldn't be surprised if it were the latter.

He threw her a wolfish grin that told her nothing beyond the fact that she was surrounded by a bunch of swashbuckling adolescents. She looked to Max for guidance. He merely shrugged. She said, "I guess it's a good thing you were going to use a small one."

Linda moved to her side, as if she were an anchor in their craziness, and said, "Don't worry. We do know what we're doing."

"I'm glad you do because I sure don't."

Hanley left twenty minutes later in an RHIB, towing an inflatable boat. He and his four-man crew shot straight out to sea for about five miles before turning southward, so there was no chance of being spotted from shore. Max brought along a gasoline-powered high-pressure pump he planned to use to excavate the bones. The needle of heated water it threw could be dialed up to four thousand psi, more than enough to melt away the permafrost covering the bodies. As he said when they left, "No picks and shovels for Mrs. Hanley's favorite son."

Juan had a decidedly more difficult job today. With the Chinese surveying the bay where the wreck was located, Mike Trono and his team couldn't resume their work. That freed up the Nomad submersible, with its air lock. The perpetually twilit sky was dark enough to provide visual cover, and the Argentines' oil rigs and hot-air bubbling system would screen the sounds of his work.

Down in the underwater operations room, Cabrillo dressed to dive. Under his Viking dry suit he wore a mesh garment embedded with more than a hundred feet of tubing. Warm water would be circulated through the tubes from an umbilical attached to a jack on the submarine. He knew the Argentines were heating the bay, but he couldn't risk encountering freezing water during his trip. The umbilical also carried his communications system and his air, so there was no need for bulky tanks.

The full-face helmet was equipped with powerful lights, which he dimmed down by covering half the lenses with paint. It would make it much more difficult to work but also much harder to be spotted from the surface. He would need to keep reminding himself to never look up and send the beams flashing toward the surface.

Linda would pilot the minisub while Eddie Seng would be Juan's dive master.

As soon as they launched, Linda guided them to the *Oregon*'s stern. Just below the naked flagpole, a hatch had been opened to reveal a huge drum of tow cable. Rather than steel, it was made of woven carbon fiber, with a quarter of the weight and five times the strength of a traditional line. As an added bonus, it was neutrally buoyant. Linda grabbed the end with the Nomad's powerful mechanical arm and fitted it into a slot where it couldn't come loose.

Then they started making their way to the Argentine base. The drag of line wasn't bad at first, but the three of them knew by the time they had enough played out the submersible would be struggling. They had timed their launch so the Nomad would ride into the bay with the tide.

It took more than an hour to reach the

pylons supporting the gas-processing plant that Juan and Linc had spent so much time studying the night before. Because the bay was kept artificially warmed, sea life teemed around the thick ferroconcrete piers. Dull-brown crabs scuttled along the bottom and fish darted between the columns, which were encrusted with barnacles and shellfish.

The Nomad was sixty-five feet long, but with multiple thrusters placed strategically on her hull she was wildly maneuverable. Linda had her bottom lip pinched between neat white teeth as she moved them under the industrial complex and around one of the columns. There she lowered them to the bottom.

She switched over to the arm once again. While the carbon-fiber cable was strong, it remained susceptible to abrasion, and being scraped across the rough surface of the pier would weaken it substantially. To protect it, she used the arm to scrape away the accumulation of mussels. The small bivalves snapped their shells violently when dislodged and propelled themselves into the gloom.

Next, she swiveled the grasping hand to pull a bundled length of commercial plastic pipe from a storage bin. It was the same material used in domestic plumbing and would be a common item found anywhere at the base. Their presence, in the unlikely event they were ever found, would not raise suspicion. They would just be other pieces of junk that had fallen into the sea. The pipes had been glued together to form a semicircle that fit around the back of the pier. It would be the smooth plastic that the cable rubbed against and not the cement.

She fitted the protective half sleeve into place and looped the submersible around the far side of the column.

"Good job," Juan said as they slowly backed away. The black towline slid easily over the bundle of PVC pipes. "One more stop to go."

She pivoted the Nomad and started back across the bay. The weight of the line and the need now to fight the tide, which had yet to slacken, strained the submersible's engine. The batteries drained almost twice as fast as normal, and their speed was down to a crawl, but they still made headway.

Twenty minutes later, they were under the *Admiral Guillermo Brown.* Her anchor was paid out and rested on its side on the rocky seabed, its heavy chain rising up to the surface. Less than twenty feet of water separated her keel from the bottom.

"Strange name for an Argentine ship.

Brown," Eddie said as he handed Juan his helmet.

"His name was really William Brown, and he was born in Ireland and then emigrated to Argentina. He's credited with forming their Navy in the early 1800s to fight the Spanish."

"How could you possibly know that?" Linda asked from the cockpit.

"What? I Googled him when we first saw the cruiser. I thought it was an odd choice of name, too."

Juan waddled to the tiny air lock, laden with a belt from which he hung his tools. Strapped to his back like a World War II flamethrower were two cylinders. Once he was in and the door secure, he jacked his umbilical into a port and checked over his connections, making certain that warm water was flowing through his suit and that he had good airflow and good comms with the sub. Only when Eddie was satisfied did he open the valve that flooded the closet-sized compartment.

Water foamed and hissed as it climbed his body, pressing the rubber suit against his legs when the pressure grew. It was a comfortable temperature, but he wouldn't discount running into icy pockets once he was outside. He could see Eddie watching him through a small window in the air-lock door. Juan gave him the traditional divers signal that everything was okay. Eddie returned it.

Moments later, the water had closed in on the ceiling. Juan reached overhead to open the outer hatch. A few stray bubbles burst free as it swung up. He climbed out of the sub, making sure to keep his head down and his lights pointed away from the surface. He felt reasonably confident that the Argentines didn't have lookouts posted in such freezing conditions, but he hadn't thought he and Linc would run into a guard last night either.

The low vibration in the water came from the cruiser's secondary power plant, which produced enough energy to run the ship's systems and keep the men warm. The main engines were off. He knew this already by observing that only a small amount of smoke escaped the warship's single raked funnel.

He jumped free of the sub, floating down to the bottom in a graceful arc. His boots hit and kicked up a little silt that drifted gently away. One of the six-inch-thick conduits for the bubbler was to his left. Air rose from its length in thin streams of silver.

Juan turned his attention to the *Admiral*

Brown's anchor. It looked to be about eight feet long and would probably weigh in at about four tons — more than enough to keep the ship stationary against the tides. A small pile of extra chain lay next to it in a rust-colored heap.

"How are you doing out there?"

"No problem so far. I'm looking at the anchor now."

"And?"

"I should be able to unshackle it from the chain. The lynchpin is held in place with bolts."

Cabrillo bent over the anchor and pulled an adjustable wrench from his belt. He fitted it over the first bolt and used his thumb on the oversized adjusting wheel until it was snug. It fought him the entire way. Tiny bits of paint lifted from the bolt head when it first moved an eighth of a turn, and it would turn no more than that. Juan heaved on it until finally bracing his legs against the anchor and pulling until he though he was going to pass out. The bolt gave another eighth turn. It took ten backbreaking minutes to remove that first bolt, and Juan was bathed in sweat.

"Shut down the hot suit, Eddie. I'm dying out here."

"It's off."

The next bolt spun out so easily that, once he had it started, he could twist it with his fingers. The third and fourth weren't quite as easy, but nowhere near as bad as the first. He clipped the wrench back to his belt and grabbed a rubber mallet. He used rubber to avoid making any noise.

He swung at the lynchpin, the water hindering his actions, but the blow was enough to knock it an inch out of alignment. Three more shots, and it was almost free of the anchor. It would still hold the ship in position against the normal flow of water into and out of the bay, but any hard jolt would slip the pin entirely, and the *Admiral Brown* would be left to the vagaries of the sea.

"That's it. Oh, man!"

"What?"

"I was just hit by a pocket of cold water. Damn, that is brutal."

"Want the hot suit back on?"

"No. It drifted away."

Juan started walking across the seafloor for the minisub, gathering up loops of his umbilical as he went so it wouldn't tangle.

He unclipped the carbon-fiber tow cable from its slot and dragged it back to the anchor. He added a little air to his buoyancy compensator to make his ascent easier and, hand over hand, he climbed the chain. For now, he left the cable on the bottom.

He paused when he reached the underside of the four-hundred-foot warship. Her bottom was coated with red antifouling paint and was remarkably free of marine buildup. His next task was to spot-weld eight metal pad eyes to the bow. That's what the two tanks he carried were for. They were high-capacity batteries for a handheld arc welder. The gear was normally used to make quick repairs to the *Oregon.*

He adjusted his buoyancy again and slid eye protection over his helmet so he could work comfortably next to an electric spark brighter than the sun. The curvature of the cruiser's hull shielded him from above, and in twenty minutes he had all eight welds completed. There were so many in case one or more of the welds failed. Juan carried no illusions that he was an expert at this particular skill. Ten minutes after that, he had the tow cable threaded though all of them. Over the very tip of the cable he clamped in place a steel box about the size of a paperback book. The box served as the belay point for the cable while inside was an explosive charge. A signal from the *Oregon* would detonate the small amount of plastique, and the box would disintegrate, freeing the cable so it could be yanked away from the ship. The only evidence left behind was the eight pad eyes. Chances were, they wouldn't survive what Juan had planned.

No sooner had he returned to the Nomad and closed the outer hatch over himself than Linda powered her up and they were under way.

"Operation Crack-the-Whip is on," he said when Eddie helped him off with the helmet.

"Any problems?"

"Smooth as silk."

"More good news," Linda said. "Eric's tracking a storm headed our way. Should hit tomorrow at what passes for dawn in these parts."

"Call Eric back and have him pull the ship off beach a bit. Also, tell him to drain the starboard ballast tanks but leave the port side flooded. That should give the old girl a convincing list." Juan had an anticipatory gleam in his eye. "I hope the Argentines have enjoyed their time ruling this part of world because it's about to end."

By five that afternoon, the Chinese survey boat had motored past the *Oregon* where she lay just off the beach. She was still close enough in that an occasional large wave would cause her hardened bows to slam against the bottom. There was little doubt they would report the *Norego* had unbeached herself and was starting her soulless wanderings once again. An hour later, an exhausted and frozen Max Hanley returned with his team and their grisly cargo.

"That sucked," Hanley proclaimed when the RHIB was winched inside the boat garage along the ship's side. "Not only is it colder than a brass monkey's you know what out there, but that cemetery would creep out Stephen King. The headstones are all carved whale bones, and there's a fence around it made up of ribs as tall as me. The arched gate is built of skulls the size of Volkswagens."

"Any problem recovering the remains?"

"Do you mean besides the eternal damnation of my soul for desecrating holy ground?"

"No."

"In that case, everything went fine. The graves were only about a foot deep, and the men were laid to rest in canvas bags sewn from sails. I was surprised to find they had mostly decomposed."

"The ground would have been too frozen to bury them in the winter, and in spring it's just warm enough for bacteria to do their thing."

"So now what?"

"You get yourself warmed up. Mike Trono and his gang just took off back to the wreck. By the time they return and we get the Nomad prepped again, it'll be showtime."

"Weather coming in?"

"Eric said it's going to be a bitch out there come dawn."

"It isn't exactly skittles and beer now."

"As the saying goes, 'You ain't seen nothing yet.'"

TWENTY-SEVEN

Major Espinoza laid the weather report back on Luis Laretta's desk. The small office, with its obligatory picture of Generalissimo Ernesto Corazón on one wall and a poster of a scantily clad girl on the other, was thick with their cigar smoke.

"This storm would be perfect cover for an American Special Force strike. They'll be expecting us to sit down here all snug in our bunks while they sneak around and place explosives all over the camp." He brooded for a moment. "I'm going to push out the perimeter patrols another couple of miles. If they're here, they would have parachuted in well back from the coast and would need to come overland."

"Surely you don't think they'll attack," Laretta said, waving his Cohiba airily.

Espinoza stared at him flatly. "I am paid to be prepared, if they do. I don't have the luxury of opining."

"We each have our jobs," the facility director replied, thinking it was better the soldiers freeze out there than his people.

There came a knock on the door.

"Come," Laretta bellowed.

In walked Lee Fong, the head of the Chinese search team. He was grinning ear to ear.

"Fong, how are you?" Luis greeted.

"Most excellent. We found the *Silent Sea*."

The director came halfway out of his chair. "So soon? That's wonderful. Here, have one of my cigars." When he sat back down, he retrieved a bottle of brandy and some paper cups from his bottom drawer.

"I don't normally smoke," the soft-spoken engineer said, "but under the circumstances . . ."

"Are you sure about your find?"

Lee pulled out his PDA and clicked through to a picture. He handed the small device to Espinoza. "After we got a solid sonar return, I sent down a camera. I admit the resolution is poor, but you are looking at the stern of one of the biggest junks ever built."

To Jorge, the picture just looked like a dark blur. "I'll have to take your word for it."

"Trust me. It's the *Silent Sea*. Tomorrow

we will dive on the wreck and bring back irrefutable proof. I tried to report this when we were out there and have you send a boat with divers right away, but we couldn't seem to transmit." He accepted a drink from Laretta.

Espinoza declined. "I'm on duty."

"Your loss." The director saluted him, then toasted Lee Fong. "Congratulations. From this moment, there can be no questioning our rights to this land and the riches off her coast. I've got to be honest with you guys. Ever since we started construction, I've always been afraid our operation would be discovered and we'd be booted out. Well, no more. We are here to stay."

"Have you contacted you superiors?" Espinoza asked Lee.

"Yes, just now. They are most pleased," he beamed. "My immediate boss says I will be awarded a medal and that our company will be guaranteed a lifetime of government contracts."

"Hold out for a big raise," Laretta told him, pouring more brandy into his glass. "Make them know you're worth it."

"I might just do that. Oh, I forgot. The ship on the beach."

"What about it," Espinoza asked sharply. He'd been suspicious about that boat, and

505

even seeing with his own eyes that she was a derelict didn't allay his concerns.

"She's off the beach and starting to float away."

"You didn't see any engine smoke?"

"Oh, no. And she's leaning heavily to one side. I think she will flip over soon."

Espinoza was regretting his moment of earlier charity. He should have let Sergeant Lugones lay some charges and blow her to pieces. It wasn't too late. He could ask the captain of the *Guillermo Brown* to sink the old scow with a missile, but he could think of no valid reason why the Navy would waste such expensive munitions on his paranoia. With any luck, the storm would either sink her or blow her so far away that he wouldn't have to worry about her presence any longer.

"Mr. Laretta, might I have some more of your brandy?"

"It would be my pleasure," Luis slopped some more into Lee's paper cup.

The Major stood abruptly. Something wasn't right. It wasn't instinct but the cold tickling of premonition that was setting his nerves on edge. The Americans would come. Tonight or tomorrow, when the storm picked up, and they would lay waste to what these two men were so smugly proud of.

"Gentlemen, I needn't remind you that until the world formally recognizes the Antarctic Peninsula as sovereign Argentine territory, we are at risk."

"Come, come, my dear Major." Laretta had no head for alcohol. He was already slurring his words. "There is no harm in celebrating our success."

"Maybe so, but I believe you are being a little premature. Get word to your workers that curfew tonight starts in one hour, and there will be no exceptions. My men are going to be on patrol with orders to shoot. Do you understand?"

That sobered him up. Laretta nodded. "Curfew, one hour. Yes, Major."

Espinoza turned on his heel and left the office. He'd been pushing his soldiers hard since their arrival and tonight he'd push them harder still. By the time he and Raul had them all deployed, there wouldn't be one inch of uncovered space around the oil terminal, and, knowing the American proclivity for coming to the rescue of others, he would double the guard on their captives.

Juan pulled the straight razor from his neck and swirled it in the copper basin of his sink. The *Oregon*'s steep list forced him to brace himself with his other hand. He made one more pass, rinsed the blade, and dried it very carefully on the towel. His grandfather had been a barber and had taught him that the secret of keeping a razor sharp was never to put it away wet.

He pressed the plunger to drain the sink and splashed his face with palmfuls of water. He looked himself in the eye in the mirror over the vanity. He wasn't sure what he saw. He was proud of the decision he had made, yet he also thought they should have cut and run and headed for South Africa, where five million a week for the next three weeks was guaranteed for doing nothing more than babysitting a head of state who had no enemies.

He dried his face with a towel and pulled on a T-shirt. They had turned up the heat somewhat, but his arms and chest were covered in goose pimples.

He hopped across to his walk-in closet and selected a leg for the day's mission among the five artificial limbs he owned. They were lined up on the floor like a bunch of left-only cowboy boots. A few minutes later, he was finished dressing and on his way to the moon pool. He knew he should eat something, but his stomach was too knotted.

The underwater operations center was a

hive of activity, with teams of technicians working on the Nomad 1000 that had just returned with Trono and his group. Mike reported that the charges were planted and ready to go. His team had been drilling into the underside of the glacier, hanging over the bay and packing the holes with enough explosives to calve off a hundred thousand tons of ice.

Juan keyed in some of the outside cameras at a workstation. The low-light cameras revealed a world gone mad. Swirling snow buffeted the ship from every direction as the wind shifted constantly. The seas heaved up waves that ran high enough to explode across the deck, and when they hit shore they had the power to move hundred-pound rocks back and forth like pebbles. He checked the meteorological display. The temperature was minus twelve, but the windchill brought it down to thirty below.

Eddie Seng and Linc showed up a couple minutes later. Because of the number of passengers they would hopefully be returning to the ship, the raiding party had to be small. The Nomad was designed for ten people, and somehow they were going to shoehorn twenty-one into it.

As before, they wore arctic clothing to resemble the Argentine soldiers, and they'd packed enough extra parkas for the captive scientists into a waterproof bag strapped to the sub. Another similar bag contained the bones of the long-dead Norwegians. Juan still wasn't sure how he was going to make up for disturbing their eternal rest.

Maurice appeared at Cabrillo's side bearing a serving tray. It was three o'clock in the morning, and he looked fresh and impeccably turned out as always. "I know you rarely eat before a mission, Captain, but you need to. In these conditions, the body burns calories too fast. I don't know if I ever mentioned, but I deployed with the Royal Navy the last time the Argies became uppity in the South Atlantic. The boys who retook the South Sandwich Islands returned as stiff as Stonehenge."

He pulled off the cover and presented Juan with an omelet stuffed with ham and mushrooms. The aroma seemed to untie the knots in his belly. It also reminded him of something he'd forgotten, and he sent Maurice back to the kitchen on an errand.

The launching went smoothly, and they were soon on their way. The first inkling that something had changed happened when the minisub passed close to the *Admiral Guillermo Brown*. Juan could hear over the other ambient noise that she had fired up her main engines. The sound and vibration carried through the water and echoed inside the steel pressure hull. It wouldn't alter their plan, but Juan didn't take it as a good omen.

Unlike before, when they had docked near the workboats, this time they surfaced at the far end of the pier, closer to where the prisoners were being held. The storm's fury overwhelmed the sound of the Nomad broaching under the dock.

Linc had the hatch open a moment later. He climbed from view, while Juan struggled into his parka and settled his goggles. The big SEAL came back a moment later.

"We got problems."

"What's up?"

"I just scoped the dock using infrared and counted three guards."

"On a night like this?" Eddie asked.

"Exactly because it's a night like this," Juan told him. "If I were in Espinoza's shoes, I'd plan for the storm to hide an assault and deploy my forces accordingly."

Juan took the night vision binocs from Linc and did his own survey, lying flat on the pier. He saw the sentries Linc had spotted, and as he scoped the rest of the base he could see more ghostly images moving around. In one minute, he counted no fewer than ten men on duty.

"Change of plans."

All along, they had intended to free the prisoners and get them at least into the submersible before going after the Argentine cruiser. With so many men patrolling the facility, the chance of them being discovered was too high. Now they would use the warship as a distraction. He explained what he wanted the men to do, and made sure that Max back on the *Oregon* was listening in.

"I don't like it," Hanley said when Juan was finished.

"Not much of a choice. We won't get within ten feet of those scientists otherwise."

"Okay. Just tell me when you're ready."

"Get as close to the jail as you can," Cabrillo told the other two men with him, "and wait for my signal."

They exited the submersible together, Linc and Eddie each taking one of the waterproof bags in tow. They had to crawl on their bellies and move inches at a time, not to attract attention. It would take twenty minutes for them to just reach the temporary prison.

Juan went in the opposite direction. The wind tore at his clothing and made each pace a struggle. It would come at his face and then reverse itself and send him staggering. His scarf drooped, and it was like his skin had been splashed with lye.

He had to time his movements for when the Argentines were turned away from him. The wind did provide one thing of use. Most of the soldiers moved with their backs toward it, giving Cabrillo a chance to cover more ground when the gusts became constant.

Visibility remained dismal, and he almost blundered on one soldier who stood in the lee of a bulldozer. He froze, no more than five feet from the sentry. The man was in profile. He was close enough to see the fur trimming around his hood whipping furiously. Juan backed up a step, and then another, but froze once again when a second guard approached.

"Jaguar," the first guard called out when he saw his comrade.

"Capybara," the second responded.

These were their recognition codes. Juan smiled tightly. That was an intelligence coup. When he had cleared around the duo, he radioed that information to Eddie and Linc in case they were challenged.

From here on, Juan moved more swiftly, and when he came up on a guard the man turned on him sharply, his gun not at the ready but raised in an aggressive manner.

"Jaguar."

"Capybara," Cabrillo said confidently. The other man lowered his machine pistol.

"The only thing that makes this worthwhile," the guard said, "is knowing that the Major is out here with us and not warm inside."

"He's never one to ask us to do something he wouldn't." Juan had no idea if this was true, but he'd seen enough of Espinoza to think he wasn't a lead-from-the-rear kind of soldier.

"I guess. Stay warm." The soldier moved on.

Juan kept going. Ten minutes and three cold and bored guards later, he reached the gas-processing building. "I'm here," he called to his men. "Where are you?"

"We're still shy of our target," Linc said. "It's like Rio during Carnival out here, there's so many people."

"Max, are you ready?"

"Ballast is pumped clear and the engines are purring sweetly."

"Okay. Stand by."

Juan opened the plant's personnel door next to the giant overhead door and moved into the entry vestibule. He was challenged by a guard instantly. "Caiman."

Cabrillo swallowed. They had different

514

code words for when someone came into a building. He mentally cursed Jorge Espinoza's foresight, as he frantically ran though the names of all the native South American animals he could remember. Llama. Boa. Anaconda. Um, Sloth. From there, he drew a blank.

A half second had passed, and the sentry was about to become suspicious. Capybara is to Jaguar as what is to a Caiman? Predator and prey. Caimans eat fish. It's a fish. Which one? He said the only one he could think of. "Piranha."

The soldier lowered his weapon, and it took all of Cabrillo's self-control not to show his relief.

"You know you aren't supposed to be in here."

"Just for a second. I need to warm up a little."

"Sorry. You know the Major's orders."

"Come on, man. It's not like he's around right now."

The soldier thought for another second, then a look of compassion crossed his face. "All right, go ahead inside. But five minutes, and if Espinoza or Jimenez shows up I'm gong to tell them you've been hiding in there since before I came on duty."

"Five minutes. Promise."

Juan moved past the guard and walked into the overheated facility. He had to pull back his hood and unzip his parka. Machinery hummed as it processed the natural gas flowing in from the offshore pipes, while, on the other side of the yawning space, the blast furnaces were hard at work keeping the bay from freezing over. Cabrillo was again amazed at the size and complexity of the Argentine facility.

"Max, I'm in. Go for it."

Juan found one of the main trunk lines for incoming gas. He pulled out a small explosive and set the motion sensor. It wasn't particularly sensitive, but for what was coming it didn't need to be.

He turned to go just as four men entered from the vestibule. They had removed their arctic coats, and at once Cabrillo recognized Major Espinoza. With him was the Sergeant who'd been aboard the *Oregon* and two other NCOs. Juan moved behind a piece of machinery before they spotted him.

"We saw you come in here," Espinoza shouted above the industrial din. "Don't make it harder on yourself. Come out now, and I won't charge you with desertion."

Cabrillo looked at the bomb, then back at the burly soldiers staying by the door while Espinoza and Sergeant Lugones started fanning out to find him.

"Max," he whispered urgently. "I might be blown, but don't stop. You read? I'll get out somehow."

"Roger," Max said tersely, knowing full well that the Chairman was lying about the last part.

Hanley stared into space for a moment and then forced himself into action. "Mr. Stone, bring us up to five percent, and set some tension on the cable, if you please."

"Aye." Eric dialed up the *Oregon*'s unrivaled engines and moved her forward at a quarter knot.

A tech stationed in the fantail locker where the cable drum was located called out when the line started showing stress.

Even with wind and waves pummeling the ship, Eric didn't need to be told when she was pulling against her tether. He knew how she responded in almost any circumstance.

"Tension on, Mr. Hanley," he said with customary op center formality when a mission was under way.

"Okay, steady acceleration. One hundred feet per minute. Don't jerk the thing, lad."

"Aye, sir."

A mile astern of them, the cable looped around the pier and back to the bow of the

Admiral Brown became as rigid as a steel girder when the magnetohydrodynamics encountered the cruiser's deadweight. The forces in play were massive. Imperceptibly at first, the big cruiser started to move, but not so much that her crew thought it was anything other than a swing of the wind pushing against her stern.

One foot became two, then ten. And then she came up hard against her anchor.

Eric kept piling on more power, causing the *Oregon*'s stern to dig deep as water rocketed through her drive tubes. But the stubborn lynchpin that Juan had so carefully sabotaged refused to give that last fraction of an inch.

One of his welds holding a pad eye popped, increasing the strain on those remaining. The *Oregon* pulled harder still, and a second pad eye popped off the hull, leaving only six. Metal ground against metal as the stubborn anchor pin struggled to do its job.

It released, and the energy stored in the carbon fiber during that frantic tug-of-war was suddenly discharged. The *Admiral Guillermo Brown* went from a virtual standstill to six knots, fast enough to knock crewmen to their knees. The captain happened to be on the bridge at this early hour, and he looked up from the report he was perusing. He knew immediately what had happened, while his less experienced crew looked confused.

"Good God, the anchor chain's snapped. Helm, give me power. All back one third."

"All back one third, aye."

With a pair of gas turbine engines capable of a combined twenty thousand shaft horsepower, he felt confident he could best whatever wind was thrown at him. But when he checked the gauge of their speed over the bottom, it wasn't slowing but rather accelerating.

"Helm, all back one half. Quickly, man!" The dock was only a half mile away, and it looked as though they were headed toward one of the processing plants. In seconds, he realized that the wind was stronger than anything he'd ever experienced. "Full power!"

The *Oregon* could handle the cruiser's twenty thousand horses without breaking a sweat. Eric had them up to eighty percent and noted with satisfaction that they were now pulling the *Admiral Brown* at sixteen knots. Over the distance and the storm, he could hear a klaxon begin to scream out a collision warning.

The cruiser was as helpless as an unmasted schooner as she arrowed straight for the gas plant. Her captain was at a loss to explain it. He'd ordered left full rudder to sheer them away from a direct collision, and the boat responded by simply crabbing sideways in the wind. Fate or destiny was going to slam her where she wanted to go, and to him it seemed the desires of man counted for nothing. A moment before impact, he looked again at their speed over the bottom and was aghast at how wind could push his warship at almost twenty knots.

For Cabrillo, there was no time for subtlety. Whatever happened in this building and the evidence it left behind would be incinerated when the *Admiral Brown* came barreling through the front wall. He deftly fitted a silencer on his FN Five-seveN and waited until Espinoza and the Sergeant were out of view.

He used the tangle of pipes as cover and crossed closer to the door. The two guards were on the constant lookout, their eyes never at rest, but the massive hangar-sized space was poorly lit, and Juan had more than ample cover. He kept looking back to make sure the others hadn't inadvertently flanked him. He was lining up to take his shot when a pressure-release valve directly behind him hissed out a jet of steam into the air. The guards both looked in his direction, and one of them must have spotted him because his gun came up and he loosed a three-round burst.

How the spray of rounds didn't puncture a critical valve and immolate them all was a miracle.

Juan ducked but came up almost instantly and dropped one of them with a double tap to the chest. The sentry who had let Cabrillo into the building burst through the door, his weapon held high and tight against his shoulder. The second guard had dived flat behind a clutch of fifty-five-gallon drums.

Cabrillo fired twice more, and the sentry collapsed. The doors closed behind him.

In the distance, he could hear Espinoza barking orders.

The guard peered out from around the barrels. Juan put a round two inches from his eye to keep him pinned in place and then charged with everything he had. The distance was less than twenty feet. He reached the barrels and pumped up in one easy bound. The guard was still flat on his stomach, never hearing the assault or expecting it.

Juan's mistake was assuming that because liquid poured from the side of the barrel where the high-velocity round had punctured it, all the kegs would be full. They weren't.

His foot touched down on the lid of one of the barrels, and his momentum toppled it and the three right next to it. He fell in the middle of the clanging mess and for a second had no idea what happened. The guard came to his wits an instant quicker. He got to his knees and swung his machine pistol toward Cabrillo. Like a greenhorn, Juan had dropped his pistol when he landed, so he kicked out with one foot and pushed one of the barrels into the guard, fouling his aim. His three-round burst pinged off the I-beam rafters.

Cabrillo grabbed the empty barrel in a bear hug and threw himself at the guard. When they collided, the soldier went down, and Juan used his impetus to drive his full weight, plus the barrel, into the man's chest. Ribs snapped like twigs. The man was down but not out. Juan frantically searched for his automatic, and was bending to retrieve it from between two more barrels when the wall behind him was stitched with a string of 9mm holes.

Espinoza recognized him immediately. His

eyes went wide and then narrowed with satisfaction when he realized that the man who had caused him so much difficulty and shame was twenty feet from him and unarmed.

"I know you are alone," he said. Sergeant Lugones appeared at his side. "Sergeant, if he moves a muscle, shoot him dead."

Espinoza set his machine pistol onto an electrical-transformer housing and pulled his sidearm from its holster and placed it beside it. He came up to Juan with a smug look, the look of a bully who had cornered the weakest neighborhood kid. He didn't stop even when a nautical horn sounded an alarm outside.

"I don't know who you are or where you came from, but I assure you that your death is going to be especially enjoyable."

Juan fired off a lightning right jab that caught Espinoza square in the nose and rocked him back a pace. "You talk too much."

The Argentine charged in a blind range. Cabrillo let him come, and as they were about to collide chest to chest he turned to the side and shoved Espinoza in the back as he went past. He crashed into the wall hard enough to make the metal ring.

"And you fight like a girl," Juan taunted.

"Lugones, shoot him in the foot."

The Sergeant didn't hesitate. The single shot was especially loud, and Juan went down hard, clutching at the ruined member and screaming in agony.

"Okay, now let's see how you fight," Espinoza sneered. "On your feet, or the next shot takes out a knee."

Juan tried twice to stand on his own and both times he collapsed back onto the cement floor.

"Not so tough now, is he, Sergeant?"

"No, sir."

Espinoza moved to Juan's side and yanked him to his feet in a savage thrust. Cabrillo swayed drunkenly and fought to keep from crying out. Espinoza kept one hand on Juan's arm and fired two powerful punches into his gut. Juan sagged, and nearly dragged the Argentine down to the floor with him.

"Pathetic," Espinoza said.

He reached down again for a repeat performance. Juan sat meekly until Espinoza's head was a foot away. Then he reached out with both hands, one on the man's chin, the other on the occipital bulge at the back of his skull. From a disadvantaged position on the ground, he still managed to generate enough torque that when he twisted Espinoza's head, the spinal column snapped cleanly.

The corpse went rubbery as it fell, and nearly blocked him from picking up the Five-SeveN. He raised it and fired before Sergeant Lugones's brain had processed what had just happened. The first round blew through his stomach and emerged on the other side, the second caught him in the forehead.

The horn sounded again, one long, continuous blast of sound that originated not fifty feet from where Juan sat. He managed to get to his feet, his prosthetic leg undamaged by the bullet, and he'd started for the door when a titanic crash seemed to rock the building's foundation and the knife-edged prow of the battle cruiser *Guillermo Brown* exploded through the wall of the processing plant.

Six seconds later, the shock waves generated by collapsing steel and crushed concrete was enough to detonate the bomb.

The building started to go up like the *Hindenburg* over Lakehurst.

Twenty-Eight

Linc and Eddie were in position under the prison when the ship's horn began to blare. The wind made the mournful sound warble like the dying cry of a ravaged animal. They waited a beat, and, sure enough, one of the guards stuck his head out the door to see if he could find the cause of the noise. Of course, he couldn't see more than a dozen feet, and he quickly withdrew.

Franklin used a small cordless drill to create a hole in the floor above him no more than an eighth of an inch in diameter. From their earlier reconnaissance, he'd approximated where the furniture was and had drilled under a threadbare sofa so the hole wouldn't be seen by the guards. Into this, Eddie inserted the nozzle of a gas canister. The gas was a potent knockout agent that would render the average person unconscious in about five minutes, with the effects lasting up to an hour depending on the concentration. They'd earlier disabled the building's ventilation system by merely unplugging the exterior unit.

Very soon, the muffled voices of the guards' idle chatter grew quieter and quieter until there was the crash of bodies hitting the floor and then silence.

The two men crawled out from under the structure and entered through the vestibule. Eddie had the parkas in a vacuum-sealed bag, to cut down on its size, while Linc carried the bag of bones. They hadn't brought eighteen complete skeletons but rather just enough to convince the Argentines. The sack still weighed in at over two hundred pounds, yet he struggled far less than Eddie, with his sixty pounds of coats.

Once they had their gas masks on, they hurried through the door that gave access to the guard area so as to not dilute the gas. There were four of them. Two slumped over on the couch, one on the floor, and the other at a desk with his head down as if to take a nap. Eddie released a little more of the gas below each man's nose to keep them down, and then he and Linc rushed into the back, making sure to unlock the door first.

The rear section of the building was divided into six rooms by a central hallway.

It had been housing for oil workers before the scientists were kidnapped from their research stations. Linc stayed on guard near the door so he could hear any of the soldiers stirring.

Eddie opened the first door on his right and flicked on the switch. Three women stared up at him from the floor. Their days of captivity had rendered them numb, so they just stared blankly. He was relieved to see that the jailers had left them their shoes. Seng peeled off his gas mask, and when they saw he was Asian their interest grew.

"My name is Eddie Seng, and I'm going to get you out of here." When no one said anything, he asked, "Do any of you speak English?"

"Yes," a stocky woman with straw-colored hair replied. "We all do. We're Australian. Who are you?"

"We're here to rescue you." He flicked open a pocketknife and cut the seal that had kept the parkas flattened. The bag expanded to three times its original size.

"You sound American. Are you with the Army?"

"No. It's not important now. Are any of you hurt?"

"They've treated us all right. I don't think they've hurt anyone."

"Good. Help me free the others."

Minutes later, all six cells were open, and the eighteen scientists were free. Eddie was bombarded with questions about why they'd been captured, and he did his best to answer them. The questions died, however, when he opened the second bag and pulled out a human skull.

"We need the Argentines to think you all burned in a fire," Eddie explained before anyone could ask. "There are severe diplomatic repercussions if they suspect you escaped."

The horn on the *Admiral Brown* began blasting a long, single note. Eddie quickened his pace. He salted the right number of remains in each room while Linc went to give the guards one last dose of gas. Next came smearing the walls and floor with a purple jellied fuel. They couldn't carry as much as they would have liked, but Eddie was more than adept at arson and knew the best patterns to lay out so the building would burn completely.

"Hold your breath when we go through the next room," he cautioned. "And once outside, stay in a tight group and follow me."

A massive explosion filled the night.

■ ■ ■ ■

When the warship hit the processing plant and set off the bomb, the blast ruptured the undersea gas line coming in from the rigs. The drop in pressure registered instantly, and check valves on the offshore platforms closed to prevent a dangerous blowback. The impact of the *Admiral Brown* had damaged the shoreside valves so that as the great ship was dragged farther into the structure, the gas in the pipes wasn't contained. With a fireball mushrooming over the facility, flame licked at the gas in the conduits and ignited it.

The bay erupted.

Miles of gas lines lit off in a cataclysmic blast that sent sheets of water soaring into the night, while the flash lit up the sky from horizon to horizon. Three of the disguised rigs were blown off their piers.

Secondary and tertiary explosions rippled the exterior walls of the gas factory until they were blown flat and sent flaming debris out across the bay and over the buildings of the station.

Aboard the *Admiral Brown,* the ship's heavy armor protected all of her crew except the men on the bridge. They could have saved themselves by simply ducking but to a man had stood in awe as their cruiser caromed into the plant. They were sliced to ribbons when all the windows imploded, turning the bridge into a hailstorm of glass.

Unnoticed in the maelstrom of fire, another small charge exploded under the cruiser's bow. It was the device Juan had clamped over the tow cable to release it. When it went, the carbon fiber was pulled free of the remaining pad eyes, and the *Oregon* no longer had her in tow.

As soon as the plant blew, Mark Murphy toggled the explosives Mike Trono and his team had planted in the glacier overlooking where the *Silent Sea* had been sunk by Admiral Tsai Song five centuries earlier. They had drilled deeply into the ice and repacked the holes with water that had frozen solid so as to contain the blast. The multiple explosions were timed precisely and built a harmonic resonance that was powerful enough to shear off a massive slab of ice as neatly as a knife. The newly calved berg was the size of a Manhattan office tower. Two hundred and fifty thousand tons of ice slammed into the bay and actually fractured when it crashed against the seafloor. The wave it spawned encompassed the entire water column and swept from shore to shore. Its momentum was such that anything caught in its path was borne away like leaves in a gutter. The magnificent Treasure Ship, so long preserved in its frigid realm, was no exception. The wave tumbled it across the seafloor and onto the long slope that led down into the deep waters of the abyssal plain. When the waters finally calmed, there wasn't a trace that it had ever existed at all.

Eric Stone felt it the second the ship was free, and he cut the power to the drive tubes.

"That's it," he said, staring at the big monitor on the front wall of the op center.

The camera that was mounted in the nose of an unmanned aerial drone revealed hell on earth, with fire shooting a hundred feet and higher over the processing plant and pockets of gas above the bay still aflame. It looked as if the very seas were burning. Gomez Adams was at the tiny plane's remote controls, and he used a joystick to fly it across the sprawling facility. It was a testimony to his skills as a pilot that he could keep the unstable craft flying through the storm. Small pockets of fire dotted the landscape where debris blown from the gas plant continued to burn. But another fire drew his attention. A building well away from the blast had flames licking through its roof.

"Looks like Eddie and Linc are making their move," he said.

A second later, Eddie's panting voice filled the high-tech room from ceiling-mounted speakers. "Eighteen present and accounted for."

Max Hanley couldn't care less. "Have you heard or seen the Chairman?"

"Negative. Last I knew, he was in the plant. He hasn't gotten word to you?"

"No, damn it! All he said was, he'd find his own way out."

"What do you want us to do?"

As much as Max wanted to delay, he knew that Eddie and his group of freed captives would eventually draw attention. "Get to the submersible as fast as you can. Maybe Juan's already on his way. His radio could be dead."

"We're moving."

Hanley tried calling Cabrillo on every preset frequency their radios picked up. He got no response. He knew in his gut that Juan hadn't gotten clear when the gas processor blew. There hadn't been enough time. He'd sacrificed himself to stick to their plan.

■ ■ ■ ■

The scene on the ground was absolute pandemonium. Lieutenant Jimenez couldn't find the Major, and the discipline they had drilled into their men seemed to have evaporated. This was the start of the American attack and yet many of his troopers abandoned their positions to gawk at the conflagration. He screamed at them to return to their posts and get ready for the assault. Noncoms added their snarls, and slowly they started getting the soldiers to pay attention to their duty.

Oil workers ignored the curfew and poured from their dormitories to see what had happened. When Jimenez yelled at them to return indoors, he was met with derision. Within minutes of the blast, a hundred men or more were outside.

A Corporal approached and saluted. "Lieutenant, it's not the Americans."

"What? What did you say?"

"It's not the Americans, sir. The *Guillermo* broke free from her mooring and drifted into the big processing plant. That's what caused the explosion."

"Are you certain?"

"I saw it myself. It looks like a quarter of

the ship is buried inside the building."

Jimenez couldn't believe it. An accident caused all this? "Have you seen Major Espinoza?"

"No, sir. I'm sorry."

"If you see him, tell him I'm investigating the plant."

"Sir. Yes, sir."

Jimenez was about to start across the complex when he heard the unmistakable chatter of an automatic weapon. This was no accident. He took off at a run toward where the gunfire originated.

When the explosion rocketed into the storm-torn sky, Linc started hustling the prisoners out to the entry vestibule while Eddie used a lighter to ignite the flammable jelly. It went up even better than he'd hoped. The wood paneling was the cheapest product available and was made of sawdust and glue that burned furiously. In seconds, the top layer of space was a dense cloud of smoke.

He made sure he was the last person out. He rushed across the room where the guards still slept. They left the door open so fresh air would revive them, though the reason behind this was to feed the fire and not offer these men any humanity.

As Cabrillo had predicted, the Argentines had temporarily lost control of the situation. Soldiers had left their patrol sectors, and civilians were mingling in with the troops.

A half mile away, the fire at the gas plant glowed orange and yellow through the curtain of blowing snow. Eddie didn't have to see it to know the building was a total loss. Without that facility, the men had no way of powering their base. In one fiery instant, the Corporation turned the Argentines from masters of the Antarctic Peninsula to people who were going to need rescuing within days or risk freezing to death. Their hope of annexing this region was over. The world would not sit idly back and let them rebuild.

All that remained now was, getting away with it.

He didn't like that they were such a big group. Large numbers attract attention; however, no one seemed to be paying them heed. Most were making their way closer to the huge blaze to see what had happened.

He made his report to the *Oregon,* and was as troubled as Max about Juan's disappearance. But he knew the Chairman and had a pretty good feeling that he was boarding the minisub this second.

They kept moving at a pace that wasn't quite a jog but more than a walk. The buildings were packed tightly together, and it was only a matter of time before they rounded a blind corner and ran into a sentry.

Linc had given the point position to him so that once they reached the Nomad, Eddie could go directly to the cockpit without having to climb over their guests.

The guard had his back turned when Eddie saw him. In the distance, he could see where the white ground gave way to the black ocean. The pier was less than a hundred yards away.

Sensing more than hearing anything, the soldier spun in place, his weapon held ready. "Jaguar," he challenged.

"Capybara," Eddie returned.

The soldier asked a question. Seng spoke no Spanish, and realized Linc should have stayed on point. Eddie cupped his glove to his hood as if to say he didn't hear the question. Ignoring Seng's pantomime, the sentry moved closer to look at the people with him. Though they were shapeless under the heavy parkas, there was no disguising that three of them were much shorter than average. Short enough to be women, something the complex had none of.

He went straight for the blonde, whose

name was Sue, and pushed back her hood to reveal her cherubic face. He whipped up his H&K and aimed it point-blank between her eyes. No one would ever know if he intended to fire. Linc dropped him with a three-round burst.

In a fit of inspiration, Eddie raised his own machine pistol and loosed an entire magazine into the air. The soldiers were nervous, had no information about what was going on, and had doubtlessly been told since their arrival that American commandos would be hitting them any day. Even the most seasoned veteran would be panicky right about now, so a moment after Eddie's burst some young recruit on the other side of the base saw a shadow he was certain was a Green Beret and opened fire. Like opening a floodgate, men began shooting indiscriminately, the chatter of autofire rising above the roar of the burning gas plant and the shriek of the wind.

Linc got it immediately. He toed the corpse. "This poor sap got hit by his own guys."

"That's how it'll read. I'll be surprised if they actually don't shoot a few of their own themselves."

They took off again and made it to the dock moments later. The gunfire didn't let up one bit, which worked to their advantage right until the instant a stray bullet caught one of the scientists in the leg. He crashed to the ground, clutching at the wound and moaning.

It wasn't a life-threatening wound, at least at that moment, so Linc picked him off the snow and threw him over his shoulder with barely a break in stride.

The Nomad had drifted a bit out from under the dock, so Eddie had to haul it back on its line. He jumped aboard and opened the hatch.

"Juan?" he called, even as he lowered himself into the craft. The Chairman wasn't back yet.

"Eddie," Linc said from the top of the hull. "Help me here."

The former SEAL lowered the injured man through the hatch. His pant leg was stained with blood, and more of it dripped from the wound. His femoral artery had been nicked. He laid the injured scientist on one of the padded benches and was about to get to work on the wound when another of the prisoners leapt down into the submersible and shouldered him aside.

"I'm a doctor."

Eddie didn't need to hear anything further. He scrambled forward to the cockpit and threw himself into the pilot's seat.

"Max, can you hear me?" he said into his mike, while he got busy prepping the sub for its return to the *Oregon.*

"Any sign of Juan?" Hanley asked.

"No. We're loading onto the Nomad now. He isn't here."

The silence stretched to fifteen seconds. Twenty. Max finally asked, "How long do you think you can hang there?"

"I don't think at all. One of the scientists was shot. Looks like he could bleed out. He needs to be in the OR as fast as we can get him there." Whenever there was a mission under way, Dr. Huxley and her staff were standing by in Medical ready to treat anything that came their way.

Eddie glanced over and down the length of the submersible. Already the bench seats were full, and people were starting to sit on each other's laps. It didn't help that the wounded man took up four places while the doctor worked to save his life. They remained quiet, but all of them threw smiles Eddie's way when they caught his eye.

"Doc," Eddie called. "It's going to take a half hour to reach our ship, but there's a level-one trauma team standing by. What are his chances? Another man's life might depend on your answer."

The physician, a Norwegian on sabbatical down there in Antarctica because of his thirst for adventure, took his time and considered all the variables. "If it is as you say, this man will live if we leave in the next five minutes."

Eddie turned back to his radio. "Max, I can give Juan ten minutes, then we have to go." He figured the doctor would have given himself a little cushion.

"Every second you can spare. You hear me? Every second."

Twelve minutes later, the sub sank into the black waters of the bay.

Cabrillo hadn't shown.

TWENTY-NINE

Thirty-six hours elapsed before the weather was clear enough for the Argentine government to send down another C-130 Hercules. In that short time, Antarctica reminded the men left stranded on the peninsula why humans were merely temporary interlopers on her shores. While not quite forced into cannibalism like some Uruguayan soccer team, the men were nearly helpless without the steady supply of natural gas. They'd been forced to use portable stoves to heat food and shared body heat to keep warm. Despite her damage, which included a holed bow, the *Admiral Brown* took on more than two hundred of the survivors, while the rest congregated in two of the dormitory buildings, huddled miserably while the interior temperatures plummeted.

General Philippe Espinoza was the first down the ramp when the big cargo plane came to a stop on the ice runway behind the base. Raul Jimenez was waiting and threw him a smart salute. The General had aged ten years in the week since Jimenez had seen him. Thick bags the size of grapes clung to his lower eyelids, and his normally florid complexion had gone pale.

"Any word of my son?" he asked immediately.

"I'm sorry, sir. No." They stepped up into a waiting snowcat. "It is my duty to report that a group of four men were seen entering the gas-processing plant just a few minutes before the accident. Nothing of their remains has been found."

Espinoza took this news like a body blow. He knew his son would never abandon his post, so the odds were that Jorge had been one of the four. "First my wife and now this," he muttered.

"Your wife?" Jimenez asked too quickly.

Espinoza didn't pick up on the young Lieutenant's enthusiasm, and such was his state of mind that he actually explained himself to a subaltern. "She took our children and left me. Worse, she has betrayed me."

Jimenez had to fight to keep the emotion from his face. Maxine had left him, and he knew she had done it so they could be together. His heart rate went into overdrive.

The news was the happiest he had ever heard, so the next words out of the General's mouth were especially painful.

"I managed to get two agents to meet her plane when it landed in Paris after I was told by customs that she had left the country. She was met by two men and was taken immediately to the headquarters of the DGSE."

He knew that was the French spy agency, their version of the CIA.

Espinoza continued. "I don't know if she was their agent all along or if they turned her, but the truth is unavoidable. She is a spy."

At that instant, Jimenez understood that she had gotten as much information from him as she had the General. He recalled that last time, along the banks of the stream, when he had told her about abducting the American professor and how she was being kept in the Espinozas' Buenos Aires apartment. Maxine had relayed that information to their superiors, and they had arranged her rescue.

"And now my Jorge is dead." He fought to contain his grief and finally managed to compose himself. "Tell me this was the work of the Americans so that I may have my revenge."

"I have been working closely with Luis Laretta, the director, and Commander Ocampo, who is the first officer aboard the *Admiral Brown.* Our preliminary conclusion is that the ship's anchor came loose, which allowed the vessel to drift into the gas plant and cause the explosion. Secondary fires destroyed three other buildings, including a workshop and the dormitory we were using to house the scientists we had taken from other bases."

"Doesn't that strike you as too convenient? The two things the Americans want, the base reduced to ashes and the prisoners set free?"

"Sir, they weren't freed. They all died in the fire, their remains burned to bits of charred bone. All told, there were sixteen fatalities, not including the foreigners. Eight were on the bridge of the cruiser, four plus a sentry in the plant, two died in the fire with the prisoners, and two more were killed when men panicked and started shooting at shadows." That last piece of news was especially hard to deliver because Jimenez had been in charge, and the lack of discipline reflected on him. "We have found absolutely no evidence that this was anything more than a tragic accident."

The General didn't comment. He was still

grappling with the quadruple loss — his wife and their two young children, his son, and, most assuredly because of this calamity, his career. He stared fixedly ahead, his body moving only when the snowcat bounced over a rough patch. They rounded the last hill, and the base was spread before them. Seen from above, the damage to the gas-processing plant looked bad. From ground level, it was far worse.

Half of the building, which had been big enough to park two jumbo jets, was a smoking hole in the ground in the center of tons of torn and blackened pipes. The *Admiral Guillermo Brown* was tied to the pier, her back half appearing normal, while from her bridge forward she was a charred husk. It was a testament to her Russian builders that more men aboard her hadn't perished.

Out across the bay stood the legs of three of the production platforms. Of the rigs themselves, only the spindly arms of deck cranes poking above the waves marked their locations. Ice was already forming around them, and within another few days the bay would be a solid sheet.

"Mr. Laretta says that we can still pump oil to the storage tanks from the surviving rigs, but, without any means to process the natural gas, we have no way to power the operation," Jimenez said when the silence became too much for him. "But he did say that portable machines can be brought in that will give us some processing capabilities and allow us to start rebuilding."

Espinoza continued to sit like a stone.

"We still need to evacuate most of the staff until we can get fuel down here and the processor is up and running. Laretta says he needs just twenty men, at first. There will be more later, to be sure, but for now there aren't enough resources to keep the rest alive. I forgot to ask, General, when are the other planes coming?"

They had pulled up close to the smoldering remains of the processing plant. Espinoza threw open his door and jumped down to the ice. He didn't bother pulling up his parka hood, as if in defiance of this place. There was nothing more Antarctica could do to him. He stood mutely as the wind howled off the ocean, the air heavy with the smell of seared metal.

"Jorge," he whispered.

Jimenez was actually surprised at how badly the General was taking his son's death. From stories the Major had told him over the years, and seeing the two together, he had come away with the sense that the father looked on his son as just another soldier under his command.

"Jorge," Espinoza repeated softly. Then his voice firmed and became angry. "You have failed and don't have the courage to face me, do you? You stupidly died to avoid answering for your mistakes. You rode my coattails for so long that when it came time to step off, you could no longer stand on your own."

He reared on Jimenez. "Planes? There will be no planes. You men will live or die by your wits. You will get this facility running again or you will all freeze to death. So long as our Chinese friends back our play, you must remain here and legitimize our claim. Now, tell me of this mystery ship that beached near here."

Espinoza had gone from lamb to lion so quickly that Jimenez took a second too long to respond, so the General shouted, "Lieutenant, your dereliction has already been noted, do not make it worse!"

"Sir!" Jimenez came to attention. "As soon as the weather cleared, I ordered our helicopter to conduct an aerial survey off the coast because that vessel was an unexplained anomaly that your son told me had bothered him. They failed to spot the craft, and, given its situation when it was last sighted, it is my belief that it sank during the storm."

"Sank?"

"Yes, sir. When we boarded it several days ago, her lower levels were flooded, and when she floated off the beach, the day before the storm, she had a severe list. It is unlikely that she survived more than a few hours when the weather front hit us. A storm strong enough to snap the *Admiral Brown*'s anchor chain would have easily had the power to capsize the old freighter."

This was another coincidence that Espinoza didn't like. However, an earlier check of the Lloyd's of London database showed that a ship named *Norego* that matched the description from his son's report had been reported lost with all hands nearly two years ago. It was just plausible enough that she had drifted all that time and her presence here was innocent.

He didn't know that Mark Murphy and Eric Stone had hacked the insurance giant's computer system and planted that information. They'd done the same at the International Maritime Safety Board as well, in case anyone became really nosy.

In the end, it all came down to what their Chinese allies would do. If they continued to support Argentina, then they had the protection to rebuild the base. If, however, they withdrew their support, then Espinoza would have no choice but to order a full evacuation, despite his earlier bluster.

Two hours later, Espinoza was in Luis Laretta's office, listening to the director's plans for reconstruction, when a radio report came in from the survey boat. Lee Fong and his team had left when the storm abated with plans to dive on the wreck of the *Silent Sea* and return with conclusive evidence, enough to convince the world that Beijing had a legitimate stake in the peninsula.

The marine transceiver was on a side table closest to the General, so he fielded the call.

"No, this isn't Mr. Laretta," he explained. "My name is General Philippe Espinoza. I am in his office with him."

"General, it is an honor to speak with you," Lee replied. "And let me extend the condolences from my government on the loss of your son. I knew him only briefly, but he seemed an excellent officer and a fine man."

"Thank you," Espinoza choked out, his voice a mix of shame and grief.

"General, it is not my wish to add to your burden, however, I have to report that the *Silent Sea* is no longer here."

"What?!"

"There is a glacier overlooking the bay

where she sank, and a large part of it broke off during the storm. One of my men believes the concussion of the explosion might have done it, but the reasons are not important. What is important is that the wave it created when it hit the water swept the wreck away from her resting spot. We have searched her most likely track and have found no evidence of the ship."

"You will keep looking." It was more question than statement.

There was an apologetic pause before the Chinese surveyor replied. "I am sorry, but no. I have contacted my superiors and apprised them of the situation. They have ordered me to call off the search and evacuate my team as soon as possible. With the loss of our submarine, the base so heavily damaged, and no solid evidence that my nation was the first to explore this region, they are unwilling to risk further international condemnation."

"Surely you can find the *Silent Sea* in a day or two. You know she's out there."

"We do, but the seafloor drops away just outside the bay to more than five thousand feet. It could take a month or longer, and we still might not find her. My government is not willing to risk our searching for that long."

That was the final nail in the coffin. At dawn the next morning, the Hercules took off again for Argentina, carrying the first wave of men off the peninsula. Unlike Caesar, they had crossed the Rubicon only to be beaten back by what they thought was fate but in truth were Juan Cabrillo and the Corporation.

A dark pall hung over the *Oregon* as she cruised northwest on her way to South Africa. They would be a couple of days late to provide security for the Kuwaiti Emir's state visit, but a quick renegotiation on their fee had settled the matter.

The ship was like a zombie now. She could function, but she had no soul. Juan's presence was everywhere aboard her, therefore so was his absence. Four days had passed since his death, and the crew were no further along in their grieving than the first instant when they realized he wasn't coming back.

Without Juan to lead it, there was talk of dissolving the Corporation altogether, talk that Max Hanley was doing nothing to quell.

Mark Murphy was seated at his desk in his cabin, playing mindless games of Internet backgammon. It was well past midnight, but the thought of sleep was impossible. More than anyone, he feared for the future. His IQ had kept him socially isolated his entire life, and it wasn't until he'd joined the Corporation that he found a place where he not only fit in but flourished. He didn't want to lose this. He didn't want to return to a world where people thought he was a freak or used him as a walking computer, like when he'd worked in the defense industry.

The people on the *Oregon* were his family. They embraced his idiosyncrasies, or at least tolerated them, and to Murph that was enough. If they cashed out, he had enough money socked away and would never need to work again, but he knew that the sense of isolation that had plagued him his entire life would come roaring back.

He polished off another player, his eleventh in a row, and was about to start a new game when he saw his e-mail icon blinking. Hoping for a more interesting distraction than another round of 'gammon, he toggled to his e-mail page. Three messages. Their mainframe did a good job of filtering spam for the rest of the crew, but, for whatever reason, Mark allowed a lot through to his computer. Junk messages were better than none.

One was spam. One was a move in a long-running series of chess matches he was playing against a retired Israeli professor. He'd have the man in mate in another four moves, and the old physicist didn't yet see it coming. He dashed off his reply, and glanced at the address for the final message.

He didn't know anybody at Penn State, but the subject line looked intriguing. It read "Lonely." Probably some lame college dating service, he thought, but he opened it anyway.

Hi there. Remember me? Until recently, I was the chairman of a major corporation. Now I'm the king of a penguin colony here at the Wilson/George Research Station. My friends had to leave me behind. They didn't know I'd gotten clear of the gas plant and escaped in the confusion after it blew. I guess I shouldn't have broken my radio in a fight. I have spent the past four days hiking through the snow to reach this place, surviving on nothing but the protein bars I'd loaded into my smuggler's leg, the one with the hollowed-out calf. I've got the generator going and have plenty of food, so my main problem is loneliness. Any suggestions?

Cabrillo had signed it, *Abandoned in the Antarctic.*

ABOUT THE AUTHORS

Clive Cussler is the author or coauthor of forty previous books, including twenty Dirk Pitt® adventures, eight NUMA® Files adventures, six *Oregon*® Files books, and the Isaac Bell historical thrillers. His most recent *New York Times*–bestselling novels are *Corsair, Medusa, Spartan Gold,* and *The Wrecker.* His nonfiction works include *The Sea Hunters* and *The Sea Hunters II*; these describe the true adventures of the real NUMA, which, led by Cussler, searches for lost ships of historic significance. With his crew of volunteers, Cussler has discovered more than sixty ships, including the long-lost Confederate submarine *Hunley.* He lives in Arizona. Visit Cussler's website at www.cusslerbooks.com

Jack Du Brul is the author of the Philip Mercer series, most recently *Havoc*, and is the coauthor with Clive Cussler of the *Or-*

egon® Files novels *Dark Watch, Skeleton Coast, Plague Ship*, and *Corsair.* He lives in Vermont.